WAKING UP TO
DR GORGEOUS

BY
EMILY FORBES

SWEPT AWAY
BY THE
SEDUCTIVE STRANGER

BY
AMY ANDREWS

The Christmas Swap

A holiday they won't forget!

Nurse Luci Dawson and Dr Cal Hollingsworth
have both had their lives turned upside down.
So when they get the chance to swap houses
in the run-up to Christmas it could be just what
they need to start afresh for the festive season!

Find out what happens in:

Waking Up to Dr Gorgeous
by Emily Forbes

and

Swept Away by the Seductive Stranger
by Amy Andrews

Available now!

WAKING UP TO DR GORGEOUS

BY
EMILY FORBES

MILLS &
BOON

Published in Great Britain 2016
By Mills & Boon, an imprint of HarperCollins*Publishers*
1 London Bridge Street, London, SE1 9GF

© 2016 Emily Forbes

ISBN: 978-0-263-91515-0

Our policy is to use papers that are natural, renewable and recyclable products and made from wood grown in sustainable forests. The logging and manufacturing processes conform to the legal environmental regulations of the country of origin.

Printed and bound in Spain
by CPI, Barcelona

Dear Reader,

I wrote my first ten books with my sister, and in my experience the first thing everyone asked was, 'How do you do it?' The truth was I'd never written a book any other way—that was all I knew. I have now written fifteen stories solo, but when I was asked if I would be interested in writing a duo with Amy Andrews of course I said yes. We have known each other for a long time, and Amy has also written books with her sister, so we're both used to plotting with other writers—and sometimes negotiating! ☺

Working out our characters and our stories and how we were going to fit them together was great fun. Our brief was simply to write two stories in which our characters swapped houses; the rest was up to us. We took one character from the country and sent her to the city, and moved one hero in the other direction. One country girl, one city boy—both out of their depth.

Seb and Callum Hollingsworth are gorgeous, smart, sexy brothers, and Luci and Flick are best friends. Even though it might have made sense to make the girls sisters, as that is what we both know so well, it was more interesting to make the boys siblings— two brooding loners in need of a bit of loving.

I really hope you enjoy both stories.

Happy reading,

Emily

For anyone who has ever fallen in love
when they didn't intend to—it's never the wrong time!

Emily Forbes is an award-winning author of
Medical Romances for Mills & Boon. She has written
over 25 books and has twice been a finalist in the
Australian Romantic Book of the Year Award, which
she won in 2013 for her novel *Sydney Harbour Hospital:
Bella's Wishlist*. You can get in touch with Emily at
emilyforbes@internode.on.net or visit her website at
emily-forbesauthor.com.

Books by Emily Forbes

Mills & Boon Medical Romance

The Hollywood Hills Clinic
Falling for the Single Dad

Tempted & Tamed!
A Doctor by Day…
Tamed by the Renegade

Sydney Harbour Hospital: Bella's Wishlist
Breaking the Playboy's Rules
Daring to Date Dr Celebrity
The Honourable Army Doc
A Kiss to Melt Her Heart
His Little Christmas Miracle
A Love Against All Odds

Visit the Author Profile page at
millsandboon.co.uk for more titles.

Praise for
Emily Forbes

'*The Honourable Army Doc* was a wonderful, emotional and
passionate read that I recommend to all readers.'

—*Goodreads*

CHAPTER ONE

'OMG, FLICK, I wish you'd been able to see this place.'

Luci had spoken to her best friend several times already today but she couldn't resist calling her again to update her on her good fortune.

'It's nice, then?' She could hear the smile in Flick's voice.

'Nice! It's amazing.' Luci wandered around the apartment while she chatted. 'It's right on the harbour. The beach is just across the road. I'm looking at the sea as we speak.' She could hear the waves washing onto the shore and smell the salt in the air. 'I don't know how Callum is going to manage in my little house.'

It was a bit odd to be walking around a stranger's apartment. Luci had spent her whole life surrounded by people she knew so to travel halfway across the country to swap houses with a stranger was odd on so many levels. It had all happened so quickly she hadn't had time to consider how it would feel. Callum Hollingsworth's apartment on the shores of Sydney Harbour was modern and masculine. While her house wasn't particularly feminine it was old and decorated in what she guessed people would call country style. No surprises there, it was definitely a country house. It was clear that her house-swap partner's taste in decorating was quite different from hers. She felt self-conscious, wondering what he would think of her place, before she realised it didn't matter. She didn't plan on meeting the guy.

She heard the whistle of the Indian Pacific through the phone. The two friends had spent the past few days chilling on Bondi Beach, a girls' getaway that Flick had suggested before Luci settled into her house swap and study course in Sydney, and Flick returned to South Australia on the iconic trans-continental train.

'Are you on the train?' Luci asked.

'Not yet,' Flick replied. 'I'm just grabbing a coffee and waiting to board.'

'Make sure you call me when you get home,' she told her.

'Of course I will. What are you going to do with the rest of your day?'

'I think I'll take a stroll around my new neighbourhood. The hospital is a half-hour walk away so I might head in that direction. Work out where I have to be tomorrow. I don't want to be late.' Luci was enrolled in an eight-week course in child and family health being run through the North Sydney Hospital and she needed to get her bearings. 'Look after my mum and dad for me.'

That was her one big concern. As an only child of elderly parents—her mother called her their 'change of life' baby—Luci was nervous about being so far away from them, but Flick had promised to keep an eye on them. It wasn't hard for her to do as Luci's dad was the local doctor and Flick worked for him as a practice nurse.

'I will. Enjoy yourself.'

Luci ended the call and had another wander around. It wasn't a massive apartment—there was an open-plan kitchen, living and dining room with a large balcony that looked out to the beach across the road. Two bedrooms, two bathrooms and a small laundry finished it off, but it had everything she would need. She dumped her bags in the spare bedroom. Having the two bedrooms was a bonus because she didn't feel comfortable about taking over Callum's room. That felt too familiar.

The sun shone on the water of Sydney Harbour, white boats bobbed and the houses peeked out between eucalyptus trees. Luci couldn't believe how perfect it looked. She'd grown up in country South Australia, born and bred in Vickers Hill in the Clare Valley, and she'd never travelled far. Her father very rarely took holidays and when he did they spent them on the coast, but the coast she was familiar with was the Gulf of St Vincent with its calm waters, like a mill pond. It never felt like the real ocean.

Then, when she'd married her high-school sweetheart at the age of twenty-one, they'd had no money for holidays. She'd married young, as had most of her friends, but she hadn't found the happy-ever-after she'd wanted. Like so many other marriages, hers hadn't lasted and she found herself divorced and heartbroken at twenty-five.

But now, perhaps, it was time to travel. To see something of the world. She couldn't change what had happened, the past was the past. She had grieved for a year, grieved for the things she had lost—her marriage, her best friend and her dream of motherhood—but she was recovering now and she refused to believe that her life was over. Far from it. She had a chance now to reinvent herself. Her teenage dream needed some remodelling and this was her opportunity to figure out a new direction, if that's what she decided she wanted. She was finally appreciating the freedom she had been given; she was no longer defined by her status as daughter, girlfriend or wife. No one in Sydney knew anything about her. She was just Luci.

It was time to start again.

* * *

Luci turned off the shower and wrapped herself in one of the fluffy towels that she'd found in the guest bathroom. She pulled the elastic band from her hair, undoing the messy bun that had kept her shoulder-length bobbed blonde hair dry, then dried herself off. She was exhausted and she was looking forward to climbing into bed. She was far more tired than she'd expected to be. She'd spent the past three days sitting in lectures. She'd thought that would be easier than the shift work on the wards that she was used to, but it was mentally tiring.

Still, it was almost the end of her first week. Only two more days to go before the weekend. Perhaps then she'd have a chance to see something of this side of Sydney. She and Flick had walked from Bondi to Bronte and back and had spent the rest of their time relaxing. Sightseeing hadn't been high on their agenda but Luci had never visited Sydney before and she wanted to get a feel for the city.

She was familiar with the route from Callum's apartment in Fairlight to the hospital on the opposite side of the Manly peninsula as she was walking that route every day. She was getting to know the local shopkeepers and was exchanging 'good mornings' with a couple of regular dog walkers. It was a far cry from Vickers Hill, where she couldn't take two steps down the main street without bumping into someone she knew, but she was starting to feel a little more at home here. She kept herself busy, not wanting to give herself a chance to be homesick. Being somewhere new was exciting, she told herself, and she had limited time so she needed to make the most of her opportunities.

The people in her course were getting friendlier by the day. It seemed city folk took a little longer to warm up to strangers but Luci had gone out to dinner tonight with a few of them, just a burger in Manly, but it was a start and Luci knew she'd feel even more at home after another week.

She knew where to catch the ferry to the city and she'd walked on the beach but she hadn't yet had time to test the water in the tidal swimming pool that was built into the rocks. That would be added to her list of things to do. She hadn't done nearly as much exploring as she had planned to, and if all the weeks were this busy, her two months in Sydney would fly past. She'd have to make time to see the sights, but first she needed some sleep.

She hung the towel on the rail in the bathroom, went through to her bedroom and slid naked between her bedsheets. She kept the window blinds up and the window slightly open. From the bed she could see the stars in the sky and the sound of the ocean carried to her on the warm spring air. The ocean murmured to itself as it lapped the shore. It was gentle tonight and she could imagine the waves kissing the sand, teasing gently before retreating, only to come back for more.

She dozed off to the sound of the sea.

It felt like only moments later that she woke to an unfamiliar sound. A slamming door.

She was still getting used to the different sounds and rhythms of the city. She could sleep through the early morning crowing of a rooster and the deep rumble of a tractor but the slightest noise in the middle of suburbia disturbed her. Rubbish trucks, the tooting of ferry horns, slamming of car doors and the loud conversations of late-night commuters or drinking buddies on their way home from the pub all intruded on her dreams, but this noise was louder than all of those. This noise was close.

She heard footsteps on the wooden floorboards and

saw light streaming under her bedroom door as the passage light flicked on.

Shit. There was someone in the house.

She put her hand on her chest. Her heart was racing.

What should she do?

Call out?

No, that would only draw attention to herself.

Find a weapon of some sort? She'd seen a set of golf clubs but they were in a cupboard near the front door. She couldn't get to them and there was nothing in the bedroom. Maybe a shot of hair spray to the face would work—if only she used hairspray.

Should she call the police? But how quickly would they get here? Not fast enough, she assumed.

She had no idea what to do. She'd never had to fend for herself.

She sat up in bed, and scrabbled for her phone in the dark. She was too afraid to turn on the light, worried it would draw the attention of the intruder. She clutched the sheet to her chest to cover her nakedness. Perhaps she should find some clothes first. She didn't want to confront a burglar while naked.

She could hear him crossing the living room. The tread of the steps were heavy. Man heavy. She could hear boots. The steps weren't light and delicate. He wasn't making any attempt to be quiet. There was a loud thump as something soft but weighty hit the floor. It didn't sound like a person. A bag maybe? A bag of stolen goods?

Her heart was still racing and the frantic pounding almost drowned out the sound of the footsteps. That made her pause. This had to be the world's noisiest burglar. She hadn't had much experience with burglars but surely they would generally try to be quiet? This one was making absolutely no attempt to be silent. Plus he had turned the lights on. Definitely not stealthy.

He was a terrible burglar, possibly one of the worst ever.

But maybe he thought the house was empty? Perhaps she should make some noise? Enough noise for two people.

She heard the soft pop as the seal on the fridge door was broken. She frowned. Now he was looking in the fridge? Making himself at home. She was positive it wasn't Callum. Luci had spoken to Flick earlier in the day. Callum had well and truly arrived in Vickers Hill and according to her friend he was creating a bit of a stir. Luci hoped he wasn't going to prove difficult—he was supposed to be making things easier for her dad, not harder, but she couldn't do much about it. All it meant to her was that it wasn't Callum in the apartment. And she was pretty sure by now that it wasn't a burglar either, but that still meant a stranger was in the house.

She needed to get dressed.

She switched on the bedside light and was halfway out of bed when she heard the footsteps moving along the passage. While she was debating her options she saw the bedroom door handle moving.

OMG, they were coming in.

'You'd better get out of here. I've called the police,' she yelled, not knowing what else to do.

The door handle continued to turn and a voice said, 'You've done what?'

When it became obvious that the person who belonged to the voice was intent on entering her room she jumped back into bed and pulled the covers up to her chin, grabbing her phone just in case she did need to call the cops.

'I'll scream,' she added for good measure.

But the door continued to open and a vision appeared. Luci wondered briefly if she was dreaming. Her heart was racing at a million miles an hour but now she had no clue whether it was due to nerves, fear, panic or simple lust. This intruder might just be the most gorgeous man she'd ever laid eyes on. Surely someone this gorgeous couldn't be evil?

But then Ted Bundy sprang to mind. He was a good-looking, charming, educated man who just happened to be a serial killer. 'Don't come any closer,' she said.

He stopped and held his hands out to his sides. 'I'm not going to hurt you, but who the hell are you and what are you doing in my room?' he said.

'*Your* room?'

Was this Callum? She was certain she'd chosen the guest bedroom but, anyway, what was he doing here? He couldn't have got back to Sydney that quickly. He was supposed to be a thousand miles away, staying in her house. That was how a house swap worked. 'Why aren't you in Vickers Hill?'

'What the heck is Vickers Hill?'

Luci frowned. 'Who are you?'

He couldn't be Callum. So whose room was she in exactly?

'Seb. Seb Hollingsworth.'

Seb.

'You're not Callum?'

A crease appeared between his superb blue eyes as he frowned. 'No. I'm his brother.'

Luci almost missed his answer, distracted as she was by the thick, dark eyelashes that framed his eyes.

'Brother!' Why hadn't Callum warned her? She sat up in the bed, taking care to make sure the sheets prevented any sort of indecent exposure. 'Callum didn't mention you.'

'So you do know Cal, then?'

'Sort of.'

He lifted one eyebrow but said nothing.

Luci could play that game too. And she used the silent seconds to examine the vision a little more closely.

He truly was gorgeous. Tall, really tall, with thick dark hair, chestnut she'd call it. He had eyebrows to match that shaded piercing blue eyes and a nose that may or may not have been broken once upon a time. His lips were full and pink, and a two-day growth of beard darkened his jaw.

His torso was bare but he held what appeared to be a black T-shirt in his hand. Just what had he been planning on doing? she wondered, before she was distracted again by his broad shoulders and smooth chest. He reminded her of someone, she thought as her eyes roamed over his body.

The statue of David, she thought, brought to life. He was made of warm flesh instead of cool marble but had the same, startling level of perfection.

Her heart was still beating a rapid tattoo. Adrenaline was still coursing through her system but not out of fear. Now it was a simple chemical, or maybe hormonal, reaction.

'I think you have some explaining to do,' said the living, breathing statue.

In Luci's opinion so did Callum, Seb's absent brother, and she was blowed if she was going to explain herself while she lay in bed naked. She clutched the sheet a little more tightly across her breasts. 'Let me get dressed and then we can talk.'

The corner of Seb's mouth lifted in a wry smile and there was a wicked gleam in his blue eyes. Luci felt a burst of heat explode in her belly and she knew that the heat would taint her body with a blush of pink. She could feel the warmth spreading up over her chest and neck as Seb continued to stand in the doorway. Did he know the effect he was having on her? She had to get rid of him.

'Can you give me a minute?' she asked.

'Sure, sorry,' he replied, looking anything but sorry. 'And while you're at it,' he added, glancing at the phone that was still clutched in her hand along with the sheet, 'do you think you could ring the police and tell them it was just a misunderstanding? I don't want the neighbours getting the wrong idea.'

'I didn't actually ring the police,' Luci admitted.

He turned and left the room, pulling the door closed behind him, and she could hear him laughing, a deep, cheerful sound that lifted her spirits.

Luci waited to hear his footsteps retreat before she was brave enough to throw off the sheets once more. She climbed out of bed on shaky legs and pulled on a T-shirt and a pair of shorts. She padded down the hallway to the open-plan lounge and kitchen to find Seb with his head in the fridge, giving her a very nice view of a tidy rear covered in denim. His bare feet poked out of the bottom of his jeans.

She stepped around a pile of luggage that had been dumped beside the couch. A brown leather jacket was draped over a duffel bag and a motorbike helmet sat on the floor beside a pair of sturdy boots, the boots that had been stomping down the passage. There was a thick layer of reddish-brown dust covering everything.

She ducked through the kitchen and into the dining area, where she stood on the far side of the table, putting some distance between them. Despite the fact that he looked like something created by Michelangelo and appeared to be related to the owner of the house, she wasn't prepared to take his word for it just yet. Until she'd decided he wasn't a serial killer she wasn't taking any chances.

He stood up and turned to face her. His chest was now

covered by his black T-shirt—that was a pity—and he had two small bottles of beer in his hand.

'Beer?' he asked as he raised his hand.

Luci shook her head.

He put one bottle back in the fridge, closed the door and then twisted the top off the other bottle and took a swig. He watched her as she watched him but he didn't seem as nervous as her. Not nearly.

He stepped over to the table, pulled out a chair and sat down. He pushed the chair back and stretched his legs out. He was tall. His legs were long. He was fiddling with the beer bottle and she couldn't help but notice that his fingers were long and slender too.

He lifted his eyes up to meet her gaze. 'So, sleeping beauty, do you have a name?'

'Luci.'

'Luci,' he repeated, stretching out the two syllables, and the way the 'u' rolled off his tongue did funny things to her insides.

'So where's my big brother? And why are you in my bed?'

Luci swallowed nervously. His bed? Of course, his room, his bed. That warmth in her belly spread lower now, threatening to melt her already wobbly legs just a little bit more.

'I didn't know it was your bed. I didn't know anyone else lived here.'

Callum hadn't said anything but she'd never actually spoken to Callum. Not that she was about to divulge that bit of information. That would just come across as odd. Her dad's practice manager had organised the whole house-swap thing. Luci had exchanged emails with Callum and had been intending on meeting to swap keys but he had messaged her to say his plans had changed. He'd left Sydney a day earlier than they had discussed so he'd left a key under a flowerpot for her, but she was certain he hadn't mentioned a brother. Not at any stage.

So what did this mean for her house-sitting plans? Would Seb ask her to leave? Would Callum?

'So where is he?' Seb wanted to know. 'Should I be checking the rest of the house? You haven't done away with him, have you? Did he treat you badly and you've sneaked in here to have your revenge?'

Luci laughed and wondered about the type of women Seb associated with if that was the direction his thoughts took him. 'He's in Vickers Hill.'

'Ah, Vickers Hill. You mentioned it before. Where is that exactly?' Seb arched his right eyebrow again and Luci found herself wondering if he could also do that with the left one. The idea distracted her and she almost forgot his question.

'In South Australia. In the Clare Valley,' she explained as she stepped into the kitchen. She needed to put some distance between them. To give herself something to do, she switched the kettle on, taking a mug and a green tea bag from the cupboard.

Seb took another pull of his beer. 'What is he doing there?'

'He's gone to work in a general practice. It's part of his studies.' She didn't mention that he was working with her father. If Callum wanted his brother to know what he was up to, he could tell him the finer details. But Seb not knowing Callum's movements only led to more questions. Where had Seb been? Why didn't he know what was happening? His room certainly didn't look inhabited. It had looked exactly like a guest room, which was what Luci had expected. There had been no sign of his presence other than a few clothes in the wardrobe, which she had assumed was the overflow from Callum's room. But perhaps those clothes belonged to Seb.

'So, if Cal's in Vickers Hill, what are you doing here?'

'We've done a house swap,' she replied as she poured boiled water into her mug.

'A house swap?' he repeated. 'How long are you staying?'

'Eight weeks. Until Christmas.' *Please, don't ask me to leave tonight*, she thought. She was half-resigned to the fact that her plans were about to change but she really didn't want to pack her bags and find somewhere else to stay in the middle of the night. This was her first trip to Sydney. 'If that's all right,' she added, pleading desperately. She had no idea where she'd go if he asked her to leave. Back to Bondi, she supposed, but the prospect of doing that at this late hour was not at all appealing.

Seb shrugged. 'It's Cal's house, whatever plans you've made with him stick. I just crash here when I'm in town. I called it my room but, I guess, technically it's not.'

Luci wondered where he'd been. Where he'd come from. But she was too tired to think about that now.

'I'll stay in Callum's room,' he added.

'Thank you.' She threw her tea bag in the bin and picked up her mug. 'I guess I'll see you in the morning, then.'

She took her tea and retreated. Seb looked interesting and she was certainly intrigued. He was giving her more questions than answers and she needed, wanted, to find out more, but it would have to wait. She had to get some sleep.

But sleep eluded her. She tossed and turned and wondered about Seb. Maybe she should have just stayed up and got all the answers tonight. Instead she lay in bed and made up stories in her head, filling in all the blank spaces about the handsome stranger with imagined details.

It wasn't often she got to meet a stranger. And a gorgeous, fascinating one to boot. In Vickers Hill everyone knew everyone else and their business. Meeting someone new was quite thrilling compared to what she was used to. Excitement bubbled in her chest. A whole new world of possibilities might open up to her.

She smiled to herself as she rolled over.

Things had just become interesting.

CHAPTER TWO

SEB PUT HIS empty beer bottle down on the kitchen table and stared out at the dark ocean through the branches of the eucalyptus. He could hear the waves lapping on the shore and could see the lights of the yachts rising and falling on the water. He'd missed the sound of the ocean but he wasn't thinking about the water or the boats or the lights now. He was thinking about the woman he'd found in his bed. The absolutely stunning, and very naked, woman.

It had been a surprise, to put it mildly. He detested surprises normally—experience had taught him that they were generally unpleasant—but he couldn't complain about this one. He'd found women in his bed unexpectedly before but he couldn't recall any of them being quite as attractive as Luci.

He closed his eyes but his mind was restless and he couldn't settle. He should be exhausted. He'd had a long and dusty eight-hour ride from Deniliquin and he'd been looking forward to a shower, something to eat and then bed. In that order. That had been his plan until he'd discovered Luci in his bed. His plan had been delightfully disrupted by a gorgeous naked woman.

He wasn't sure that he really understood why she was here. Or why Cal wasn't. He hadn't spoken to his brother for several weeks. They didn't have that sort of relationship. Seb wasn't even in the habit of calling ahead to let Callum know he would be in town. They were close but unless there was a reason for a call neither of them picked up the phone. And when they did their conversations were brief, borne out of necessity only and usually avoided if possible.

Seb had tried to talk to Cal after Cal had been injured in a cricketing accident, an accident that had almost cost him his left eye, but even then they had never got to the heart of the problem. Neither of them were much good at discussing their feelings.

But despite their lack of communication they still shared a brotherly bond. They had relied on each other growing up. The sons of high-achieving surgeons, they had spent a lot of time by themselves, supervised only by nannies. Perhaps that was why they had never learned to discuss their feelings—the nannies certainly hadn't encouraged it and Seb couldn't remember many family dinners or even much support in times of crisis. Not that there had been many crises, just one big one for each of them in their adult lives. They'd been lucky really.

But their childhood bonds had remained strong and Cal had always had a bed for him. Until now. Which brought him back to the question of what Luci was really doing here. And what did it mean for him?

He ran his hands through his hair. It was thick with dust and sweat from hours encased in a helmet. He still needed a shower. The sea breeze wafted through the balcony doors, carrying with it the fresh scent of salt. Perhaps he should go for a swim instead. The cool water of Sydney Harbour might be just what he needed to stop his brain from turning in circles.

There was no light coming from under Luci's door so he stripped off his jeans in the living room and pulled a pair of swimming shorts from his duffel bag. He left his house key under the flowerpot on the back balcony and jogged barefooted down the stairs and crossed the road to the beach. The sand was cool and damp under his feet and the water was fresh.

He didn't hesitate. He took three steps into the sea and dived under the water. He surfaced several metres off-shore but the water was shallow enough that he could still stand. The sea was calm and gentle and refreshing but it wasn't enough to stop his head from spinning with unan-swered questions.

Vickers Hill, South Australia. He'd never heard of Vick-ers Hill. How the hell had Callum ever found it? But if the girls there looked like Luci, he couldn't blame him for wanting to visit.

He turned and looked back across the beach to the apartment block. It was a small complex, only three floors, and Callum's apartment took up the top floor, but there was nothing to see as it was all in darkness. But he could imagine Luci, sleeping in his bed. The image of her, at the moment he'd first seen her, filled his mind.

In his bed with the sheets pulled up to her chin, her blue-grey eyes huge with apprehension. He'd got just as much of a shock as she had but at least he'd been semi-clothed. He'd been unable to see anything but he'd known that beneath those sheets, his sheets, she had been as naked as the day she was born.

As she had sat up in bed the covers had slipped down, exposing the swell of her breasts, before she'd clutched the sheet tightly, pulling it firmly across her chest. He'd had his T-shirt in his hand, halfway to the shower when he'd discovered her, and he'd had to surreptitiously move his hand so the T-shirt had covered his groin and his reaction. It had been pure and primal. Lust, desire.

He knew he'd let his eyes linger on her for a few seconds too long to be considered polite. Had she noticed?

Her eyes had watched him carefully. Her face was round with a heart-shaped chin and she had lips like a ripe peach. She was thin but not skinny and she had firm, round breasts that it was impossible not to notice. He'd seen them rise and fall under the sheet as she'd panicked. He could have happily watched her breathing all night.

His eyes had been drawn to four small, dark freckles that made a diamond shape against the pale skin on her chest. One sat about an inch below her collarbone, another on the swell of her right breast with a matching one on the left, and the fourth one, the one that formed the bottom of the diamond, was tucked into her cleavage. The pattern was stamped on his memory.

He should have given her some privacy, backed out of the room, but he'd been transfixed.

He closed his eyes now and floated on his back but he could still see Luci's pale skin decorated with the perfect diamond imprinted on the backs of his eyelids. It was late and he was physically exhausted but he knew there was no way he'd be able to sleep. Not yet.

He flipped onto his front and swam further into the harbour. In the pale starlight he could see the outline of his boat tied to its mooring. With long, fluid strokes he passed several other boats floating on the water as he swam out to his cabin cruiser.

His hands gripped the ladder at the stern and he pulled himself up onto the small ledge at the rear. He ran his hand over the smooth, sleek lines of the cabin as he made his way round to the large, flat bow. He stretched, resting his back against the windscreen. This boat was his sanctuary. He'd bought it almost three years ago as a project. It had good lines and plenty of potential and had been advertised as needing some TLC or a handyman's touch. He was no builder but he was good with his hands and he'd figured the learning curve would keep his mind occupied, which was just what he'd needed at the time. He had needed a project, a focus, something to keep him busy, so he could avoid dealing with his alternate reality.

Three years down the track he had made good progress emotionally but he couldn't say the same about the boat. It was still far from finished, although he had managed to get it to the stage where he could enjoy a day out. The engine worked, as did the toilet, but the kitchen and sleeping berths still needed serious attention. That was his current project, one he intended to finish while he was back in Sydney this time. He had an appointment scheduled for tomorrow evening to meet a cabinet-maker who was, hopefully, going to make new cupboards for the kitchen. While it was far from perfect, it didn't matter. It was perfect for him.

The boat represented freedom.

Seb didn't want to be tied down and the boat gave him a sense of having a place in the world without commitment. Eventually, when the renovation was completed, he planned to live aboard. Having a boat as his place of residence appealed immensely as he could close it up and leave or take it with him. It would be a fluid living arrangement, transient enough that he didn't have to think of living aboard as settling down. It wasn't a big commitment.

He wasn't ready for commitment. He'd tried it once, with disastrous results.

Luckily for him Callum didn't show any signs of settling down either, which meant he always had a place to crash. It was reassuring to know that he had a place to stay that didn't require any commitment from him. Was that immature behaviour? Perhaps. Irresponsible? Maybe. He

hadn't thought about what he'd do if Callum ever did settle
down. At least he hadn't until tonight.

Seeing someone else in his room—he always thought of
it as his, even though he was an infrequent visitor—seeing
Luci in his bed, made him wonder what he would do if Callum ever wanted to make changes. What if he wanted to rent
out that room or live with a girlfriend? Either one would put
him out on the street.

Was he being selfish? Taking advantage of Callum's
generosity? Was it time he grew up and stopped relying
on his big brother?

But no matter what Cal's intentions were, being tossed
out onto the street by Luci was still a possibility if she was
uncomfortable about having him share her space. He'd told
her he would stick with Callum's plan but what if she decided she didn't want him there?

One thing at a time, he decided. He'd only been back
for five minutes. It wasn't worth wasting time worrying
about things that might not happen. It was far more enjoyable to spend his time thinking about a pretty blonde who
was curled up in his bed.

Seb laced his fingers together and rested his hands behind his head as he looked up at the sky. There were no
clouds, the sky was dark and clear, the stars bright against
the inky blackness. He picked out the Southern Cross, its
familiar diamond shape marking the sky reminding him
of the other diamond he'd seen earlier.

Things were about to become interesting.

Luci was up early. She showered and grabbed a piece of
fruit for breakfast, trying to keep the noise to a minimum.
There was no sound from Seb's room and she didn't want
to disturb him. She hadn't heard him come back in last
night but his motorbike helmet, jacket and boots were still

piled on the living room floor so she assumed he was sleeping. She stuffed her laptop into her bag and slung it across her body, biting into her apple as she walked out the front door.

Today was her last full day of lectures. Tomorrow she and the other nineteen registered and enrolled nurses would have orientation at whichever child and family health centre they had been assigned to for their placements, and the course would then become a mixture of theory and practice. Luci was looking forward to getting out of the lecture room and dipping her toe into the world of family and community health.

The lectures had been interesting but she wasn't used to sitting down all day. The training room was an internal one in the hospital. It was small and windowless and by the end of the day Luci was itching to get outside into the fresh air. She was planning on taking a walk along Manly beach to clear the cobwebs from her mind. She stretched her arms and back and rolled her shoulders as the group waited for the final lecturer of the day. The topic for the last session was indigenous health, which had the potential to be interesting, but Luci didn't envy the lecturer their four o'clock timeslot. She doubted she was the only one who was thinking ahead to the end of the day.

Luci heard the sound of the door click open and swing shut. It was followed by a murmur from the back of the room that intensified in volume as it swept down the stairs. The room had half a dozen rows of tiered seating and she was sitting near the front. The room was buzzing and Luci turned her head to see what had got everyone so excited.

Seb was at the end of her row, about to step down to the front of the room. What on earth was he doing here?

He shrugged out of his leather jacket and dropped his motorbike helmet on a chair. He was dressed casually in sand-coloured cotton trousers and a chambray blue shirt that brought out the colour of his eyes.

He looked seriously hot.

He pulled a USB stick from his shirt pocket and plugged it into the computer. *He was the lecturer?*

He looked up, ready to address the room, and his eyes scanned the group, running over the twenty or so attendees. Luci's stomach was churning with nerves and her palms were sweaty as she waited for him to pick her out in the room. It didn't take long.

He spotted her in the front row and smiled. His blue eyes were intensely bright in his ridiculously handsome face and Luci swore the entire room, including the two male nurses, caught their collective breath. Her knees wobbled and she was glad she was already sitting down.

'Hello.' He was looking straight at her and everything around her dissolved in a haze as she melted into his gaze. 'I am Dr Seb Hollingsworth.'

Dr! Did he just say Dr? The motorbike-riding, leather-jacketed, living, breathing marble statue was a doctor? Somehow he'd let that little piece of information slide.

Luci missed the rest of his introduction as she tried to remember if she'd told him what she did. She'd talked about the house swap but perhaps she hadn't told him she was a nurse, which might explain why he hadn't mentioned he was a doctor. It was hard to remember anything when he was standing right in front of her, looking at her a bit too often with his bright blue eyes.

His voice was strong and deep and confident and Luci could feel it roll through her like waves rolling onto the shore. His voice caressed her and she was tempted to close her eyes as she listened. Maybe then she would be able to concentrate.

He was talking confidently about the cultural differences between the indigenous communities and those families with European backgrounds and the impact that had on the health of the children.

'Indigenous families are often reluctant to bring their children to the health clinics because of the lessons history has taught them. Many are fearful but we know that early intervention and health checks save lives. Education is the key, not only by the health professionals but also by the schools. We know that educated people have a better standard of living and better health. We have been running playgroups and early learning sessions to encourage the families to come to the clinics and the hope is that the parents will then feel comfortable enough to enrol their kids in school. Our current focus from a health perspective is on nutrition and family support so for any of you who will spend time working with these communities during your placements you'll need to be aware of the cultural sensitivities.'

Luci knew she should be taking notes but she was too busy watching and listening. She hadn't been able to keep her eyes closed. It was too tempting to watch him. And she knew where to find him if she had any questions.

'Funding is an issue—nothing new there,' he was saying, 'but the health department will continue to lobby for that. Our stats show there are benefits with these early intervention health programmes.'

There were lots of questions as Seb tried to wrap up his session. Luci guessed they all wanted to prolong the time that he spent in the room and even when he dismissed the class several of them crowded around him like kids around the ice-cream truck.

Luci gathered her notebook and laptop and shoved them into her bag. She wasn't going to hang around. If he was finished by the time she was packed up she'd stop and talk

to him, otherwise she'd leave. She picked up her bag and
started up the steps.

'Luci! Can you wait a moment?' Seb's voice stopped
her in her tracks.

She hesitated. She had nowhere she had to rush off to.
She had no reason not to wait. She dumped her bag on a
chair and sat down, aware that some of the other girls were
looking at her curiously. That was okay. She was used to
being stared at and talked about.

Seb finished his discussions with the other students
and came over to her.

'*Dr* Hollingsworth?' Luci was determined to get the
first words in but that didn't seem to faze Seb.

'Nurse Luci.' He was smiling at her, making her insides
turn somersaults. Again. 'Have you got time for a drink?'

'Why?'

'It seems we have some things to discuss, I thought it
might be nice to share our secrets over a drink.'

'I don't have any secrets,' she fibbed.

His grin widened. 'Everyone has secrets,' he said. He
had his jacket and helmet tucked under one arm and he
picked up Luci's bag with his other hand. 'Come on, I'll
give you a lift.'

'Where are we going?'

Seb smirked, obviously sensing victory, and replied,
'The Sandman, it's about halfway down the beach.'

The bar was on North Steyne Street, a little over a ki-
lometre away. Luci had walked past it before. 'I'll meet
you there,' she said. The walk would give her a chance to
clear her head and hopefully time to get over her jitters.
She wasn't sure if this was a good idea but she couldn't
think of an excuse on the spot. She couldn't think of anything much when Seb looked at her and smiled.

Luci took her bag from Seb and slung it over her shoulder. When she reached the beach she rolled up the legs of her khaki pants and slid her canvas sneakers off her feet and walked along the sand. The late-afternoon sun bounced off the waves, turning the water silver. Kids with surfboards ran in and out of the ocean, their shouts drowning out the screeching of the seagulls. The beach was busy. She didn't know a soul but she was fine with that. Back home she couldn't walk down the street without bumping into half a dozen people she knew and it was a pleasant change to have anonymity, especially after the past six months. It wasn't always so great having everyone know your business.

She stepped off the beach opposite the bar. She walked on the grass to brush the sand from her feet then slipped her shoes back on. Seb had beaten her there and he lifted a hand in greeting as she crossed the street. As if she wouldn't have noticed him—the bar was busy but he was easily the most noticeable person there.

Somehow, despite the crowd, he'd managed to grab a table with a view of the beach. He stood up as she approached and offered her a stool, his motorbike helmet on a third stool, like a chaperone.

'What can I get you to drink?'

'What are you going to have?'

'A beer.'

'That sounds great, thank you.'

Sturdy Norfolk pines lined the foreshore, guarding the beach, and Luci watched the ocean through the frame of the trees. She took her phone out of her bag as Seb went to the bar and snapped a photo of the view. She sent it to Flick captioned, After-work drinks, could get used to this! But she resisted saying anything about the company she was keeping. There was no way to describe how he made her feel. Nervous, excited, expectant. She was silly to feel those things, she knew nothing about him, and she knew she couldn't share her thoughts, Flick would think she'd gone crazy.

She slipped her phone into her bag as Seb came back to the table.

He handed her a glass. 'So, you're a nurse?'

'And you're a doctor.'

'I am. Is that how you met Callum? Through the hospital? How come I've never met you?'

Luci laughed. 'Which question do you want me to answer first?'

'Your choice.'

He was looking at her intently and her heart pounded in her chest. He made her feel nervous—a gorgeous man paying her attention. It was such an unfamiliar situation but she would have to admit she rather liked it. She didn't even mind the nerves. It was exciting.

She took a sip of her beer as she thought about which answer to give him.

'I've never actually met your brother. And I've never been to Sydney before, which would be why we've never met. Callum needed a place to stay and so did I. The house swap was convenient for both of us. Nothing more than that.'

Luci had been restless since her divorce and Flick had been pushing her to get out of Vickers Hill, but she'd needed more than a push. She was buying her ex's share of their house and she couldn't afford to pay her mortgage and rent elsewhere so it wasn't until the house-swap idea had been suggested that she'd been brave enough to actually put a plan in motion. Having the opportunity to study *and* have free accommodation had been a big deciding factor for her. Which brought her back to the matter at hand.

Where was she going to be able to stay now? It would be extremely inconvenient if she had to change her plans.

'Callum didn't tell me that he had any other tenants,' she said. 'I suppose I could look into nurses' accommodation through the hospital if you want me to move out. Do you know if the hospital has any student accommodation? I'm afraid I don't know anyone in Sydney to stay with.'

Seb shook his head. 'You have more right to be there than I do. I told you, whatever plans you made with him stick. It's his place and I'm not even technically a tenant. I only crash there when I come to town. I can ask one of my mates to put me up.'

'When you come to town?' Luci queried. 'You're not employed at North Sydney?' She had assumed he was a staff doctor. 'Are you just a guest lecturer?'

'Not exactly.' Seb picked up his glass and Luci's eyes followed the path of his drink from the table to his lips. She watched as he took a long sip. She could scarcely believe she was sitting at a bar, having a drink with a stranger. She'd never been out with a man she'd just met. Not one on one. For as long as she could remember she had been part of a couple.

Seb made her feel nervous. But it was a good kind of nervous. An exciting kind.

He swallowed his beer and continued, 'I'm employed by the state health department and I'm based out of North Sydney Hospital but I spend most of my time in rural areas. There doesn't seem to be much point paying rent in the city, especially not at Sydney prices, for the few nights a month that I'm in town so I crash at Cal's.'

Disappointment washed over her. He was only in town a few nights a month. Did that mean he'd be gone again soon?

'If you're only here for a few days then I'm sure we

can manage to share the space,' she suggested, hoping she sounded friendly and hospitable rather than desperate, but the truth was she'd quite like the company. While she was enjoying her anonymity she'd never lived on her own before—she'd left home and moved into university accommodation and then married Ben. She was finding Callum's apartment a bit too quiet. She liked the idea of having company and she had a feeling she could do a lot worse than Seb's.

'I need to be honest,' he replied. 'I'm here for longer than a few days this time, it'll be closer to six weeks, and in the interests of full disclosure I'll be working out of the community health centre attached to the hospital. Where will you be doing your placement?'

'There.' Because Luci was from interstate she'd been given the most convenient placement.

'So we'll be working together too,' Seb added, 'but if you're happy to share Cal's space for a few days, we could give it a trial and see how we go.' He smiled at her and Luci's heart flipped in her chest. 'If it doesn't work out, I'll find somewhere else to stay. How's that sound?'

It sounded all right to her but she paused while she pretended to give it some thought. She nodded. 'Okay.'

'That's settled, then.' He tapped his drink against hers. 'House mates it is.' He sipped his beer and asked, 'So tell me about Vickers Hill. Your family is there?'

Luci nodded. 'My parents. I work at the local hospital.'

'Is it a big town?'

'Big enough to need a hospital. Your typical country hospital. We have obstetrics and some aged-care beds and we do some minor surgery as well.'

'So why the change to family and community health?'

'I needed to get out.'

'Of the hospital?'

Luci shook her head. 'Of Vickers Hill.'

'Why?'

Luci sighed quietly. There was no point keeping everything a secret as she figured he'd find out most of it eventually anyway. His brother was in Vickers Hill, working with her father. There would be no secrets. Not that her father would talk about her but Luci knew there were patients who couldn't resist gossip. And if Callum looked anything like Seb did, Luci knew there'd be no shortage of patients booking appointments with the new doctor. 'I got divorced six months ago and I just felt I needed to get out of town for a while.'

'Has it been messy?'

'Not messy so much as awkward. My dad is the local doctor—Callum has gone to work in his clinic,' she explained, 'so everyone, and I mean everyone, knows me. My ex-husband and I grew up together, we dated since high school, got married at twenty-one and divorced at twenty-five.'

'You were together, what, ten years?'

'About that.'

'That's a long time. This must be tough for you.'

No one else, other than Flick and her parents, had really understood how her divorce had impacted on her but Seb had hit the nail on the head immediately.

Her divorce had turned her world upside down. Every day of her life had included Ben. He was part of her history. Their friendship and relationship had shaped her into the person she was today and it had been difficult to separate herself into her own person. Ben was wrapped up in her identity and she was having to shape a new one for herself. It had been tough. Really tough.

Perhaps it was the distance lending Seb perspective. Everyone at home seemed to be having just as much difficulty adjusting to Luci being single as she was, which was partly why she had decided, or agreed with Flick's suggestion, to leave. The locals weren't moving on as quickly as she would like, which had made things even more difficult for her. It had taken her a lot of adjusting but she was finally coming to terms with the end of her marriage, and she felt the process would be faster if she didn't have to contend with local opinion as well.

'It has been rough,' she admitted. 'I reckon a divorce is sad and stressful enough, without having an entire town involved. Because everyone knew us, had seen us grow up, they all seemed to think that our divorce was somehow their business. I was tired of everyone either feeling sorry for me because I couldn't keep my husband or offering to set me up with their nephew, grandson or best friend's boy.'

'So you ran away?'

He was watching her closely and Luci could feel herself starting to blush. She wasn't used to such close attention. She turned away, breaking eye contact. 'It was time for a change.'

Feeling sorry for herself was self-indulgent. She needed to move on but in a town where everyone knew her business that was hard to do. The truth was she hadn't coped well at all but that was none of their business. That's why Flick had been able to talk her into this crazy idea to take a study break in Sydney, and looking around her now she had to admit that it hadn't been such a mad idea after all. She was actually feeling like she was able to put her marriage behind her. But the demise of her marriage had also cost her the chance of motherhood and that wasn't so easy to come to terms with.

But she preferred to think she was running towards her future rather than away from her past. She didn't want to get pigeonholed, which was the danger if she'd stayed put, but there was no need to explain everything. Seb didn't need to know it all. Unlike at home, she could choose to keep her secrets. This was her opportunity to tell people only what she wanted them to know and she intended to make the most of it.

'Well, I reckon there's plenty in Sydney to keep you so busy that you won't have time to think. And I promise not to introduce you to any eligible men. Unless you ask me to,' he added. He finished his beer, pushed back the cuff of his shirt and looked at his watch. 'I have a meeting to get to but can I give you a lift home first?' he asked as he picked up his helmet.

'That would be great,' she said, but she should have said no.

Seb offered her his leather jacket to wear for protection, just in case something untoward happened. His hands brushed hers as he slid the jacket over her arms and when his fingers brushed her neck as he fastened the strap of his spare helmet under her chin Luci thought she might melt on the spot. And she still had to get on the bike and sit behind him and wrap her arms around his waist. She wasn't sure her brain could be trusted to convey all those messages.

She should have declined his offer, she'd remember that next time.

But it was too late now. She'd been on a motorbike before. It was probably no different from cycling—it would all come back to her once she got on. Her ex had a trail bike that he'd used to ride around his parents' property and to school. He would pick her up every morning and give her a lift, but they'd been seventeen then. She couldn't remember the last time she'd ridden on the back of his bike, and as she wrapped her arms around Seb's waist and felt his body heat radiating into her she thought she certainly didn't remember feeling like this.

The bike vibrated between her thighs. She pressed her legs into the seat as she held on tight. Her face was tucked against his shoulder blade and she could smell him. He smelt fresh and tangy; there was a trace of citrus in his aftershave, lime perhaps.

She probably should have walked home but she was glad she hadn't. She was quite happy right where she was.

CHAPTER THREE

LUCI'S MORNING STARTED with orientation at the family and community health clinic attached to North Sydney Hospital. She spent the morning getting her ID, setting up her email and running through the safety policies and procedures for the site. Once the administration side of things had been dealt with, she would start work. The course participants would be given a case load as the service tried to get through their waiting list. The system was under the pump, there were always more people who needed the service.

Her diary showed her running an immunisation clinic. It was an easy, straightforward introduction that didn't require her to have detailed backgrounds or rapport with the clients. She worked steadily through the hours after lunch. She had bumped into Seb once but it seemed that the staff worked autonomously and she was almost able to forget that he was there. Almost.

But all that changed when her two-thirty client didn't keep her appointment. Melanie Parsons had booked her son, Milo, in for his six-month check and immunisations. When she failed to arrive Luci pulled up her file on the computer. There were numerous entries and lots of red flags.

This woman was a victim of domestic violence. Her

past medical history included three full-term pregnancies, one miscarriage and a long list of broken bones and medical treatment for bruising and lacerations. And they were only the things she'd consulted a doctor about. Luci would bet her house that there were more incidents that had gone unreported.

Luci picked up the phone and dialled the client's number. The community health centre's policy stated that all no-shows had to be followed up with a phone call. She checked the file again. It was possible that Melanie had just forgotten her appointment or was catching up on some sleep; it couldn't be easy having three children under the age of five.

But the phone went unanswered.

Luci needed to be able to record a reason for the non-attendance. In instances where that wasn't possible she had been told to let the co-ordinator know. She went to discuss the situation with Gayle, the health centre co-ordinator, to find out what the next step in the process was.

Gayle brought Melanie's notes up in her system.

'Can you discuss this with Dr Hollingsworth?' she suggested. 'He knows Melanie, he's treated her before.'

Luci heard the unspoken words and she'd seen the supporting evidence in Melanie's file. Seb had treated her for injuries sustained at the hands of someone else.

She knocked on Seb's open door.

'Have you got a minute?' she asked. He was entering notes into the computer system. He looked up and smiled. His blue eyes sparkled and Luci felt herself start to blush.

'Sure.'

She stepped inside and closed his door. She didn't want anyone else to overhear the conversation. 'Melanie Parsons. Do you know her?'

Seb nodded. 'Is she here?'

'No. She had an appointment to get her baby's six-month immunisations but she hasn't shown up. Gayle suggested I talk to you about her.'

'Have you called her?'

'Yes. There was no answer.'

'Do you know her history?'

Luci nodded. 'I've read her file.'

'Someone will need to call past her house and check on her. What time do you finish?'

'I don't think I should be the one to do a home visit,' Luci objected. 'She doesn't know me from a bar of soap.' She was not the right person for that particular job. Someone who had already established some rapport with Melanie would be far more suitable.

'I agree. But if our timing is right we can go together. You can immunise the baby and I'll see what's up with Melanie,' Seb replied. He clicked his mouse and opened his diary. 'I should be finished by three-thirty. Let me know if that works for you.'

Seb was waiting at Reception for her when she finished her clinic. 'Do you want me to drive or navigate?' he asked her as he signed out one of the work cars and collected the keys.

'I don't think I'm game to drive on your roads,' Luci replied. The streets of Sydney were narrow, winding and steep, not at all like the wide, straight roads she was used to. 'But I should warn you, my navigating skills might not be much good either as I'm not familiar with Sydney.'

'No worries. I'll get the map up on my phone.' Seb handed her his phone and she followed him out to the car.

It wasn't long before Seb pulled to a stop in front of a squat red-brick house. It had a low wire fence and a front lawn that needed mowing. There was an old station wagon parked under a carport at the side of the house and a couple of kids' bikes were lying abandoned behind the car in the driveway. The house could do with a coat of paint but it looked lived in rather than neglected. Luci had seen plenty of houses just like it in country towns in her district.

The driveway gate squeaked as Seb pushed it open, announcing their arrival. He closed it behind Luci before leading the way up the concrete path to the veranda. He knocked but there was no answer. The screen door was locked but the front door was ajar. Someone was home. Luci could hear the sound of children playing.

'Melanie?' Seb called out. 'It's Dr Hollingsworth. You missed Milo's appointment at the clinic. I need to know that you are okay.'

Through the screen door Luci could see movement in the dark passage. A woman came to the door but didn't unlatch it. She stood, half-hidden behind the door with her face turned away from them to her left.

'Hello, Melanie.' Seb struck up a conversation as if it was perfectly normal to talk through a door. 'Milo was due for his six-month check-up and vaccinations today. This is Luci Dawson.' He lifted a hand and gestured towards Luci. 'She's a nurse at the health centre. Seeing as we're here and you're home, can we come in and see the kids?'

Melanie nodded. She unlocked the door and stepped aside. She was thin. Luci knew they were the same age but Melanie looked older. Her shoulder-length brown hair was lank but her skin was clear. However, Luci didn't really take any of that in. She couldn't when all she could see was Melanie's black eye. Her left eye was slightly swollen and coloured purple with just a hint of green. The bruise looked to be a day or two old.

'Thank you,' Seb said, as he stepped into the hall and

reached for Melanie's chin. Luci expected her to flinch or pull away but she didn't. She must trust Seb.

Luci knew Seb had looked after her before. He'd filled her in on his involvement on the drive over here but Luci hadn't anticipated that she would see the evidence of Melanie's husband's abuse for herself. She hadn't been expecting that.

Seb turned Melanie's face to the right.

'You're hurt.'

'I knocked into the corner of the car boot.' Melanie's eyes were downcast.

'I haven't heard that one before.'

'It's nothing. I've had worse. You know I have,' she said, as she turned away and led them into the house. They followed her into a tired-looking sitting room. The arms of the couch were ripped and stained but Melanie had put a sheet over the cushions in an attempt to brighten the room or maybe disguise the state of the furniture. Everything looked well worn and tired. A bit like Melanie.

She collapsed onto the couch and Seb pulled an upright dining chair closer to the couch and sat on it, facing Melanie. 'What was it this time?'

'It's not his fault, Dr Hollingsworth. I'm pregnant again.'

'And how is that not his fault?' Seb's voice was quiet. He wasn't judging her but Luci could tell he was frustrated.

'He says we can't afford more kids.'

'It takes two, Melanie. He can't blame you.'

Melanie kept her eyes downcast. She had her hands in her lap, clenched together, and Luci knew she was close to tears. Luci wanted to tell Seb to let it go but she knew he couldn't. They couldn't ignore what was going on here. She knew from Melanie's file that she already had three kids—Milo, who was six months old, a two-and-a-half-year-old toddler and a four-year-old. That was a handful for anyone, let alone a woman with an abusive partner.

Seb had told her that he had advised Melanie to take her kids and leave. She had left once but had then gone back, making the usual excuses about him being the kids' father and saying that she loved him. Luci knew it was a difficult decision and something that was hard to understand unless you'd been in that position yourself or had worked with victims of domestic violence. The women were often trapped by their circumstances and Luci suspected that would be the case for Melanie. With three kids under five it was unlikely she had time to work, which meant she had no source of income if she left. And potentially no roof over her head either.

Even while Luci realised it wouldn't be easy, she couldn't stop the twinge of jealousy that she felt when she heard that Melanie was pregnant again. Luci would give her right arm for a family.

But she knew she had to put her own issues aside. Her job, their job, was to help Melanie. Luci wanted to jump in, she had suggestions on how to assist Melanie to change her situation, but Seb must have sensed her desire to offer her opinion and he put a stop to it by asking her to do Milo's health check. Did he think Melanie would open up more if she wasn't in the room? He was probably right. Melanie was unlikely to want to discuss her problems in front of a stranger.

'Milo hasn't had a cold or been unwell?' Luci clarified with Melanie. 'Any concerns at all?' she asked, figuring that as Melanie had three children she would know what to look out for by now.

Melanie shook her head. 'He's been fine. He's on baby

formula now and some solids. He's in the room across the hall.'

'No ear infections, colds or reaction to any other immunisations?'

'No.'

Luci picked up her nursing bag and crossed the hall and found herself in a child's bedroom. A bunk bed stood against one wall and Milo's cot was in the opposite corner. He was lying in his cot but he was awake. His eyes followed her as she came towards him.

There was a change mat leaning against the cot and she put it on the bottom bunk. She chatted softly to Milo as she lifted him out of the cot. She could smell a dirty nappy. She laid him down and undressed him, removing his nappy and singlet. She needed to check his hips and testes and it would also give her a chance to check for any bruises or other signs of maltreatment. She was relieved to find nothing. His soft baby skin was unmarked and besides his dirty nappy he was perfectly clean and seemingly well cared for. She found a clean nappy and his blue health-care book on a shelf. She changed his nappy and listened to his chest then recorded his length and weight. He was in the average range for both. He seemed like a happy, healthy little boy.

She gave him his oral polio vaccine and then his immunisation injection and then she couldn't resist a cuddle. She took a deep breath, getting her fill of tiny baby smell. He smelt like talcum powder and baby lotion and the smell made her heart ache. She closed her eyes and wondered if coming to Sydney to study family and community health had been the right decision. She'd been so keen to escape Vickers Hill that she hadn't really considered the ramifications of taking the course. She was going to be exposed to plenty of babies and pregnant mothers. Perhaps she should have enrolled in an aged-care course instead.

Milo was grizzling a little after his injection so Luci took him back with her and handed him to his mum. She recorded the details of the vaccinations in the little blue book while she listened to Seb's conversation with Melanie.

'It's worse when he's been drinking,' she was saying.

'Today is Friday. I suppose he'll be going to the pub after work tonight?' Seb asked. When Melanie nodded he continued, 'Is there someone you could ask to come over? A friend, your mum or a sister? If you are going to stay here then I think it would be wise to have someone else here with you for support when he gets home.'

Melanie wouldn't maintain eye contact and Luci knew she had no intention of following Seb's suggestion.

'Your decision, Melanie,' Seb said as he stood up. Perhaps he realised he was getting nowhere. 'But I will be checking to make sure you keep the appointment that I'll make for you with the counsellor, okay?'

He gathered his things and Luci went with him out to the car.

'We can't just leave her there,' Luci exploded as she clicked her seat belt into position. She'd been fighting to keep her temper under control and had just managed to hold it together until they had some privacy.

'What else do you suggest we do?' Seb asked. 'She doesn't want to leave and when she has left in the past it's never been for long. She always goes back. We have to pick our battles.'

'But she should be thinking about the children.'

'Melanie says he's never hurt them. Did you see anything to indicate otherwise?'

'No.' Luci shook her head. 'Milo was perfectly healthy

and happy but still it's no way for those children to grow up. They shouldn't have to see that, plus it perpetuates the cycle of abuse.'

'I know that. Trust me, we're working on it. I will make an appointment for her to see a counsellor. For us to be able to make any real difference we need to support Melanie to find a way out of this. She will need somewhere to live and she will need money. There is new legislation that can force the perpetrator to leave the premises so that the victim can stay in their home, but I'm not convinced that is a workable solution. It makes it far too easy for the abusive party to find the victim. Court orders ordering them to stay away are violated on a regular basis. This is a problem that can't be fixed overnight and it can't be fixed unless Melanie wants it to change, but I promise I will be doing everything I can.'

Luci nodded. 'I'm sorry,' she apologised. She should have guessed Seb would do what he thought was best. 'I jumped down your throat.'

'It's okay. I know it's hard to understand when you're strong and independent how someone else can put up with circumstances that you would never dream of tolerating. But try to see it from Melanie's point of view. She feels she doesn't have any other option. Again it's about education and support. But these things take time. Not everyone can just up and leave. If you want to work in community health you're going to need to have patience and empathy. Don't stop wanting better things for people but don't expect them all to be like you.'

Luci got off her high horse. She knew all that. She didn't have to look too hard to find the similarities between her situation and Melanie's. She understood how much effort and energy and strength it took to leave the familiar. She hadn't left Vickers Hill without a push from

Flick, and her circumstances were far better than Melanie's. She'd only had to leave behind an ex-husband—one who had never beaten her, just one who'd decided he wanted a different life. She knew she couldn't be critical of Melanie or Seb.

'Now, let's talk about something else,' Seb said as he turned onto the main road. 'Something happier. What are your plans for the weekend?'

'I should be studying,' she replied, as she tried to put Melanie and her circumstances out of her mind. Seb had said he would monitor the situation and she had to trust him to do that. 'I have an assignment due Monday.'

'How long do you need?'

'I'm not sure. Why?'

Seb shrugged. 'You said you've never been to Sydney before. I have a free day tomorrow. If you like, I could show you around.'

She should get started on her assignment but when faced with a choice between spending her day with a gorgeous tourist guide or her laptop it was a no brainer. If she got started on her assignment tonight she should be able to finish it on Sunday. She'd get it done on time even if it meant staying up all night. She wasn't about to knock back Seb's invitation.

'I'd love that, thank you.'

There was a sticky note from Seb stuck on the kettle. In two days he'd figured out that the first thing she did every morning was switch the kettle on. She smiled as she read the note and waited for the water to boil.

Meet me on the beach at ten a.m. Bring togs, a hat and sunglasses.

Excitement swirled in her belly. She knew she needed to get her assignment finished but she'd just work all day tomorrow. She wasn't going to miss this opportunity for sightseeing or spending time with Seb. In just a couple of days she could already feel herself changing, becoming the person she thought she could be. She was leaving the old Luci behind. Leaving behind the doubts and the failures. This was her time to start again, to step through the doorway and into her future, and it felt like Seb could help open the door.

She slipped a white cotton sundress over her black bikini, sunglasses over her eyes and a soft, straw hat onto her head. Figuring she'd need a towel if she needed her bathers, she stuffed one and some sunscreen into a bag and headed to the beach across the road.

The beach was small, really only a cove, and apart from a couple and their dog it was empty. Luci scanned up and down along the sand but she couldn't see any sign of Seb. Assuming he wouldn't be far, she sat on the sand and looked out to sea. Little boats bobbed on the water at their moorings, but there were a lot fewer than normal. People must have headed out for the day. The weather was perfect for boating, the sky bright blue and cloudless, the water relatively calm, and the sun was already warm.

Movement to her right caught her eye and she watched as a man rowed a dinghy towards the shore. He had his back to her and was bare to the waist, and she watched the muscles in his back flex and relax as he pulled the oars through the water. As the boat got closer she realised the oarsman was Seb. She barely knew him and it wasn't like she could recognise his movement patterns or even the shape of his shoulders and torso yet, but she recognised the funny fluttery feeling in her stomach that she got when he was nearby.

The boat ran aground and he stowed the oars and jumped out in one fluid and graceful movement. He turned and smiled when he saw her waiting there. His hair was wet, it looked darker than his normal chestnut, and his bare chest was lightly tanned and perfectly sculpted. His swimming trunks were damp and clung to his thighs. She swallowed as the fluttery feeling in her stomach intensified.

'Good morning,' he greeted her.

'Good morning,' she replied, hoping the sun was hiding the blush that she could feel stealing over her cheeks.

He reached out a hand and helped her to her feet. His hand was warm and strong but his grip was gentle. The butterflies in her stomach went crazy.

'You're ready?' he asked her.

'Where are we going?'

'Out on the harbour.'

Luci looked doubtfully at the boat at the water's edge. 'In that?'

Was he kidding? The boat was barely ten feet long and had no motor.

'At first.' He was laughing at her discomfort. 'You're not a sailor?'

'I grew up in the country. This looks a little small,' she said, as she stood and surveyed the little vessel.

'It's okay. I have a bigger boat.' He smiled at her and Luci noticed that his eyes were the same bright blue as the sky. 'This is just the tender to get us out there. Hop in.'

He took her bag and held her hand as he helped her into the dinghy. Her body came to life with his touch. The butterflies took flight and swarmed out of her stomach and lodged in her throat. She didn't think she could breathe. But he had to let go of her to push the boat off the beach and then she was able to inhale a lungful of salty sea air.

He spun the boat around and jumped in, sitting on the seat opposite her. Their knees were almost touching.

He gripped the oars and pulled through the water. She could see his muscles straining. His biceps and triceps alternately tensed and relaxed. His pectoral muscles flexed in his chest. His abdominal muscles were taut. She could feel a blush deepening on her cheeks. She looked out at the harbour as she tried to get herself under control.

'What is your boat called?' she asked, as she scanned the yachts, reading the names painted on the hulls.

'She doesn't have a name yet. She needs a bit of work and once she's finished I'll work out what to call her. It will depend on how she feels.'

'She?'

'All boats are female.'

'Why is that?'

'I'm not sure.' He grinned and she suspected he was about to spin her a story. 'Probably because no matter how much money you spend on them, it's never enough.'

'Hey, that's not fair,' she argued, as he laughed. 'We're not all high maintenance.'

'Well, I hope *you're* not because you might be disappointed by today if you are.'

Luci doubted that. In her opinion the day was already off to a very good start.

Seb pulled the dinghy to a stop beside a sleek white cabin cruiser, then secured the tender before stepping on board and reaching for her hand. Luci was prepared for her reaction to his touch this time and managed to take a deep breath before she took his hand. He helped her on board and then picked up a boathook and dragged a mooring rope closer and tied off the tender.

'Come, I'll give you a tour before we take off.'

'A tour?' Of what? she wondered. Surely there wasn't much to see?

He opened a small gate at the rear of the boat and Luci stepped off the back ledge. There was a steering wheel with a driver's seat and a small bench seat ran perpendicular to that along the left-hand side of the boat. Luci knew that left and right weren't called that on a boat but she didn't know much else.

Seb put her bag on the seat. 'Follow me,' he said as he ducked his head and made his way down three small steps into the front of the boat.

Luci hadn't noticed the steps until Seb showed her but she did as she was told, finding herself in a compact cabin. A kitchen bench complete with a sink ran along the wall to her right and a small table surrounded by a bench seat sat to her left. In front of her, at waist height, raised above a bank of cupboards, was a large flat wooden surface. But all of that barely registered. Seb was still shirtless and the small confines of the cabin meant he was standing only inches from her. She realised that he must have swum out to the boat to retrieve the tender before rowing back to shore to collect her. His chest was smooth and almost hairless and she could see the white spots where the salt had dried on his skin.

'This is it.' Seb's head was almost brushing the ceiling and his left hand almost brushed against her as he gestured to the space around them. 'I have to install new kitchen cabinets and appliances, these have seen better days, and...' he slapped his palm a couple of times on the flat wooden platform '...get a decent mattress for my nautical futon and then I'll be able to take her out for more than just day trips.'

'You'll be able to sleep on the boat?'

'I already have but only in my swag. But if I'm going

to live on her I want something a little more comfortable and permanent than that.'

'Live on it?'

'That's my plan. There's a bathroom in here, the toilet is working,' he said as he opened a narrow door next to the bed, 'and once the shower is operational and the new kitchen is installed I'm good to go.'

'But it's so small!' Luci looked around. It possibly had everything a man might need but there was no getting away from the fact that it was at the compact end of the scale spectrum.

'Haven't you ever had a holiday in a caravan?'

Luci laughed. 'A holiday, yes, but I'm not sure I'd want to live in a caravan.' *Or on a boat.*

'I've spent plenty of nights in my swag under the stars with just my bike and a camp fire for company. This will be five-star compared to that. And whenever I get tired of one place I can just haul up the anchor and be off.'

Luci didn't want to rain on his parade. It wasn't her place to comment on his choice of accommodation and she supposed it did sound romantic—for a while.

She wondered what it would be like to be so free. She was busy trying to pay off the mortgage on her house and it would be years until she was free of that commitment. But while she could see the appeal of being debt-free, she knew that deep down she would still want a home. She needed that security.

'It sounds like fun,' she said, determined not to be a naysayer.

She looked around. It didn't take long. The boat was only big enough for one person to live on—just. It looked like Seb wasn't planning on sharing it with anyone on a permanent basis and she wondered why. He was a smart, attractive man; he must have women lining up at his door.

Why would he choose to hide away on a boat built for one? A boat that for all intents and purposes seemed very much like a bachelor pad?

The tour over, she followed him back up the steps.

'Have a seat,' Seb said, indicating the bench seat to the left of the wheel. 'There are cold drinks in the ice box and life jackets and a bucket under your seat. Fire extinguisher here.' He pointed to a small red cylinder attached to the side of the steering mechanism. 'And that concludes the safety briefing.'

'You're making me nervous.'

'I may not have finished the cosmetic side of things but I promise she's seaworthy,' he said as he pushed a button and the engine roared to life. He released the boat from her mooring, put it into gear and headed out of the cove.

The boat's engine rumbled under her feet and the noise made conversation difficult but Luci didn't care. She stowed her bag beneath her seat and stretched out, enamoured with the view of both scenery and the driver. North Head and South Head jutted out into the ocean to their left. Luci could see a lighthouse on top of South Head and whitecaps on the water of the Pacific Ocean through the rocky outcrops, but Seb veered to the right, staying within the harbour, and followed the Manly ferry on its way to Circular Quay.

Seb pointed out the Prime Minister's house and Taronga Park Zoo as they motored further into the harbour. It was incredibly beautiful. And busy. It seemed like half of Sydney must be out on the harbour but that didn't detract from the experience.

The Opera House blossomed on the foreshore to their left and Seb slowed the boat down as they approached the iconic building. The drop in speed was accompanied by a decrease in engine noise, allowing them to talk normally.

'This is just brilliant. Thank you so much,' she said as Seb took them under the Harbour Bridge. She looked up at the massive steel structure that spanned the harbour. 'Have you walked across it?' she asked.

Seb laughed. 'You know you can drive across it? Or catch a train? Walking across is the sort of thing tourists do.'

'Well, I'm a tourist.'

'Add it to your list. But you might prefer to climb it or the south pylon. You get a pretty good view of the harbour from up there.'

She was disappointed. It didn't sound like Seb would offer to keep her company if she did want to walk across the bridge.

She rummaged in her bag for her phone to take some pictures. She might not get this view again.

'What, no selfie?'

She turned to find he was grinning at her.

'I'm not that photogenic,' she said, but she suspected that he was. It was a good excuse to capture a picture of him. She stepped beside him and held the phone at arm's length. He put his arm around her and she leaned in and snapped a photo of the two of them.

She checked the photo. Still shirtless, Seb was lean, muscular, gorgeous and definitely highly photogenic. She'd managed to capture the bridge in the background but she doubted anyone could look past Seb. Not that she planned on showing that photo to anybody, it was strictly for her eyes only.

He circled the boat, turning in front of Luna Park and the clown over the entrance gate grinned manically at them as they passed the jetty. Luci could hear kids screaming on the roller-coasters and she hoped he wasn't planning on taking her to the sideshows. She wasn't keen to spend the afternoon surrounded by a bunch of kids. She needed something less stressful than that but thankfully Seb kept going, steering the boat back towards the Opera House.

'Hand me your phone and I'll take a photo of you,' he said as he put the boat into neutral and idled in front of the Opera House.

Luci passed him her phone and Seb looked at the screen. The tiles that covered the sails of the building sparkled and shimmered in the sunlight, blindingly white against the brilliant blue of the sky. Luci shone just as brightly in the foreground.

She was sublime. She'd taken her hat off for the photo and her golden hair glowed. The sun was on her face, the tip of her nose was going slightly pink and her cheeks were flushed from the breeze. Her eyes were hidden behind sunglasses but she was laughing as he pressed the shutter. Her sundress framed her diamond-shaped freckles. He checked the photo, wishing he'd thought to take it on his phone. That way he would have had a copy to keep.

He tried to ignore the stirrings of lust as he put the boat into gear and cruised between Mrs Macquarie's Chair and Fort Denison and headed for Milk Beach. Luci was like a breath of fresh air in his stale world but his world was no place for her. She was gorgeous but she seemed far too delightful and pure for someone as jaded and disillusioned as he was. Too innocent. The women he'd chosen of late had been just as disheartened by life as he was. There had been no agenda other than short-term, mutual satisfaction, no danger of him damaging anyone's fragile psyche. Girls like Luci were not for him. Or, more specifically, he was no good for girls like her.

He cut through the wake of dozens of other boats, powering through the churned-up water that crisscrossed the blue of the ocean with white foam. The harbour looked magnificent and as they rounded Shark Island the mansions of Point Piper and Rose Bay clung to the hills on their right, adding to the picture-perfect view they had from his boat.

Milk Beach came into sight ahead of them and he pulled back on the throttle as he eased the cabin cruiser into the bay. He cut the engine and dropped anchor a hundred metres off the beach. From this spot they could look back towards the Sydney skyline and, as the boat swung around so her bow faced the city, he heard Luci's intake of breath.

'Wow!' She turned to him and smiled. 'Did you park here deliberately?'

The Harbour Bridge rose majestically across their bow.

'I did.' He was pleased with the reaction he'd elicited, it was just what he'd hoped for. 'The view's pretty good, isn't it?'

'It's incredible.'

It was, he thought. Luci was looking across the water to the bridge but he was watching her. 'I thought we could stop here for lunch and a swim,' he said. The small beach was busy with day trippers but he had been careful to anchor his boat away from the few others that were also enjoying a day out, in order to give them some privacy.

He grabbed the ice box and some cushions from the bench seat and took Luci around to the bow of the boat, where there was room to stretch out. He dropped the cushions on the deck, they would need some padding as the fibreglass hull of the boat could get a little uncomfortable after a while.

Luci spread her towel over the cushions and pulled her sundress over her head, revealing a very tiny bikini. Four triangles of black fabric tied together with black ties. His eyes were drawn to the diamond freckles that nestled between the swell of her breasts.

She pulled a tube of sunscreen from her bag and rubbed it into her shoulders and chest. Seb's brain pounded in his head and his heart raced, sending blood rushing through his body into all five of his extremities. He squatted down and took the lid off the ice box, giving himself a minute to regain his composure. He breathed deeply. He could smell the sea air and sunscreen. He thought he could also smell Luci. Fresh and floral. This girl was doing his head in. She was quite unselfconscious, apparently quite comfortable stripping off in front of him. He guessed there was no reason why she should worry. She had no reason to think he wouldn't be able to keep his eyes off her and people showed just as much flesh on Bondi Beach. But seeing her in a tiny bikini was sending his hormones wild. Not that it was her fault.

He was worried now, worried that she might prove irresistible, worried that he could find himself in hot water. She was down to earth, gorgeous, funny and she smelt sensational. And now she was stretched out beside him wearing nothing but a string bikini. He wasn't sure how he was going to be able to keep his hands to himself.

He wasn't sure he wanted to.

Actually, he knew he definitely *didn't* want to but he had no idea what she thought. Maybe she was looking for some fun, maybe she was disillusioned after her divorce and was looking for some short-term satisfaction, but he suspected it was just wishful thinking on his part. He didn't even know how long she'd been divorced. It could be five minutes or five months. She could have sworn off men altogether.

He offered to rub sunscreen onto her back. That was a legitimate way of not keeping his hands to himself and was possibly the best idea he'd had in a long time, along with inviting her out for the day. Her skin was soft and velvety smooth under his fingers. She lifted her hair away from the nape of her neck, getting it out of his way, and he was sorely tempted to press his lips to the knobbly bone at the base of her neck where it met her shoulders.

Instead, he stepped back, opened the ice box and offered her a drink. God knew, he needed something to help him cool off. He passed her a bottle of water. She sipped her water and then lay back, lifting her face to the sun and closing her eyes.

Seb turned back to the ice box and began to assemble a small plate of cheese, crackers and fruit. He was trying to keep busy, to keep his mind on mundane things and off the fact that a very attractive and semi-naked woman was lying inches away from him. He was unaccustomed to feeling this nervous, and to make matters worse Luci appeared completely at ease and unaware of the effect she was having on him. Which was probably just as well.

He could probably learn a thing or two from her. She was relaxed, easygoing and she didn't appear to have let her failed marriage stop her from having fun. She certainly hadn't shut herself off from others, like he had. He knew he had laughed more often and smiled more frequently in the past three days than he had in the past three years. And the only thing that had changed was that Luci had come into his life. He had separated himself socially, his focus had been on his work and his boat for the past three years, and he had kept any interaction with others to a minimum. His chosen response to any invitation was to decline it politely and yet Luci hadn't hesitated to say yes to all three of his invitations—an after-work drink, a lift home on his bike and now a day on his boat.

For a man who had knocked back most opportunities to spend time with other people over the past three years he didn't want to think about why he was suddenly inviting someone into his life. He must be crazy. Maybe his solitary lifestyle was slowly driving him mad.

What was it about Luci that made him feel the need to spend time with her?

He knew what it was. It was the way she made him feel.

Three years ago he'd lost everything, including a large chunk of his heart and soul, but Luci was waking him up again. He'd been holding his breath, marking time, treading water, and now he felt like he could breathe again.

He put the fruit platter into the shade and ran his eyes over her still figure. Her skin was already turning golden in the sun, her breasts were round and firm, her stomach flat, her legs were toned and athletic, and her toenails were painted pale pink.

Luci sat up. Had she felt him staring at her? Maybe, but she didn't seem perturbed.

'This is much more fun than studying,' she said as she sliced a piece of cheese and popped it onto a biscuit. 'I have never spent a day like this before. All the boat trips I've ever been on involved fishing with my dad in the Gulf of St Vincent in a little tinny, much like the one you rowed before. Nothing nearly as fancy as this.'

'Wait until I finish her. Then we'll be talking fancy.'

'Really?'

Seb laughed. 'No. I don't need fancy. She just has to be comfortable. A decent bed and a fridge and I'll be happy.'

Luci stretched her arms over her head and her breasts lifted. They were barely contained in her minuscule bikini and Seb couldn't help but notice. He was finding it extremely difficult to ignore her. He really was in trouble.

'Poor Callum,' she said with a half sigh as she surveyed their surroundings. 'I wonder what he's up to this weekend. I think he might have drawn the short straw in the house-swap stakes.'

Seb smiled. 'I'm sure he'll be okay.'

'Have you spoken to him?' she asked.

'No. I sent him a text, saying I was in town and that I was crashing at his place—after discussion with you. He replied saying he's not fussed.'

'I hope he's settling in.'

'You said he's working with your dad?'

'Yes. And with my friend Flick.' Luci laughed, a warm, rich sound. 'God, I hope he survives. There'll be plenty of patients inventing illnesses in order to get a look at the new doctor. I hope he's made of stern stuff.'

'You don't need to worry about us Hollingsworths. We're tough.' They were definitely the strong, silent type, masters of putting on a brave face and keeping their own counsel. Sometimes he wasn't sure how they had managed to get through the couple of traumatic events they had faced in their lives but he didn't want to think about those days now. Today was about Luci and he was keen to find out more.

'You haven't spoken to your dad?'

'No, I've spoken briefly to Mum but not Dad. He works such ridiculous hours, I don't like to interrupt unless it's something really important. He's supposed to be retiring this year. I know Mum is looking forward to that. Perhaps they'll finally be able to do some of the things they've been putting off. But, of course, that depends on Dad finding someone to take over the practice. Even though Vickers Hill is only a couple of hours from Adelaide, not everyone wants to work in the country and he won't leave his patients in the lurch.'

'Vickers Hill is north of Adelaide?' Seb asked, even though he knew the answer. He'd looked it up, intrigued to know where Luci had come from.

Luci nodded. 'Known for its wine. Dad has bought a

small acreage and he and Mum are going to grow grapes and have chickens and ducks. That's the plan anyway. I think they should move further away otherwise Dad will find it hard to retire completely. Old patients will still come to him with their troubles if they see him around town but I guess that's for him to sort out.'

'Can you see them leaving?'

'Not really.'

'And what about you? Are you missing home?'

'Not one bit. How can I be missing home when I'm surrounded by this? So far I don't have any regrets about coming to Sydney. I'm going to make the most of my time here.' She looked up at Seb and he wondered if spending time with him qualified as making the most of things. He hoped so. 'I jumped at the chance to come to Sydney. Well, not so much jumped, Flick pushed me, but now that I'm here it seems like it was a really good decision.'

She rolled over onto her stomach and Seb struggled to keep his eyes off her very shapely behind.

'You have no idea how nice it is to just relax and do my own thing, without everyone telling me what they think is best for me. I'm old enough to work that out for myself.'

He did have some idea what it was like to have everyone interfering in his life in what they thought was a helpful way. That's why he loved having the boat. It had been his escape route and he was convinced it had saved his sanity. He'd been able to disappear and avoid talking to anyone.

Luci might profess that she had chosen to take Flick's advice to study interstate but he still thought a large part of her motivation stemmed from having a reason, an excuse, to leave. He still thought she was running away. She might deny it but he recognised the signs. He had seen those same signs in himself. He knew exactly what it was like—he'd been running for three years. He recognised the need to get away from all the people who knew you and your past and your story.

But even though he thought Luci was running away from Vickers Hill he knew he was in no position to judge her for it. He'd shut himself off from the world completely. At least she was still living.

He knew that was the difference between them. For the past three years he hadn't been living. He hadn't thought he was allowed to enjoy life. It hadn't felt right but was it okay? Was it allowed? Did he have to continue to ignore the world?

Possibly. It was the only way to ensure it didn't hurt him again.

But he knew it was going to be hard to ignore Luci.

'And what is it you should be doing?' he asked, continuing the conversation she had started.

'I don't know yet.' She laughed. 'That's a little ironic, isn't it, but it's early days still. I'll figure it out. On my own. My life is different from how I pictured it. I just have to figure out what I want it to be like from now on. And one benefit of being divorced is that I can figure it out for myself. It's up to me.'

'What did you think your life would be like?'

She shrugged and averted her eyes. 'Married with kids.'

He supposed that was quite different from being divorced with no kids. 'Your husband didn't want kids?' he asked. Maybe that was why they'd got divorced.

'No, he did. We both did.' Luci was restless. She rolled back over so she was sitting up now. 'But he decided he didn't want them with me.' She stood up and dropped her hat and sunglasses onto her towel. 'I think I might go for a swim.'

It was clear she wanted to avoid this particular conversation. There was obviously more to the story but he wasn't going to push her. It was none of his business. He would listen if she wanted to talk but from what she had already said she was tired of interference. He decided he would just let her be but he wondered about her ex-husband. What sort of man was he? Luci had told him they had been together for almost ten years. What sort of man took that long to decide that he didn't want to be with someone? What sort of man married a girl like Luci and talked about raising a family together, only to leave her right when they should have been starting that future?

Seb felt a sudden surge of anger towards Luci's ex. He wasn't normally a violent man but he could see the hurt in her eyes and hear it in her voice and something within him made him wish he could fix it. But that reaction was out of character for him. He expected other people to leave him alone, not to interfere in his life, and he had learnt to do the same. But he wanted to help her and had no idea what to do.

He suspected she was not over the divorce and not over the loss of her dreams for the future but he had no idea what she needed. He could almost feel steam coming out of his ears and knew he needed to cool down. Calm down.

Luci was treading water a few metres from the boat, looking towards the shore. He dived in after her. He would keep quiet. He was good at that, it was easy not to speak about his thoughts and feelings or anything emotional. He floated on his back and waited to see what Luci would do. After a few minutes she drifted over to him.

'If you weren't messing about in boats when you were growing up, what did you do on weekends?' he asked.

'Chased the boys,' she replied.

Her mood had shifted, she was happy again. He thought that by nature she was a sunny person and that drew him to her even more. She balanced out his sombre side. He hadn't always been dark but the events of three years ago made him more reserved, less carefree and more sceptical about the good things in life.

'I thought the boys would have been chasing you.'

'There wasn't much chasing going on, if I'm honest. The girls played netball in winter and tennis in summer. The boys played footy and cricket. Our parents tried to keep us busy. We'd ride around town on our bikes and during harvest we'd often lend a hand if we had friends who had vineyards or farms. There was plenty to keep us out of trouble.'

Her stomach rumbled.

'Time for lunch?'

She nodded. 'Swimming always makes me hungry.'

Sex always made him hungry and Luci made him think of sex. Therefore he was hungry too but he didn't mention that.

Luci was looking back at the boat. 'I didn't think that through when I went for a swim.'

'What?'

'How I was going to get back on.'

'Swim to the back, and I'll help you up the ladder.' The ladder was short but it required substantial upper-body strength to haul yourself out of the water. 'I'll go first and give you a hand.'

They swam side by side and when they reached the boat Seb stretched up for the top rung of the ladder and pulled himself up onto the deck.

'Reach up and give me your hand.' He leaned down and grasped her hand in his. 'Grab the ladder with your other hand,' he said as he pulled her up into the boat and into his arms. Luci might not have thought about the logistics of getting back on the boat but Seb hadn't thought about the logistics of helping her. There wasn't much room at the back, just the small ledge. His back was to the gate and to open it he had to turn round and let her go. He didn't want to do that. They were squashed into a space less than a metre square. Her body was soft against his, slick with water. Her skin was cool and he could feel her heart beating in her chest, beating against his.

She looked up at him.

They stared at each other in silence until he could stand it no longer.

He didn't stop to think about what he was doing. He couldn't think. All he could do was see and smell and feel.

He saw her blue-grey eyes looking at him, the freckles dusted across the bridge of her nose, the tip of it turning red with the sun. Saw the pink rosebud of her lips and wanted to taste her.

He couldn't ignore her and he couldn't resist. He bent his head, making his intention clear, waiting for her to tell him to stop. But she remained quiet. He couldn't hear the sound of the ocean or the other bathers. All he could hear was the sound of their breathing, heavy in the stillness. He could see her eyes watching his and then they flicked down to his lips. He knew she understood his intention but she didn't protest and that was all the invitation Seb needed.

CHAPTER FOUR

HE BENT HIS HEAD.

Luci lifted her chin, offering her lips to him, and he claimed them. Claimed her.

He kissed her firmly, just like he'd been wanting to.

He pressed his lips to hers. She tasted of salt and she smelt of sunshine.

She parted her lips, opening her mouth to him. His tongue darted inside, tasting her, touching her. He couldn't control his desire. She was irresistible. But while his own lack of control surprised him she surprised him more when she kissed him back. His hands slid down her back and over the bow of her bikini top. With one flick of his fingers he could untie that bow and he would be able to feel the swell of her breasts pressed against him, skin to skin. But this time he did resist. He moved his hands lower until they cupped her buttocks instead. Firm and round, they fitted perfectly into his palms.

He pulled her into him, pressing her against him as he deepened the kiss. Her mouth was warm, soft and inviting. Her body was cool and soft under his hands.

His body was hard and firm and he held himself back. He didn't want to overpower her.

He felt her hands on his chest. They were cool over his racing heart.

She pushed gently against him, pulling away.

She looked up at him. Her blue-grey eyes were enormous, her pupils dilated. She was panting softly. She was out of breath, they both were.

They stood in silence, looking at each other, waiting for someone to say something. He wasn't going to apologise for kissing her. It had been the right time and the right place and she certainly hadn't resisted. But now she looked unsure. Albeit thoroughly kissed.

Her lips were dark pink now, almost red. She didn't look upset. Just uncertain.

He didn't think she wanted an apology. She hadn't objected but now she looked wary.

'Should I stop?' he asked.

She didn't reply immediately. She just stood, wrapped in his arms, staring up at him, and he could almost see her thoughts spinning in her brain, swirling behind her eyes.

'I don't know what you should do. I don't know what *I* should do,' she replied. 'I can't think.'

'Did I make you uncomfortable?' He wasn't going to apologise for kissing her. He wasn't sorry and he didn't think she was either.

'It's not that.' She paused and stepped away. 'But I wasn't expecting it.'

'The kiss?' he asked. He was pretty sure she'd seen it coming.

She shook her head. 'No. How it felt.'

He thought it had been amazing but his heart stopped for a second as he wondered if perhaps she hadn't been quite so astounded. 'And how was that?' he couldn't stop himself from asking. He had to know.

'Different.'

'Good different?' He had never fished for compliments

before but he had to know if the kiss had rocked her world in the same way it had his.

'Good *and* different. I don't know if there's such a thing as "good different". I'm not used to different. I think that's the unexpected thing. I'm not used to kissing a man I've just met. I'm not used to kissing anyone except my ex-husband.'

'Really?' That was it? She'd had one relationship?

'Ben and I were together since I was fifteen. I've only been divorced six months.'

In that sentence lay the answers to several of his questions, the first being how long she had been divorced, but the second answer was even more telling. If she'd been ready to move on from her marriage then six months was a reasonable length of time, but if the end of her marriage hadn't been something she'd chosen then a period of re-adjustment was only normal. She'd said her husband had met someone else. Seb guessed she wasn't ready to do the same. But that didn't preclude them from having some fun. Not if she wanted to. It was all up to her.

'I get it. You need time.'

'Don't get me wrong. It felt good but I don't know if it felt right. I'm not sure what I should be doing. I don't know if I need more time but part of me feels like I should be a bit cautious and the other part is saying just close your eyes and jump.'

'Only you can make that decision,' he said. He wanted her to jump, he desperately wanted her to jump, but he knew that wasn't his call. 'Let me know what you decide. I'm not going to put any pressure on you but I will say this—you're only here for a few weeks. We can enjoy each other's company, no strings attached, no commitment, and then say goodbye. But it's up to you. Think about it. You know where to find me.'

He dropped his arms from around her waist and leaned back to open the gate, allowing them to step into the boat.

They spent the rest of the afternoon talking. Conversation flowed easily, there were no awkward pauses, but the awareness was always there. He could feel the tension in the air around them, crackling and sparking, but they both ignored it. They talked about work, about places he'd visited and her home town; they talked about everything but the kiss they'd shared and where they were going to go from there.

He was serious about his suggestion, though. He was pretty sure she wasn't the one for him long term, it was obvious she wanted to settle down and have a family, something that was definitely not on his agenda, but she was only in town for eight weeks and he was only committed to Sydney for six weeks. There was no reason they couldn't have some fun together. They could enjoy each other's company and then say goodbye. But he would give her space. For now. This had to be her decision.

Luci towelled herself dry and slipped her sundress over her head. She'd had enough time in the sun but the extra layer wasn't to prevent sunburn, it was to provide her with a bit of a barrier. Not that it afforded much protection but she needed all help she could get to ensure she didn't just throw herself back into Seb's arms.

She should be having doubts and reservations. She had known him for less than three days and she had *never* kissed a man she barely knew before. She'd never properly kissed anyone other than her ex-husband.

She should be having doubts and reservations about kissing him, full stop, but that wasn't the issue. It wasn't Seb who was making her nervous but the consequences of her actions.

She didn't want to make a mistake or do anything that might jeopardise her time in Sydney. There were more important things than kissing a handsome stranger. They had to live together and work together. There were a whole lot of reasons why she should keep her distance and only one thing, her hormones, was telling her differently.

She was a single adult, there was no rule saying she couldn't take this further, but she really wasn't sure if she was ready. She needed some ground rules. She'd never done 'no strings attached' and she wasn't sure if she could. Until she had processed the idea she felt it would be wise to keep her distance.

The kiss had been amazing. She'd seen it coming and she hadn't stopped him. She hadn't wanted to. She'd wanted to touch him, to taste him, but she hadn't realised how hard it would make it to deny herself more. It was going to be difficult. She would have to find other ways of keeping busy. If she was busy she wouldn't have time to think about him.

Seb had pulled some more food out of the ice box and assembled a picnic lunch. Luci was starving and she was more than happy to sample the selection. While she was eating she couldn't talk but when they did talk Seb kept the conversation neutral. They talked about inconsequential things, a polite conversation between two virtual strangers, skirting around the issue that she couldn't stop thinking about.

But not talking about the kiss didn't stop her from thinking about it.

Seb shoved the crowbar behind the last of the kitchen cabinets in the galley of his boat. He had spent most of his spare time for the past week hunkered down, removing the shower and the kitchen cabinetry. The carpenter had told him not to expect the new fittings to be ready for installation for another fortnight but he needed to dismantle the old fixtures and he needed to keep himself occupied.

The demolition work was achieving three things—he was progressing nicely with his renovations, he was keeping his mind occupied, to a point, and he was keeping his distance from Luci. He had promised to give her time and space but over the past couple of days he'd found that if he spent too much time in the same space as her it was becoming increasingly difficult to resist the pull of attraction. It was difficult to be around her and not touch her. All he wanted to do when she was around him was to explore their attraction but he had promised not to push her.

Once again his boat was his sanctuary but this time he didn't need it to help him over his heartbreak. This time it was to keep his mind off his desire rather than his despair. The physical work was a good antidote for the desire. He was so knackered by the end of the day that he would fall straight to sleep when he went to bed. That was a fourth benefit of the demolition work.

He'd had several brief affairs over the past three years but he had been very careful to avoid meaningful relationships. If Luci was willing there was nothing stopping them from having some fun, as her time in Sydney was limited anyway, but he realised she might still be working through her own issues. It would probably be wise to spend some time working out whether her issues were major or minor. He wasn't prepared to get involved in anything too emotional—a physical relationship was fine but he didn't want anything more serious than that.

There were all sorts of reasons why he should avoid Luci and he knew them all, he'd been running over them constantly.

She had led a sheltered life. A *very* sheltered life.

They had to work together.

They had to *live* together.

It was all a little bit too close.

But that didn't alter the fact that he was excited by Luci and it had been a long time since he'd been excited by anything.

Although he knew it still might be better to avoid her he couldn't avoid her completely. They had to work together and on Friday afternoon she knocked on his consulting-room door. He could smell her before he saw her. She smelt of frangipani.

'Hi,' he said as he looked up. 'How's it going?'

'Good.'

She smiled at him and her blue-grey eyes sparkled. She looked happy. She glowed and he had the sense that she was filled with light that then spilled out to brighten everyone else's day. At least, that's how he felt when she was around.

'Melanie Parsons is in the clinic today,' Luci told him. 'She has an appointment with the psychologist and then I'm going to do the health check on her four-year-old. I wasn't sure if you wanted to see her.'

'Good idea. What time is she booked in with you?' he asked as he looked at his diary.

'She's next. I'm just going to grab a coffee and by then she should be done with the psych consult. Give me ten minutes to get started on the toddler check and then come in.'

Luci was just helping Harper down from the exam table when Seb knocked on the door. She took Harper out of the room to the play area where Harper's two-year-old brother was busy with the building blocks while Seb caught up with Melanie. When she returned Seb had been given the update on the two psychologist appointments Melanie had already had.

'We are working on my responses so that I can try to manage the situation,' Melanie told him. 'And then we're going to tackle the best way to get Brad in for a session as well.'

Milo was strapped into his pram in the corner of the room. He started to grizzle.

'Sorry,' Melanie apologised, 'He's due for a feed.'

Seb thought it was interesting that Melanie felt she needed to apologise for something that was perfectly understandable. She started to get out of her chair to attend to the baby when Luci offered her help.

'Don't worry about him. I'll see if I can settle him for a bit, let you finish with Dr Hollingsworth.' Luci lifted Milo out of the stroller. She blew a raspberry on his foot and his grizzles stopped, becoming happy chortling instead. She laid him on the exam table and distracted him with a mirror and a game of peek-a-boo, allowing Melanie to continue.

The young mother was watching Luci play with Milo while she spoke to Seb. 'And I think I need to make an appointment to discuss a more reliable form of contraception. After this next one I reckon I'm done. Some days I feel like I'm not even managing with the three I already have.'

Seb's antennae went up. 'I'll speak to the psychologist and recommend that you continue with regular visits until a few months after this next baby is born.' He didn't want to let Melanie slip through the cracks in the system. If she needed help and support he wanted to make sure she got it. For her sake and for her children's sake.

'Thank you,' she replied with a nod as she stood up, preparing to leave. She picked Milo up from the exam table to put him back into his stroller. 'Do you have kids, Luci?' she asked.

Melanie was bending over, strapping Milo into his pram, and she missed Luci's expression. But Seb didn't. She looked like someone had slapped her.

'No, I don't,' Luci replied.

'You should. You're a natural.'

'Mmm-hmm.' Luci turned away and Seb wasn't able to see her face. He couldn't tell if her expression had changed or not.

'I don't seem to have the energy,' Melanie remarked.

'I imagine managing them twenty-four-seven is very different from seeing them for ten minutes at a time,' Luci said. 'I'm not surprised you're tired.'

'Exhausted is the word, I think. But I'll get through it. What other choice do I have?' she remarked as she pushed the pram towards the door.

'Are you okay?' Seb asked Luci the moment Melanie left the room.

'I'm fine.'

She didn't look fine.

'I'm concerned about Melanie, though,' she said, changing the subject. 'Do you still think the kids are safe?'

'How was Harper's health check?' he asked, letting her change of topic go—for now. 'Were there any red flags with her weight or teeth or any unexplained bruises?'

Luci shook her head. 'Everything was within normal ranges.'

'I've never seen any signs of neglect or abuse. The kids are clean and well fed. I think she's coping. Maybe just, at times, but I don't think the kids are in any danger.' If he thought the children were in any danger he wouldn't sit on his hands. 'Her kids' welfare comes before her own, which is part of the problem, but also why I'll insist that she continue with regular psych reviews. If anything changes, hopefully we'll pick up on it.'

Luci was nodding but she still looked upset. He felt that he'd learned to read her expressions in just a few days and he was still worried about her. He wanted to find out why she'd looked so shocked. He ignored his self-imposed ban. He wanted to spend time with her. 'Have you got plans tonight?' he asked.

'Only to cook up a stir-fry.'

'Would there be enough for two?'

'You'll be home?'

So she'd noticed that he'd been MIA. He wondered if she had missed him. He nodded and offered, 'I'll bring wine.'

'Sure.'

'Dinner smells good.'

Seb's voice startled her and made Luci jump. She had her head over the wok and the sizzle as she fried the garlic and crushed chilli had blocked out all other sounds.

'It's just chicken and noodles,' she said as she scraped the marinated chicken strips into the pan. The aroma of fried garlic always smelt good but she hadn't really thought about the practicalities of serving up a dish laden with garlic. Oh, well, she supposed it was one way to make sure Seb didn't kiss her again.

She glanced over her shoulder when she heard the familiar snap as Seb broke the seal on the screw top on the bottle of wine he held. He poured two glasses and handed one to her before leaning back on the kitchen bench.

Was he planning on hanging around in the kitchen while she cooked?

She'd been surprised that he was free tonight. He'd barely been home all week. She'd heard him come in late at night but he definitely hadn't been home for a meal and she'd expected he would have other plans. She'd wondered if he had been deliberately avoiding her and had thought about shooing him out of the kitchen now, but dinner would only take five minutes so she may as well enjoy his company. Sitting home alone was no fun.

The house had been far too quiet this week without Seb. She still wasn't used to being on her own. After her divorce she'd formed a habit of eating at her parents' house a couple of times a week or sharing a meal with Flick. But being in Sydney, where she didn't have a large network of friends, had made her nights long and lonely. She'd never really been on her own before and she'd discovered she didn't like it. But that didn't mean she was going to fall for the first guy to cross her path. She needed to develop some resistance along with her independence.

She sipped her wine, hoping it would calm her nerves. It felt like they were on a date. Not that she really knew how that felt. She and Ben had been together since high school and she couldn't even remember their first date, but she guessed it would have been at a school friend's birthday party. They had probably played silly party games and drunk some wine they'd pinched from a parent's cellar.

She wished she was cooking something a bit more complicated than a stir-fry, something that required more attention. Something that would require her focus but, as it was, she could whip up a stir-fry blindfolded and that meant she had plenty of time to think about Seb.

Even though she hadn't seen much of him that week she could always tell when he'd been to the apartment. She could smell him. The air was different and even now, despite the aroma of garlic and chilli, she could still smell him. He had showered after work—that must have been while she'd been at the supermarket—and she could smell soap and aftershave. He'd changed into a pair of stone-coloured shorts with a fresh navy T-shirt. His feet were bare and he looked relaxed and comfortable. He certainly didn't look nervous or like he was dressed for a date.

Luci took another sip of wine and concentrated on copying Seb's calm approach as she served up the stir-fry and sat at the table opposite him.

He tucked into the bowl of noodles, scooping up several forkfuls before he paused to take a breath.

'This tastes great, thank you,' he said, as he topped up their wine glasses.

Luci had intended to do some studying after dinner but she could fast see that plan disappearing if she had too much wine but she didn't refuse the top-up. After a week of lonely nights it made a pleasant change to share a meal with someone. And it was even more pleasant when that someone was Seb.

'Two weeks down, how's it been going?' he asked her as he sipped his wine. 'Have you recovered from Melanie's visit?'

'What do you mean?'

'Something she said upset you.'

'You noticed that?'

'I did. What was it?'

'I know she didn't mean any harm but if I had a dollar for every time someone asked me if I had kids I'd have paid off my mortgage. I just don't understand why so many clients feel they have a right to ask personal questions.'

'I think she thought you were a natural with kids. She meant it as a compliment.'

'I realise that but I didn't expect that every second person would ask me if I have children. I bet they don't ask you the same thing, do they?'

'Some do,' he admitted, 'but I guess it probably is more of a question between women.'

'They all seem to assume that if a woman is working in family health or paediatrics or obstetrics she would either have kids or want them.'

'But you do want them.'

'Yes, but I don't want to think about it all the time. Obviously my divorce has changed my plans somewhat. I'm not exactly in a position to start a family but I don't want to tell clients my life story.'

'Fair enough.'

'I guess I hadn't anticipated that the subject of children would be raised so often. I need to find an answer to the most popular question, which is, "So, Luci, do you have children?"'

'Why don't you just tell them that you're only young? You've got plenty of time.'

It wasn't a bad suggestion. It wasn't Seb's fault that time wasn't on her side but he didn't know that.

'A lot of these mothers are younger than me. I don't want them to feel I'm judging them. If I had my way I *would* have had children by now. All I've wanted, all my life, was to have kids and to be a young mum. My parents are old. Dad is almost seventy and Mum is a couple of years younger. They are wonderful parents but growing up I really noticed their age. Especially in my town where so many people start their families young, my parents could have been my grandparents and I didn't want to be like that. I also want more than one child. I was an only child and I didn't want that for my kids. Having a family has been my dream since I was a teenager.'

'Why don't you tell them you're waiting for the right man, then?' He scooped up the last mouthful of his dinner and didn't speak again until he'd finished it. 'Or do you think you had the right one in Ben?'

'Obviously I did when I married him.' She had thought that was it for her. As far as she'd been concerned, her life had been sorted when she'd walked down the aisle and become a wife. Until she'd found that it could easily be unsorted.

Ben couldn't have been the right man for her. If he had been, surely they'd still be together? Or perhaps she just wasn't the right woman for him. But when they'd got married she hadn't known what else was out there. Neither of them had. Ben had found someone he felt suited him better and Luci had to hope that there was someone else out there for her too.

What would her perfect man be like?

She looked across the table. She suspected he would be a lot like Seb. That was dangerous territory. She needed a change of topic. A safer direction. 'How was your week?' she asked. 'I barely saw you. Have you changed your mind about sharing the house?'

'No. I wanted to give you some space. Being around you was testing my limits. It's been difficult to put you in the "friend" zone so I thought it would be best if I stayed out of the way. I've been working on my boat.'

Hearing Seb put their situation like that made her wonder if she wanted to be in the 'friend' zone. She didn't think she did but she was still confused about what she should be doing. It was still safer not to do anything. He hadn't apologised for kissing her. She was glad about that. The kiss had been good, she didn't want an apology, but she wasn't ready to revisit it either.

He was looking at her so directly but she couldn't respond. It was safer not to reply to his comment. To break eye contact, she stood and picked up their empty bowls, clearing the table. She took the bowls to the sink and rinsed them, keeping her back to Seb.

'You don't need to stay out of the house, that doesn't seem fair.' She found her voice once she wasn't looking at him.

'I thought it was easiest for both of us. I promised I wouldn't make you uncomfortable.'

'I'm not uncomfortable. I just can't jump into another relationship.' Even though she was tempted. 'I know I should spread my wings but jumping into something with the first man who crosses my path doesn't really fit that. I think I need to test the water. I've never even been on a proper first date. Maybe I should be the one who spends more time out of the house. Maybe I should meet some more people.'

Seb had been hoping to hear Luci say she'd made a decision. His ego had let him believe that if he gave her time and space she'd miss him. But perhaps she had a point. Perhaps she *did* need to meet other people. Perhaps then she would see that he could be the perfect person with whom to test the water.

But maybe he had a solution to this dilemma.

'I've been invited to a dinner party tomorrow night. If you'd like to come with me it would give you a chance to meet some other people.'

He hadn't actually thought about going until just now. The whole premise of the evening hadn't appealed to him but now, with Luci's provisos, it was suddenly more attractive.

When Ginny had invited him he'd declined the invitation. That had become his habit over the past three years but he knew Ginny wouldn't mind a last-minute change of mind. They had been friends since high school and she had made a lot of effort to keep in contact, especially recently. Even when Seb had been difficult and unsociable, Ginny had kept him in the loop, inviting him to parties and functions. He'd declined almost all of her invitations but he appreciated the fact that she hadn't given up on him. Perhaps it was time he said yes.

'Like a date?' Luci queried.

CHAPTER FIVE

'NOT EXACTLY.' HE wished he could offer to take her on a proper first date but if she was going to insist on meeting other people then tomorrow night's party would be a good compromise. If everything went according to his plan he could organise a first date after that. 'A friend of mine is hosting a "dates with mates" party. It's for singles. Each guest is expected to bring a partner who they are not romantically involved with—it's a way of meeting new people, of broadening your set of acquaintances and potentially meeting someone who you could date. So it fits within your rules. We'd be going as friends and you'll get to meet new people. What do you think?'

She nodded. 'Sure. I'd like that.'

He was surprised by her immediate reaction. There was no hesitation, no further questions. She was far more adventurous and sociable than he was.

Luci pulled her hair into a sleek ponytail and applied a coat of pale pink lipstick before zipping herself into the strapless black jumpsuit she'd bought that day. She'd seen it in a shop window that she passed on her way to work and had loved it but had had no reason to buy it. Until today. She'd told herself she hadn't bought anything new in ages so it was a justified purchase. She told herself a lot of things. That she wasn't looking forward to the date, that it wasn't really a date and that she was keen to meet other people when, in fact, she was nervous about pretty much all of it. She was nervous about whether or not she looked okay, whether she'd fit in to the crowd, whether Seb would like her outfit, and what he would be thinking about their 'non-date'.

Seb looked her up and down when she joined him in the lounge room. 'Wow. You look sensational.' Luci relaxed. At least now she knew what he was thinking. 'I was going to suggest we take my bike but perhaps we should call a cab.'

'The bike is fine,' she replied. She enjoyed going on the bike. It gave her a chance to wrap her arms around him and hold on tight. What wasn't to like about that? 'Just let me grab my boots.' She swapped her gladiator sandals for her old work boots and carried her sandals down the stairs to put on when they reached the party. Seb unlocked the compartment under the seat of his motorbike and pulled out his spare helmet, exchanging the helmet for Luci's sandals and the wine. He had his spare jacket tucked under his arm and he held it for her while she slipped her arms in before helping her to fasten her helmet.

He started the bike and Luci straddled the seat behind him. She wrapped her arms around his waist and held on tightly as he rode through the streets of the North Shore to Cremorne Point. He parked his bike on the road behind the house and helped Luci off. She changed her shoes and checked her hair in the mirror, then took a deep breath. She'd come up with the idea of meeting new people but the reality of walking into a party where she knew just one person was more daunting than she would have thought. It was another new situation for her. Something else she'd never done.

Seb took her hand and squeezed it. He must have known she was nervous but having him hold her hand only intensified the feeling. At the same time it felt so good that she didn't want to object.

The party was already under way and music filled the night air. Seb opened the back gate and led her along a narrow path that followed the side of the house. When they emerged into the front garden Luci caught her breath. The house sat right on the harbour and the view was incredible. A white, open-sided marquee had been erected in the centre of the lawn with a dining table positioned beneath it, and closer to the water's edge Luci could see a long bar, loaded with glasses and drinks, that framed the view across the harbour to the Opera House and the bridge.

The garden was lit with hundreds of lights—fairy-lights, up-lights and down-lights—and the Opera House glowed as the sun set. It looked spectacular.

Ginny came to greet them and Seb introduced her.

'Welcome,' Ginny said, and she kissed Luci on both cheeks. 'I'm so glad you agreed to come. It's been ages since I've seen Seb and I was afraid he was going to turn down this invitation too.'

'Thank you for including me,' Luci said as she gestured to the garden. 'This looks amazing.'

'Thanks but I can't take all the credit. The decorating is my work. I'm a food stylist by trade, but the house belongs to another friend of mine—Michael. Come with me, I'll introduce you.'

Seb and Luci followed Ginny across the lawn to the bar where the other guests had gathered and Luci tried to keep track of who was who during a whirlwind introduction. First up was Paulo, a Spanish chef, who Ginny had met on an assignment. She introduced him with the comment, 'I can make food look pretty but I can't cook so I invited Paulo.' Then there was Michael, who owned the house, and he was followed by a model, a footballer, a massage therapist, Ginny's brother, who worked in finance, a lawyer he knew, an actor and a food blogger. Luci was unsure what a food blogger actually did but the woman was extraordinarily thin so Luci assumed it didn't actually involve eating. It was an interesting assortment of people and Luci thought the evening would either be a lot of fun or a huge disaster.

Ginny had a seating plan arranged and they were told it would change between each course. Luci started the night between Paulo, the Spanish chef, and Michael, her host.

Michael was smooth, dark and good-looking, with a European heritage, Luci suspected. Besides this gorgeous house, he also owned three restaurants. A fact he successfully mentioned within the first few minutes and several times thereafter. He seemed to think Luci should be suitably impressed. She was, but not by him. He was obviously wealthy but that wasn't high on Luci's list of priorities. He also had a very high opinion of himself but no sense of humour. Luci preferred someone who could make her laugh and would let her be herself. She suspected Michael was not that sort of man. She wasn't interested in material objects. She wanted a family and she would give up everything else if she could have that. Nothing else was that important.

Paulo, to her left, was outrageously handsome and quite charming but he wasn't her type of man either. He didn't make her heart race or her breath catch in her throat. He didn't give her the fluttery feeling she got in her stomach whenever Seb was near. If nothing else, this dinner party was helping her to narrow down her type of man.

Somehow she managed to survive the first course and conversations that she wasn't particularly interested in. For the main course she found herself sitting between the actor and the footballer, a rugby league player. He had limited conversation, appearing to be restricted to the topics of rugby and golf, neither of which Luci knew anything about. Her mind drifted to the opposite side of the table where Seb was now seated. She never seemed to have any difficulty talking to him. They had discussed all manner of topics.

She turned her attention to the actor on her other side, leaving the rugby player to try to strike up a conversation with the girl on his right. The actor turned out to be 'between jobs' and working as a barista and he was pleasant enough, although she was pretty sure he was gay. Not that it mattered as she wasn't interested in him anyway, but she wondered who had invited him.

Somehow, through all the various seat changes and movements, she managed to keep one eye on Seb and hoped no one noticed. She thought she was being subtle but it was hard to know. She did her best to concentrate on what the other guests were talking about but as the evening wore on she found it increasingly difficult. All she wanted to do was to swap seats and plonk herself next to Seb.

Even though he made her feel nervous, Luci knew it was the right kind of nervous. The exciting kind. The possibility that something could happen if she was willing. She wondered what the rules were if you decided that the mate you came with was the same one you wanted to go home with. So far, in her opinion, no one could compare to Seb. He didn't need to be the perfect man, it didn't even matter if he was the first one to cross her path, she just knew that she wasn't going to get him out of her system without exploring the possibilities.

If she was honest she'd admit—to him and to herself—that she'd thought about little else for the last week. She didn't want to live in the past. Her marriage was over and at some point she was going to have to try again. And she was more than happy to try again with Seb.

She looked across the table and found him watching her. She blushed and hoped he couldn't read her thoughts. No. It was time to share those thoughts. If she wanted to be a grown-up she had to take the leap. She wanted to stretch her wings and she hoped Seb would give her the opportunity to do just that.

She smiled at him and stood up as dessert was cleared away. Guests gathered in smaller clusters as coffee was served in the garden but before Luci could make her way to Seb she was cornered by Michael. At the beginning of the evening she had thought the evening would either be interesting or a disaster. It looked like it was heading down the path of complete disaster.

She stood patiently for another few minutes as Michael talked some more about himself. She searched the crowd for Seb as she waited for a polite time to escape. Seb was on the other side of the garden, talking to the model who was Ginny's brother's date. Their eyes locked and Michael and his conversation receded into the background. Why was she wasting time with him?

'Would you excuse me?' she said.

She saw Seb break away from the model at the same time. He was coming for her. Luci waited and fell into step beside him, following him in silence down to a wooden garden seat that sat at the harbour's edge.

Finally it was just the two of them.

As she sat next to him her thigh brushed his leg and she wondered if she should move, if he needed some space. But she didn't want to move, so she stayed put. The now familiar butterflies careened around in her stomach. She wanted to touch Seb. Wanted to feel him.

A light breeze blew off the harbour, sending a shiver through Luci.

'Would you like my jacket?' Seb offered.

'No, I'm okay.'

He put his arm around her shoulders and pulled her into his side. He was warm and solid and Luci wanted to close her eyes and soak up the feeling of being in his arms again.

'Are you having fun?' he asked her.

'Not really,' she replied. 'The rugby player is boring, Michael is only interested in himself and Paulo was nice but a bit too smooth for me.'

'Too smooth? I wouldn't have thought that was a thing.'

'It most certainly is, and I think the barista-slash-actor is gay.'

'Really?'

'Yep.'

Seb laughed.

'Why is that funny?' Luci asked.

'It means there's one less bloke in the running.'

'In the running for what?'

'For your attention.'

Luci hesitated for a fraction of a second, wondering if she should tell him what she thought. She decided she should. 'It doesn't matter. I've found the one.'

'Ginny's brother?'

'No. Not him.'

'There isn't anyone else.'

'Yes, there is, but I'm not sure if it's within the rules of the night. Are you allowed to go home with the same person you came with?'

'Go home with? As in together?'

She nodded.

'Are you serious?'

She nodded again. 'As long as it's not against the rules.'

'I don't give a damn about the rules,' Seb said as he stood and reached for her hand. 'Let's get out of here.'

They barely stopped to say thank you and goodnight to Ginny before making a beeline for Seb's bike. Luci ignored Ginny's knowing smile. She didn't care what anyone thought. What happened between her and Seb was their business, no one else's. Luci was going to do exactly what she wanted for a change and if anyone tried to tell her it was a bad idea she wasn't going to listen.

She slid her hand under Seb's shirt as she sat behind him on the bike. She rested her hand against his chest and imagined what the rest of the night would be like.

They barely made it up the stairs and into the apartment before their clothes started coming off.

Seb kicked off his boots and Luci did the same with hers. He tossed his leather jacket on the floor and pulled his shirt over his head, discarding items of clothing on the passage floor. Luci's jacket followed.

He lifted her up and she wrapped her legs around his waist as he pushed her against the passage wall. He bent his head and kissed her. She opened her mouth and kissed him back.

Her hands were pressed into his shoulder blades. His skin was firm and smooth. He looked as though he'd been carved from marble but he was warm and pulsing with life. He carried her further into the apartment and she could feel his erection pressing between her thighs.

'Your room or mine?' he asked.

'Yours. It's closer.' Luci didn't think she could wait much longer.

He put her down and reached behind her to unzip her jumpsuit.

'The zip is on the side.'

His hands found the zip and he bent his head as her

jumpsuit fell away and pressed his lips against the diamond-shaped freckles on her chest.

'I've wanted to do that since the first time I saw you.'

His fingers brushed over her breasts as he released her bra. He cupped one breast in his hand as he took the other into his mouth, making Luci think she might burst into flames.

She reached for his waistband and unzipped his trousers, discarding them on the floor along with her outfit.

Seb scooped her up and laid her on the bed. His boxer shorts joined his trousers as Luci admired him.

The marble angel in all his glory. His chest was broad and tanned from hours on his boat. Her eyes followed the line of his sternum where it divided his pecs, down to the ridges of his abdominals. Below his belly button a light trail of hair led her eyes further to where his erection was proudly displayed. He was absolutely gorgeous. Perfectly sculpted and ready and waiting for her.

She swallowed feeling moisture pooling between her thighs. She hooked her fingers under the elastic of her knickers, wanting to discard them, but Seb leaned forward and moved her hands. He lifted her hips and gently tugged her underwear down. His fingers brushed the backs of her legs and she felt like she might explode right now. He slid her knickers down over her calves and dropped them on the floor.

Now they were both naked but Luci didn't have time to feel self-conscious. She wasn't thinking about how she looked, she could only focus on how Seb made her feel.

He knelt at the foot of the bed and spread her legs, pushing her knees gently apart. He ran his tongue along the inside of her thigh, starting at her knee. He kept moving up and Luci lifted her hips as his tongue delved and flicked and tasted her.

She reached for him and pulled him up onto the bed. He knelt between her thighs and she circled his erection with her hand, running her thumb over the tip of his shaft. Felt him quiver.

He bent his head and took her breast in his mouth. His tongue was hard and wet as it flicked over her nipple. Luci moaned and arched her back. It had been months since she had felt this way, and couldn't wait any longer.

'Take me now, Seb,' she begged. The tension of the last few days made her impatient. There would be time later to explore, but right now she needed release.

He reached into the bedside drawer and handed her a condom. Luci tore the packet open and rolled it onto him before guiding him into her. She lifted her hips and let him fill her.

She met his thrusts, timing them with her own. She had to learn a new rhythm, faster and harder. He consumed her and she let him.

CHAPTER SIX

SHE CRIED OUT as she came and felt him shudder as he joined her.

It was different.

But good.

There was such a thing as good different after all.

They had made love fast and impatiently, unable to restrain themselves, and then they made love slowly, getting to know every inch of each other. Luci was adventurous and brave as she discovered the joys of sex with Seb. There was no routine, there was no expectation or pressure. It was all new and exciting.

Luci could remember when sex had been like that—when she and Ben hadn't been able to get enough of each other. When they had been young and first married they had grabbed every opportunity and then again when they'd decided it was time to start a family. She'd had plenty of sex but somewhere along the line it had lost the fun and become a chore. At some point it had become another thing on the list of jobs that had to be done.

She knew when that had happened. When, month after month, her dreams of falling pregnant hadn't eventuated. She'd started worrying, constantly taking her temperature, changing her diet, insisting on sex on certain days of the month, certain times of the day—and it had taken the fun out of it. Was it any wonder Ben had started looking elsewhere? She'd blamed him for destroying their marriage single-handedly when the reality was that she'd played her part too.

Remembering how much fun sex could be cheered her up immensely. She still knew how to enjoy life.

She smiled as Seb tucked her in to his side and trailed his finger down her arm. The night hadn't been a complete disaster after all.

'So how was the water?' Seb asked, as his fingers ran over her hip bone and down to the top of her thigh.

Luci's brain had turned to mush. 'Pardon?'

'The water?' Seb repeated. 'You wanted to dip your toe in. I want to know if it was to your liking.'

Luci grinned. 'Very much so. I've decided there is such a thing as good different. But this is all new to me. I need some guidelines.'

'What do you mean?'

'I need to know if we are dating or just having sex.'

'What do you want?'

'I need to have some fun but I also want to see what dating is like in the modern day. When I leave Sydney I need to know what to expect. I need some practice.'

'I think you'll find you'll be fine. Trust me,' he said. 'But I'm happy to be of service for the next four weeks while I'm still here. We can have fun until I leave or until you get sick of me.'

Luci appreciated the fact that he didn't suggest he'd get tired of her first.

'But I do have one condition,' Seb added.

'What's that?'

'We are exclusive while it lasts. No dating anyone else.'

Luci nodded. She had no intention of looking elsewhere. She couldn't imagine needing to.

'So when Michael calls and asks you out, you'd better have an excuse ready.'

'Really? Michael? I thought I made it perfectly clear that I wasn't interested.'

'For some men that only makes you more appealing. For some it's all about the chase. I can see I have a lot to teach you,' he said, as he kissed her shoulder. 'So much to do and so little time.'

'Where do you want to start?' Luci replied with a smile.

'How about we start with this?' he said, flipping her onto her back and ducking his head under the covers.

Luci closed her eyes and gave herself up to him. There was no room in her head for thoughts of anything other than the waves of pleasure that consumed her.

Seb knew exactly what he was doing. This might just be the best decision she had ever made.

Seb woke her in the morning in the same way he'd said goodnight, then got up to make her a cup of tea.

'We might be going about this a little backwards but I have a first date planned,' he said as she sat up in bed and took the tea.

'Now?'

'You might have time for a shower.' He grinned.

The shower took a little longer than normal. Having Seb in there with her, offering to wash her back, wasn't necessarily the timesaver one might expect.

She dressed in jeans, canvas sneakers, a T-shirt and Seb's spare leather jacket and climbed on the back of his bike. Her thighs complained as she stretched them over the seat but she wasn't complaining. She might be a bit stiff and sore but it was an ache she was more than happy to put up with.

'Where are we going?' she asked.

'I'm taking you out for breakfast.'

That sounded good. She was starving.

Seb rode to Milson's Point on the north shore and pulled into a parking spot beside the harbour bridge. There were numerous cafés along the opposite side of the street and Luci wondered which one he had chosen, but Seb didn't cross the street. Instead, he took her hand and led her along the ramparts of the bridge and up a flight of stairs.

'You're going to walk across the bridge with me?' Luci asked as they reached the top and she found herself on the pedestrian walkway that ran along the eastern side of the bridge. 'I thought this was the sort of thing only tourists did?' she teased.

'I figured you're worth making an exception for. But if I'm going to do this then this is the best time of day. It's quiet enough on a Sunday morning to still be relatively peaceful. We can take our time and we'll have breakfast at the other end.'

The view was spectacular, better than Luci had imagined. The Opera House, the botanic gardens and the city skyline were laid out before them as they headed south across the bridge. The sun was still low in the sky to their left and the Opera House sparkled like a sugar-coated meringue on the edge of the harbour. She'd seen it from the water, in daylight and at night-time and now from a higher vantage point. It didn't disappoint, no matter what. She thought it was an incredible building and she knew it would always remind her of Seb.

There was a light breeze blowing, just enough to get the flag on top of the bridge moving but not enough to be unpleasant. They stopped numerous times to watch the ferries crisscross the harbour and the tiny yachts dart across the water. By the time they descended onto Cumberland Street in The Rocks Luci was famished. The combination of sex and walking had certainly fired her appetite. Seb ordered a big breakfast—bacon, eggs, tomato, spinach, mushrooms, hash browns. Luci had smashed avocado on toast with bacon on the side. She needed an energy boost.

'Can I ask you something?' she said as she cut into her bacon.

'Sure.'

'Why don't you have a girlfriend?'

'You mean, what's wrong with me that you haven't noticed yet?'

'No. Maybe.' Seb was teasing her but she was serious. 'Why *is* a guy like you single?'

'A guy like me? What *am* I like, exactly?'

'Oh, no, don't go fishing for compliments. Just answer the question.'

'Well, as long as you were thinking complimentary things, I'll explain,' he said. 'I want the freedom to do the things I want to do, to go where I want to go. Last year I spent about forty weeks in the country in four different towns. I don't see the point in long-distance relationships. I don't have a girlfriend because I don't want a serious relationship.'

'Have you *never* had a serious relationship?'

'Only one but that ended three years ago and I'm used to doing things my way now. I can't really see the need to commit to one person, not when so many relationships end badly.' He speared a mushroom with his fork before he looked up at her. 'Would you go through it all again?'

Luci nodded. 'I would. I liked being married,' she said honestly. 'I didn't like how my marriage *ended* but I'm not going to let that dictate how I spend the rest of my life. I liked being part of a couple, sharing my life.' It would be a long, lonely existence if she vowed never to go down that path again and if she was going to achieve her dream of motherhood she needed to be in a committed relationship. It wouldn't work any other way. Not for her at least, who had always dreamed of the whole package. 'You don't want that? Someone to share your life with? A family of your own?'

'No.' Seb drained the last of his coffee and pushed his chair back. 'I don't,' he said as he stood up.

Clearly that conversation was over. Luci would remember not to raise that topic again. She didn't want to rock the boat. There was no need to. They didn't need to have in-depth, detailed discussions about their hopes and dreams. This was all temporary, she reminded herself. It was supposed to be just a bit of fun.

They spent the next hour wandering through the markets in The Rocks before Seb took her to climb the south pylon of the bridge on their way back across the harbour. Their conversation stayed neutral, away from anything that could be considered remotely emotional, but Luci wasn't going to let it ruin her day. There was no rule that said he had to open up to her, and besides that he was the ideal date. He was attentive, funny, thoughtful and gorgeous. It had been a perfect first date.

Over the next ten days Seb took her on several dates that were almost as good. They visited the zoo and shopped in Paddington. They ate dinner in Chinatown, oysters beside the Opera House, burgers in Manly and fish and chips in Watson's Bay. But her favourite date was the day they'd hired a kayak and paddled to Store Beach. Just thinking about it now made her smile. She had been surprised by how many secluded coves there were around the harbour and she loved being able to escape the city so easily.

Store Beach was only accessible by boat, which meant it was quiet. She preferred the quieter beaches to the bustle of Bondi and Manly. Perhaps it was the country girl in her or perhaps it had something to do with the fact that when they had a beach to themselves they took advantage of that. They had made love in the water that day, something she was positive they wouldn't have been able to do at Bondi, and she knew she was going to file these memories away and revisit them when Seb was gone from her life. This might be temporary but she would always have the memories.

Spending time with Seb was therapeutic, mentally as well as physically. She felt happier than she had in a long time and she no longer thought about babies and failed marriages or Ben and his new wife, Catriona, every day. She had other things on her mind. She was becoming the person for the next stage of her life and she was starting to feel that she would be okay. She still wasn't sure that she'd be okay on her own but Seb was showing her how to put herself out there again. She knew that if she had been able to do it with him she'd be able to do it with the next guy. And maybe the next guy would be the one.

Her life was far from over. She would take her second chance. She would achieve her dreams, one way or another. Seb was right, she had time on her side and she wasn't going to let Ben take it all away from her. She would go after her dream and she would make it happen. She would learn as much as she could about herself while Seb was giving her that chance so she could grow and move forward.

Luci's time in Sydney was almost half-gone. The time was flying past; her days were busy and so were her nights. She wasn't sure how she was going to manage back in Vickers Hill. She couldn't remember how she used to fill her days. Work, housework, dinner with her parents and a game of netball once a week didn't seem like much now compared to what she was packing into her days in Sydney. So she'd better make the most of it.

She was feeling more confident and comfortable at work. She'd decided not to be so precious about comments and questions from clients as to whether or not she had children. They didn't know her circumstances so she replied with, 'Not yet,' and left it at that. She wasn't wearing a wedding ring so at least she was spared from those expectations that she and Ben had had. From the moment they'd got married that had been the next question. She'd initially used the excuses of 'We've only just got married' or 'We're saving for a house' but the questions hadn't really bothered her until she'd been trying to fall pregnant. She had needed to develop a tougher skin.

Spending time with Seb was definitely helping. He kept her mind and body busy and she no longer thought about having kids every hour of every day. She had relaxed. She had a little over four weeks remaining and she was determined to enjoy every second. The rest of her life could start after that. She had time.

But she very quickly got used to spending her days and nights with Seb and when he told her he needed to go away for a few days for work she found the prospect of being alone again quite daunting.

'I have been asked to go to Budgee to work in their community health clinic for a few days later this week. The doctor's wife and daughter have been injured in a car accident and the doctor has flown down to Sydney to be with them. There's no hospital there any more so there's no other cover.'

'Why have they asked you?'

He shrugged. 'I was there about eighteen months ago

for six weeks so they figure I'll be more familiar with the work than others. And, besides, it's what I do.'

She knew that. He'd told her he spent a lot of time travelling to different parts of country New South Wales.

'You could come with me if you like.'

'How do you figure that?'

'The doctor's wife is a nurse so with her out of action the town has lost their nurse and doctor. I could arrange a few days there for you as part of your course.'

Luci didn't care if people accused Seb of favouritism. Going with him was preferable to being left alone in Sydney, even if it was only for three days, which was how she found herself being driven down the main street of Budgee two days later.

It was a pretty town three hours west of Sydney over the Blue Mountains, with a small-town feel. The main street was wide, not dissimilar to main streets in most country towns across Australia, and this one was planted with oak trees and lined with beautiful old public buildings. A wide, grassy strip ran down the centre of the road. A military memorial stood at one end near the pub; a majestic building with wraparound balconies and elaborate wrought-iron railings. The two-storey red-brick post office stood in the middle of town opposite the limestone town hall. Further down the street, past the police station, the Catholic church faced off across the road from the Presbyterian one, standing sentinel at the end of town.

They had left Sydney early and arrived at the clinic by ten. They were going to spend the morning working there before visiting an aboriginal settlement in the afternoon.

'Budgee used to have a small hospital,' Seb explained as he turned off the main street, 'but the services gradually dwindled as the community decreased in size and as the roads and transport improved, making it unnecessary for each country town to have its own facilities. The government "consolidated"—their word—the services, which was all well and good in most cases except for emergencies. Budgee lost its hospital but retained a community health centre, which was moved into the old hospital ironically, and the local doctor spends two days a week here and three days a week in surrounding towns.'

Seb pulled into the car park of the old hospital and Luci followed him inside. She spent what was left of the morning doing health checks, just like she would have done in Sydney, along with fielding the same personal questions interspersed with questions about the health of the local nurse and her daughter.

For lunch she and Seb grabbed a meat pie from the local bakery and ate in the car as Seb drove them to the aboriginal settlement thirty minutes out of town. Budgee was in the centre of a wine-growing region and the town was surrounded by vineyards. It reminded Luci of Vickers Hill, having the same look and feel of home. Did Vickers Hill still feel like home? She wasn't sure. She'd changed since she'd been in Sydney. She was different now and she wasn't sure if she would be able to settle back into her old life.

Was it living in a big city that had changed her or was it Seb?

She didn't know the answer to that either, although she suspected the latter.

As they drove through the countryside she almost felt as though they were on a date. Seb was dressed casually in an open-necked, short-sleeved shirt that showed off his muscular forearms. His long fingers were wrapped around the steering wheel. Last night they'd been caressing her breasts and bringing her to another orgasm, and she could still feel some tenderness between her thighs after another night of lovemaking, but it was definitely not an unpleasant sensation.

Seb was tapping his index finger and humming along in time to the song that was playing on the radio. She looked at his face, at his perfect profile as the scenery flashed past. They were still driving past rows and rows of vines, dense with green foliage, and she was tempted to tell him to pull over. She wondered if they had time for a quick make-out session in the car. She hadn't behaved like that for years but something about him made her feel like a teenager again, a reckless, rebellious teenager with only one thing on her mind.

He turned his head to look at her; he must have felt her scrutiny. He took one look at her expression and winked, and she knew he could tell what she was thinking.

She blushed and he laughed, rich and throaty, as he turned his attention back to the road.

'Hold that thought,' he said. 'There'll be time for fooling around later but we can't turn up at the settlement looking like we've just tumbled out of bed. Or out of the bushes.' He grinned and his eyes flicked briefly back to her.

A quick glance at her chest and Luci could feel the heat rising from her. The only thing stopping the windows from fogging up was the fact that it was almost as warm outside the car as inside.

If he looked at her like that once more she was going to have to pull on the handbrake and have her way with him.

'Pity,' she said as she reached across the console, ignoring the handbrake, and rested her hand at the very top of his thigh. She slid her hand between his thighs so her fingers rested against his groin. If he was going to make her sweat she was going to make sure he joined her. Two could play at that game. 'We could pull over and sneak down between the rows of grapes and make love on the ground between the vines.'

'You'll get covered in dirt.'

'I was planning to go on top,' she responded.

'Luci,' he groaned. 'That's not playing fair. I need to concentrate.'

'Are you sure we haven't got time for a quick stop?'

'Positive,' he said, removing her hand from his groin and putting it back in her lap. 'But we will have all night and I promise I'll make the wait worth your while,' he said as he drove past the signpost that welcomed them to the settlement of Frog Hollow.

She sighed and looked around as Seb drove down the main street. She needed to get her mind back on the job.

'So tell me again what I'll be doing here,' she said, trying to focus less on Seb and more on her duties.

'It does depend on who turns up but general health checks are the norm. BP, cholesterol tests, with referral for any high readings, plus counselling will take up most of your time. Just keep in mind there are different issues facing this population. Diabetes, eye disease, cardiovascular conditions, kidney disease and ear infections all tend to be more prevalent in the indigenous community and a lot of the problems arise because they don't have access to health care.'

'I remember what you told us when you gave the lecture.'

'Well, you're about to see it first-hand, although because the community of Frog Hollow made a decision to be a dry settlement we do see fewer issues here than elsewhere. There won't be scheduled appointments as such, we just see whoever turns up in whatever order they turn up, but expect to be busy as these remote clinics are only run once a month.'

Seb turned off the main street onto a side road that was made of dirt. Apparently only the main road in and out of town was tarred but the buildings were modern. Luci could see plenty of free-roaming chickens and dogs, as well as a number of kids riding bikes and playing in the street. There seem to be an awful lot of children not in school.

'There's no school in the settlement,' Seb explained, when Luci commented. 'The kids need to go into Budgee on the school bus but a lot don't make it in time. Today quite a few parents would have chosen not to send their kids to town because we were coming,' he said as he parked the car and switched off the engine.

Luci could see several people waiting, sitting on the veranda of the hall. She helped Seb to unload the medical kits from the car and take them into the hall. A temporary clinic had been set up at one end near the kitchen. There were two stations, one for her and one for him, basic and identical save for the fact that Seb's had an examination bed tucked against the wall, sectioned off behind a privacy screen.

They worked their way steadily through the locals who seemed quite content to sit and wait. They didn't seem impatient. They didn't seem to be watching the clock, like the clients in the city who always seemed to have somewhere else they needed to be. The pace suited Luci. It was nice to have time to stop and take a breath occasionally.

There were some things about home she hadn't missed—the lack of privacy, for example—but she hadn't realised just what a whirlwind life in Sydney was. The pace was frenetic, with everyone constantly on the go, but it wasn't until she had a chance to slow down that she realised how rushed she'd been.

From her station she could watch Seb working. He

seemed to be primarily checking ears and eyes as frequently as she was checking blood pressures.

He looked up and smiled at her and she felt a warm glow suffuse her. They worked well together. They did other things well together too and she hugged that thought to herself. She was looking forward to the end of the day, looking forward to tonight.

She stripped off her gloves as she finished with her patient and went out to the veranda to call the next one, only to find there was no one else waiting. She wondered if their day was done, if they could return to Budgee and finish what she'd started.

She went back inside the hall and was preparing to pack away her things when she saw Seb incline his head at her and nod at his patient, and she knew he wanted her to join them.

Seb was looking into the ears of a little boy who looked about three or four years of age. The boy's mother sat beside him. She was heavily pregnant and the fabric of her summer dress strained across her belly.

'Nadine, this is Luci Dawson, one of the community health nurses,' Seb said as he switched sides to look into the little boy's left ear. 'Luci, would you mind checking Nadine's blood pressure for me while I finish up with Byron? This is Nadine's fifth pregnancy and she hasn't had any problems, but she hasn't had any antenatal care either and she's not sure of her dates. She thinks she might be about seven months but seeing as we're here I thought we'd do a bit of a check.'

'Sure.' Luci smiled at Nadine.

The woman looked much further along than seven months. Luci couldn't imagine not having any antenatal care herself but Seb had warned her that things were different out here. Nadine looked relaxed but Luci knew Seb was worried.

It was hard to pinpoint her age. Her brown skin was smooth and glowed but her eyes looked tired. She could be anywhere from twenty-five to thirty-five. Even so, a fifth pregnancy was a lot.

Luci wrapped the blood-pressure cuff around Nadine's arm and pumped it up. She popped the stethoscope in her ears and listened for the heartbeat followed by silence as the cuff deflated. Her blood pressure was fine.

'All normal,' she told Seb.

'Good.' Seb nodded. 'Byron seems to have another slight middle-ear infection, swimmer's ear most likely. I'll give him a course of antibiotics but no swimming for a week, okay? And before you go I'd like to listen to the baby's heart and take a couple of measurements, if that's all right. Can you just hop up on the bed behind the screen for me?'

Seb rifled through one of the medical bags and found the medication he wanted. He wrote Byron's name and the instructions on a label and attached it to the bottle.

Luci took the bottle and handed him the stethoscope. She picked Byron up and popped him on her hip and followed Seb around the screen. Protocol dictated that she needed to be present for the exam.

Nadine had already hoisted her dress up to expose her belly, which was as tight as a drum. Luci felt a familiar pull of longing and jealousy when she saw the woman's heavily pregnant frame but she tried her best to ignore it. She was a professional, she could do this.

Seb placed the bulb of the scope on Nadine's tummy and moved it around, listening for the baby's heartbeat. Luci watched him. She saw him frown and reposition the stethoscope. She could see Nadine hold her breath but then Seb smiled and Nadine relaxed and exhaled.

Seb pulled the stethoscope out of his ears and looped it around his neck. Luci handed him a tape measure, which he took but didn't immediately use.

'Well, that explains a few things,' he said as he smiled at Nadine. 'You're having twins.'

'Twins?' Nadine and Luci said in unison.

Seb nodded and his blue eyes sparkled. 'Now I know you've done all this before but this is the first set of twins you've had. I want you to have some antenatal care. I want you to make an appointment at the hospital in Dubbo—actually, I'll make it for you,' he said as he helped Nadine to sit up on the edge of the bed.

He pulled his mobile phone out of his pocket and scrolled through the address book, looking for the number. Nadine stood up and slipped her feet back into her flip-flops before taking Byron from Luci.

Seb had been put through to the right department and covered the speaker with his hand as he spoke to Nadine. 'Can you make it to Dubbo tomorrow afternoon?'

Nadine nodded and Seb confirmed the time.

'They will do an ultrasound scan,' he said as he ended the call. 'It's important that they try to confirm your dates and check that everything is on track. Any dramas, make sure you call the Budgee clinic. I'll still be there tomorrow and I'll phone Dubbo for an update,' he added, wanting to make sure that she understood he'd be around to keep an eye on her. He handed Nadine a card with the Budgee clinic number on it and added the number for the Dubbo hospital, along with the appointment time.

'Do you think she'll keep the appointment?' Luci asked as they hit the road a little later for the return trip to Budgee. Flocks of galahs and sulphur-crested cockatoos were feeding at the side of the road. The cockatoos rose up in a squawking mass as the car passed them but the little pink and grey galahs seemed oblivious. They kept their heads down, pecking away at the gum-nut seeds that were strewn on the ground.

'I hope so. Twins are obviously trickier to deal with, and gestational diabetes is high in the indigenous population so I'd like her to have the proper care. It'll be another month before anyone is back out at Frog Hollow. Anything could happen in that time.'

Luci's muscles groaned in protest as she lowered herself onto a child-sized kindergarten chair. Muscles she'd forgotten she had ached and every time she moved she was reminded of the night before. She'd been stretched, bent and contorted into all sorts of positions last night but she wasn't complaining even if her muscles were. She and Seb had barely made it back to the motel before tearing each other's clothes off. Their desire had been building all afternoon until it had reached fever pitch and they had almost sprinted to her room and spent the rest of the evening making love, stopping only briefly to shower and grab some food before they'd gone back to her room. Luci knew they must have looked like they had been having frenzied sex but she hadn't cared any more. It hadn't been like home. She could behave as she pleased out here and it pleased her to misbehave with Seb.

She smiled to herself as she thought about what they'd got up to, until she realised that the preschoolers sitting at the table with her weren't going to give her time to daydream.

She was spending the afternoon in the child-care centre and kindergarten attached to the community health clinic. The work was pretty much the same, assessing the development of the children, but the approach was different. Instead of a formal appointment, Luci played with the children in the kindergarten environment, doing surreptitious development checks. Sitting with the kids while they drew pictures or constructed masterpieces out of cardboard rolls, boxes, egg cartons and metres of sticky tape gave her a chance to assess their hearing, speech and fine motor skills. Later she'd play outside with them in the sandpit and on the climbing equipment, observing their balance, co-ordination and gross motor skills.

If she noticed any issues she could then make referrals to the visiting therapists but, again, making appointments didn't necessarily work. Appointment times were not generally considered fixed and Luci had been told that a lot of the time the health-care staff just had to hope that some of the kids were in attendance at playgroup when the visiting therapists were in town.

Luci was writing a child's name on the cardboard robot that he'd made when she noticed Nadine and Byron coming into the centre.

Nadine looked tired today, definitely not as fresh as yesterday. The circles under her eyes had darkened and Luci thought her face looked a little pinched and drawn, as if she was in pain. Luci stood up. 'Nadine, hello. Are you on your way to Dubbo?'

Nadine nodded. 'I thought I'd drop Byron here while I went for my appointment, if that's okay. He knows this kindy.'

Budgee was about halfway between Frog Hollow and Dubbo. Nadine had had to pass through town in order to reach Dubbo.

'Sure,' Luci replied as Byron ran off to play. 'Are you feeling all right?'

'I didn't sleep well and my back is a bit sore. I think I might have pulled a muscle when I picked Byron up this morning.'

'Have you got time for a cup of tea or water? Why don't you sit down and I'll get you something to drink?' Luci offered. But before she could usher her to a chair Nadine clutched her stomach and looked as if she was about to burst into tears.

'What is it?' Luci asked.

But Nadine didn't answer, she just looked down at the floor. Luci followed her gaze.

Nadine was standing in a pool of water.

CHAPTER SEVEN

'THAT'S NOT GOOD,' Nadine said.

Luci agreed but at least Nadine was in town, and Seb was only metres away in the building next door.

But before Luci had a chance to say anything further Nadine gasped and doubled over.

'Contraction?' Luci asked.

She looked up at Luci and her dark brown eyes were filled with fear. She nodded and said, 'It's too early.'

Luci knew that Nadine was unsure of her dates and today's appointment had been an opportunity to narrow them down, but there was the distinct possibility that it was far too early. In some cases labour could be delayed, even if the membranes had ruptured, but that was a clinical decision and once the contractions had started Luci knew there was very little they could do.

'Dr Hollingsworth is just next door,' Luci said, trying to sound calm and reassuring even as she fought back her own concerns. 'Do you think you can walk or shall I fetch a wheelchair?'

'I can walk if I can lean on you.'

Jenny, the child-care director, had seen what was happening and she came across the room, carrying an armful of old towels. Being a centre filled with preschoolers, they were well equipped for dealing with accidents similar to this.

'Jenny, we need to leave Byron here,' Luci said as Jenny dropped the towels on the floor.

'Of course.' She squatted down to mop up the mess. 'What about your older children?' she asked Nadine.

'They'll go home on the school bus,' Nadine managed to say, before another contraction swamped her. She gripped tightly onto Luci's arm. The contractions were close together and strong. Luci didn't like the look of this at all. She needed to get Nadine next door to Seb. And quickly.

Byron was engrossed with a big box of building blocks and trucks and didn't look up as Luci ushered his mother out of the centre.

'Heather, can you call Seb, please?' Luci started speaking to the receptionist in the community health clinic as soon as she and Nadine walked through the clinic doors. 'And an ambulance. Nadine is in labour.'

Heather stood up from behind the desk. 'Take her through here,' she said, directing Luci into one of the old hospital rooms. She wheeled a trolley over to the bed and handed Luci a hospital gown. 'There are gloves, scissors and basic clinical supplies on here. I'll call Seb and the ambulance and then check back to see if there's anything else you need. We're not fully equipped any more but I'll do my best.'

Luci nodded her thanks. 'You'd better phone ahead to Dubbo and warn them too. Nadine was on her way there for an antenatal appointment,' she added as Heather left the room. She turned back to Nadine, who was still clinging to her arm. 'Let's get you into this gown so that Dr Hollingsworth can examine you when he gets here.'

'Can you stop the labour? It's too early.'

Luci shook her head. 'Once your waters have broken

there's nothing much we can do. These babies are on their way.' The best they could hope for was that the ambulance arrived before the babies did.

Seb hurried in just as Luci had finished helping Nadine to change.

'Nadine! I wasn't expecting to see you today. What's going on?' He sounded cool, calm and collected but there was no doubt he'd come at a run.

Luci handed him a paper hospital gown and he slipped his arms into the sleeves and waited as Luci tied the strings before he repeated the process for her. He washed his hands and pulled on a pair of surgical gloves as Luci wrapped a BP cuff around Nadine's arm.

'Let's see what's happening,' he said, as he positioned himself at the foot of the bed and got Nadine to lie back and bend her knees. 'Eight centimetres dilated,' he said.

There wasn't going to be much time to spare. But just as Luci was praying that the ambulance was close by Heather came into the room and dashed her hopes.

'The ambulance is forty-five minutes out of town at the scene of a car accident. They'll get here as quickly as they can but expect them to be a while,' she informed them.

Nadine was in the middle of another contraction and Luci didn't think she'd heard a word Heather had said, which was probably just as well. It wasn't great news but it didn't appear to faze Seb.

'It looks like your babies are going to be born in Budgee,' Seb told Nadine once her contraction had passed. 'Luckily for you, we've done this before.' There wasn't a trace of panic in his voice and he even had Luci believing it would all be all right.

'You okay?' He looked at Luci and mouthed the question. Nadine wouldn't be able to see his lips as her belly was blocking her view.

Luci wasn't sure. She didn't want to deal with a woman in labour. She'd managed to cope with Nadine's pregnancy yesterday, but actually delivering babies was a different thing altogether. But Seb didn't need to hear about her issues now. He needed her help. Somehow she'd get through this. She would focus on one thing at a time.

She nodded. Seb needed her. She would do her best to keep it together and wouldn't think about things that were out of her control.

'How quick were your other labours?' Seb asked Nadine. 'Have you been caught off guard before or have you been able to get to the hospital?'

'My third one was fast. She was born out at Frog Hollow.'

'But other than that it all went fine?'

Nadine nodded, unable to speak as another contraction gripped her. She was covered in a sheen of sweat and Luci wiped her forehead with a flannel.

'Were there any complications with your other deliveries?'

'No,' she puffed.

Seb picked a stethoscope up from the trolley and listened to the babies' heartbeats. They were both around one hundred and forty beats per minute—perfectly normal. Everyone else might be stressed but at least the babies weren't.

Heather returned and this time she was wheeling two small cots side by side. She parked these in the corner of the room and lifted out a pile of blankets and a set of scales. She wiped out the cots and folded some of the blankets, putting them back into the cots to act as makeshift mattresses before covering them with clean sheets. 'We had these in storage but there's not much else,' she said. 'There's pethidine if you need it but that's about it.'

Seb got the message. He doubted he had time for pethidine to work to provide any pain relief for Nadine—these babies were in a hurry and Heather's underlying message was that there was nothing else on hand to help him manage premature infants medically. There were no drugs, no Vitamin K injections, no heat lamps and no emergency team standing by.

Babies had been born for thousands of years without all the modern interference but Seb knew the survival rate of premature twins had been low in those days. He would do his best and hope that the ambulance arrived soon. He prayed silently that everything would go right.

His gaze swept the room, looking for anything at all that might come in handy. There was an oxygen tank attached to the wall. He looked at Luci and then back at the cylinder. 'Can you see if that works?' he asked her.

Luci put down the flannel and crossed the room. She had been very quiet and he hoped she was coping okay with the drama, he wasn't really sure how much experience she had with this sort of situation. But her movements were practised and efficient. She knew the basic procedures and he just had to hope that he could prevent an emergency.

Luci opened the valve on the oxygen tank. She nodded.

That was one thing he had up his sleeve if needed, he thought as he turned back to Nadine.

Her labour was progressing quickly. That wasn't surprising given that it was her fifth pregnancy and delivery, but Seb wished it wasn't so. He would much prefer it if she could hold on until the ambulance reached them but that was looking highly unlikely because he could see the first baby's head crowning.

'I want to push,' Nadine told him.

He'd barely had time to check the position of the babies but there was no going back now. 'Okay. We're ready to go.'

Nadine's knees were bent. Luci stood beside her, holding her hand.

'Push,' he instructed.

He reached between her thighs and eased the baby's head out.

'Okay, relax now. Wait for the next contraction.'

Nadine panted swiftly between contractions and with the following one Seb delivered the baby's shoulders. The little girl slid out swiftly and he hoped it was because Nadine's body was familiar with the process and not because the other baby had kicked it out. He didn't want to deal with a breech presentation as well as the premature delivery of twins.

'It's a girl,' he told Nadine. She came out yelling and Seb placed her on Nadine's chest. Luci had loosened the hospital gown at Nadine's neck so the baby could lie skin to skin on her mother but Seb couldn't leave her there for long. She needed to be checked and kept warm and he needed to get ready to deliver the second baby.

'Can you do the Apgar test?' he asked Luci as he cut the cord.

Luci nodded and reached for the baby. 'I'll just check her out,' she explained to Nadine. 'You've still got some work to do.'

Seb briefly watched Luci holding the baby. It suited her. She had an expression of contentment and he hoped for her sake that she had a child of her own one day. He knew that was what she wanted.

'One minute Apgar eight out of ten. Pulse ninety-six, tinge of blue in the fingers,' Luci said as she put the baby on the scales. He was aware of her weighing the baby as she updated him. 'Two point four kilograms,' she said as she wrapped the baby. There was no time to clean her up as she needed to be kept warm and Luci needed to be ready to help with the second delivery.

Nadine's contractions were continuing strongly. The second twin was on its way. He checked what was happening and breathed a sigh of relief when he felt Twin B moving down into the pelvis.

Seb had to rupture the membrane for Twin B and the next thing he saw was the baby's head crowning. Thank God it wasn't breech.

'Five-minute Apgar nine out of ten,' Luci said, updating him on Twin A. 'Colour is good, heart rate ninety-eight.'

He nodded in acknowledgement to Luci but spoke to Nadine. 'Okay, time for number two. You can push with the next contraction.'

The second twin was slightly bigger but was delivered just as easily. He handed the little boy to Nadine then checked the cord before clamping and cutting it. Nadine had a quick cuddle before Luci took him to assess.

'Six out of ten. Pulse ninety-four. Sluggish reflexes, blue extremities, resp. rate thirty-five.'

The little boy was bigger, but not as healthy as his sister.

'He needs oxygen,' Luci said, and Seb knew she was looking to him to fix the problem. They had oxygen but how was he going to get it into a premature infant?

He looked around the room for inspiration as he prayed that the ambulance would hurry.

His gaze rested on the acrylic bassinettes.

'Can you connect some tubing to the oxygen cylinder?' he asked Luci as he covered Nadine with a blanket. The little boy was his priority now and there was nothing else he could do for Nadine until the ambulance arrived. If he could manage to hold the two bassinettes together he would be able to fashion a makeshift oxygen tent, which would be better than nothing in the short term. Taking the little boy from Lucy he placed him in a bassinette along-side his sister. He emptied the second bassinette and in-verted it over the first. He grabbed a roll of medical tape and ran it around the edges of the cribs, taping them to-gether. There was an opening where the sides had been cut down that would allow the carbon monoxide to escape. The 'tent' would be less efficient than he would like but it would be good enough.

Luci had connected the tubing to the oxygen cylinder. She passed the end to him and he slid it into the bassinette, taping it in place too.

'Run it at eight litres per minute,' he said as Heather came back into the room.

'The ambulance is five minutes away,' she told them, and Seb thought that was the best sentence he'd ever heard. He could handle five more minutes.

He left Luci to keep an eye on the babies as he spoke to Nadine. 'Your babies are okay. Your daughter is doing well, your little boy is having a little bit of difficulty breathing so we need to give him some oxygen, but the ambulance is almost here and will transfer them to Dubbo hospital.'

'What about me?'

'You'll go too.'

'Byron?'

'I've put him on the school bus with your other kids,' Heather said as she returned to the room with the ambu-lance officers in tow. 'Will there be someone home in Frog Hollow to take care of them?'

Nadine nodded. 'My husband is there and my sister will give him a hand.'

The next fifteen minutes passed in a flurry of activity as the ambos stabilised the babies and Seb gave Nadine an oxytocin injection and delivered the placentas.

Somehow they got the whole family into the back of the ambulance and Seb breathed a sigh of relief as he closed the back doors and watched the ambulance take off.

When he went back into the community health clinic Heather was rescheduling the rest of the day's appointments. She was proving to be worth her weight in gold today.

He left her to it and went to help Luci tidy up the makeshift delivery suite.

She was stripping the bed and had her back to him but he saw her lift her arm and wipe her hand across her face and he realised she was crying. Were they happy or sad tears? Her shoulders were shaking and as he got closer he could hear her sobs. It sounded like her heart was breaking.

He put a hand on her shoulder. 'Luci, what's the matter?'

She turned around but she was crying so hard she couldn't talk. He wrapped her in his arms and held her tightly until her tears eased but didn't stop completely. He brushed her hair from her forehead and kissed her gently. 'What is it, Luce? Tell me what's wrong.'

'I can't do this any more,' she sobbed.

'Can't do what?'

'Deliver babies. It's one of the reasons l left Vickers Hill, seeing other women holding their newborn babies. I can't do it.'

He frowned. 'You'll get your turn,' he told her. 'We've talked about this.'

But Luci was shaking her head. 'You don't understand.'

'Explain it to me, then.'

'Not here. I need to go home.'

'Home?' he asked. 'To Vickers Hill?'

She shook her head and gulped air as she tried to get her emotions under control. 'No. Back to the motel.'

He was happy to call it quits. It was almost the end of

the day and hopefully Heather had managed to reschedule the remaining appointments. Rarely was anything so urgent with community health that it couldn't be pushed back. He would start earlier tomorrow if necessary, before they headed back to Sydney. Right now Luci was his priority.

He had bundled her into the car and driven her back to the motel and now she was sitting on the edge of the bed. Her face was blotchy and her eyes were red but she had stopped crying. He boiled the kettle to make tea, wondering if he should call room service for something stronger, but decided to wait.

He handed her a cup of green tea. 'What's going on?' he asked.

'I don't like delivering babies.'

He frowned. 'What's not to like? I agree, sometimes things can get a bit difficult but we had a really good outcome today, all things considered.'

'I know and I'm happy for Nadine but I find it soul destroying. It just reminds me that the thing I want most in my life isn't a possibility.'

'What are you talking about? We've had this conversation…you're young, you've got time.'

'It's not time I need,' she said with a shake of her head. 'There are some things I love about small country towns and there are things I can live without. Like delivering babies. That's part of the reason I wanted to get out of there. I don't want to deliver other people's babies. Not when I can't have my own.'

'What do you mean?'

'I can't have kids.'

He wasn't sure if he was following the conversation properly. 'But you told me you and your ex-husband were planning on starting a family.'

'We were trying to get pregnant. It didn't happen.'

'But that doesn't mean you can't have them. It just means it hadn't happened yet.'

'We tried for eighteen months. Nothing.'

'It still doesn't mean the problem lies with you.'

'I'm pretty sure it does. Ben has remarried and is expecting a baby with his new wife.'

Wow. He hadn't seen that coming.

'Why haven't you told me this before?' he asked.

'Because it was irrelevant to you.'

He was momentarily affronted until he realised she was right. Their relationship had no strings attached.

But that didn't change the fact that Luci was upset and his natural instinct was to try to fix things. Although this could be a slight problem. He might be out of his depth.

'I guess it's not,' he agreed. 'You've spoken about wanting to have kids but you never mentioned you couldn't.' He was surprised at how hurt he felt that she hadn't confided in him but he wasn't stupid enough not to realise that he hadn't confided in her either. There was plenty of information he had kept to himself so why should he be upset to find she was no different? He didn't normally have double standards. 'Do you know what the problem is?'

Luci shook her head. 'No.'

'You haven't been tested?'

'It's a long story.'

'I'm not going anywhere.' Never had a truer word been spoken. They were in the middle of New South Wales. They had nowhere to go, nothing else to do. He had all the time in the world.

Luci sipped her tea. 'The doctors said the same thing as you did initially. They told us we were young and healthy and there was no reason to worry. They said we should try to relax, try to just enjoy it, and if, after a year, we weren't pregnant then they'd do tests. So we listened and decided to keep trying. I had no idea how hard it would be to "relax" in that situation. We kept working. We thought we'd pay off some more of our mortgage and Ben wanted to expand the family business and suddenly eighteen months had passed. So we went back to the doctor and tests were suggested.

'We started the process but by now we were worried. We started discussing what we would do if the tests showed a problem. Would we go down the IVF path? That's expensive and we weren't sure how we would afford it. We were already stressed and things just got worse, and then Ben met Catriona. When Ben left me there didn't seem any point in continuing the testing process and when I heard that Catriona was expecting a baby I figured I had my answer.' She shrugged. 'It didn't matter what the tests showed. The problem was with me.'

Seb could understand her devastation and her logic but that didn't mean she was right. 'But it could have been any number of things.'

'Well, until I find someone who I want to try again with it doesn't matter. What matters is trying to get on with my life. Ben took away my marriage and I've recovered from that, but he also took away my dream of having a family. Even if the problem lay with me as a couple we could have adopted or fostered kids, we could have made something work, but now I either have to give up on my dream or start again. I decided to start again. I will do it. I want this more than anything but it still hurts when I see pregnant women or women with their babies. It reminds me of what I might never have and it's part of the reason I wanted to move away from working in a country hospital. I had to assist with deliveries and I'd want to be happy for the parents but every time it just felt like my heart was breaking.'

'Working in family and community health might be just as difficult.'

'I know. I'm coming to realise that,' she sighed. 'But it's still an area that interests me. It's a double-edged sword in a way. I want to work with kids but I didn't think about the fact that so many women with young children would be pregnant with another one. But I'm hoping that eventually I'll feel better about it. It will either wreck me or help me but I don't expect it to happen overnight. One thing at a time.

'I've got over the end of my marriage, perhaps one day I'll accept that I can't have a family, but for the moment I just prefer not to talk about it. Not talking about it means I can try to ignore it. It's obvious the problem lies with me, but I'm not ready to think about what it means.'

All along Seb had had the feeling that she'd been running away and now he knew why. He couldn't blame her for not wanting to be around when her ex's new partner had the child she'd been longing for.

And now it was Seb's turn to feel as though his heart was breaking. In sympathy with Luci. *I'm so sorry.* What else could he say?

But he couldn't help her. There was nothing he could do. As much as he wanted to, he couldn't fix this. He couldn't give her what she wanted but he could take care of her. At least for now.

He lay on the bed with her and wrapped her in his arms and waited until she fell into an exhausted sleep.

But sleep eluded him. He lay in the dark and thought about Luci.

It had been a long time since anything, or anyone, had affected him this strongly. Since anyone had made his heart ache.

This was exactly what he'd been trying to avoid. He

didn't want to feel. He didn't want to hurt for someone else. And he didn't want to think about what that meant.

In the space of three weeks he had seen her ecstatic, nervous, passionate, playful, flirty and full of despair. Unlike him, she wore her heart on her sleeve. He felt he had known her for much longer and he knew he would miss her when they parted ways, but their time was limited. He would be leaving Sydney in a little over a fortnight. This wasn't a long-term proposition and her problem was not his to solve. As much as he'd like to, he couldn't fix things for her and she hadn't asked him to.

He would enjoy the next few weeks, distract her and hopefully take her mind off her problems. He would give her time to heal and then he'd let her go.

Luci picked up her wine glass and followed Seb up the steps of his boat and around to the forward deck.

The carpenter had finished installing the new kitchen while she and Seb had been in Budgee. The boat was finished, still unnamed but finished, and to celebrate Seb had invited her to spend the weekend on board. Seb had cooked a simple meal of steak and salad, the new kitchen had been tested and the new bed christened. So far the weekend was fabulous.

The boat bobbed gently on the calm waters of the Hawkesbury River. It was a beautiful warm night. There were thick clouds on the horizon and rain had been forecast. The air was heavy with humidity but so far the rain held off. The sunset had been incredible and, for now, the sky was clear and black.

Luci sat beside Seb and he slipped his arm around her shoulders, tucking her in against him. She was naked under her cotton dress and Seb wore only a pair of shorts. His body heat radiated out to her. She leaned back against the windshield of the boat and looked up at the sky. It was sprinkled with tiny stars that looked like diamonds on black velvet.

There were no other lights, on the water or on the shore. She felt like they had the world to themselves. Luci sighed. Seb was constantly surprising her with their dates and this one was particularly romantic. Lying on the deck of the boat, feeling like they were the only two people in existence, she could see the attraction of having somewhere to escape to. It was quite possibly a necessity in order to maintain your sanity if you lived in a city like Sydney, but she still couldn't imagine making this her life. As romantic as the night was, she imagined it would be a very isolated existence with no one to share it with.

'Do you think you'll ever get lonely out here on your own?'

'Maybe,' Seb replied. 'But that's a chance I'm willing to take. I've never been lonely before.'

'You've never had anyone else stay?'

He shook his head. 'No.'

'Why is that?' Luci was curious and also flattered to think she was the first, but realised there could just as easily be another explanation that had nothing to do with her. 'Was it because the boat wasn't ready?'

'No. I've stayed the night many times but I've never felt the need to share this with anyone else before.'

'Why did you ask me?'

'I thought you might like it,' he said simply.

'Not to keep you company?'

'I'm happy with my own company.'

That had been a question that had been bothering her since the first time she'd set foot on his boat. His desire to have an escape, to keep a bachelor pad of sorts had seemed at odds with someone who was so vital and charismatic.

'Have you never thought about sharing your life with someone?' She knew he'd had at least one lengthy relationship but she still wondered why it hadn't developed into something more serious. He was only thirty-one. Far too young to have decided to spend his life alone. What had happened that had made him so solitary?

Despite her divorce Luci hadn't given up on finding love again. She wasn't assuming Seb would want to share his life with her but she wondered what had happened to make him so against the idea of sharing his life with anyone.

'Once upon a time I assumed I would marry and have kids, that it was something that was in my future. But it was just that. In the future. I assumed it would happen one day but I had no real plans that it had to happen by a certain point in my life. I guess I thought I would finish my studies, get married, eventually have a couple of kids, but it hasn't turned out that way. And I'm okay with that. I'm okay on my own.'

She had shared so much of herself with him—her hopes and dreams, her failures and disappointments. She knew him intimately yet she still knew very little about what had made him into the man he was today.

What had shaped him? What had led him to the decisions he had made? What were his hopes and dreams? Surely no one really hoped to spend their life alone, did they? Something must have happened to bring him to that conclusion.

'Yet now you've decided that you don't want that future. What has happened that has made you think you'd be better off alone?'

'I lost someone unexpectedly.'

'Your girlfriend?'

She felt his answering nod.

'What happened?'

'She was killed in a hit-and-run accident.'

'Oh, Seb.' Luci felt awful now. She'd forced the admission out of him and perhaps it wasn't something he'd wanted to share. She didn't know what she could say to make things better but before she could say anything Seb continued.

'It happened right outside our house. It was the day we were moving in together. Emma had parked opposite the house and she was carrying boxes inside. A car came round the corner and ran her over. I don't know whether she couldn't see where she was going, she might have stepped into the path of the car, but she hit her head when she fell. I guess she didn't have time to put her arms out. When I got home there was an ambulance in the middle of the street but it was too late. *I* was too late.

'She died from head injuries. I like to think she never knew what had happened but I don't think that's true. She didn't die instantly. It messed me up for a long time. Thinking about what she went through. How she suffered. And I don't want to experience anything like that again. That's why I've chosen to live my life the way I am.'

Finally Luci was able to understand. She couldn't imagine going through that experience. The trauma, the guilt, the despair. She knew he would have felt all those things, especially guilt. He would blame himself for not getting there sooner, not being there to help his girlfriend with the boxes. He would think he could have made the difference. Luci knew him well enough to know that he would struggle to forgive himself. She finally understood.

'Did they ever find the driver of the car?' she asked.

'No.'

He'd lost everything that day. He'd thought losing Emma had been the worst thing that could happen but things had got worse from there, much worse. But Seb wasn't sure if Luci could handle hearing about what had happened next. He lapsed into silence as he fought his demons. Fought with the guilt that still haunted him. He had never forgiven himself for not being there earlier. He had been held up at work, agreeing to see an extra patient. If he hadn't he would have been there. *He* would have been carrying those boxes and he wouldn't have lost everything.

'Seb?' Luci interrupted his thoughts.

Maybe if he explained everything to her she would understand why he was so different from her. Why he was the darkness and she was the light. Why he struggled to see the beauty in the world.

He continued. 'The coroner ordered a post-mortem. The cause of death had to be officially determined in case Emma hadn't died from injuries sustained in the accident. They had to determine whether it had been natural causes or manslaughter. Not that it mattered in the end as the driver was never found,' he said, and he could hear the bitterness in his voice, 'but the post-mortem found that Emma was pregnant. I was going to be a father.'

CHAPTER EIGHT

HE FELT LUCI squeeze his hand in the darkness and heard her little intake of breath but she didn't speak, allowing him to continue.

'Emma had told her sister about the baby and apparently she was planning on telling me that night. She wanted it to be a surprise on what would have been our first night in the house. I've hated surprises ever since.'

He had lost everything. Not just his girlfriend but his future. He hadn't really ever thought seriously about being a father, he'd just assumed it would happen one day, but to be given that news and then have it taken away from him immediately had devastated him.

'Losing something I never had and never knew I wanted; I didn't understand how that could hurt so much.' It had destroyed his belief that good things could happen and he had only seen darkness for a long time after that. Mostly that was still all he saw.

'I imagine the feeling is similar to knowing that the thing you want most in the world is never going to happen for you.'

Luci's voice was thick with tears and he realised she did understand how he felt. She would have had the same feeling over and over again, every month, when she had been desperate to fall pregnant and it hadn't happened. Month after month. But she'd got through it.

Had his confession been hard on her?

'I didn't mean to upset you,' he told her. He'd wanted her to understand. He wasn't sure why but it seemed important that he share his past with her but he hadn't meant to upset her.

'I'm okay. I'm upset for you.'

'My whole life changed in the space of a few minutes. I took a new direction after that. I never moved into the house. I couldn't bring myself to do it. I sold the house and bought my motorbike and this boat instead. I couldn't settle, I was restless, I still am. That was my attempt at domesticity, at living a normal life, and it didn't turn out as I'd planned. I lost everything at once, things I didn't even know I had, and it took me a long time to feel like my life was back under control. I think it's enough now to be responsible just for my own life. I don't ever want to go through that pain again.'

Over the past three years he had slowly recovered from Emma's death but he hadn't forgotten how he'd felt and he wasn't sure that he wanted to put himself out there again for love. 'I don't want to put myself in that position again.' He didn't ever want to be vulnerable again. He had worked hard to get back on top of things and he didn't ever want to lose his way again. He was determined to be the master of his own destiny but that made it very difficult to let someone else in.

He had moved on, to a degree, but he knew the events of that day had changed him and he never again wanted to feel that pain of loss that he felt was inevitable if he opened up his heart. So he had lived a solitary existence.

He didn't want to have a home. He didn't want to put down roots. Becoming invested in something, attached to something, scared him. He knew how easily it could be ripped away. 'When you love someone it isn't for ever. It can't be. Life doesn't work like that.'

'No one is meant to live a whole lifetime alone,' Luci argued. 'There are highs and lows, disappointments and tragedies, as well as happiness and joy in life, and *I* think it's better to share those times with someone else. Sharing those feelings can soften the lows and enhance the highs. Joy and sadness are both better shared. Let me show you.'

She stood on the deck and lifted her dress over her head. She wore nothing underneath the thin cotton shift. She stood before him, naked and gorgeous, and offered him solace.

His reaction was immediate. He knew how the pleasures of the flesh could wipe out the traumas of the past, even if only temporarily. He'd had plenty of experience in that method of recovery over the past three years but never had he felt the satisfaction that he felt when he was with Luci. He got a sense of peacefulness with her and that was something that had never lasted before. Along with the physical release Luci was somehow able to provide emotional release too.

He pushed his shorts down and over his feet so he too was naked and knelt before her. His erection stood to attention, stiff and strong, but he ignored it.

He ran his hands up the insides of her thighs, parting them.

She opened her legs wider for him as his fingers reached the junction of her thighs. He slid his fingers inside her. She was warm and moist.

She moaned and pushed against him as he ran his thumb over the bud at her core. He replaced his thumb with his tongue and all his troubles were forgotten as he licked and sucked until she shivered with his touch. He cupped her buttocks with his hands and held her against him, burying himself in her, losing himself in the sweet saltiness of her.

She gasped and held his head with her hands. She moaned again, a little louder. Spread her legs a little wider. Let him in a little deeper.

He felt her legs start to shake. He rose and lifted her off her feet and she wrapped her legs around him. He was vaguely aware of thunder rumbling in the distance as he turned and pushed her against the windshield. The storm was on its way.

He locked her between his body and the slope of the glass. Bent his head and licked her breasts as he drove himself deep inside her.

Her skin glowed ghostly pale in the moonlight and he could see the four freckles, dark against her skin, on the swell of her breast. Over her right shoulder he could see the Southern Cross, the diamonds in the sky that would always remind him of her.

He ignored the storm and the stars and the memories as he focused on feeling, touching and tasting. He rode the waves of pleasure with Luci.

He didn't miss Emma any more. He hadn't missed her for a long time. He'd taught himself to be alone but as he lost himself in Luci he realised all the other things he'd been missing. All the things that not feeling had deprived him of. The pleasure of sharing not just physically but emotionally.

He had shut himself off and Luci was helping him to open up again. She saw the good in the world. The brightness and the light. He had blocked that all out. Not wanting to risk being hurt, he had shut out all the beauty as well.

Her arms were around his neck and he felt her legs tighten around his waist as she met his thrusts, urging him to go faster. She was warm and wet as she clung to him.

She was brightness and light. Even after what she'd been through she hadn't given up on the idea of love.

'Now, Seb. Now!'

She arched her back as she came, trembling in his arms.

He shuddered with the release as a fork of lightning split the sky, followed by a clap of thunder booming overhead just as they came together, sharing the pleasure.

He could smell her. She was warm and sweet. He pressed his lips against her shoulder as he tasted her. She was salty and sweet.

Clouds drifted overhead, obscuring the stars, and he smelt the rain just before it began to fall. Fat, warm drops fell on their bare skin.

Luci was still in his arms and he carried her downstairs to his bed, their clothes abandoned on the deck as the storm raged overhead.

It passed quickly but he didn't notice. They lay in peaceful, contented silence. He wasn't thinking about love and loss. He wasn't thinking about anything other than the satisfaction and pleasure of having someone to hold.

Perhaps Luci was right. Maybe having someone to share things with could sometimes make things better.

He fell asleep with Luci in his arms as the storm rolled to the east.

Luci stowed her suitcase in the luggage compartment under the bus that was going to take her back to Vickers Hill. She climbed on board with mixed emotions. Her uncle had died three days ago so the trip home was tinged with sadness but while she was looking forward to seeing her family she wasn't sure if she was quite ready to be back in Vickers Hill. She didn't feel as if she'd been gone long enough to erase people's perceptions of her. Would they still think of her as 'poor Luci', the girl who couldn't keep her husband? Or would they have moved on to something else?

She was also wary about seeing Ben but she knew there would be no avoiding it. Her uncle had been married to his great-aunt. There weren't enough degrees of separation in country towns. She would have to see both Ben and his new wife, Catriona, and just to complicate things further Luci knew Catriona would be heavily pregnant. She was due to give birth any day now.

She could use Seb's cool head and rational thinking but he was hundreds of miles away. She knew he'd been worried about how she was going to cope with all the different stresses but she'd assured him she'd be fine. She didn't want him to worry, even though she was worried herself. She was a big girl. She'd have to cope. She couldn't expect Seb to fight her battles, he wouldn't always be there for her, but she admitted to herself it would have been nice.

Despite the fact that it had only been a few hours since he had dropped her at Sydney airport to catch the flight to Adelaide she was missing him already. But she was only planning on being gone for two days. She could last that long.

She had got used to his company very quickly. He made her laugh. He listened when she talked. He made her feel happy and positive. Plus he was gorgeous and smart and good in bed. What wasn't to like?

The only problem was that he didn't want to settle down.

So ultimately he wasn't the man for her. She knew that but it didn't stop her from wishing things were different.

She wanted to find the person she was supposed to spend the rest of her life with. There must be someone out there for her. It wasn't Ben and it wasn't Seb, not unless she could change his mind—an unlikely event—and she was running out of time.

She'd known from the very beginning that his time in Sydney was limited, as was hers, but his holidays started in eight days and she knew he was planning on leaving then. He was heading off on his boat, leaving her to finish her stint in Sydney. She would have another fortnight in Sydney on her own after Seb left and she was already dreading it, not looking forward to being on her own again. She wasn't looking forward to being without Seb, but there wasn't anything she could do about it.

Things were out of her control. She couldn't control his plans and she couldn't conjure up a man. She would just have to be patient.

At least she knew now that she could open her heart. Finding love shouldn't be impossible if she was open to it.

She closed her eyes and rested her head on the window as the bus chugged through the northern suburbs of the city. She fell asleep dreaming of Seb and woke as the bus slowed on its approach into Vickers Hill.

She'd forgotten how dry and brown the countryside could get, even when it was only the beginning of summer. In five weeks she'd already grown used to being surrounded by water, by the ocean, and the blue and sometimes rainy grey of Sydney was very different from the brown and pale, washed-out grey of the Clare Valley.

The scenery was unfamiliar but the smell was the same. She could smell the dust in the air. It smelt like home but did it feel like home? She wouldn't know until she got off the bus.

The bus pulled up in the main street of Vickers Hill. She wanted to go and see Flick, there was so much to tell her, but she needed to see her parents first. She checked her watch. They would be having lunch. Her father would have taken the day off to bury his brother, Callum would have him covered, but even when he was working her parents had a tradition where her father would break for lunch and go home and eat with her mother. Luci would join them and then attend the funeral. There would be time to see Flick later.

The funeral had gone as well as could be expected. A death was always sad but her uncle had been old and it had been his time. Luci couldn't help thinking that her father might be next, though. She would feel so differently if it had been her father's funeral. He was younger than his brother, but not by many years, and she wanted him to live long enough to see his grandchildren. She wanted to give him that gift. Her parents had nieces and nephews and great-nieces and great-nephews but Luci knew it wasn't the same thing as grandchildren.

Ben along with several of Luci's cousins and nephews had been the pallbearers for her uncle's coffin. She had watched Ben as he had helped to carry her uncle out of the church and into the graveyard beside it. Her parents supported her uncle's wife, her aunt by marriage and Ben's great-aunt, as they buried her husband.

Luci chatted to her cousins as everyone made their way from the church to the wake, which was being held in the beer garden at the back of the local pub. She spent the next half-hour talking to familiar faces but she felt out of place. Having changed in the past few weeks, she wasn't sure she belonged here any more.

She was thinking about leaving, about excusing herself to get some breathing space, when she saw Ben approaching. She looked for Catriona but couldn't see her. She hadn't noticed her in the church either. It was too late to escape now as he was heading right for her, so she waited; she couldn't avoid him for ever.

He greeted her with a kiss and Luci waited to see what

effect that had but she felt nothing. No regret. No desire. It was like greeting an old friend and she supposed that's now what they were. They had been friends for too long to cut him out of her life altogether. She could do platonic kisses.

'Hi, Luce, you're looking well.'

In contrast, she thought he looked tired. He was a little greyer at the temples. Perhaps a little bit heavier. It had only been a few months since she'd last seen him so how much could he have changed? Or was she just comparing him to Seb?

She pushed Seb out of her mind.

'Hello, Ben. How are you? How's Catriona? *Where's* Catriona?' Luci wondered if Catriona was too pregnant, too uncomfortable to stand at the funeral.

'She's in hospital. Our baby was born yesterday.'

'Oh.' Luci was taken by surprise. Why hadn't her mother told her? Warned her? Was everyone still trying to protect her?

Or perhaps with everything else going on in her family this week it had slipped her parents' minds. Her mother had a habit of telling her things twice or not at all, getting confused between what she'd told Luci's father and what she'd told Luci. Luci supposed she couldn't blame her for forgetting in the scheme of things. Ben and Catriona's baby didn't really matter to Luci, and why should it matter to her mother?

She didn't need protecting. She was sad for herself, but she didn't begrudge Ben his happiness.

She really had moved on, she realised. She'd been talking the talk but without really knowing. This was the test and it was good to find she could be happy for Ben.

'Congratulations,' she said.

Ben was watching her closely. 'I'm sorry. I didn't realise you didn't know. I thought someone would have said something. I wasn't planning on being the one to tell you.'

'It's okay. I would have found out sooner or later. What did you have?'

'A daughter.'

A baby girl. 'Details?' she asked, pleased to know she could remember the niceties.

'Seven pounds three ounces and we've named her Mia.'

Luci breathed a silent sigh of relief. She'd been worried that Ben might choose one of the names they had picked out and she was glad he hadn't. It was highly unlikely that she would get to use the names she'd chosen, Eve for a girl or Joe for a boy, but even so she didn't want Ben to use 'their' names.

'I'm happy for you,' she told him truthfully. She knew he wanted children just as much as she did. She couldn't begrudge him that happiness, but it didn't negate the sadness she felt that she was still childless.

She should go and find Ben's parents, her ex-in-laws, and congratulate them. She knew that by doing that, it would help to stop any unwanted smalltown gossip. She would be doing herself a favour. And it would give her a reason to say goodbye to Ben. She was ready for that. She didn't want him back but she couldn't deny that she was jealous of his new life. He had everything she wanted.

She excused herself and was relieved to see Flick making her way through the pub and into the garden. Luci forgot about seeking out her ex-in-laws and made a beeline for her friend, wrapping her in a big hug.

'God, it's so good to see you,' she said.

'Sorry I couldn't come to the funeral,' Flick replied as she hugged her back. 'Callum was covering the clinic for your dad so he needed me to help him.'

Flick had a sparkle in her eye. She looked well. Happy.

But Luci was too preoccupied to pay any more attention than that.

'Why didn't you tell me Ben and Catriona had the baby?'

Flick shrugged. 'She was only born yesterday. I figured your mum would tell you and we'd talk about it today. Who did tell you?'

'Ben.'

'Oh, hell. Are you okay?'

Luci nodded. 'I think so. Sad for me, if I'm honest, but otherwise okay. I'll hold it together. I'm not going to give anyone here the satisfaction of seeing me fall apart. I'm tired of being the one everyone talks about.'

'Well, don't get your hopes up.' Flick laughed. 'No doubt they'll be talking about you again now that you're back and everyone has seen you talking to Ben.'

'I'm not back for good,' Luci responded, and wondered whether that was really how she felt. Could she come back permanently?

She wasn't sure.

But where else would she go?

She had no idea.

'You're not thinking of staying in Sydney, are you?' Flick asked. 'Are you enjoying it that much?'

Luci kept quiet, which was a mistake.

Flick jumped straight to a conclusion. 'OMG, is it Seb?'

She'd told Flick a little bit about him. Not everything. She wanted to keep some of what they'd shared to herself but it had been obvious in her conversations that they'd been spending a lot of time together and Luci hadn't been able to keep the happiness from spilling into her voice.

'I'd stay in a heartbeat if he asked me to but I can't see that happening.'

When Luci saw the expression on Flick's face—eyes

wide open, jaw dropping—she realised she'd said the words out loud and remembered that Flick was working with Seb's brother. 'Promise me you won't say anything to Callum!' she hissed.

'Why would I? But does Seb know how you feel?'

Luci shook her head. 'Of course not. It's just a bit of fun.'

'Seriously? That doesn't sound like you.'

'What do you mean by that?'

'Well, you have to admit that even for around here you settled down early. You were always the one who was going to have the serious relationships.'

'Seb is only in Sydney for another week. I can't afford to get serious.'

'So you're just using him for sex.'

'Shh!'

'Well, you are doing the deed, aren't you?'

'Yes.' Luci blushed, thinking about the sex. Where and when and how good it had been. 'And often,' she added, wanting to see Flick's reaction.

Flick laughed. 'You go, girl! So why is it just a bit of fun? Why can't it be more serious than that? It doesn't matter if he's leaving Sydney. You could go with him.'

'No.' Luci shook her head again, knowing she was trying to convince herself as much as Flick. 'It's not a long-term proposition. Not at all. We want different things out of life. He's great but he doesn't want to settle down. I can't afford to waste time on someone who doesn't want the same things as me.'

It was a pity. Such a pity. Luci understood why he felt that way but it was still a shame. He didn't know what he was missing.

But did she? Why was it that she was so desperate to have kids? Could she be content without them?

She didn't know what she was missing either but she just knew that something was. There was a yearning in her heart. Not only for a partner but for a family. She knew what she needed to make herself complete. A man wouldn't be enough. And if she knew that she needed to be a mother without ever having been one, who was to say that Seb couldn't know he didn't want to be a father? That wasn't for her to judge.

Flick opened her mouth and Luci had the suspicion that she was about to tell her something important but right at that moment the crowd went silent. All at once.

Heads turned as the noise ceased and all eyes were focused on the door that led from the pub out to the garden.

Standing in the doorway was Seb.

CHAPTER NINE

IT WAS IMMEDIATELY obvious that he wasn't from around here and it had nothing to do with the fact that he was a tall, dark, handsome stranger. You could always expect a few strangers at a funeral but Seb wasn't wearing the country uniform. All the male mourners were wearing smart jeans, their polished boots and a shirt that was obviously kept for best. Seb was wearing neatly ironed chino pants, a black T-shirt and his leather jacket. The other men all had suntanned faces with white foreheads where their hats sat, and despite the hours Seb spent on the water he didn't have the same weathered look of years spent outdoors.

The stunned silence was followed by a swell of murmuring as everyone tried to figure out who this man was. Luci could hear people asking each other if they knew him.

'OMG, what is he doing here?' she muttered.

She could feel Flick looking from her back to Seb and back to her and she knew Flick's jaw had dropped open again.

'Is that him?'

Luci nodded. She couldn't speak.

'Holy…' Flick said under her breath. 'He looks like more than just a *bit* of fun. He looks like a whole *lot* of fun.'

'Shush,' Luci said, whacking Flick on the arm before making a beeline for Seb. She had to get him out of the pub. People had only just moved on from discussing her and Ben and she knew there was no way they'd be able to resist talking about her again now that they'd laid eyes on Seb and realised he was here for her.

Was he here for her? she wondered as she was halfway across the room. Maybe he was here to see Callum? Although that made no sense whatsoever. She knew that the two brothers didn't even talk that often, so why would he have travelled halfway across the country to see him?

He was grinning widely by the time she reached his side. His blue eyes sparkled and to keep herself from jumping into his arms she grabbed his elbow and pulled him back through the doorway, out of the garden and into the pub. She would have kept walking too, wanting to get him right out of the building and into the street, away from flapping ears and prying eyes, but Seb planted his feet and once he did that she had about as much chance of moving him as a mosquito had in a cyclone.

'What are you doing here?'

They were in a short, narrow corridor between the pub kitchen and the rest rooms and it was only a matter of time before they were interrupted, but Seb didn't seem to mind. He leaned against the wall and pulled her into him. She could see he was about to kiss her and she wasn't going to let him do that. Not in front of her family and the rest of the town.

She put her hands on his chest, keeping them separated by a few inches of air, but the gesture hardly afforded her any protection. His chest was firm and solid under her fingers and his thighs were strong and powerful against her legs. She could feel herself melting into him as her resistance weakened. She might as well have let him kiss her, the effect would have been the same.

'I thought you might be finding things difficult,' he said. 'I wanted to be here for you.'

She was touched that he had even thought that, let alone jumped on a plane and somehow made it to Vickers Hill just hours after she had. He was gorgeous. She couldn't believe he was standing in front of her, in her home town, looking at her with his blue eyes and ridiculously long, dark eyelashes. She'd been wishing he was here and somehow her wish had come true. She wasn't going to deny that it was good to see him.

'I love it that you're here,' she told him. And she did, except for the fact that the gossip mill was going to go into overdrive again, but that wasn't his fault. She couldn't expect him to understand how her home town worked. She'd just have to deal with the questions later. 'But my uncle was old so while a funeral is never the best situation it's okay. I think my dad is going to find it hard but I'm all right.'

'I wasn't thinking about your uncle. I was thinking that you would be seeing Ben and Catriona. I thought that would be hard on you. I wanted to be here to support you.'

'Oh.' He really was incredible. She couldn't believe he had come all this way for her. 'Catriona had the baby yesterday.'

'Did you know?'

Luci shook her head.

'How are you feeling?'

'Mixed emotions, if I'm totally honest. I'm actually pleased for Ben that he's found happiness and I'm not sorry that he's had a child, but I am sorry that it might not happen for me.' She didn't want Ben, there was no sense of longing, of wishing they were still a couple. The spark was well and truly extinguished, but she did want what he had.

'I'm here for you. Just tell me what you need me to do. Do you want to get out of here?' he asked.

She did. Desperately. She wanted Seb to take her away from all this. Now that he was here she knew he would be all she could think about. But he'd asked her what she needed, not what she wanted. And she needed to have dinner with her parents.

She shook her head. 'I'm supposed to be having dinner with my family.' She didn't want to introduce him to anyone, she wasn't ready for that. She didn't want to explain or start any rumours. It wasn't worth it when it would all be over in a week. These considerate gestures that Seb insisted on making—turning up here to offer support, walking with her across the harbour bridge, bringing her a cup of tea every morning in bed—not to mention being simply gorgeous, were going to make it hard to walk away, but there was no other option. That was the agreement they had made. She wasn't ready for the end yet. But it wasn't her choice.

'Why don't you do that, then, and I'll see if I can catch up with Cal and meet you later. After dinner.'

He didn't push her for an invite. He seemed to know what she needed before she did. She wanted to go with him now but knowing he would be waiting for her at the end of the day was enough. She was glad he was here.

She nodded. 'Okay. Where are you staying?' she asked, hoping he wasn't staying at Callum's. That was her house. That would be weird.

'I booked a room at the hotel.'

She didn't need to hear any more. That was perfect.

'Room eleven,' he added with a wink and a grin, and Luci nearly gave in right then. She was sorely tempted to ditch the family dinner in favour of jumping into bed with Seb.

But instead she had to be content with grabbing a fistful of his shirt and pulling him towards her. She kissed him hard, not caring who saw them. She didn't care any more. He had come all this way for her and she didn't want to waste a minute of the time they had left together.

She'd be gone again tomorrow. Let them talk.

'I'll see you later,' she said as she pushed him out of the pub.

Luci sneaked into her parents' house just before sunrise, avoiding the fourth and ninth floorboards in the hall because she knew they creaked. She felt like a teenager again, even though she knew she shouldn't have to worry. After all, she'd been married and divorced, but old habits died hard.

She hoped they were asleep. She didn't want to explain where she'd been, what she'd been doing. She had spent the night in Seb's bed and after saying goodbye he'd headed off early in order to make it back to Adelaide in time for his return flight.

Luci climbed into her old bed but she couldn't sleep. Her mind was turning in circles.

She needed to start planning her next move. To work out how she was going to fulfil her dreams. Seb wasn't going to be a part of that. She knew he didn't want a proper relationship and she was determined to fulfil her dreams of motherhood one way or another. She assumed it would have to be through adoption and she wanted to find a partner who would support her in that. She couldn't afford to waste time on Seb. They had eight more days together and then it would be over. They would go back to their own lives. She couldn't focus on Seb, there were more important things for her to worry about.

The decisions were hers to make and hers alone.

* * *

Luci disembarked from the plane in Sydney and switched on her phone. As expected, there was a message from Seb asking her to text when she arrived safely, but there was also one from her GP, asking her to call back. Luci waited until she got back to the apartment to return the call.

'Could you come in for a chat?' her GP asked. 'There's something I need to discuss with you.'

Her GP was in the neighbouring town to Vickers Hill. Luci hadn't wanted to see anyone with ties to her dad's clinic so ever since she'd got her driver's licence she'd made the fifteen-minute drive along the highway.

'Actually, I can't,' she said. 'I'm in Sydney. Is there a problem? I'll be here for another three weeks.' Luci couldn't imagine what it was about. She was perfectly healthy and so was everyone else, as far as she knew.

'Can you talk now?'

'Yes,' she said, sitting on the couch.

'I received a letter today from the lab that did your fertility tests. The letter contains your test results. Apparently they were upgrading their computer system at the same time that you went for testing and some of the results were mistakenly filed as "sent" when they were actually pending. The lab has only just realised their mistake. I'm sorry, I never realised that these weren't forwarded to you. You haven't been in for an appointment.'

'It doesn't matter,' Luci replied. 'It turns out the results were irrelevant.'

'What do you mean?'

'It was obvious that the problem was with me. Ben had no trouble getting Catriona pregnant. The results don't matter, it's not like I'm in a situation to have a baby now. I'm divorced and single, I'm not trying to get pregnant any more.'

'I still think you should know the results. It's not quite as simple as you think. The tests indicated that the problem wasn't solely with you.'

'What does that mean? Ben's reproductive system seems to work fine.'

'The problem was with the two of you together.' Luci frowned as Veronica continued. 'Your body was producing antibodies against Ben's sperm. It's very uncommon and especially rare to see in women, but it meant that your body was having a kind of allergic reaction to the sperm. The antibodies attach to the sperm and impair motility, making it harder for the sperm to penetrate the cervical mucus and therefore fertilise the egg. IVF would have been a relatively simple procedure for you. In your situation there would have been a high chance of success for the two of you.'

'What?' Luci couldn't believe what she was hearing. 'We could have had children?' They could have had the family she'd dreamed of?

'With IVF assistance, almost certainly,' Veronica agreed.

'How?'

'The sperm would be injected directly into the harvested egg. If the sperm aren't swimming freely there would have been no opportunity for your body to attack. The antibodies wouldn't have had a chance to attach to the sperm. With IVF a viable embryo would have been created and it would then have been implanted.'

'So I can have kids?' Luci still wasn't absolutely sure that she was getting the right message. Was that what Veronica was telling her? She held her breath as she waited for the final confirmation.

'Yes. Either with the right partner or with IVF.'

Luci breathed out as tears welled in her eyes.

'It's rare for a woman to produce anti-sperm antibodies

so it's quite likely that with a different partner you wouldn't have the same issues,' Veronica went on, but Luci was only half listening. She was still processing the idea that she could have children.

'But don't forget, this condition is very successfully overcome with IVF assistance. Identifying this is a good thing.' Veronica was still speaking. 'You and Ben may have been incompatible but that doesn't mean all men will be. And there's more good news. Your eggs were healthy. You're young and fertile. You have time. It will happen for you, I'm sure of it.'

'Thank you.'

Tears spilled out of Luci's eyes and rolled down her cheeks as she ended the call. Mixed emotions engulfed her. The news was incredible but it was tinged with anger and regret. Just when she felt she had come to terms with the demise of her marriage to find out that Ben's betrayal had robbed her of her dream of motherhood was almost too much to bear. When she had thought she couldn't fall pregnant she'd been able to forgive him for leaving her. She had blamed herself as much as him. But now?

If he had stayed they could have worked this out. With IVF *she* could have been the one who had just had a baby. She could be a mother now.

She needed to think. She needed a walk to help focus her mind. She changed into a pair of shorts and her sneakers and headed for the beach.

As she walked she realised it was unlikely that her marriage would have survived regardless. They had broken up because of the stress of infertility but Ben had very quickly moved on. If she'd been unable to rely on him to stick by her through that situation she knew she wouldn't have been able to rely on him for anything else. Quite possibly he would have run for the hills the moment the going had got tough. Quite possibly she would have ended up divorced with a baby.

Would she want to be a single mother?

Yes.

If she could have a baby without a partner she knew she would take that opportunity. She had never imagined herself as a single mother but she knew that if that was her only option she wouldn't hesitate any more. She still wanted a baby more than anything.

More than she wanted Seb?

Yes. Her heart ached with longing and her womb ached with emptiness. A baby was very much her priority.

She had fallen in love with Seb but planning a future with him had never been realistic and especially not now. He was her second ever boyfriend and she wasn't even sure she could call him that. They weren't thinking about the future and he didn't want commitment. He didn't want to settle down and she was pretty sure he wasn't going to want kids.

She would have to break up with him. It was her only option.

She wanted it all but if she couldn't have it all she was going to choose motherhood, or the possibility of it at least, and if her dream was to become a reality she needed to find the man who could help her to make that happen.

Which meant she needed to break up with Seb.

He was starting his holidays at the end of the week. He was heading off in his boat so their relationship wasn't going to last any longer than that anyway, no matter what she wished for, so the best thing to do would be to end it now. Quickly and swiftly. Waiting a couple more days wasn't going to make it any easier. She needed to move on to the rest of her life.

The decision was made. Now all she had to do was tell him.

Telling him would give him the chance to change his mind if he wanted to and she knew she was still hopeful that he would make that choice. Perhaps he would decide that she was worth it.

The sun was low in the sky as she returned to the apartment. Her phone buzzed in her pocket. She pulled it out and looked at the caller ID. Seb.

'Where are you? Is everything okay?'

He sounded worried but she didn't think she could put his mind at ease so she opted for a simple reply. 'I'm almost home. I'll see you in a minute.'

But Callum's apartment wasn't home. And Vickers Hill hadn't felt like home either.

Luci knew she wouldn't be going back to Vickers Hill. She'd felt like a fish out of water there. Everyone was settled or, worse, if they weren't she had known them all her life and she knew she wasn't going to find the man she was looking for amongst them. She needed new faces. New places. She had no idea where she would go but she knew she wouldn't go back.

She would need to find somewhere that felt right.

Also, she needed a man, or his sperm at the very least, and a place to live. But one thing at a time. Her first priority was to speak to Seb. She needed to tell him her decision. There was no point delaying. She needed to get on with things. She was a girl with a mission.

The door to the apartment was open. Seb was waiting for her. He still looked worried. There was a little crease between his eyebrows and his blue eyes were dark with concern. But she almost didn't notice. It was a hot night and he was dressed only in a pair of shorts. Shirtless and bare-chested, she found it hard to notice anything else.

He looked incredible. She'd almost forgotten how gorgeous he was. She should ask him to put a shirt on, she wasn't going to be able to concentrate when he was semi-naked, but she resisted. Why deprive herself of her last chance to see him like this? She could use the memory.

He greeted her with a hug. God, that felt good. His arms were strong, his embrace warm, and Luci could have stayed there quite happily for the rest of her life.

'I've missed you,' he said as he let her go. 'Is anything wrong?' He ran a thumb under her eye and Luci's knees buckled slightly at his touch. 'Have you been crying?'

Her tears had dried long ago but she knew her eyes would still be puffy and red. She wiped a hand across them. 'Yes. But they were happy tears, I think.'

'You think? What's going on?'

'I need to sit down.'

Seb ushered her to the couch. 'Can I get you anything?'

She shook her head. 'No. But I need to talk to you.' Luci launched into her news. She knew if she waited she'd chicken out. She was sorely tempted to spend one last night with Seb and tell him tomorrow but it wouldn't be any easier then. She needed to do this now. 'I had a phone call from my GP today. She was calling about some test results. Results that I should have got ages ago but the lab made a mistake. I didn't really notice that the results hadn't come back because of everything else that was going on at the time between Ben and me.'

'Are you okay?'

'Yes. I'm perfectly okay. That was what she was ringing me about. Apparently I am perfectly healthy and fertile. I can have children. The problem wasn't with me. It was with *Ben* and me. But even so we could have had a family together if we'd stuck it out. IVF would have fixed it.'

'Wow.' Seb sat back and ran his hands through his hair. The muscles in his arms and chest flexed and Luci averted her gaze so she wasn't tempted to throw herself into his arms. 'Does Ben know?'

She shook her head. 'No.'

'Are you going to tell him?'

'I hadn't thought about it. Probably not. It doesn't matter to him any more. He's moved on. I have too. My marriage is over but now I have a chance to fulfil my dream of having a family. I *am* going to chase that dream. Which means I need to find the man who wants to follow that same dream, the man who wants to share my future. I know that's not what you want so I need to say goodbye.'

'Now?'

Luci nodded. She knew it would be hard. It was so tempting to spend their last remaining nights together but she knew the longer she waited the harder it would get. If her heart was going to break she wanted to get it over and done with.

'You'll be gone in a few days anyway. We both knew it was only a bit of fun, just a temporary arrangement. It was always a matter of when, not if, and I need to move on to the next phase of my life. I appreciate every minute, everything we have shared, you have helped me more than you'll ever know. I know I'm ready to let someone else into my life now.'

'What are you going to do?'

'I'm not sure yet. Finish off my last two weeks here while I try to work out what this all means and then I don't know what. But I'm not going back to Vickers Hill. I doubt the man for me is there and I'm not sure that a big city is for me either.'

'So that's it? This is goodbye?'

She nodded, forcing herself to stay strong. 'We don't want the same things, Seb. We've both been honest about that. I was always going to want to find a way to have a family. You've always said that isn't on your agenda. I need to go.'

Now was his chance to tell her he'd changed his mind. That he couldn't live without her. She held her breath, waiting to see what he would do.

'Okay.' Seb sat forward, resting his elbows on his knees, and sighed. Luci stretched out one hand, wanting to run it over his back, but she hesitated just inches from his skin then pulled her hand away. She didn't know if he wanted or needed comfort.

Seb pushed himself to his feet and turned to face her. His blue eyes were still troubled but his voice was strong. He nodded his head. 'I respect the fact it's your decision to make. I'll just grab a few things and I'll sleep on the boat.'

Disappointment flooded Luci's chest and surged through her belly. She'd pinned her hopes on him changing his mind, even though she'd known it was a long shot, and it was devastating to know that he wasn't going to argue with her. That he wasn't going to change his mind. But neither was she.

She wanted to tell him that he didn't need to leave tonight but then realised it was probably better if he did. He wasn't the man for her future. He had been a perfect interlude but she couldn't let emotion derail her dreams.

But saying goodbye to Seb took some of the gloss off her dream. Gaining the knowledge that she could have kids meant she was losing him. She needed to remember he had never really been hers in the first place.

This was goodbye.

She loved him but that was irrelevant. She had said she

would give her right arm to have a chance at motherhood; giving up Seb was much harder.

She wasn't going to let the chance to have a baby feel like a consolation prize. She wanted a child more than anything. She had to remember that. But that didn't stop the tears from flowing again as she watched him walk out the door with his duffel bag and bike helmet. He travelled light, leaving only with what he'd come with, and taking her heart with him.

CHAPTER TEN

SEB HAD FINISHED his stint at the family and community health clinic. He was gone and Luci was doing her best to focus on her job. She had two days left before she went back to Vickers Hill for Christmas. She still hadn't decided what she would do after that. She'd make a final decision after the Christmas break. Hopefully by then her head would have cleared and she'd be able to think straight. She was having difficulty focusing, her thoughts turning constantly to Seb, and her heart was hurting so badly it was making her feel nauseous. She knew she had done the right thing, saying goodbye to him, but that wasn't making it any less painful.

The nausea was so bad today that she'd actually vomited up her breakfast and hadn't been able to keep anything down since. She felt like she might have contracted a virus. She had five minutes before her next appointment so she quickly took her temperature while she checked her emails. There was one from the doctor's wife in Budgee and Luci noticed it had been copied to Seb. She scanned the message. The doctor's wife had forwarded it from Nadine. She had wanted to send photos of her twins to Seb and Luci.

Luci opened the attachment. The twins appeared to be thriving. It was amazing to see how much they had developed in four weeks. They were both starting to fill out and their chocolate-brown eyes were shining. Luci felt a pang of envy but she had hope now and the knowledge that one day she might be holding a baby of her own in her arms was making it easier to cope with all the pregnant clients and newborn babies she seemed to have on her list.

After an uncertain start in community health she was now enjoying getting to know her patients and being able to give continuity of care was rewarding. It was very different from working in a hospital and she had managed to establish good relationships with several of the regular clients, which was extremely satisfying. Melanie Parsons was a good example. She and her kids had been in to see her several times and Melanie appeared to be coping much better. She and her husband were both attending counselling and her husband had also joined AA. Luci was pleased that she had been able to witness what she hoped would be the start of something better for their family. Seeing the change in Melanie and getting emails from patients like Nadine made her feel that she was making a difference and doing something worthwhile, even if her heart was breaking.

The thermometer beeped and Luci closed her emails and read the display as her diary flashed to indicate that her next client had arrived. Her temperature was slightly elevated—she'd take something for that after she'd finished her next consult.

'What can I help you with today, Shauna?' she asked as her client sat and settled her toddler on her knee.

'I think I might be pregnant again.'

Luci waited for the usual stab of jealousy but it didn't come. She didn't need to feel jealous any more, she was certain pregnancy would happen for her one day. 'Have you done a test?'

'I've done a couple,' Shauna said. 'One came back positive and one was negative but I've got all the usual symptoms. I feel sick, my boobs hurt and I need to go to the toilet constantly. I thought maybe you could do another test.'

Luci took a jar for a urine sample from the cupboard and handed it to Shauna.

She tested it when Shauna returned. 'It's negative. When was your last period?'

'Three weeks ago.'

'It might just be too early.'

The conversation made Luci think of her own situation. When had her last period been? she wondered. She did a quick mental calculation. It had been almost six weeks ago.

She and Seb had practised safe sex most of the time but that night on Seb's boat, during the thunderstorm and in the heat of the moment, protection had been the last thing on her mind. She hadn't thought anything of it then. Sex that night had been spontaneous, contraception hadn't been an issue for her then, and she hadn't given it a moment's thought.

Maybe she was pregnant?

But that eventuality was more than likely just wishful thinking. Mind over matter. She was probably putting two and two together and getting five, she thought. But the minute Shauna left the consulting room she took a standard pregnancy test from the cupboard for herself.

She took it into the bathroom. She knew what she was looking for. She'd done dozens of these. She was looking for two pink lines.

She waited. She'd never seen the two pink lines before. Until today.

She double-checked the window. She leaned over the basin and triple-checked but the lines still remained.

Her knees buckled and she sat back on the toilet seat.

That explained the nausea and her slightly elevated temperature.

Her hand went to her stomach.

She was pregnant.

Seb was into his second week of holidays. He should be somewhere far away from Sydney. His plan had been to take his boat and travel but he hadn't been able to bring himself to leave. Not while Luci was still in town.

He'd realised too late that he should never have left so hurriedly the night Luci had said goodbye. He should have stayed and argued his case, only he hadn't known he'd had a case. Not then.

His knee-jerk reaction had been to leave. He didn't want to settle down, to commit—at least, that was what he'd been telling himself for three years—and it had taken him a while to realise he'd changed his mind. That *Luci* had made him change his mind. She had brought the light back into his life and her absence had taken it away again.

They had said goodbye but he hadn't been able to sever the ties so he sat on his boat, alone, in Fairlight Bay, watching the lights go on and off in Callum's apartment and wondering what Luci was up to. How she was doing. If she was missing him.

For the past three years he had been working toward fixing his boat, making it habitable on a permanent basis, but now he felt trapped. It was supposed to be his sanctuary but instead it felt like a prison cell. He escaped its confines every day, taking his bike from the garage he'd rented and cruising the highways, but the feeling of freedom never lasted. He didn't want to be free. He didn't want to be able to come and go as he pleased. He didn't want to be alone. He wanted to be with Luci.

He shouldn't miss her and he knew he should be pleased for her. She had an opportunity to be a mother, had a chance to get what she'd always wanted. But he wanted that to be him.

He had spent the last three years convincing himself, and everyone else, that he was fine, that he was happy to be alone, but he hadn't stopped to see if he actually was and now that Luci was gone from his life and he was alone again he realised that he wasn't okay. He needed her in his life.

He needed her.

He loved her.

And he didn't want to think about Luci finding another man. He didn't want to give someone else the chance he'd thrown away.

Once again he hadn't realised how badly he wanted something until it was gone but, unlike last time, it wasn't too late. He wanted Luci in his life and he would do what he could to keep her.

She wanted a family and he wanted her. Could he give her what she wanted?

He was going to have to because he couldn't imagine his life without her in it.

All he needed to know was whether or not she wanted him.

He knew she was due to leave Sydney tomorrow but he didn't know where she was headed. What were her plans? What was she going to do?

He only had a few hours to find out. It was two days until Christmas and Luci was due to leave Sydney on Christmas Eve.

He had one last chance to see her.

* * *

Luci had finished cleaning the apartment. She was leaving tomorrow. She would be back in Vickers Hill for Christmas.

She went into Callum's bedroom, just for one final check to make sure it was clean and tidy, although she knew it was. Seb had changed the sheets and tidied up. She knew because she was in here every day, thinking about him. She sat on the bed and ran her hands over the covers. They were tucked tight, not a stray crease in sight. Almost as if Seb had never been there.

She thought about the first night they'd made love. It had been in this bed. They'd been in too much of a hurry to get any further; they'd barely made it to here. But the bed showed no sign of their intimacy. It was almost as if it never happened.

But she had proof that it wasn't a dream.

Her hand went to her stomach.

There was the proof of what they had shared. She had all the proof she needed.

She had two things left to do—pack her bags and then see if she could get hold of Seb.

She had debated about when she should speak to him, when she should give him the news. She had thought about waiting until thirteen weeks, or maybe even eighteen, after her first scan, until she knew everything was all right, but she had decided it would be better to tell him face-to-face while she was still in Sydney, and she knew part of her wanted an excuse to see him one last time before she left.

There would be no easy way to share her news and she knew he didn't like surprises but he had the right to know about the baby. Their baby.

He had the right to have the opportunity to choose to be

involved. Or not. She had no idea what he would choose to do but that was his prerogative.

Luci hadn't really ever expected to end up a single mother. Before the phone call from her GP she had assumed she would have to adopt in order to have a family and adopting in South Australia meant she needed a partner. She had assumed she would need to find a man.

But now she had the opportunity she'd been wanting—the chance to be a mother. A month ago she would have leapt at the chance, any chance, to hold a baby of her own in her arms, so why did she now want more? She knew she could manage on her own. She knew she didn't need a partner. The trouble was, this wasn't about what she needed. It was about what she wanted.

So she was getting what she'd always wanted, except now she wanted more. She wanted Seb too.

Although she knew she should be content with what was in store for her, it was hard when her heart ached constantly for what was missing from her life. She had traded one heartache for another. Why couldn't she have it all?

She stood up. She needed to get moving. Procrastination never solved anything.

She was staring at the clothes in her wardrobe, wondering where to start, when she was interrupted by a knock on the door.

She opened the door and burst into tears.

Seb was standing on the other side.

'Luci, what on earth's the matter?' he asked as he stepped across the threshold. He opened his arms and gathered her up, holding her close.

She let him comfort her. She was right where she wanted to be. If only she could just stay here, maybe everything would turn out as she hoped.

She cried into his shoulder and sniffed as she said, 'Nothing, I'm just tired. I haven't been sleeping well.' *Plus I'm an emotional wreck and I'm carrying your baby.* But that was *not* the way to deliver her news.

'Are you unwell?'

He stepped back, releasing her from his arms but not letting go completely. It felt good to have her in his arms again but he'd needed to see her. He'd needed to make sure she was okay. She looked like she had lost weight and her blue-grey eyes were filled with tears, but otherwise she looked fantastic. Her skin glowed and she looked perfectly healthy.

'No,' she said. 'I'm fine. I'm glad you're here.'

'Are you sure? You don't look happy to see me.'

She laughed and Seb breathed a sigh of relief. She sounded like the Luci he loved, full of laughter and happiness even if she had just been sobbing in his arms.

'Of course I am. I've missed you.'

Good. That cheered him up. Perhaps things would turn out in his favour. 'I've missed you too.'

She was looking up at him. Her eyes were shining and her pink lips were slightly parted, like an opening rosebud. He had come here to talk to her, to beg her for another chance, but he couldn't resist. He bent his head and kissed her.

She sighed gently and leaned into him and he felt her arms loop around his neck as she kissed him back. Soft and supple in his arms, he could feel his soul being restored as he held her. She tasted like heaven and he wished he could stay like this for eternity.

But he needed to find out if that was possible.

'Luci,' he sighed as he pulled away. He kept a finger

under her chin, keeping her face tilted up at him. 'I need to talk to you.'

'Oh.' Something flashed behind her eyes. Was it disappointment?

He took her hand and led her to the couch. The place was spotless and its tidiness served to remind him that his time was limited. If he didn't get this problem resolved tonight, it would be too late. She would be gone.

He kept hold of her hand as they sat, making her sit close to him.

'What is it?' she asked. 'Is something wrong?'

Seb nodded. 'Yes. I've made a mistake. A big one. But I'm hoping it's not too late to fix it. I've discovered a pattern.'

'A pattern?'

'It's a problem I have,' he told her, 'where I can't seem to work out I want something until it's gone. But I'm hoping this time I haven't left it too late.'

'I'm not following you. Left what too late?'

'Us. I don't want to lose you. I don't want to let you go.' He picked up her other hand, holding them both, keeping her close. 'You have brought light back into my life. A purpose. An energy. A reason to look forward to the day. I didn't know what my life was lacking until you came into it. I thought I was okay on my own. Happy even. But I was kidding myself. I was surviving. I wasn't living and I definitely wasn't happy.

'I've missed you,' he said honestly. 'I look for you, I listen for you. I want to hear your laugh, I want to see your smile. I want to be the one who *makes* you smile. I don't want you to leave. I came here tonight to ask if you would consider staying in Sydney. With me. I want to see if we can make something of this thing between us. Before it's too late.'

He very rarely spoke about his feelings and he certainly hadn't bared as much of his soul in the past three years but it didn't seem to make any difference. Luci was shaking her head. 'It *is* too late. I'm going home.'

'Back to Vickers Hill?'

She nodded.

Seb's heart plummeted like a stone and settled heavily and morosely in his abdomen. He was losing her. 'I thought you'd decided that wasn't the place for you.'

'My circumstances have changed.'

How much could have changed in two weeks? Did she feel nothing for him?

'Have you met someone else?' Surely she couldn't have moved on that quickly? He didn't want to think of her with other men. He didn't want to imagine her searching for someone else to share her dream. What was wrong with him? Why couldn't she choose him?

'No, of course not. This is a practical decision. A financial one. I can't afford to start again.'

Despite the flicker of hope that had come to life as soon as Seb had started talking, Luci had other things to consider now. Another *person* to consider. She couldn't allow herself to get carried away until she was sure of Seb's feelings. Vickers Hill had been good enough for her growing up, it was a good place to raise a family and she would have support there. All the things she had hated at times about a small country town were now the reasons she was moving back. She knew people would rally around her. If she was going to be a single mother she wanted to do it somewhere familiar. Somewhere safe. 'This is the next stage of my journey.'

'Can you take that next stage with me?'

She shook her head, still determined not to jump head first too soon. 'You know I can't. You know what I want. Being a mother is something I've always wanted. If I have to choose between having a family and having you, I will choose children. I'm sorry. I wish I could have both but that's up to you.'

Luci had dreamed of Seb choosing to be with her but he had to choose everything. He had to choose her dream as well as her. This was her chance to see how he felt without telling him about the baby. She didn't want to force his hand, she didn't want him to feel that he had to make promises he wouldn't be able to keep, but she had nothing to lose now. If he didn't want a family she could still walk away.

'Luci, I love you and I want a future with you.'

'You love me?'

'I do. I know you want a family and I'm asking you to give me a chance. Let's see if we can have that future together.'

'I can't afford to wait. I haven't got time to see if it all works out. I can't.' She took a deep breath. It was now or never. She was either going to get what she wished for or not but either way the time had come to share her news. 'I'm already pregnant.'

'What? When? How?'

'The usual way, I suppose. Ironic, isn't it? I didn't think it could happen for me the usual way but it must have been that night on the boat.'

'In the storm?'

Luci nodded. 'I'm sorry. I know you hate surprises but you need to know.'

'Don't be sorry.' Seb shook his head and his eyes filled with tears. 'I'm going to be a father?'

Luci nodded. She took his hand and put it on her stomach as her nerves escalated another notch. Her dream was so close she could almost taste it and she couldn't stand the thought that it might all slip away. She tried one last time to convince him that things could work out. 'I know loving someone scares you and I understand that this is a big step for you, but you have to have faith that things will be okay. Bad things can happen but they don't always happen. You can't close yourself off just in case you get hurt. I intend to live my life and I want you to live yours. But I would like us to live our lives together, I'd like us to share our dreams. I love you and I think we can make this work but it's up to you. I know this will be a shock, it's a lot to take in and I don't expect you to decide what you want to do tonight, but you should know that I am going to have the baby.'

'Of course you are. And I'm going to be there with you. Every step of the way.'

'Are you sure?'

'Positive. I'm ready for this. I know you didn't want to fall for the first guy who crossed your path and I wanted to give you a chance to decide if you wanted me. That was why I thought we could take our time and see what happened but I know I want you. I know I want a future with you. And a family. I have thought about nothing else for the past two weeks.'

Seb reached for her. Brushing her hair from her face, he bent his head and kissed her and Luci could feel herself blossoming under his touch.

'I love you, Luci, and I promise that will never change.' He smiled at her and his blue eyes sparkled as he added, 'And now you need to invite me home with you for Christmas.'

'You want to come with me?'

'Where else would I be? I want to spend the rest of my

life with you and that starts now. Plus I think it's time I met your parents. I need to ask your father for your hand in marriage.'

'You want to get married?'

'I do.'

'My father won't expect you to ask his permission.'

'I think he will and I'd like to do things properly. I need to at least tell him I intend to make an honest woman out of his only daughter before I tell him I knocked her up.'

Luci laughed. 'They probably wouldn't believe you. It's incredible, isn't it?'

Seb nodded. 'It's amazing.' He got off the couch and went down on one knee. He slid his hands under the hem of her shirt, exposing her belly. He kissed it gently and the touch of his lips sent flames of desire racing through her. His hands were on her knees and she felt her thighs fall apart under the caress of his fingers as she waited for him to slide his hands up her legs, but his fingers went no further. He knelt between her thighs but his focus was on her face.

'I came here to see if I could convince you to give me a chance to prove my love. I want to share your dreams with you. I want to share your life. Will you let me love you and our children for the rest of our lives? Will you marry me? Will you be my wife?'

Luci pulled Seb to his feet and wrapped herself in his arms. She kissed him deeply, fighting back tears. Her dreams were coming true but it was not the time for tears. She was getting everything she'd wanted since the moment she'd first laid eyes on Seb. This glorious, gorgeous man wanted to make a life with her and she wasn't going to refuse him.

'I will.'

EPILOGUE

Luci sat on the front veranda and watched the sun rise over the ocean as she nursed her baby. This was one of her favourite times of day.

She and Seb had the best of both worlds. They had moved to the coastal town of Shellharbour after their wedding but were still only a two-hour drive from Manly. They could have a day in the city if they wanted and return to the relative peace and quiet of a large country town. They both had jobs at the local hospital in family and community health, and Luci was considering studying midwifery, but she had time to make that decision. Their daughter, Eve, was only four months old, she still had a couple of months of maternity leave and would only be going back to work part time. They had jobs they enjoyed, a lifestyle they loved, but most importantly they had their family.

Sometimes Luci could hardly breathe when she thought about how wonderful her life was and how much it had changed. Blessed with a daughter, a gorgeous husband and a new life in Shellharbour, she still sometimes wanted to pinch herself.

She lifted her daughter from her breast and held her up against her shoulder, inhaling her scent of talcum powder, baby lotion and love.

She looked up as she heard soft footsteps on the wooden

floorboards. Their house was full of visitors but she'd recognise that rhythm anywhere.

Seb stepped out onto the balcony, followed by the two-
year-old Labrador they had somehow inherited with their
house. She smiled as she thought about the man she had
first met—the motorcycle-riding man who'd been adamant that he was going to live a bachelor life on his boat.
Now he was a husband, a father, a home owner and a pet
owner who had swapped regular trips to the country with
a permanent job in a country town. He had traded his
motorbike for a family car but he still had his boat, which
he'd named *Diamond Sky*, which was moored in the ma-
rina five minutes from home. Their lives had changed
dramatically in the course of a year but she knew he was
happy and content.

'Merry Christmas, my love.'

Luci lifted her face for a kiss as Seb put a mug of green
tea beside her and plucked Eve from her arms.

'Come here, my gorgeous girl.'

Eve gurgled and laughed and reached for her father with
chubby little hands. She was a real daddy's girl but Luci
didn't mind. She was living her dream.

'You're up early,' Seb said.

He was bare-chested and Luci felt the familiar stirring
of longing as she looked at him. Even the sleepless nights
associated with a new baby hadn't been able to diminish
her desire for her husband.

'You know I love it out here and I didn't want to wake
everyone else.'

Seb's parents were staying with them for Christmas.
Seb's dad in particular was smitten with Eve and Luci
knew that her in-laws saw this time as an opportunity to
enjoy the things they'd missed out on with their own boys.
Luci's own parents, not wanting to be separated from their

first grandchild, had decided to retire to Shellharbour and lived just down the road, and Callum and Flick were also under their roof. Eve was being christened tomorrow and Cal and Flick were to be her godparents.

'We haven't taken on too much, have we? Hosting Christmas and then having Eve's christening?' Seb asked.

Luci shook her head. She was surrounded by family and she couldn't be happier. 'No. This is just what I wanted. Having everyone here with us is perfect.' She stood up and wrapped her arms around Seb and their daughter. 'Life is perfect,' she said as she raised herself onto her toes and kissed her husband. 'I love you. I love you both.'

* * * * *

Look out for the next great story in
THE CHRISTMAS SWAP *duet*

SWEPT AWAY BY THE SEDUCTIVE STRANGER
by Amy Andrews

And if you enjoyed this story, check out these other great reads from Emily Forbes:

FALLING FOR THE SINGLE DAD
A LOVE AGAINST ALL ODDS
HIS LITTLE CHRISTMAS MIRACLE
A KISS TO MELT HER HEART

All available now!

SWEPT AWAY
BY THE
SEDUCTIVE STRANGER

BY
AMY ANDREWS

Published in Great Britain 2016
By Mills & Boon, an imprint of HarperCollins*Publishers*
1 London Bridge Street, London, SE1 9GF

© 2016 Amy Andrews

ISBN: 978-0-263-91515-0

Our policy is to use papers that are natural, renewable and recyclable
products and made from wood grown in sustainable forests.
The logging and manufacturing processes conform to the legal
environmental regulations of the country of origin.

Printed and bound in Spain
by CPI, Barcelona

Dear Reader,

When I was asked to write a duo with Emily Forbes centring around a house swap I leapt at the chance. I simply adored the movie *The Holiday*, and thought the concept would be great to play around with. There are no snowy cottages or Jude Laws in this one, but there *is* Outback Australia, a delicious wounded doc and a no-nonsense small-town nurse who's super-wary of love—particularly when it comes in the form of a very temporary locum.

I was also thrilled finally to be able to put a train in a book! In 2012 my husband and I travelled on the Indian Pacific from Sydney all the way across the country to Perth, and I have been wanting to put that trip in a book ever since. Growing up as the daughter of a railway man, I've always felt that trains are in my blood, and some of my happiest childhood memories involve train trips with the family. There's just something so romantic about saloon cars, moonlit landscapes flitting by, and two strangers making love all night to the clickety-clack of the rails against the track.

I hope you enjoy the journey through this book as much as I did bringing it to you.

Happy reading—and all aboard!

Amy

To my dear friend and colleague Emily Forbes.
It was a blast—let's do it again some time!

Amy Andrews is a multi-award-winning, *USA TODAY*
bestselling Australian author who has written over
fifty contemporary romances in both the traditional
and digital markets. She loves good books, fab food,
great wine and frequent travel—preferably all four
together. To keep up with her latest releases, news,
competitions and giveaways sign up for her newsletter—
amyandrews.com.au/newsletter.html.

Books by Amy Andrews

Mills & Boon Medical Romance

Rescued by the Dreamy Doc
Just One Last Night…
Waking Up With Dr Off-Limits
Sydney Harbour Hospital: Luca's Bad Girl
How to Mend a Broken Heart
Sydney Harbour Hospital: Evie's Bombshell
One Night She Would Never Forget
Gold Coast Angels: How to Resist Temptation
200 Harley Street: The Tortured Hero
It Happened One Night Shift

Visit the Author Profile page at
millsandboon.co.uk for more titles.

Praise for
Amy Andrews

'A lovely and sweet romance, but with plenty of heat and
some ripping sexual tension.'

—*Goodreads* on
It Happened One Night Shift

CHAPTER ONE

CALLUM HOLLINGSWORTH WOULD have had to be completely blind not to notice the sexy blonde in his peripheral vision. Thanks to a combination of excellent medical care, the passage of time and her being on his right, he wasn't.

Although it was her laugh he'd noticed first.

She was talking on her phone and even though her tone was hushed her occasional laughter practically boomed around the busy café. It was so damn...unrestrained, so carefree, he couldn't help but stare.

Callum hadn't had much to laugh about in recent times and a hot streak of envy tore through his chest as he ogled her from behind his sunglasses. Long honey-coloured hair with curly ends that brushed her shoulder blades. A glimpse of sun-kissed skin at her throat and on toned, tanned arms. Legs clad in denim that were shapely rather than skinny and knee-high fringed boots that looked more country girl than dominatrix.

She didn't wear any make-up or jewellery. In fact, there was a lack of anything flashy or ostentatious about her yet she shone like a jewel in the old-fashioned café in Sydney's Central Station as the sun streamed in through the high windows overhead.

Maybe it was the way she laughed—with her whole

body—that held his attention. Maybe it was the jeans and the boots. Maybe it was her lack of pretension. Whatever, he was just pleased to be provided with some relief from the burden of his thoughts as he sat waiting for his train to depart.

For God's sake, he was about to embark on one of the great train journeys of the world. He was leaving Sydney and going somewhere else for two months where nobody knew him or about the tumble his career had taken. He could reset the clock. Reinvent himself.

Come back refreshed and show them all he didn't give a damn.

The sooner he got to grips with his old life being over, the sooner he could get his act together. This was his chance to finally get his head out of his backside and work on being impressively happy once again. Because he sure as hell was sick of himself and the dark cloud that had been following him around for the last two years.

Nothing like moving fourteen hundred kilometres away to send a strong message to himself about the new direction of his life.

'All passengers for the Indian Pacific, your train is now ready for departure from platform ten.'

Callum gathered his backpack at the announcement over the loudspeaker. The woman on the phone crossed her legs and kept talking and a pang of disappointment flared momentarily. She obviously hadn't been waiting for the same train. Visions straight from a James Bond movie of a glamorous night between the sheets with a mystery woman on a train as a brilliant way to kick-start his new life fizzled into the ether.

He gave himself a mental shake, his lips twisting at the insanity as he headed towards the exit to the platforms.

* * *

A thrill of excitement shot through Felicity Mitchell's system as she stepped into the luxurious carriage and was ushered to her compartment by a man in a smart uniform who had introduced himself as Donald, her personal attendant. She passed several other compartments with their doors open and smiled at the couples who beamed back at her.

Booking a double suite in platinum class on the Indian Pacific was a hideous extravagance. She could have done the Sydney to Adelaide leg in the sitting compartment or even the gold class and saved a lot of money, but it had been a lifelong dream of hers to watch the world chug by as she lay on her double bed, looking out the window. She'd spent the last of her inheritance on the fare but she knew her grandpa, wherever he was now, would be proud.

They passed a compartment with a shut door before Donald stopped at the next one along. 'Here you are,' he said, indicating she should precede him.

Felicity entered the wood-panelled compartment dominated by a picture window. A small plate of cheese and biscuits sat on a low central wooden table. A long lounge that would become her double bed sat snugly against the wall between the window and a narrow cupboard where her bags had already been stowed.

'This is your en suite,' he said, opening a door opposite the lounge to show her the toilet and shower. It was a reasonable size considering the space constraints.

Donald gave her a quick run-down on her compartment and other bits of information about the service before asking if she'd like a glass of wine or champagne as the journey got under way.

Would she? *Hell, yeah.*

'Thank you, Donald, I would love a glass of champagne.'

He smiled at her. 'One glass of bubbles coming up.'

Felicity waited for him to leave before she danced a crazy little jig then collapsed onto the lounge in a happy heap. Workers scurried around on the platform outside, ready for the train's departure in a few minutes. She couldn't believe she was finally sitting in this iconic train about to begin the trip of a lifetime.

Donald returned quickly and handed her a glass full of fizz. 'You're just with us until Adelaide, that's right, isn't it?'

'Yes, that's right. I'd love to go on all the way to Perth. Maybe one day.'

The Indian Pacific was so called because it travelled the width of Australia between the Indian and Pacific oceans. The full trip from Sydney to Perth took three days. Her leg of the journey was only twenty-four hours.

'I think you'll enjoy yourself anyway,' Donald said.

'Oh, yes,' Felicity agreed. 'I have absolutely no doubt. I've been looking forward to this for most of my life.'

'So, no pressure, then?'

Donald laughed and Felicity joined him as the train nudged forward. 'And we're away,' he said.

Felicity looked out the window. The platform appeared to be moving as the train slowly and silently pulled away. 'Let me know if you need anything. Dinner's served at seven.'

Felicity nodded then turned back to the window, sighing happily.

Felicity emerged from her compartment half an hour later. She'd stared out the window, watching the inner city give way to cluttered suburbs then to the more sparse outlying areas as it headed for the Blue Mountains. And now it was time to meet her fellow travellers.

Her neighbour's door was still firmly closed as she headed out. Maybe she didn't have one yet. Maybe they'd be joining the train at a later stop? Quelling her disappointment, she headed for the place she knew people would be—the lounge.

And she hit the jackpot. Half a dozen couples smiled at her as she stepped into the carriage, her legs already adjusted to the rock and sway of the train. She stopped at the bar and ordered a glass of bubbles from a guy called Travis. It was poured for her immediately and she made her way over to the semicircular couches where everyone was getting acquainted.

'Hi,' she said.

The group greeted her as one. 'Sit down here with us, love,' said an older man with a Scottish accent. The woman with him moved over and made some room. 'If you don't mind me saying so, you don't exactly look in the same demographic as the rest of us.'

Felicity laughed. 'I have an old soul.'

Every other person in the lounge would have to have been in their sixties. At twenty-eight that made her the youngest by a good thirty years. Luxury train travel was clearly more a retiree option than a hip, young, cool thing to do.

But that was okay. She'd never been particularly hip or cool. She was a small-town nurse who genuinely liked and was interested in older people. She had a bunch of oldies at the practice who she clucked around like a mother hen and she knew this lot would probably be no different despite what would be a short acquaintance.

'What do you do, dear?' a woman with steel-grey hair over the other side of the lounge asked.

Felicity almost told them the truth but a sudden sense of self-preservation took over. If she told them she was a nurse, one of two things would happen. She'd have to give medical advice about every ache, pain or strange rash for the next twenty-four hours because, adore them as she did, too many people of the older generation loved to talk obsessively about their ailments. Or they'd pat her hand a lot and tell her continually that she was an angel.

If she was really unlucky, both would happen.

She might be a nurse but she was no saint and certainly no angel. In fact, that kind of language had always made her uncomfortable.

And she didn't want to be the nurse from a small community where everyone knew her name on this train journey of a lifetime. She didn't want to be the girl next door. She wanted to be as sophisticated and glamorous as her surroundings. She wanted to dress up for dinner and drink a martini while she had worldly conversations with complete strangers.

Nursing wasn't glamorous.

'Oh, I'm just a public servant,' she said, waving her hand dismissively as she grabbed hold of the first job that came to mind. She doubted it was very glamorous either but it was one of those jobs that was both broad and vague enough to discourage discourse. Nobody really understood what public servants did, right? They certainly didn't ask them about their jobs.

Or tell them about their personal medical issues.

'What do you do?' Felicity asked, and relaxed as the woman, called Judy, launched into a spiel about her job of forty years, which kicked off a conversation amongst them all about their former jobs, and that segued into a discussion about the economy and then morphed again into chatter about travel.

Felicity was in heaven. She was on a train surrounded by witty and enthusiastic companions on the inside and the rugged beauty of the Blue Mountains on the outside. For twenty-four hours she was determined to be a different person.

Tomorrow afternoon she'd be back home where everyone knew her name and stopped her in the street for advice about their baby's fever, their weird allergies or their shingles. Where everyone called her 'Flick' and the guys called her 'mate' and the older women of the town tried to matchmake her with any remotely available male.

Tomorrow would be here soon enough. Today nobody knew her and she was going to revel in it for as long as she could.

The first thing Callum noticed when he entered the restaurant at seven sharp was the sexy blonde from the café. He blinked once or twice just to make sure it was her—his vision wasn't the best after all. Then she laughed at something her companions were saying and it went straight to his chest and spiked through his pulse.

It was definitely her.

If he'd known she was in the platinum carriage too he wouldn't have wasted the last few hours catching up on some essential reading his new boss had emailed and insisted he read before he started work.

'Can I find you a dining companion, sir?' Donald asked.

'No,' Callum said. The beautifully dressed tables seated four and there were several spare chairs around the elegantly appointed dining car but his gaze was glued to the empty one beside her. 'I've found one.'

The corner of Donald's mouth lifted a fraction. 'Good choice, sir.'

It took him only a few more seconds to reach the empty

chair next to blondie. 'Excuse me,' he said. The conversation stopped as all three diners turned to look at him. 'Is this seat taken?'

Her eyes widened slightly. They were smoky grey and fringed by sable lashes. She stared at him for long moments and he stared right back. He liked that she seemed as confused by her reaction to him as he was to her.

She'd changed into a dress, a slinky black thing that showed off her neck and collarbones and crisscrossed at her cleavage. She was wearing lip gloss. Pink. Light pink—the colour of ballet shoes. The ends of her honey hair seemed curlier or maybe that was just a trick of the overhead light.

The old guy sitting opposite welcomed him heartily. 'Sit down, young fella. Save this pretty young thing from having her ear bent off by us old fogies.'

Callum didn't wait to be asked twice. He wasn't someone who believed in instalove but he sure as hell believed in instalust. He may be rusty but he knew sexual interest when he saw it.

She sure as hell wasn't looking at him with pity, like too many women had these past couple of years.

No more pity sex for him.

'I'm Jock, this is my wife Thelma and the odd one out is Felicity.'

Callum shook Jock and Thelma's hand and reached for blondie's. *Felicity.* 'Nice to meet you,' he murmured, their eyes meeting again, an awareness that was almost tangible blooming between them.

'You were in the café,' she said after a beat or two, sliding her hand out of his.

He let it go reluctantly. 'Yes.' A purr of male satisfaction buzzed through his veins. She remembered him. Had she been checking him out at the same time he'd been ogling her?

'I didn't realise you were in the same carriage.'

'I had some work to do.' Callum grimaced. 'I shut myself away for a while. I'm in number eight.'

'Hey, you're in nine, right?' Jock asked Felicity jovially. 'You're neighbours.'

Callum smiled at her as he sent a quick thankyou up into the universe. Things were definitely looking up for him. She smiled back and for the first time in a long time his belly tightened in anticipation. His libido had taken a real battering since the accident, so it was a revelation to feel it rousing.

'So, what do you do?' Jock asked.

Callum dragged his gaze off Felicity and forced his attention on the couple opposite. She wasn't the only person on the train and this was the way these social situations worked. You ate a good meal, drank good wine and made polite and hopefully interesting conversation with strangers.

God knew, he needed something like this to get himself out of his head. But he promised himself that later he would do his damnedest to shamelessly monopolise the woman beside him. They might not end up in bed together but he intended to flirt like crazy and see where it went.

'I'm a technical writer,' he said.

The well-practised lie rolled smoothly off his tongue. He still wasn't used to the real answer. Becoming a GP after being an up-and-coming vascular surgeon was taking some getting used to. And he only had to look around at the age demographic of the other passengers in the carriage to know that admitting to being any kind of doctor would probably result in an avalanche of medical questions he just didn't want to answer.

He didn't want to be any kind of doctor tonight. He wanted to forget about the bitter disappointments of his career and just be a regular Joe. He wanted to be a man chatting to a woman hoping it might end up somewhere interesting.

'Oh?' Thelma asked, as she buttered the bread roll Donald had just placed on her plate. 'What does that entail?'

'Just boring things like industry articles and manuals,' he dismissed. 'Nothing exciting. What about you, Thelma? Are you still working?'

It was a good deflection and Thelma ran with it. The conversation shifted throughout the sumptuous three-course meal and it felt good to stretch his conversational muscles, which were rusty at best. Felicity, on the other hand, was a great conversationalist and Callum found himself relaxing and even laughing from time to time.

His awareness of her as a woman didn't let up but the urgency to get her alone mellowed.

Like him, she seemed reluctant to talk about herself, expertly turning the conversation back to Thelma and Jock or himself and more neutral topics, such as travel and movies and sport. Consequently, the meal flew by as Felicity charmed them all. It was hard to believe he'd sat for two hours and not thought once about the accident and its repercussions on his life.

That wasn't something *anybody* had achieved in the past two and a half years.

He went to bed thinking about it, he woke up thinking about it, and it dominated his thoughts far more than it should during the day.

He suddenly felt about a decade younger.

'A few of us are retiring to the lounge for some after-dinner drinks,' Jock said as he placed his napkin on the table. 'I hope you'll both join us.'

'Of course,' Felicity said, smiling at their companions before turning that lusciously curved mouth towards him. 'You up for that? Or do you…have more work to do?'

Callum wanted nothing more than to invite her back to his compartment for some *private* after-dinner drinks. Their gazes locked and her cheeks pinked up and he wondered if she could read his mind. She was a strange mix of eagerness and hesitancy and Callum didn't want to push or embarrass her.

But he could see in those expressive grey eyes that she didn't want him to lock himself away again either.

'I'd love to,' he said, resigning himself to sharing her for a bit longer, to go slowly, to drag out a little more whatever it was that was building between them.

Anticipation buzzed thick and heavy through his groin.

Felicity found it hard to concentrate for the next couple of hours, aware of Mr Tall-Dark-and-Handsome sitting beside her in a way she hadn't been aware of a guy in a long time. Every time he spoke or laughed it rumbled through his big thigh pressed firmly against hers and squirmed its way into her belly.

There was a sense that they were marking time and she was equal parts titillated and terrified. This being a whole other person thing wasn't as easy to pull off as she'd thought but she'd never felt so alive either. So utterly *buzzed*.

Not even with Ned. Sure, he'd been the love of her life and being dumped by him had been crushing, but their love had grown out of friendship and a slow, gentle dawning.

This…*thing* was entirely different.

Was she seriously going to do this? Pick up a stranger on a train? Or let *him* pick her up? She might have limited experience of the whole pick-up scene but she was pretty sure that's exactly where they were heading. When she'd booked her train ticket, meeting a good-looking stranger hadn't been part of her plan.

But here they were with a night full of possibilities stretching ahead of them.

One by one their companions left, withdrawing to their beds, making jokes about old bones and early nights. Felicity contemplated doing the sensible thing and following them. Retiring to her bed and the moonlit landscape flying by outside her window, tuning into the clickety-clack of the wheels as they rocked her to sleep.

But she didn't.

'Well,' Jock said, standing, helping Thelma up as well. 'This is way past our bedtime and my indigestion is playing up so we'll be off too.'

Felicity smiled at them and bade them goodnight, excruciatingly conscious of Callum's eyes on her as she watched their companions disappear from the lounge.

And then there were two.

'Whew,' he murmured, his gaze brushing over her neck and mouth, a smile tilting his lips into an irresistible shape. 'I thought they'd never go to bed.'

Felicity blushed but she didn't deny the sentiment. She'd thought exactly the same thing.

He tipped his chin at her martini glass. 'Another drink?'

She hesitated. This was it. This was the moment. Was she going to be the sophisticated woman on the train or the girl next door?

'It's only eleven,' he coaxed. 'I promise to have you back to your compartment before you turn into a pumpkin.'

Oh, God, oh, God, oh, God. The man had a PhD in flirting. 'Yeah. Okay. Sure.'

He grinned. 'Good answer.'

Felicity's mouth quirked in an answering grin. 'Good question.'

She flat-out ogled him as he walked to the bar. She'd seen him in the café and had been struck by his presence but he'd seemed so brooding and intense, so closed off she hadn't bothered to go there. He hadn't put a foot wrong tonight, however.

Sure, there was still a brooding quality to the set of his shoulders and the line of his mouth, but he'd been witty and charming and great with all the oldies and, good Lord Almighty, the way he'd looked at her had been one hundred percent high-octane flirty.

Nothing brooding about it.

Even the way the man leaned against the bar was sexy. His expensive-looking charcoal trousers pulled nicely against his butt and hugged the hard length of his thighs.

And they *were* hard. And hot. She could still feel the imprint of them along her leg.

He'd worn a jacket to dinner but had since shed it to reveal a plain long-sleeved shirt of dark purple. The top two buttons had been left undone and about an hour ago he'd rolled up the sleeves to reveal tanned forearms covered in dark hair.

Those forearms had caused a cataclysmic meltdown in her underwear.

He turned slightly and smiled at her and Felicity sucked in a breath. The man was devastating when he smiled and it went all the way to his green eyes. It did things to his face, which was already far too handsome for any one man. Square jaw covered in dark, delicious stubble, strong chin, cheekbones that women would kill for and sandy-brown hair longer on the top and shorter at the sides.

Hair made to run fingers through.

His laughter drifted towards her as Travis handed over the drinks and said something she couldn't quite hear. She liked how it sounded. How it rumbled out of him. She got the sense he didn't do a hell of a lot of it, though, which was a shame. That laugh was turning her insides to jelly.

The military should employ him as a secret weapon.

He headed in her direction, his gait compensating for the rock of the train. She probably should be glued to the window, watching the moonlit bush whizzing by, and not be so obvious, but she figured they were beyond the point of being coy and, frankly, he was too damn hard not to look at with his long stride and knowing smile.

He placed her glass down and sat opposite her this time, a low table between them. She couldn't decide if she was relieved or disappointed. Neither, she concluded as he filled her entire field of vision and everything else became pretty much irrelevant.

'To strangers on a train,' he said, lifting his whisky glass, that smile still hovering.

She tapped hers against it. 'I'll drink to that.'

CHAPTER TWO

FELICITY WAS CONSCIOUS of his gaze as it followed the press of her lips then lowered to the bob of her throat as she swallowed. She was grateful for the cold, crisp martini cooling her suddenly parched mouth.

'So…what's a *young 'un*—' he injected Jock's Scottish brogue into the words and Felicity smiled '—like yourself doing on a train with the cast from *Cocoon*? Lots more people your age down in the cheap seats. Unless… Wait, are you some kind of heiress or something?'

'No.' Felicity laughed at the apt description of their travelling companions and at the thought of her being some little rich girl, although she had inherited enough money from her grandfather to buy a small cottage. 'I'm not. And you don't look like you're of retirement age either. You're, what? Thirty-five?'

She'd been wondering how old he was all night and this seemed like as good an opener as any.

'Close,' he murmured. 'Thirty-four. And you?'

'Twenty-eight.'

'Ah…' He gave a long and exaggerated sigh. 'To be so young and carefree again.'

Felicity laughed at his teasing but was struck by the slight tinge of wistfulness. 'Oh, no,' she teased back. 'You poor old man.'

He grinned at her and every fibre of her being thrilled at being the centre of his attention. 'Seriously, though,' he said, sobering a little, 'why the train?'

'My grandfather was a railway man through and through. Fifty years' service as a driver and he never got tired of trains. Of talking about them, photographing them and just plain loving everything about them. We'd go on the train into the city every day when I used to stay with them in the school holidays and he'd take me to the train museum every time without fail.'

He frowned. 'Didn't that get boring after a while?'

Felicity shook her head. 'Nah. He always made it so exciting. He made it all about the romance of train travel and I lapped it up.'

'Romance, huh?' He raised an eyebrow as his gaze dropped to her mouth. 'Smart man.'

Felicity's belly flopped over. 'That he was.'

If tonight was anything to go by, her grandfather was a damn genius.

She stared into the depths of her frosty glass as her fingers ran up and down the stem. 'He spent his entire life saying that one day he was going to take my grandmother on the Indian Pacific for a holiday of a lifetime. Then, after my grandmother died when I was twenty, he used to tell me one day he and I would go on it together. He died last year, having never done it, but he left me some money so…here I am.'

The backs of Felicity's eyes prickled with unexpected tears and she blinked them away.

'Hey.' His hand slid over hers. 'Are you okay?'

'God, yes,' she said, shaking her head, feeling like an idiot. *Way to put a downer on the pick-up!* 'Sorry. I didn't mean to get so maudlin. I'm stupidly sentimental. Ignore me.'

'Nothing wrong with that.' He smiled, removing his hand. 'Better than being cold and hard.'

Felicity returned his smile. She appreciated his attempt to lighten the mood. Sometimes, though, she had to wonder. If she was a little more hard-hearted she probably wouldn't fret so much about her patients or become so personally involved. It would make it much easier to leave it all behind at the end of the day.

'What about you?' she said, determined to change the subject. To get things back on track. 'Why the train?'

'I guess I'm a bit like your grandfather. Always loved trains. Doing all the great train journeys of the world is a bucket-list thing for me and when I had to travel to Adelaide I thought, Why not?'

It was stupid to feel any kind of affinity with a man—this man—because he was a train guy. Especially when up until about eight hours ago she hadn't even known him. But somehow she did. Her grandfather had always said train people were good people and, even though he'd been biased, right at this moment Felicity couldn't have agreed more.

Callum was ticking *all* her boxes.

'So...' He took a sip of his whisky. 'Felicity...'

Goose-bumps broke out on her arms and spread across her chest, beading her nipples as he rolled the word around his mouth. She'd never heard her name savoured with such carnal intensity. It sure as hell made her wonder what it would sound like as he groaned it into her ear when he came.

Lordy. Another box ticked.

'Is that a family name?'

She cleared her throat and her brain of the sudden wanton images of him and her twisted up in a set of sheets.

'Nope. My mother just liked it, I think. And I don't really get called that anyway.'

'Oh?' He frowned. 'You get Fliss?'

Felicity grimaced. 'Flick, actually.'

'Flick.'

He rolled that around too but it didn't sound quite the same as when he'd used her full name. She didn't hate the nickname, she'd never known anything else, but she didn't want to be a Flick tonight.

Tonight she wanted to be *Felicity*.

She shrugged. 'My cousin couldn't pronounce my full name when she was little and it stuck.'

He lazed back in his chair, his long legs casually splayed out in front of him, the quads moving interestingly beneath the fabric of his trousers. 'You don't look much like a Flick to me,' he mused.

Felicity's pulse fluttered as she suppressed the urge to lean across and kiss him for his observation. The sad fact was, though, in her everyday life she did look like a Flick. Her hair in its regulation ponytail, wearing her nondescript uniform or slopping around in her jeans and T-shirt.

'Thank you,' she murmured, raising her glass to him and taking a sip.

'My brother calls me Cal.'

Felicity studied him for a moment. 'Nope. You *definitely* don't look like a Cal.'

'No?'

Felicity smiled at the faux wounded expression on his face. 'No.'

'What *do* Cals look like?'

'Cals are the life of the party,' she said, happy to play along. 'They're wise-cracking, smart-talking, laugh-a-minute guys. You're way too serious for a Cal.'

He laughed but it wasn't the kind of rumbly noise she'd

come to expect. It sounded hollow and didn't quite reach his eyes. *Crap.* She'd insulted him somehow. Way to turn a guy off, Flick.

She had to fix it. *Fix it, damn it!*

'Anyway,' she said, hoping like hell she sounded casual instead of panicked. Nothing like ruining their evening before it had progressed to the good bit. 'I like Callum. It's very…noble.'

A beat or two passed before he laughed again, throwing his head back. It was full and hearty with enough rumble to fill a race track. It rained down in thick, warm droplets and Felicity wanted to take her clothes off and get soaking wet.

The laughter cut out and he fixed her with his steady gaze. 'Just so you know, I'm not feeling remotely noble right now.'

Felicity's belly clenched hard and she swallowed. *Eep!* This was really going to happen. He downed his whisky and put the glass on the table. 'Would you like to come back to my compartment?'

She cursed her sudden attack of nerves. But this wasn't her. She didn't do this kind of thing. Could she pull it off?

'Hey,' he said, leaning forward at the hips and placing his hand over hers. 'We don't have to. I just thought…'

Yeah. He'd thought she was interested because she'd practically done everything but strip her clothes off and sit in his lap. *God, she must look like some freaked-out virgin.* Or some horrible tease.

Felicity could feel it all slipping away. She didn't want to pass this up, damn it, but she hadn't expected to feel so…conflicted about it when it came to the crunch.

So she did what she always did in lineball calls. She picked up her phone.

He quirked an eyebrow at her. 'What are you doing?'

'I'm asking Mike what he thinks I should do.'

A bigger frown this time. 'Mike?'

'Yeah. You know, the guy in my phone who talks to me and tells me stuff like why the sky is blue and where the nearest hairdresser is.'

He chuckled. 'Yours is a dude?'

She shrugged. 'You can choose and Mike sounds like Richard Armitage so it was a no-brainer.'

'And do you always let your phone decide such things?'

'Sometimes. It's the modern-day coin toss, right?'

He chuckled again. 'Well, this ought to be interesting.'

Felicity grinned as she pushed a button and brought her phone up closer to her mouth. 'Mike, should I go back to Callum's?'

The phone gave an electronic beep then a stylised male voice spoke in a sexy English accent. 'Is he good enough?'

They both laughed then he grabbed her wrist and brought the phone closer to his mouth. Her pulse point fluttered madly beneath his fingers as their gazes locked. A smile played on his mouth again as he spoke into the microphone, his eyes firmly fixed on her. 'He's very good, Mike.'

Felicity's toes curled in her pumps at the sexually suggestive reply. *That wasn't what Mike had meant.*

'Does he know how to treat a woman?'

He didn't laugh this time, just eyed her intently as he replied. 'Oh, yeah. He knows *exactly* how to treat a woman.'

'Then you don't need me to decide, Felicity.'

He released her hand, slowly, still holding her gaze with a red-hot intensity. 'Looks like the ball is in your court.'

Felicity's heart tripped as he fixed her with a gaze that left her in no doubt they were both going to be naked within about ten seconds of the door shutting. Her breath hitched but she was aware of Travis, still at the bar, in her peripheral vision.

What would he think if they left together? Would he gossip about it with the rest of the crew? Would everyone know in the morning that she and Callum had spent the night together?

If she was back home in Vickers Hill, *everyone* would know.

But she wasn't. Was she? She wasn't *Flick* here. She was *Felicity* and *nobody* knew her.

Felicity picked up her glass and swallowed the last quarter in three long gulps. She stood, her body heating as his lazy gaze took its sweet time checking her out. 'Your compartment or mine?'

He smiled, downed the last of his whisky and held out his hand. She took it, smiling also, tugging on his hand, impatient now she'd taken the first step to get on with it.

Jock entered the lounge at that moment and Felicity halted, letting go of Callum's hand immediately, like a guilty teenager. The older man was in a pair of tracksuit pants and a white singlet.

'Jock,' she said, smiling as she walked towards him, aware of Callum close on her heels. 'Thought you'd be in the land of nod by now.'

Jock gave them a tight smile. 'So did I but...' He rubbed his chest. 'My indigestion is really giving me hell tonight. I thought I'd come and ask Travis for a glass of milk. That usually does the trick.'

Felicity felt the first prickle of alarm as she neared Jock. The subdued night-time lighting in the lounge hadn't made the sweat on his brow and the pallor of his face obvious.

'Jock?' She frowned. 'Are you okay?'

Callum stepped out from behind her, also frowning. 'You don't look very well.'

'You need to sit down, I think,' Felicity said, ushering him over to the closest chair.

'Do you have any cardiac history?' Callum asked as Jock swayed a little, reaching for the arm of the couch.

'No. Never had any ticker prob—'

Jock didn't get to finish his sentence. He grabbed his chest and let out a guttural cry instead, folding to his knees.

Adrenaline surged into Felicity's veins. *'Jock!'* she said, throwing herself down next to him.

But it was too late. He collapsed the rest of the way, splayed awkwardly on the floor. Felicity gave him a shake but there was nothing.

'He's having an MI,' Callum said as he helped Felicity ease Jock on his back.

Felicity blinked at the terminology. An MI, or myocardial infarction, was not a term a layperson used. Nonmedical people said heart attack. 'He doesn't have a pulse,' she said, feeling for his carotid.

'Oh, my God, what's wrong with him?' an ashen-faced Travis asked, hovering over them.

'I'll start compressions,' Felicity said, ignoring the bartender as more adrenaline surged into her system and she kicked into nursing mode.

'He's in cardiac arrest,' Callum said as he automatically moved around until Jock's head was at his knees. Felicity admired the steadiness of his voice and the expert way he tilted Jock's jaw and gave his airway support.

Technical writer be damned.

'Do you guys keep a defib?' Callum demanded. 'Some kind of first aid kit? We need more help. And we need to figure out how to get him to an ambulance.'

Felicity couldn't agree more. She had no idea if that was possible but she knew they couldn't keep him alive indefinitely. Jock needed more than they could give him here on a luxury train in the middle of nowhere.

Things were looking grim for the travelling companion she'd grown fond of in just a few hours.

'Yes. We have a defib,' Travis said, his voice tremulous as Felicity counted out the compressions to herself. 'But I've never actually used it on a real person before.'

'It's fine. I'm a doctor,' Callum said, his voice brisk.

Felicity glanced at Callum, not surprised at the knowledge given his use of medical terminology and his total control of the scene.

'And I'm a nurse.'

He glanced at her but didn't say anything, just nodded and said, 'Go,' to Travis as he leaned down and puffed some breaths into Jock's mouth.

It was satisfying to see Jock's chest rise and fall. CPR guidelines had changed recently, focusing more on chest compressions for those untrained in the procedure. But for medical professionals who knew what they were doing airway and breathing still formed part of the procedure.

And old habits died hard.

Callum's training took over and all his senses honed as he rode the adrenaline high, doing what he did best—saving lives. Travis was back in under a minute, bringing a portable defibrillator, a medical kit and the cavalry, who arrived in varying states of panic. He tuned them all out as he grabbed the defibrillator, turned it on, located some pads, yanked up Jock's singlet and slapped them on his chest.

Even Felicity in her dress and heels, pumping away on Jock's chest beside him, faded to black as he concentrated on Jock. Once this was over—which could be soon if they couldn't revive Jock—he'd think about her being a nurse. About how they'd both lied. For now he just had to get some cardiac output.

Felicity stopped compressions while the machine was

reading the rhythm. Callum opened the medical kit, relieved to find an adult resus mask. At least he could give Jock mouth to mask now.

The machine advised a shock.

'All clear,' Callum said, raising his voice to be heard above everyone talking over everyone else.

Felicity wriggled back. So did he as the room fell silent. The machine automatically delivered a shock, Jock's chest arcing off the floor.

'Recommence CPR,' the machine advised, and they both moved back in, Felicity pounding on the chest again as he fitted the mask and held it and Jock's jaw one-handed.

'Where's the nearest medical help?' Callum demanded of a guy with a radio who appeared to be the head honcho.

'We're about twenty clicks out of Condobolin. Ambulance will meet us at the station. A rescue chopper is being scrambled from Dubbo.'

'How long will it take to get to Condobolin?'

'The driver's speeding her up. Fifteen minutes tops.'

Callum wasn't sure Jock had fifteen minutes, especially if he wasn't in a shockable rhythm. He wished he had oxygen and intubation gear. He wished he had an IV and access to fluids and drugs. He wished he had that ambulance right here right now. And a cardiac catheter lab at his disposal.

But he didn't. He had a defibrillator and Felicity.

He glanced at her. He didn't have to ask to know she was thinking the same thing. Fifteen minutes was like a lifetime in this situation, where every second meant oxygen starvation of vital tissues.

'Piece of cake,' she muttered, a small smile on her lips, before returning her attention to the task at hand.

He smiled to himself as he leaned down to blow into the mask. There was controlled panic all around him, with

orders being given and radio static and the loud clatter
of wheels on the track as the train sped to Condobolin.
Somewhere he could vaguely hear poor Thelma sobbing.
But amidst it all Felicity was calm and determined and so
was he. Fifteen minutes? He'd done CPR for much longer.

'Check rhythm.'

Felicity stopped so the machine could do its thing.
When it recommended another shock they followed the
all-clear procedure again and once more the entire lounge
fell silent, apart from Thelma's sobs.

Jock's chest arced again but this time it was successful.

'Normal rhythm,' the machine, no bigger than a couple
of house bricks, pronounced.

Felicity gasped, a broad smile like the rising sun breaking over her face. 'I've got a pulse,' he confirmed, grinning back. 'Jock?' Callum pulled the mask away. 'Can
you hear me, Jock?'

Jock gave a slight moan and made a feeble attempt to
move a hand. 'Jock? Jock!' Thelma threw herself down
beside them.

'Is he okay?' she asked, looking first at Callum then at
Felicity through puffy red eyes.

'We got him back,' Callum said. Both of them knew he
wasn't out of danger but it was something.

Felicity reached across and squeezed Thelma's arm.
'He's still very unstable,' she said gently. 'But it's a good
sign.'

Callum was relieved when the train pulled into the station, even if the strobing of red and blue lights around the
iron and tin structure of the roof created a bizarre disco-
theque. Very quickly a drowsy Jock was transported out of
the train to the ambulance, accompanied by a paramedic,
Callum, Felicity, Thelma and the rail guy with the radio.

Finally Callum had access to oxygen and a heart monitor. It was worrying to see multiple ectopic beats and runs of ventricular tachycardia, though, and Callum crossed his fingers that Jock's heart would hold out until he got the primary cardiac care he so urgently needed.

Callum and the paramedic whacked in two large-bore IVs and then Felicity was helping Thelma into the ambulance and he was getting in the back with Jock. There was no question in his mind that he'd stay with the old man and hand over to the medivac crew when they landed at the airstrip in approximately fifteen minutes' time.

He glanced out the back window as the rig pulled away, the siren a mournful wail in the deserted streets of the tiny outback town. Felicity was framed in the strobing lights, staring after the ambulance. She looked exactly the way he suspected they all probably looked. A little shell-shocked as the adrenaline that had ridden them hard started to ebb.

But also strong and calm. As she had been throughout.

This was not how he'd pictured tonight would end, and as the mantle of regret settled into his bones he knew their moment had passed.

He watched her with a heavy heart until she faded from sight.

CHAPTER THREE

FELICITY LAY AWAKE on her bed an hour later, staring out the window. The train was still stationary at Condobolin station, which was in darkness after the ghoulish flashing of emergency lights. Her compartment was also in darkness, except for the slice of light coming in from the hallway through her open door.

Callum hadn't returned and she couldn't sleep.

After the ambulance had disappeared she'd gone back to her compartment and showered, standing beneath the spray shaking like a leaf as the adrenaline that had sustained her during the emergency had released her from its grip.

She'd waited around in the lounge for a while after they'd gone, thinking Callum would be back soon. Some of her fellow passengers joined her, curious to know what was happening, but they didn't linger and eventually Donald had urged her to go back to her compartment and try and get some sleep.

But she couldn't. It was hard to shut her brain down after what had transpired.

She was about to give up, switch her light on and grab a book out of her bag when Callum strode by her door.

'Oh…hi,' he said, obviously surprised to see her awake and her door open as he pulled up short. She'd deliberately left it ajar because she didn't want to miss his return.

Felicity sat up and swung her legs over the side of the bed. 'You're back.' She stood and took a couple of paces towards him, conscious, as he took up all the space in her doorway, of how different she looked now in loose yoga pants and T with bare feet, compared to the high-heeled, little-black-dress woman he'd been flirting with earlier.

He looked exactly the same. Only sexier. His calm and control when everyone else around them had been losing their heads had kicked his good looks up to a whole other level.

Why was competence so damn attractive?

'How's Jock? Did the medivac transfer go smoothly?'

'Not really. He went into VF while we were waiting for the plane and we had to shock him twice to get him back.'

Felicity pressed her hand to her mouth, a hot spike of concern needling her. 'I was worried something was going down. You were gone so long.'

'I stuck around and helped them stabilise him for transport.'

'Of course.' They'd have wanted to have everything as controlled as possible before they loaded him on the chopper to avoid any chance of midair deterioration. 'What are his chances, do you think?' she asked, folding her arms.

'I don't know. He's not very stable at the moment. It's a forty-minute chopper flight to Dubbo hospital and by that time he'll be about ninety minutes post–cardiac tissue injury. He's inside the window, so fingers crossed, with some tertiary management he should be okay. I'll check on him when we get into Adelaide tomorrow.'

Felicity nodded. 'I guess we're going to be kind of late into Adelaide.'

'I guess we are. Although Donald reckons they'll be able to make up a lot of the time.'

'I'm in no hurry,' she said, and gave him a smile because

she could stay on this train and look at him for a decade and it probably still wouldn't be long enough.

He smiled back, his gaze locking with hers. 'Neither am I.'

There was silence for a beat or two while they just stood and smiled at each other in some weird moment of shared intimacy as only two people who'd been through such a high-stakes ordeal could.

The train moved forward unexpectedly and jostled him inside the compartment, bringing him a step closer. He ducked his head down to glance out the window. 'Looks like we're off.'

'Yes,' Felicity said, as she half turned to find the dark-ened station platform appearing to slowly move.

When she turned back he was staring at her with heat in his eyes. They'd been flirty earlier but now they were just plain frank. His gaze dropped to her mouth as he took a step towards her. Her breath hitched. The atmosphere thickened and pulsed with promise.

She'd resigned herself to this not happening but sud-denly it was on again.

'So...' She swallowed to moisten her suddenly parched throat as he loomed big and broad and close enough to reach out and touch. '*Not* a technical writer, huh?'

He cocked an eyebrow. '*Not* a public servant?'

She shrugged. 'I didn't want to be regaled with a dozen different medical stories or be canonised as some kind of saint.'

'You're forgetting about the lectures on the state of the health-care system.'

She laughed. 'Those too.'

Felicity supposed she should ask him more about his medical background but right now she didn't care. Not with her pulse fluttering madly at her temple and warmth suffusing her belly. 'You were great out there.'

'So were you.'

'Not quite what I expected would happen tonight.'

He smiled. 'Me neither.' And then, 'Are you…okay? It was kind of intense. The adrenaline was flowing.'

'Sure, steady as a rock.' Felicity held up a hand horizontally. It betrayed her completely by trembling.

'So I see.'

Felicity glanced from it to him, conscious of the sway of the train. Conscious that she was far away from Vickers Hill.

It emboldened her.

'That's not from the accident.'

Her hand was trembling for reasons that were far more *primal*.

He regarded her for long moments before turning slightly and reaching for the door behind him to shut it. He turned the lock with a resounding click, the noise slithering with wicked intent to all her secret places.

They were truly alone now.

Darkness pressed in on her, the only light entering from the strip at the bottom of the door and the moonlight pushing in through the window. It was enough to allow her eyes to adjust quickly.

Enough to see Callum.

He turned to face her, stepped closer, so close his breath warmed her forehead. He reached for her hand, which had fallen by her side. 'Maybe you just need to…' he slid her hand onto his chest, flattening it over his heart, his big hand holding hers in place '…grab hold of something solid?'

Felicity dropped her gaze to their joined hands. Each thud of his heart reverberated through her palm, scattering awareness to every cell of her body. She'd never had a one-night stand or done anything so spontaneous. But on a night when she'd been reminded how precarious life could be she needed it.

She needed this. She needed him.

The clickety-clack of the wheels on the track faded. 'Maybe I do,' she murmured, the scent from his citrusy cologne filling her senses until she was dizzy with wanting him.

Like a slice of lime after a shot of tequila.

His kiss, when it came, was gentle. So gentle it almost made her cry. It was long and slow and sweet. It was everything she hadn't known she needed in this moment.

Earlier, if she'd been asked how this would go down, she would have said fast and furious. But this was infinitely better. Burning slow and bright, building in increments that piled on top of the next, making her yearn and ache and want even as it soothed and sated.

His hands slid around her waist. Her arms snaked around his neck. He drew her closer. She lifted up onto tiptoe.

Their hearts thundered together.

When he finally pulled away, they were both breathing hard. His eyes roved over her face, glittering with the kind of fever that also burned in her. What was he looking for?

Permission. *Sub*mission?

He had it.

'I knew you'd taste this good,' he muttered, the low, husky rumble stroking right between her legs.

His next kiss wasn't long and sweet and slow. It was hot and fast and dirty. Just as she'd imagined it would be. His lips were firm and insistent, his tongue seeking entry, which she gave him on a greedy moan. His hands slid under her T-shirt, tightening her belly and heating her blood to well past boiling.

She was so damn hot and horny she could barely see. She certainly couldn't think. All she could do was feel. And surrender.

Her bra snapped open and she gasped and pressed into his palm when his hand cupped a breast.

'God,' he murmured against her mouth. 'You feel good.'

Felicity moaned as his thumb taunted her erect nipple. 'Don't stop.'

He did, but only temporarily as he whisked both her T-shirt and bra off. 'Oh, yes,' he muttered, as he drank in the sight of her bare breasts, one hand sliding around her back, pulling her closer as he lowered his head to the opposite nipple and drew it deep into the warm cavern of his mouth.

Felicity sucked in a breath, her back arching, her hand sinking into the silky softness of his hair. His mouth tugged relentlessly at the nipple and it was equal parts delicious and dangerous. A tingling between her legs built with every hot swipe of his tongue as if he was licking her there instead.

Just then the train clacked loudly and jostled them apart as it got up to speed. Felicity held on to him, her hands curling around his biceps as their bodies lurched to the movement. His hard thighs bracketed hers, steadying them.

Hell. She'd forgotten she was even on a train. The noise of the wheels on the track and the sway was something she'd quickly become accustomed to.

And nothing outside the havoc of his mouth had registered.

'How about we get horizontal?' he suggested, his lips buzzing her neck, his big hands anchored to the small of her back. 'Before we injure ourselves?'

Felicity laughed at the imagery of them being found by Donald in the morning sprawled on the floor, her still half-naked.

God, this was totally insane.

She couldn't believe she was doing it. Getting down and dirty in her train compartment with a comparative stranger.

It was exciting and titillating and scandalous and there was nothing she wanted more.

She slid her hands onto his and eased them off her, keeping hold of him as she walked backwards the two paces required to reach her bed. The backs of her thighs hit her mattress and she sat down, looking up at him, their hands still joined.

She eased her legs apart slightly and was thrilled when he stepped between them. He released himself from her grip and cupped her face with both of his hands.

'You're beautiful,' he murmured.

'You're not so bad yourself.' There was a classic beauty to the angle of his jaw, the blade of his cheek, the cut of his mouth.

Lordy, that mouth.

He smiled, his fingers burrowing into her hair. 'Lie back.'

Felicity shook her head as her gaze zeroed in on his fly, which was, most conveniently, at eye level. 'Soon,' she muttered, reaching out to walk her fingers along the thick bulge testing the strength of his zipper.

He sucked in a breath and a dizzying hit of sexual power surged through her system.

'I don't think that would be a good idea,' he said, but the subtle increase in pressure through his finger pads on her scalp betrayed his true desire.

'You don't like?' she asked, blinking up at him with as much innocence as she could muster.

'Oh, no,' he said with a shaky laugh. 'I like. Probably won't last too long, though. It's been…a bit of a dry spell.'

Felicity didn't understand why that titbit of information should make her so happy, but it did. She liked the idea of being the one to break his drought.

He was breaking hers after all.

'Just a little taste.' She smiled as she reached for his belt buckle.

He dropped his hands and let her have her way. Triumph pulsed through her system, rich and heady, quickening her heartbeat and tingling at the juncture of her thighs.

Her hands trembled as she undid his belt then popped the button. She glanced at him as her fingers toyed with the zipper tab. He was watching her, his eyes hooded, his mouth full and brooding.

She couldn't wait to feel it on her again. Her mouth. Her neck. Her breasts.

Lower.

But for now it was her turn. Her mouth.

Felicity's pulse tripped as she slid the zip down and the fabric peeled back to reveal his impressive girth stretching the limits of his briefs. She looked up at him, her pulse skipping a beat to find him still watching her intently. Locking her gaze with his, she slid a hand up his thigh, inside his underwear and grasped the steely length of his erection.

He shut his eyes and groaned as she pulled it free. The sound was low and needy, sluicing over her like warm rain. His hand slid onto her shoulder and squeezed before his eyes drifted open again.

She made sure he was focusing on her before she transferred her attention to the solid weight of him in her palm and thanked whoever was the patron saint of trains for that strip of light at the bottom of the door allowing her a visual she was never going to forget.

He was big and hard and perfect. Thick and long. And for tonight—what was left of it—*hers*.

She leaned forward, placed her lips against the rigid perfection of him, kissing him there like he had first kissed her. Slowly and gently, testing things out, discovering his contours and the heady aroma of him, teasing him a little with her light kisses.

It wasn't until his quad started to tremble beneath her palm that she realised the level of control he was exercising. She glanced at him, seeing it in the taut planes of his face, feeling it in his grip on her shoulder. So she shut her eyes and let him have it all, leaning forward, pleasuring him with her mouth, taking him in as far as she could.

'Yes-s-s,' he hissed, sliding both hands into her hair. 'Yes.'

His gratification spurred her on and she went harder, revelling in the husky timbre of his breath and the utter hedonism of giving oral pleasure to a man she barely knew while she was topless in the privacy of a luxury train compartment.

She felt wild and reckless and completely wanton.

So freaking *James Bond*.

And she was never going to forget this night as long as she lived.

'Oh, God,' he groaned. 'We have to stop.'

But Felicity barely heard him. She was swept away in the moment, her pulse roaring through her ears.

It wasn't until he said, 'Stop,' again and pulled away that Felicity tuned back in.

'Sorry,' he panted. 'I'm too close…'

His forehead was scrunched, his lips tight. He looked

in pain and completely undone, looming over her almost fully dressed, still potently aroused but somehow achingly vulnerable.

He didn't look like a man who was used to that state of being. His vulnerability hit her hard in the soft spongy spot that was never too far from the surface. She'd give him just about anything right now.

'What do you need?'

'To be in you.' He ducked down and kissed her hard. 'Now.'

The compartment tilted as the dizzying effects of the kiss continued even after it had finished.

Him in her? Now? *That* she could accommodate.

She shimmied back on the bed, dragging her yoga pants and underwear off in the process, aware of him watching the jiggle of her breasts with laserlike focus.

'Well?' she said as she wriggled to the centre of the bed, her nipples responding blatantly to his unashamed gaze. 'Am I the only one getting naked?'

'Nope.' He grinned, immediately toeing off his shoes and hauling his still-buttoned shirt over his head.

Watching him strip was sexy. Him *watching her* watch him strip even more so.

Felicity salivated at the perfection of his chest. It was wide at the shoulders, narrow at the waist. The muscles of his abdomen were defined but not excessively. Tanned and smooth, there was only a fine trail of hair trekking south from his belly button.

She wanted to kiss his chest. Smell it. Lick it. Stroke her fingers over the hills and valleys of his abs, trail them between his hips and watch how it turned him on. Feel the weight of it as he pressed her into the bed.

He stripped off his trousers and underwear together, revealing long, lean legs—more athletic than meaty. Before kicking them away he quickly retrieved his wallet from his back trouser pocket and plucked out a foil packet.

'Condom,' he said, as he took the two paces to her bed.

Felicity smiled as she let her gaze roam over every inch of his body. He was six feet plus of lean male animal and he was hers. 'Just the one?'

He put a knee on her mattress, tossing the packet near a pillow. 'We'll improvise.' He smiled.

And then he was lying on his side next to her, his head propped on his hand, his other hand trailing down her neck, through the valley between her breasts, down to her stomach, swirling around her belly button before continuing south all the way down through the soft curls of her pubic hair, stopping just before he reached ground zero.

Felicity's breath hitched as his finger hovered, taunting her. She doubted she'd last long either if he were actually to touch her.

She groped for the foil packet and thrust it at his chest. *His totally freaking awesome chest.* 'In me. Now. Remember?'

He smiled, his finger circling just out of reach. 'I can play a little first.'

She shook her head. 'It's been a while for me too.'

He regarded her for a moment before taking the condom and easing onto his back to roll it on. It was a position Felicity couldn't resist, taking advantage of his momentary distraction to move on top of him, straddling his hips, his fully sheathed erection sliding deliciously through the slick heat between her legs.

'God,' he muttered, his hands drifting up her belly to her breasts. 'You look magnificent.'

Felicity smiled as she arched her back and rubbed herself up and down the length of him. 'I feel pretty damn magnificent right now.'

His thumbs brushed her nipples and she shut her eyes, revelling in the heady glow of sexual abandonment for a moment or two.

But it just wasn't enough.

Her eyelids fluttered open to find him watching her again with an intensity that practically melted her into a puddle. She held his gaze as she leaned forward, tilting her pelvis and grasping his girth. His hands fell to her hips as she guided him to where she was slick and ready.

Where she *needed* him to be.

The feel of him there, so thick and *big*, was incredible. His eyes on her as she slowly sank down and he filled her—stretched her—was a whole different level. Felicity gasped as she settled flush against him, leaning forward with outstretched arms, bracing her hands on his shoulders, steadying herself as she took a breath.

'So good,' she muttered.

'God, *yes*,' he panted.

And it was. *So good.* Too good to just sit and do nothing. Too good not to move. Not to flex up and down and back and forth and round and round. Too good not to find a rhythm that was perfect and would drive them both towards a conclusion that had been building between them all night.

Her fingernails curled into his shoulders, his fingers gripped her hips like steel bands as they did just that, staring into each other's eyes as the tempo picked up, finding a rhythm and an angle that tripped her switch. His fingers slid between her legs again, not teasing this time but going straight to the spot she needed it most and rubbing sure and hard.

Nothing fancy. Just merciless pressure.

'God, yes,' Felicity gasped, drumming her feet behind her on the bed, riding him harder, faster as the fabric of her world started to tear from the inside out. Her thighs trembled, her nails dug in a little harder, her belly pulled taut.

Her orgasm hit hard roaring from a tiny quiver to an all-consuming pleasure storm within seconds.

'Yes,' he muttered, working her harder, faster, vaulting upright to press his lips to her neck, whispering, 'Yes, yes, yes,' as she slid her arms around his shoulders and came apart in his arms.

He flipped her on her back then, his forehead pressed into her neck, driving in faster and faster, sustaining her pleasure as he reached his own, groaning long and low into her ear as he came hard, sweat slicking the valley between his shoulder blades, his biceps trembling, her name on his lips as he spent himself inside her until he had no more to give and they both lay panting to the rock and sway of the train.

CHAPTER FOUR

CALLUM WAS EATING breakfast the next morning when Felicity finally put in an appearance. He'd left her sleeping two hours ago when the train had pulled into Broken Hill and woken him. It hadn't woken her and he'd told a hovering Donald not to wake her for the tour she'd been booked on or for breakfast.

'Of course,' he'd said, nodding his head. 'It was a late one, wasn't it?'

Callum's smile had been noncommittal. Little did Donald know just how late it had been. They'd enjoyed two more rounds of 'inventive' sex due to lack of protection. He'd only managed two hours' sleep.

But, then, insomnia had been part of his life for the last two years. He'd learned that lying around in bed, willing himself back to sleep, was counterproductive. Ignoring the tour options, he'd showered and gone through some more of his reading, as well as contacting his ride to let her know to delay her pick-up.

'Good morning,' Felicity said as she sat in the empty chair opposite him. Callum had been staring out the window, watching the scenery flash by, as he sipped his third cup of coffee. He had his sunglasses on to deal with the excessive sunlight flooding in through the glass because the view was too good to pass up.

He smiled at her. She looked fresh from the shower in jeans and a T-shirt, her wet hair pulled back into a pony-tail low on her nape. An image of her riding him last night, honey-blonde strands flying loose around her bare shoulders, slid into his mind unbidden.

'It is,' he agreed. 'A very good morning.'

A small smile touched her mouth before a blush stole across her cheekbones and she dropped her gaze to the tablecloth briefly before raising it again. 'You're kind of chipper for someone who didn't get a lot of sleep.'

Callum shrugged. 'Some things are worth losing sleep over.'

'Absolutely.' She looked like she was about to say more but one of the wait staff interrupted, filling Felicity's cup with coffee. 'About last night…' she said after they departed, spooning in some sugar and stirring absently.

She seemed wary and unsure suddenly, staring at the circling spoon, reluctant to meet his gaze. Alarm bells rang in his head and his hair prickled at his nape. Was she going to suggest that they make it something more? Was she going to ask for his number? Or a date? Was she going to morph into some kind of clingy, bunny-boiler who wanted some kind of relationship?

Because, as incredible as it had been—and it had been *incredible*—he just didn't have time and space in his life at the moment for a romantic entanglement. He was trying to get his life back on track and last night had purely been the inevitable end to a couple of hours of flirting and one massive adrenaline hit.

Hadn't it?

Hell. He didn't even know her last name.

'I don't…' She placed her spoon on the saucer and glanced at him. 'I don't usually do this kind of thing.'

Callum nodded. There wasn't one part of him that thought she did. 'Yeah. I got that.'

'Not that I think,' she hastened to add, 'there's anything wrong with *hooking up*. It's just not…me, you know? Well, of course you know because I'm totally screwing this up in a very unsophisticated way, *exactly* like I've never done this before, but look… I live in this small town where everybody knows everybody else and they're all in each other's business and all the guys my age there think of me as Flick so I don't often get the opportunity to…'

He waited for her to continue but she appeared to have run out of steam. Callum couldn't figure out where she was going with this. Was the reason she was telling him she was a small-town girl her way of saying her daddy had a gun and he was now part of the family whether he liked it or not?

'Oh, God, sorry.' She grimaced, covering her face with her hand before dropping it again and shaking her head. 'I'm babbling. I *swore* I wouldn't babble.'

Callum laughed, which surprised the hell out of him. She really was quite cute when she was flummoxed. 'It's fine, don't worry about it. I'm not judging you and there *were* extraordinary circumstances last night.'

'Sure.' She picked up her cup and sipped, her gaze zeroing in on his. 'But you and I both know we were heading to bed even before our adrenaline-induced recklessness.'

There was no point denying that one. In fact, he was damn certain they'd have done it more than three times had their flirting not been so catastrophically interrupted.

'You're very direct, aren't you?' He liked that.

She laughed. 'Usually yes. Although not so much right now. It's the nurse in me.' She glanced out the window for a beat or two before looking at him again. 'What I'm trying to say—*very inelegantly*—is that I hope you don't think… I mean *want* or expect even…that this is anything more than just last night. Just two strangers on a train, in a…bubble almost. Indulging in something spontaneous. I mean, I like you but…hell, I don't even know your last name or where you live or what kind of doctor you are or even if you're going on to Perth.'

Callum opened his mouth to tell her it was okay. He got it. He felt exactly the same way about what had happened between them. About spontaneity. About getting out of his head and just not being himself for a night. But she held up her hand to ward it off.

'No. Don't tell me. I don't want to know any of it either. I'd kind of like to keep this whole thing as a big, delicious secret. This…crazy thing I did once that'll make me smile whenever I think about it. Maybe…' she smiled '…scandalise my grandkids about it one day.'

Grandkids. Of course there'd be grandkids. And kids. With honey-blonde hair and grey eyes. She was young and, despite what she said about the guys in her town, he had no doubt someone would snap her up.

Whereas he couldn't even look that far ahead.

'So,' Callum said, forcing himself to lighten the mood, 'you just want to use me for my body and callously walk away? Pretend it never happened?'

She pulled her bottom lip between her teeth as she nodded and said, 'Yes.' She toyed with her spoon again. 'Does that make me a terrible person?'

Callum chuckled at the little frown knitting her brow. He'd never met a woman who was such a compelling mix of confidence and uncertainty. 'No,' he teased. 'Relax. It was one night. We barely know one another. I promise you haven't broken my heart and I'm not about to drop down on one knee and ask you to marry me. You are not a terrible person and we should absolutely go our own ways after this with a smile on our faces and *very* fond memories of our night.'

'Is that how you're going to remember it?' she asked, placing her elbow on the table and propping her chin on her fist. 'Fondly?'

She was teasing now and he liked it. '*Very* fondly.'

She grinned. 'Me too.'

'Good. Now…' he thrust the breakfast menu at her '…order your breakfast. You *must* be hungry.'

Her gaze dropped to the menu but he could still see the smile playing on her mouth as she muttered, *'Starving.'*

Felicity ate like the train was about to run out of food. She was absolutely famished from her vigorous night between the sheets. Callum laughed at how much she put away and the happy little bubble around her grew.

It continued when they moved to the lounge. Jock's heart attack was a hot topic with their fellow travellers and everyone was agog at how they'd saved Jock's life. They were so impressed they didn't seem to mind the fact that both she and Callum had lied to them about what they did.

Or at least they didn't call them on it anyway.

The day flew and before Felicity knew it the train was rolling through the outer suburbs of Adelaide, bringing her closer and closer to home. She was treating herself to a few days in the city first, though. The last week in October was a perfect time to do her Christmas shopping and also hit the beach before the full tilt of summer. There were no beaches in the Clare Valley. Vineyards and antique shops, amazing restaurants with gourmet offerings and dinky little tearooms for sure, but no beach.

It was back to work on Monday and the magical time she'd spent in Sydney with her best friend Luci and the train trip and last night would all soon be pushed to the side as she morphed back into Flick and her life revolved around work and small-town life.

So she was going to savour this for as long as she could.

Half an hour later the train had pulled up at the platform and she was saying goodbye to her fellow travellers and Donald as she disembarked. A part of her wanted to stay on for ever, stay in this bubble for ever with Callum. But it was neither real nor possible so she channelled Flick and let it go, stepping onto the platform.

'Well, I guess this is goodbye.'

Felicity took a calming breath as Callum's familiar sexy rumble washed over her. She turned to face him, struck again by how sexy he was as her gaze roamed over his face, trying to remember every detail.

She was curiously reluctant to say goodbye. What did she say to a man who'd given her a moment in time she was never going to forget? Who had made her body sing? Who had made her feel sexy and desired?

Thank you just didn't seem enough.

'Do you have someone picking you up or…?'

Maybe they could catch a lift together? Maybe if he was also in the city for a few days they could…?

'We could share a taxi if you like. Where are you heading?'

'Oh, no, it's fine,' he said. 'I have someone picking me up.'

Of course. It was better this way really. A clean break.

'In fact…' he looked past her shoulder '…I think that may be her.'

Her. A sick moment of dread punched Felicity in the gut. She hadn't even asked him if he was involved with someone. She'd just assumed…

'Dr Hollingsworth?'

Felicity blinked at another very familiar voice as Callum waved and said, 'Over here.' She turned to find Mrs Baker, the wife of Vickers Hill's police chief, heading in their direction.

What the...?

'Mrs B.?'

'Oh, Flick, darling.' She smiled and pulled her into a big bear hug. 'What a surprise! Oh, wait…did I get my wires crossed? Julia was supposed to come but one of the receptionists had to go home sick, which left them short-staffed so she was ringing around to find someone else. I left a message on her phone that I'd do it but maybe she didn't check it and had already arranged for you to do the pick-up?'

Felicity had absolutely no idea what the other woman was talking about. 'The pick-up?'

'Yes.' Mrs Baker nodded. 'For Dr Hollingsworth here.'

Dr Hollingsworth? Felicity glanced at Callum. *He* was Dr Hollingsworth? The new locum? The one who'd done the house swap with Luci?

'*You're* Dr Hollingsworth?'

He frowned, obviously confused now too. 'Yes.'

Oh, hell… *What had they done?*

'So you're not here to pick him up?' Mrs Baker asked, looking as perplexed as Felicity but oblivious to her inner turmoil.

'No.' She shook her head. 'We've been on the train to-gether. I just didn't…' she glanced at Callum '…know it.'

'Oh, how delightful.' Mrs Baker beamed. 'What a co-incidence.'

Hmm. *Delightful* wasn't the way Felicity would describe it. She'd slept with the locum? A man she was going to have to face every day for two months?

How could she pretend it had never happened now?

'So…you know one another?' Callum asked, frowning at both of them, obviously trying to put the pieces together.

'Oh, yes.' Mrs Baker nodded vigorously. 'Flick's one of the practice nurses at Dr Dawson's surgery, aren't you, dear?'

Felicity watched as realisation slowly dawned on Callum's face. 'Oh. Right.'

'Isn't that an amazing coincidence?' Mrs Baker repeated.

'Yes…amazing,' he murmured through lips that were so tight Felicity worried they might spontaneously split open. *Fabulous.*

The man looked like he wanted to disappear. Or, at the very least, hightail it out of town. Felicity didn't know whether to be sad, mad, insulted or to push him back on the damn train herself.

'Right, well…' Mrs Baker said, still oblivious to the thick air of *what-the-hell* between them. 'Did you want a lift back home too, dear? Only we really do have to hit the road. It's a good two-hour drive, more with the peak-hour traffic.'

'Oh, no, thank you,' Felicity said, dragging her gaze off the incredulity in Callum's green eyes. 'I'm staying on for a few days.' *Thank God!* 'I'm not back till Sunday.'

'Oh, that's nice. Doing some Christmas shopping or seeing some bloke you're not telling any of us about?' Mrs Baker nudged her arm playfully.

Hardly. Given the last bloke she'd *seen* was now a certified disaster. She returned the older woman's good-natured teasing with a wan smile, changing the subject. 'Well, you're right, you'd better be off. Say hi to everyone and I'll see them all on Monday.'

She forced herself to look at Callum like he was just some guy she'd met on the train and not someone she'd torn up the sheets with in what had been, without a doubt, the most memorable—and now the most disastrous—time of her life.

'It was nice meeting you, Dr Hollingsworth,' she said, willing a smile to her lips. She wasn't entirely sure she'd managed it but she ploughed on. 'I look forward to working with you over the next couple of months.'

About as much as shoving a rusty fork in her eye.

He nodded, his mouth set in the grim line she'd first seen back at Central Station in Sydney. God—had it only been yesterday?

'Yes,' he said. 'Can't wait.'

He looked like he could do with a rusty fork too.

And then, because there *was* actually someone watching her, Mrs Baker was ushering him along and out of the station and she was staring at his back. His chinos encasing those long athletic legs, his T-shirt stretching over those big shoulders, his hair brushing his nape.

A back she'd seen naked. A back she was damn sure she'd scratched up a little at one stage. Felicity shut her eyes and allowed herself an internal groan. How was she going to work with him every day and not think about their night together?

Not remember the bunch of his muscles under her hands as he'd loomed over her, the smell of his cologne on his neck, the deep groan when he'd orgasmed—*three times*.

Not relive every moment in glorious Technicolor?

Not want a repeat performance?

CHAPTER FIVE

FELICITY ALWAYS ARRIVED at work at seven in the morning.
The practice didn't open until eight but she liked to grab
a cup of tea and set things up at a leisurely pace. She liked
to go through each of the doctors' appointment books as
well as her own to mentally prepare herself for the day.

This morning she was here at seven because she hadn't
been able to sleep. She'd driven into town deliberately after
dark yesterday so no one could just drop in for a chat. She'd
spent three days in Adelaide, trying to figure out a strat-
egy to deal with Callum, and she still wasn't any closer.

She wasn't worried that anyone would find out. She
didn't think Callum would be indiscreet. He didn't look
like the kiss and tell type.

But *she* knew. Her *body* knew.

She'd been okay with acting so wildly outside her usual
character when it had been a one-off. And she'd been fine
to walk away from it and get back to the life she knew,
loved and understood. The place, the people, the work
that defined her. But with him constantly reminding her
of something sizzling and exciting?

Constantly derailing her contented life?

She didn't need that kind of disquiet. She'd been lucky.
She'd already had her big love. She didn't need some crazy,

hot thing with a guy who was here for two months making her question all she held dear.

And even if she'd been actively looking for a man—which she wasn't—Callum did not fit the bill. She was only interested in long-term prospects and she was perfectly happy to wait. For it to happen when it happened. *If* it happened.

There wasn't any rush despite what every woman of a certain age in Vickers Hill thought.

The kettle boiled and Felicity shook herself out of her reverie. She was getting way ahead of herself. Catastrophising as usual. Also being a little egotistical. *Like she was so freaking irresistible.* Just because the man had ravished her in bed all night didn't mean he wanted anything more from her or that he wanted to carry on while he was here.

She was making way too much of it. It was two months, for Pete's sake. She could do *anything* for two months. They'd talk, set some rules and then she'd be cool, calm and collected. Polite. Professional. Friendly even. Vickers Hill was a great place to live in the middle of a famous wine region—she could play tour guide.

Felicity heard the back door open and glanced at her watch. She frowned. Dr Dawson was early today, he didn't usually arrive until seven thirty sometimes. Now he was cutting back his hours a little on his countdown to retirement he left it as late as a quarter to eight.

Felicity had worked for Luci's father for four years and would be grateful to him for ever for employing her when she'd fled back to Vickers Hill, licking her wounds post-Ned.

She turned to greet him, a smile on her face, knowing he'd come straight to the staffroom for a cuppa. But it wasn't Dr Dawson. It was Callum standing in the doorway,

all long legs and wide shoulders, looking devastating in a
dark suit and patterned tie.

Her stomach dropped. Her fingers tightened around
her mug. She swore muscles between her legs tightened in
some kind of Pavlovian response as heat coursed to all the
erogenous zones he'd taken his sweet time getting to know.

So much for being cool, calm and collected. If her body
was any hotter she'd be smoking. 'Oh. Hi.'

He nodded, his gaze guarded, reminding her of the
brooding guy in the café that day. 'Hi.'

Awkward.

But, then, she'd always known it was going to be.

'You're early,' she said, to sever the stretching silence.
'You know you don't start till one each day, right?'

She knew he'd been in a couple of times already, orien-
tating himself to the practice, because she'd been talking
to Luci, who'd rung to tell her that Callum's brother Seb
had turned up on her doorstep in Sydney and he was now
living with her, but had also mentioned Callum dropping
in to see her father and introduce himself to everyone.

He shrugged. 'Thought I'd get settled in.' He walked
into the room and set the small plastic crate he was holding on the dining table. 'I also wanted to go over the clinic
charts for this week. You know...' he gave a half-smile but
it was strained and tight '...be prepared.'

Felicity nodded stiffly. Oh, yeah, he was a regular Boy
Scout.

In any other person, she would have been impressed
by the diligence but she'd thought she'd have more time
to get her game face on this morning so she wasn't feeling terribly charitable.

'You'll have access to the appointment calendar on your
computer in your office,' she said. 'I'll send you an invite
to join but I'll just grab the printout now.'

It was her chance to temporarily escape and get herself together. He didn't try to stop her and for the thirty seconds it took her to snatch the list of today's appointments off the reception desk she was grateful.

She needed a breather. To hit the reset button.

She stared down at the list, not really seeing it. The Dawson general practice was one of two in Vickers Hill. There were two GPs. Bill Dawson was the original and had founded the practice almost forty years ago. About twenty years later he'd taken on a partner—Angela Runcorn—because the work had been too much for one and he'd wanted to have a woman for his female patients to have a choice. He and Angela each owned fifty percent of the practice.

Four years ago, and this was why Felicity had been employed, he'd taken on a part-time GP—Meera Setu. Meera and Felicity ran the afternoon specialty clinics together, which freed up a lot of appointment time. Monday was ortho clinic, Tuesday was diabetic, Wednesday was babies and Friday was immunisation. There was no clinic on Thursdays as it was Felicity's day for home visits.

But, with Meera going on maternity leave last week for two months, Dr Dawson had needed a replacement and had advertised for a locum. Given that it was for such a short amount of time, Felicity hadn't paid much heed to the process other than encouraging Luci to go to Sydney to do her course and pushing her to do the house swap with Callum when the possibility had been floated.

Except she'd only heard him being referred to as Dr Hollingsworth. And she'd never bothered to find out Callum's last name when she'd been getting naked with him between her sheets.

She made a mental note to always find out a guy's full name before doing the wild thing. Because now she'd be working closely with Dr Wild Thing *every* day.

Like right-hand woman close. And it all could have been avoided had she stopped to find out the basics—like his name!

'Here it is,' she said, injecting a lightness into her tone as she re-entered the staffroom.

He was at the sink, spooning coffee into a mug. She placed the list on the table next to the crate because there was no way she was getting any closer to him when she didn't have to.

'Thanks,' he said, picking up his mug and leaning his butt against the counter, his feet casually crossed at the ankles, which pulled the fabric of his trousers tight across his thighs.

'I'll forward you the email folder with all their electronic charts in a bit.'

'Thank you.' The silence built again. 'I checked up on Jock. They transferred him to hospital in Sydney and put in several stents. He's doing okay.'

Felicity nodded. 'Yes. Thanks. I spoke with the hospital this morning.'

Thankfully a noise in the hallway outside alerted her to someone else arriving and Felicity almost kissed Dr Dawson as he sauntered into the staffroom, his usual chipper self.

'Ah, Flick.' He smiled as he embraced her in a warm hug that smelled of the starch Julia, Luci's mum, always ironed his shirts with. 'Good to have you back. We almost fell apart without you.'

Felicity laughed, ignoring Callum in her peripheral vision. 'I'm sure Courtney caught on pretty quickly.'

Dr Dawson chuckled in that way of his that made other people want to join in as he pulled out of the hug. 'Now, then, I see you've met Cal. I think you two are going to get along famously.'

Felicity smiled at her boss then nodded in Callum's general direction. 'Yes. Callum and I have met.' She couldn't bring herself to call him Cal—he'd always be Callum to her.

'Oh, call him Cal,' Dr Dawson said. 'That's right, isn't it, son?'

At almost seventy Bill called every male under forty 'son'. It was his term of endearment.

'Cal's fine,' Callum said, ambling over to the table and sitting down. 'Most people call me Cal.'

Dr Dawson nodded, looking pleased with himself. 'You're bright and early. If you're trying to impress me, it's working.'

'Thought I'd look at the clinic appointments for the week. Familiarise myself with some charts.'

'Jolly good idea.' Dr Dawson nodded. 'Must do the same myself. Better get to it. Monday morning is always a madhouse here. I'll just make myself a cuppa and do the same thing.'

'I'll make it and bring it in for you, Dr Dawson,' Felicity offered.

She loved Bill Dawson almost as much as she loved her own father but he made an unholy mess in the kitchen and, like a lot of men, seemed completely blind to it. Also, Callum was a little too close for comfort now.

'Oh, no, Flick. Julia would rouse on me if I made the nurses get me a cup of tea.'

Felicity smiled. She knew that was the truth. Julia Dawson had been a nurse for over twenty years before Luci, her change-of-life surprise package, had come along. She'd worked part time on Reception for many years at the practice once Luci had gone to school and still helped out when things got hectic.

There was no greater advocate for the practice nurses than Bill's wife.

'I'm offering,' Felicity said, shooing him away from the sink as she approached. 'It'll be our little secret, I promise.'

Dr Dawson capitulated easily. 'Thank you.' He grinned. 'I'll see you later, Cal,' he said, moving towards the door. 'Don't hesitate to ask if you have any questions. Pop your head in or ask Angela or even our girl Flick. She knows more than all of us put together.'

Felicity kept her back turned, fiddling with the mugs as she snorted self-deprecatingly, which produced more chuckles from Dr Dawson as he exited.

She was excruciatingly conscious of Callum's gaze burning into her back as she made two cups of tea. When she was done she picked them up and finally turned to face him. It was disconcerting to find him still watching her, his brow crinkled, his mouth set in a brooding line.

'I used to be a Cal,' he said. 'Felt like one too. The life of the party. The centre of the world. The man of the moment. I used to be like that.'

Felicity wasn't sure what this was about. Was he annoyed all these days later that she'd told him he didn't look like a Cal? Because he didn't—not to her mind. *Especially not now.* Or was he trying to explain why he hadn't introduced himself as Cal right out of the blocks?

Or did he just miss that Cal guy and want to reminisce? She had to admit to being curious about him herself.

It was hard to figure out what he meant. He was so tense and shuttered, so hard to read. 'What happened?'

He shrugged, looking down into his mug. 'Life. Stuff.'

She nodded. She didn't know what he wanted her to say. Did he want her to push or leave it alone? Something had obviously happened to Callum to change him.

Was that why he was here? In the middle of freaking

nowhere? Fourteen hundred kilometres from his amazing harbourside apartment that Luci had raved about?

'You're a long way from home,' she murmured.

'Yeah.'

Felicity almost gave up. It was like pulling teeth. But she'd always been stubborn. 'Because you wanted to trade water for wine? Or…because you're running away?'

He glanced up from his mug, piercing her with his eyes. Running away it was.

Best she remember that.

'Because I'm newly trained and thought some rural experience would be good.'

It was a sound reason. Most GPs who locumed in rural areas and weren't from rural areas did so for the experience. Somehow, though, she didn't think that's what was going on here.

But whatever. It wasn't any of her business.

'Right. Well…' She looked at the mugs in her hand. 'I better deliver this, we open in fifteen minutes. I'll email you those files in a bit. Have you been set up on the computer?'

'Yes.' He nodded. 'Thanks.'

Felicity gave him a weak smile as she headed towards the door. 'No worries. Just yell if you need anything.'

But she hoped like hell he didn't.

It was almost three hours later before Felicity got around to emailing the file, although she had managed to send the appointment calendar invite through to Callum before things had got too crazy.

In the mornings Felicity was a general dogsbody. From receptionist to nursing duties, she was a jack of all trades and Mondays were always busy. It was like medical conditions multiplied over the two-day break. Plus there was a new doctor starting so that always brought out the rubber-neckers hoping for a glimpse.

Not that anybody had seen Callum yet, he was keeping his door firmly closed. A fact that didn't deter the Vickers Hill grapevine. They didn't need a sighting today. It was already in full swing because Mrs Mancini had spied him at the local supermarket, buying groceries at the weekend, and had declared him a bit of a catch.

She was surprised Mrs Mancini hadn't arrived with her gorgeous granddaughter who was a teacher at the local public school and who she'd been trying to marry off for the last two years. Three patients had already arrived bearing gifts of food for him.

Felicity picked up the plate of shortbread Mrs Robbins had brought with her. Her shortbread won the blue ribbon at the district fête every year and had been known to make grown men weep.

She took it with her to Callum's office. As far as she knew, he hadn't surfaced all morning and it was for him after all. She wanted to check he'd received the file and needed to get in there to set up for the orthopaedic clinic that started at one. There were three lots of plaster due to come off today and the plaster saw wasn't in the treatment room so it was probably in his office somewhere.

Also they needed to talk. Before the clinic. There were things to say. Although she wasn't sure how to start.

That's where the shortbread came in. If it all went badly, at least she could console herself with sugar.

She knocked on the door and opened it when she heard a muffled, 'Come in.'

Even dulled, his voice did wicked things to her pulse.

Damn. She was in trouble if his voice could make her legs weak through a closed door.

'Hey,' she said as she opened the door and shut it behind her then walked towards him all businesslike, concentrating on the plate of shortbread. 'I come bearing gifts.'

She glanced at him as she drew level with his desk and was pleased she was close enough to a chair should she collapse into it. *Glasses.* He was wearing glasses. Sexy glasses. The kind of trendy, designer wireless frames that hunky male models wore in advertisements for optometrists.

She wouldn't have thought he could look any sexier. *She'd seen him naked, for crying out loud.* But she'd been wrong. Callum with glasses was a whole other level.

'You wear glasses?'

It was possibly the dumbest thing she'd ever said. She might as well have said she'd carried a watermelon.

He peered at her over the top of those glasses. 'So do you.'

'Oh…yes.' She absently touched the frames she'd pushed to the top of her head. 'Just for reading and computer work.'

'Same here.' He took them off and tossed them on his desk and Felicity wished he'd put them on again.

He stared at her, obviously waiting for her to say something. 'Did you want something?' he asked, looking pointedly at the plate of shortbread.

His tone was brisk. Not unfriendly but businesslike. It appeared she wasn't going to have to worry about any lines they'd crossed. He'd obviously retreated as far as he could.

It was just the bucket of cold water she needed.

'I came to check you'd received the file I sent you and to bring you these. Mrs Robbins made them for the new doctor. They're the best in the district. You also have a jar of Mrs Randall's rosella jam and Cindy Wetherall has made you a mulberry pie.'

He blinked. 'But…why?'

The incredulity in his voice would have been comical had it not been utterly genuine. Felicity shrugged. 'It's the country. That's how we welcome newcomers. Also there's a rumour going around town that the new doc is hot so you've gone to the top of the eligible list.'

'Eligible?'

'Yes, you know. Marriage, babies, the whole enchilada. We don't get a lot of new blood around here.'

His face morphed from mystified to horrified, which was another salient warning. He looked like two rusty forks would be welcome about now.

Obviously marriage and babies were not on his agenda. Or not in Vickers Hills anyway.

'What did you think you were going to get when you traded the city for the country?'

If her voice was a little on the tart side she didn't care. Honestly…for someone who'd come across as intelligent and articulate on the train, he was being rather obtuse.

'Not this.'

'Well…you'd better get used to it.' She plonked the plate of biscuits down. 'You're going to be well fed around here.'

He looked at them like they were a bomb that could possibly detonate at any moment. *Oh, for Pete's sake…* She had the strange urge to pelt him with one.

'Anyway… Did you get the files?'

He put his glasses back on and her pulse gave a funny little skip despite her annoyance. He looked at his computer screen. 'Thanks, yes. I've figured out the system and I've been reviewing all the charts for the week.'

He was being thorough. That was good. Being prepared and focused. Doing his homework.

But she still wanted to pelt him with shortbread.

'It looks pretty light,' he said, his eyes still glued to the screen. 'I'd see double the amount of patients in an afternoon in Sydney.'

There was no criticism in his voice. He was being matter-of-fact but it irked Felicity. She bit her tongue against the urge to tell him he could turn right around and go back to his precious Sydney.

It appeared their *talk* wasn't going to be necessary. It was obvious he didn't want to be here. She'd been worrying about nothing.

'Trust me, it'll take us all afternoon.'

'Okay. The clinic usually starts on time?'

'Yes. There are no appointments between twelve and one so we can have lunch then afternoon clinics start at one on the dot.'

'That's very civilised.'

Felicity gritted her teeth. Again, his tone wasn't critical but anger stirred in her chest anyway.

She supposed they didn't get time for lunch in Sydney.

'Well, you know what they say, the family that eats together stays together.'

He glanced at her. 'And you're all family here.'

Why did he make that sound like they were some kind of cult? 'Well…yes.' Where the hell was the charming guy from the train? The one she'd slept with?

Talk about a Jekyll and Hyde!

He nodded as if he was absorbing her answer before returning his attention to the screen. Felicity had to stop herself from rolling her eyes. 'Do me a favour? Have a look around here for the plaster saw when you're done with the charts?'

She'd planned on looking for it herself but frankly she didn't want to be around him any longer than she had to be. And she didn't need the temptation of a plaster saw in her hand when she felt like causing him physical harm.

'Sure,' he murmured, still focused on his computer.

Felicity wasn't sure if that was his way of dismissing her or not but she took her leave anyway.

She had no idea if he noticed.

CHAPTER SIX

CALLUM GLANCED UP as the door clicked shut. He hadn't realised Felicity had slipped out. He sighed and threw his glasses on the desk again, massaging the bridge of his nose with two fingers.

Damn it. He'd been too short with her. He hadn't meant to be, she'd just caught him at a bad moment. He'd been trying to concentrate on his work, to push away the powerful feelings of regret that were threatening to swamp him, but sitting here at his desk in a Vickers Hill general practice he couldn't deny them any longer and she'd arrived in the middle of his pity party.

He was a GP. A general practitioner. The last two years he'd been in training for this so it hadn't seemed quite real. But now he was here, in his first GP job, and it was as real as it got.

Goodbye, hot-shot surgeon. No more triple As, carotid endarterectomies or vascular bypasses. His life now revolved around tonsillitis, hypertension, reflux and asthma. No more international surgical conferences or pioneering new techniques or glitzy dinner parties. No more cut and thrust of the operating theatre. It was all rosella jam and mulberry pie...

So not the way he'd pictured his life turning out.

Sure, after this he was heading back to the prestigious

north shore practice where he'd undergone a lot of his training. He'd never been given home-made anything by any of the patients there but it wasn't scrubs and the smell of the diathermy either.

Still, none of it was Felicity's fault and they had to work together so he needed to get his head out of his rear end. He hadn't been prepared for the leap in his pulse when he'd seen her again this morning. He'd spent the last few days trying to compartmentalise her in his head as the woman on the train. A fantasy. A very sexy, very real fantasy that he thanked his lucky stars for but a fantasy nonetheless.

He'd thought he'd succeeded.

And then she'd been in the staffroom and his libido had growled back to life again as a rush of memories from the train had filled his head.

She hadn't looked like the woman in the fringed boots or the little black dress. She'd been in her uniform—a pair of loose-fitting blue trousers and a polo shirt with 'Dawson Family Practice' embroidered across the pocket. The shirt was also loose and her honey-coloured hair was tied back in a low ponytail at her nape.

But she *had* looked like the woman in the yoga pants and bare feet who'd shared her bed with him and damn if that hadn't made him all fired up. And messed with his head. Why else would he have babbled on about being a Cal?

Oh, God. He'd been inept…

But it had seemed vital suddenly that she know. To make her understand that he had been a different person once. That he *was* capable, even if that guy felt lost to him for ever.

To not judge him as the man she saw now.

Which hopefully she wouldn't because that guy had just acted like an insensitive jerk.

He'd come here to get away from the tentacles of his past. To begin his new career away from judging eyes. To get some clear air before he went back to a world that was used to seeing him as an entirely different person.

To be happy, goddamn it.

Or at least less miserable.

He just hadn't realised how hard it was going to be. He'd put too much expectation on this first day. That starting it would be some miracle cure. Some invisible line in the sand that held magical powers of career satisfaction by just stepping over it when clearly it was going to take time. He was going to have to get used to it. To the change in pace and clientele and his core duties. To take one day at a time and have faith that each day would be better than the last.

It was that or become a bitter old man. And he refused to let that damn cricket ball win.

The clinic started promptly but didn't go according to what Felicity, or the patients, were used to. Callum was efficient in the extreme. No wonder he had queried the appointment numbers when he seemed to have mentally allotted five minutes to each one and zipped through the list like he was trying to set a new world record.

Usually, with Meera, each appointment would last between ten and fifteen minutes. But Callum didn't believe in pleasantries. He wasn't rude. He was polite and respectful but he didn't dillydally either, didn't open himself to chitchat, preferring to cut straight to the chase. Review the problem. Make a diagnosis. Order a test, an X-ray, a pill or dish out some medical advice.

Thank you for coming. *Next!*

Some city practice was going to lap him up with his billing rate. But that's not what they were about at the Dawson Family Practice and by the time they'd worked their way through to their second-last patient—at *four o'clock*—Felicity was cranky. The clinics always ran until at least five and usually closer to six.

She had no doubt Callum looked on it as efficiency. There were more people in the cities, therefore more demand on GP services. Double- and triple-booking were common practice. But he could keep it as far as she was concerned. Her patients deserved more than a paint-by-numbers doctor.

Old Mr Dunnich came in, bearing a bunch of roses. He was a big old wizened bloke in his mid-eighties, used to stand six-four and didn't have the belly he was sporting now in his grape-growing days.

'These are for you, Doc,' he said in his slow country drawl. 'Don't usually go around giving flowers to blokes but the wife insisted.'

Callum seemed as puzzled by the gesture as Mr Dunnich. 'Oh…thanks,' he said, taking them awkwardly and putting them on his desk before ploughing on. 'Now, let's have a look at those bunions, shall we?'

Mr Dunnich shot her a perplexed look. In fact, she knew him well enough to see a fleeting flash of offence. Mr Dunnich's prize roses were a thing of beauty, and the perfume floated to Felicity from across the other side of the room within seconds. There wasn't a person alive—including clueless men—who didn't comment on how spectacular they were.

Felicity wasn't usually a person who harboured murderous intent but she had to suppress the urge to hit Callum across the head with the nearest heavy object, which just happened to be a tendon hammer.

It *probably* wouldn't kill him should she be unable to suppress the urge to use it.

Mr Dunnich took off his shoes and socks in silence.

Normally he was always up for a chat. He could talk about his roses all day and what the man didn't know about growing grapes for wine wasn't worth knowing. But he did what all old men from the country did when feeling socially awkward—he clammed up.

Callum examined both big toes. The silence stretched, which was obviously making Mr Dunnich uncomfortable enough to try and initiate some conversation. 'The pain's getting worse, Doc, but I really don't want to have to go under the knife. I don't want to leave Lizzy alone.'

'I see,' Callum said, poking and prodding as he asked a few questions. 'Okay,' he said briskly a moment or two later. 'You can put your shoes back on.'

Mr Dunnich did as he was told. 'I'm going to try you on this new medication,' Callum said, turning to his computer and using the electronic prescription system to generate a script to give to the chemist. The printer spat it out and he handed it over. 'It's had good results for arthritic pain. One twice a day for a week then come back and see us at the clinic next week and we'll reassess.'

'Rightio,' Mr Dunnich said, taking the printout and glancing at her, obviously not sure if the consult was over. He hadn't been in and out in five minutes ever.

Felicity smiled at him encouragingly, her heart going out to him. 'I'll see you out, Mr Dunnich.'

Again, Callum hadn't been rude but he hadn't been welcoming either. He'd been brisk and efficient and oblivious to his patient's awkwardness.

'I need to find a vase for these anyway,' she said, ignoring Callum as she swooped up the roses. She buried her face in them as she caught up to the patient and linked her arm through his. 'They're gorgeous, aren't they? What are these ones called?'

The old man's wrinkled hand landed on hers as he gave her a couple of pats. 'I struck this one myself.'

Felicity was back with the roses in a vase in under a minute. She put them on his desk, desperately hoping he was allergic to them, but he didn't shift his attention from the computer, squinting at it instead as he clicked around different views to assess the X-ray on the screen.

'This radius looks good,' he declared, finally looking at her over the tops of his glasses, and it hit her again how they loaned him that extra dollop of sexy.

It wasn't a thought she welcomed. How could she have the hots for someone who didn't have a clue about connecting with his patients? Who she wasn't even sure she *liked* any more.

Because you've seen the other side...

Felicity hated it when the voice in her head was right. She had seen a very different side to Callum. One who had been competent and *compassionate* as well as chatty and flirty.

She'd liked that guy. *A lot.*

And compassion was always going to trump competence and looking great in glasses.

'It's healed very nicely.' His gaze returned to the screen. 'Can you take the plaster off then send her in to me?'

Aye, aye, sir. 'Certainly, Dr Hollingsworth.'

He looked up abruptly, a frown between his brows. 'You don't have to call me that,' he said. 'Callum is fine.'

Felicity figured 'jerk' was even better but she wisely held her tongue.

'Looks like we're going to both get an early mark,' he said, glancing at his watch, clearly pleased with himself.

Felicity's blood pressure shot up a notch or two. She didn't want a damn early mark. She wanted her patients to feel like they were more than a body part or some medical problem to cure or treat.

'I'll just see to Pauline.'

Felicity hit the waiting area with a full head of steam and a bunch of uncharitable thoughts. 'Hey, Pauline, you can come through now,' she said, forcing herself to smile so she wouldn't scare any of the waiting patients.

Pauline had slipped on the wet tiles around her pool and put her arm out to break her fall, snapping her radius instead. She was a few years older than Felicity but with three little kids she was a regular at the practice.

Felicity led her into the treatment room and Pauline sat on the central table over which hung a large, adjustable operating theatre light. It could be moved higher and lower and angled any which way required when suturing or other minor procedures were performed.

'You ready for this?' Felicity asked as she applied her face mask, grateful for her glasses being a little more glamorous eye protection than the ugly, clunky plastic goggles that the practice supplied. Cutting through plaster kicked up a lot of dust and fibres.

'I am so ready for this, Flick. Those kids of mine have sensed I'm weak and have been running riot these last six weeks. I can't wait to show them Mummy's back.'

Felicity laughed. 'All righty, then. It looks scary and it's going to be loud, okay?'

She turned it on to demonstrate. The oscillating saw with its round blade whined as loudly as any handyman's saw. She turned it off. 'The blade vibrates, it doesn't cut. If it comes into contact with your skin it can't hurt you. But it won't, I promise. Once I get down to the last layer I'll switch to plaster spreaders and some kick-arse scissors.'

'Yep. Cool.' Pauline nodded vigorously. 'Let's do it.'

It took fifteen minutes to remove the cast. Using the

loud saw was actually quite therapeutic. By the time she'd sent Pauline on her way to Callum, Felicity wasn't feeling anywhere near as annoyed as she had been.

She did, however, get some dust or fibre in her right eye, which became more and more irritating as she cleaned up the treatment room. She ambled over to the mirror hanging behind the door to see if there was anything obvious. Her eye was red from her rubbing it but there was nothing apparent in it.

Damn. She'd get a lecture from Bill for sure about wearing the correct safety equipment and she'd only have herself to blame. She'd always considered her own glasses as good eye protection—for plaster removal anyway—and now she was going to have to revise that opinion.

The irritation grew worse and out of desperation she grabbed a handful of plastic saline ampoules, twisted off their tops and moved to the sink. She leaned her head over and turned it on the side, her right eye down and bent her knees to bring her closer to the porcelain so she wouldn't make a mess.

It was an awkward position but at least the saline ran straight into the sink as she gently trickled ampoule after ampoule into her eye.

'What on earth are you doing?'

Felicity's pulse leapt both at the unexpected interruption and who it belonged to. Not exactly the most elegant position to be found in, especially as she already felt like an idiot for being in this situation. Her earlier crankiness returned. 'What does it look like?'

'You got something in your eye?' His voice grew nearer and she could see him approach in her peripheral vision, coming to a halt, his hands on his hips as he watched her, her eyes about level with his fly.

She tried valiantly not to go back to that night again but failed.

'Give the man a cigar.'

'Is this from removing the plaster?'

'Yes.'

He held out his hand for the remaining ampoules. 'Let me help.'

'I'm fine. You've got your early mark, go home.'

She may have liquid in one eye and a side view from the other but she didn't need to see his glare—she felt it all the way down to her toes.

'Are you angry at me for some reason? Do you have something against efficiency? Or is this some self-loathing guilt trip of yours because of what happened on the train, which is suddenly now wrong and somehow my fault? Because if we've got a problem then I really wish you'd just come out and say it.'

Felicity glared right back, which was difficult considering what she was doing. Yes, she was angry but it had absolutely nothing to do with the train or any kind of guilt trip. Hindsight was always twenty-twenty but she could never hate herself over that night.

This was purely about today. Unfortunately it wasn't her place to chastise the new doctor about the way he practised. Or any doctor for that matter. There were protocols and formal procedures in place for those kinds of things.

Not that she'd ever had any cause.

If Dr Dawson asked her how Callum was going she'd say he was diligent and efficient. But if there were complaints from the patients, he was on his own.

'No problem,' she muttered. She could bite her tongue over this. She *would*. If it killed her. Because she'd be damned if she did a single thing to make him think she was playing some petulant game because she was embarrassed about what had happened between them.

'Good. Now let me look at your damn eye and see if there's anything obvious.'

'I already looked. Couldn't see anything.'

He folded his arms. 'So let me check now you've treated it.'

Felicity realised her recalcitrance wasn't doing her any favours. She could act like a two-year-old or take advantage of the professional help being offered like an adult. 'Fine,' she muttered, reaching for the paper towel dispenser nearby. He beat her to it, pulling off two sheets and passing them over as she righted herself.

'Thank you.' She injected a more conciliatory note into her voice as she dabbed at her wet face. He was offering to help. It wasn't his fault she was in this situation.

'Over here,' he said, moving to the centre of the room near the examination bed. He glanced at the overhead light. 'Where's the switch for this thing?'

Felicity tossed the paper towel on the bed and went up on tippy toes to reach one of the vertical handles. She pulled it down and located the switch. Light pooled around them. He squinted and moved so the back of his head blocked the light. The halo affect was disconcerting considering she'd been thinking of him as the devil incarnate most of the day.

'Okay,' he said, sliding his hands either side of her face. 'Let me look.'

The sizzle from his contact was also disconcerting. They were standing close. Too close. Her brain rejected the nearness while her body flowered beneath it. He wore the same aftershave as he had on the train and if she shut her eyes she could almost imagine them being gently rocked.

Felicity tried to pull away but he held on tight. 'It's better, much less gritty.'

He set his thumbs beneath her jaw and used them to angle her head. 'That's good,' he murmured, obviously ignoring her as he peered into her eyes. Or her *eye* anyway. Her pulse hammered madly at every pulse point, surely he could feel it beneath the pads of his thumbs?

He instructed her to look up then down then to both sides, which she did eagerly. Frankly she was pleased to look anywhere but right at his big handsome face in those beyond-sexy glasses. Being up this close and personal to Callum was a seriously crazy temptation.

It was madness and she reached for something to evoke a bit of sanity.

Think about Mr Dunnich.

But all she could think about was how good Callum smelled and she understood a little better why some women stayed with men who weren't good for them.

'Well… I can't see anything,' he announced.

The statement made her forget she was trying *not* to look at him as she did exactly that. *'Quelle surprise,'* she murmured, their gazes locking, his green one intense as his thumbs stroked along her jaw.

It was so damn good she swayed a little.

The sensible person inside her scrambled for a reason to pull away, for something, anything to break the spell he was weaving with the seductive stroke of those clever thumbs.

It was then that she noticed it.

'Your left pupil is misshapen.' There was an area where the black of the pupil appeared to have bled into the green of his iris. 'It's larger than the other one too.'

That did it. His hands slid off her face and he took a

step back. Felicity reached for the table to steady herself as her body mourned his abrupt withdrawal.

'Yes.'

'Is that genetic or from an injury?'

The brooding line had returned to his mouth and for a moment she thought he wasn't going to answer her. 'An injury.'

She quirked an eyebrow. A rusty fork maybe? 'Are you going to make me guess?'

It wasn't any of her business but it didn't stop her being curious as hell. It was obvious from his reaction that it had been serious.

'A cricket ball.'

Felicity's wince was spontaneous and heartfelt. She almost grabbed her own eye in sympathy. 'Ouch.'

'Yeah…' His fingers fiddled with the sheet on the examination table. 'It was a bit of a mess.'

'Define mess.'

She expected him to dismiss her query and leave, and if she wasn't very much mistaken he looked tempted to do just that. But then he shrugged. 'Fractured zygoma. Blown globe. Hyphema. Partial retinal detachment.'

Her wince increased. 'Holy cow! Who was bowling to you? Mitchell Johnson?'

His lips twitched into the grimmest semblance of a smile she'd ever seen. 'One of my mates used to bowl for the under-nineteen Australian side. He's still got it.'

Maybe this was what Callum had been referring to this morning when he'd been going on about being a Cal once upon a time. He was just as tense and shuttered. 'Do you have a sight deficit?'

If anything, the line of his mouth grew grimmer. 'I only have seventy percent vision in my left eye, hence these.' He pointed at his glasses.

Seventy percent. This morning she'd been sure something had happened to Callum to change him—something big—and now she was absolutely convinced. Was the 'life' and 'stuff' he'd talked about the injury to his eye?

Had it turned Cal into a Callum?

Great. A wounded guy. Appealing to her soft underbelly. She was hopeless with them. *This* was the guy from the train, not the one she'd seen today, and she was finding it hard to reconcile the two.

'Is the mydriasis permanent?'

He grimaced. 'It's a work in progress. It's constricted quite a bit since the injury but the specialist thinks after all this time it's about as good as it'll get, and unfortunately I concur.'

'How long ago did it happen?'

'Two and a half years.'

Felicity did a quick calculation in her head. So the accident had happened six months before he'd commenced his GP training. It had probably taken that long for his eye to recover sufficiently to be useful.

Which begged the question, had it always been his plan to train to become a GP? Or had his injury caused him to change career path?

She had a feeling that was very much the case.

'So I take it being a GP hadn't been your grand plan?'

His lips twisted and his self-deprecating laugh was harsh, grating in the silence of the room. 'No.'

Felicity marvelled that such a little word could hold so much misery. This accident had obviously gutted him.

'What was your specialty before you did your GP training?'

He dropped his gaze to the sheet again. 'I was a surgeon.'

Ah. Well, now. His concentration on body parts and medical problems rather than the patient as an individual suddenly made sense. Felicity had spent some time in the operating theatres when she'd been training in Adelaide. She'd quickly come to realise she would never make a scrub nurse. Impersonalising patients and the lack of any real contact with them had driven her nutty.

She hadn't wanted to work in a place where patients were known by their operative site. The leg in Theatre Two, the appendix in Theatre Five or the transplant in Theatre Nine.

Patients had names and she liked to use them.

'What kind of surgeon?'

'Vascular.'

Felicity suppressed the urge to whistle. Impressive. She could see him all scrubbed up, making precise, efficient movements, working his way through his list, conscious of his next patient waiting. 'Did your sight issues interfere with that?'

'Oh, yes.' His tone was harsh with a bitter end note. 'My depth of field and visual acuity in the left eye were shot. A lot of the work I did was microsurgery and…' he glanced up, his gaze locking with hers '…I didn't trust myself.'

The emotions brimming in his eyes belied the hard set of his face and punched Felicity in the gut. 'But surely with time—'

His short, sharp laugh cut her off. 'They'll only give me a conditional driver's licence, they're not going to let me be in charge of a scalpel.' He shoved a hand through his hair, looked away, looked back again. 'It has improved, but not enough. Not to be a surgeon. I'm not prepared to take that kind of risk with somebody's life.'

And there was the compassion. Callum had obviously had the rug pulled right out from under him but he was a doctor first and foremost and doing no harm was the code they lived by.

It was honourable but obviously not easy. This was the man from the train. The one who had been great with Jock and Thelma and the other group of oldies. The one who had laughed and flirted with her. The one who had looked into her eyes in her compartment and *connected* with her.

She gazed at him, trying to convey her understanding. 'I'm sorry. That must have been very hard for you.'

And she *was* sorry. He may have annoyed her today but at least now she understood him a little better. Would maybe even cut him a little slack. He'd given up a lot. Having your hopes and dreams quashed wasn't easy. She knew that better than anyone.

He shook his head dismissively. 'It is what it is.'

She took a step towards him, put her hand on top of his. 'Yeah. Doesn't make it suck any less, does it?'

His gaze flicked to their hands before returning to her face and she caught a glimpse of a guy who was adrift before he shut it down and slid his hand away, tucking it in his pocket as he moved back a few paces.

'Anyway,' he said, his eyes not quite meeting hers, 'maybe take home some liquid tears to settle any residual irritation.'

Felicity didn't need him to tell her that but the way he was judging the distance to the door she figured it was just a segue to him leaving. The thought needled but she had no idea why.

'Yep, great, thanks for your help.' She turned and headed for the sink, flipping on the water and washing her hands because the other ninety-nine times today hadn't been enough.

But it gave her something to do and the opportunity for him to slip away, which he took with both hands.

CHAPTER SEVEN

CALLUM WAS LOOKING forward to the home visits even if
Felicity had seemed less than impressed by his request to
accompany her. She hadn't said no but she had queried the
necessity of it. He felt it was essential to know about this
important service, especially if he was ever going to be
called out to one of the patients during his one weekend
in three on-call days.

She hadn't had a comeback for that but her stony profile as she drove them to their first appointment spoke
volumes.

He wasn't sure what was going on with her. Despite her
protestations on Monday that they didn't have a problem
and the obvious empathy in her eyes when he'd told her
about the accident, the last couple of days had still been
awkward.

Sure, she was polite and efficient. But he wouldn't exactly say she was knocking herself out to be friendly. Not
like she was with her patients.

Not like she'd been that day on the train.

Was that where Felicity's awkwardness was springing
from? The train? Did she regret what had happened? Did
she resent that seeing him every day she couldn't put it away
in some neat little box somewhere? Or was she worried
that he'd kiss and tell and spoil her St Felicity reputation?

Because there was one thing he'd learned in his few short days at the practice—Felicity could do no wrong.

Everyone loved Felicity.

Their version of her anyway because she was a very different Felicity from the one he'd met on the train. Sure, she was as friendly and easygoing with the patients as she had been with their travelling companions, but here, in Vickers Hill, she was very definitely *Flick*. The small-town girl, the friendly nurse, everyone's mate.

She knew who everyone was and who they were related to. She knew where everything was found, everything anyone had been treated for in the last four years and, it seemed, everyone's birthdays. As well as having practically every phone number in the town memorised.

She *was* a freaking saint.

And he'd gone and thoroughly debauched her.

He didn't think the town—aside from one or two busybodies—cared what their saint did in her private time but what if she thought they did? They hadn't talked about what had happened between them, not since discovering they would be working together, so maybe it was time they did.

He glanced at her profile. Her forehead was crinkled into a frown, her lips pursed. *Maybe not.* Safer to stick to work-related topics and hope she eventually relaxed when she realised he wasn't here to make her life difficult.

'So,' he said, his sunglasses in place as the harsh October sun cut through the glass of the windscreen, 'the purpose of the home visits is?'

'A federally funded initiative to keep older and less able patients in their homes and in the community and out of care.'

She parroted the facts as if he'd pushed a button on her somewhere that read *Press here for information*. She didn't shift her gaze off the road. Didn't glance at him for a second.

Callum ploughed on, bloody-minded now. 'What kind of things do you do when you're with a patient? Are there specific things or is it just a general social call?'

Her fingers wrapped, unwrapped and wrapped around the steering wheel again. 'A lot of different things. I deal with any specific medical issues of the day but mostly patients go into the practice if they have anything acute. I do blood-pressure and blood-sugar checks as well as full yearly health checks when they come due. I make sure their prescriptions and referrals are up to date. I do a lot of ordering.'

'Ordering?'

She at least nodded this time. 'Products. Medical supplies. Incontinence products, stoma bags, peritoneal dialysis supplies, test strips as well as equipment like feeding pumps, shower chairs or Zimmer frames.'

'Sounds busy.'

'It's not all tea and scones,' she said.

He could have cut the derision with a knife. He was about to call her on it when Felicity engaged her blinker and said, 'First cab off the rank is Mr Morley.'

Callum looked out the window to see an old-fashioned, low-set cottage that could do with some TLC. She undid her seat belt then looked at him for the first time since he'd sat in the car.

'These people know me. They trust me. They're often wary of strangers and prefer talking to a nurse about their issues over a doctor. They might be suspicious of you. Just try to…'

Callum thought she was going to say 'not screw it up' but she continued, 'Stay in the background, okay?'

She didn't give him time to reply, reaching for the handle and stepping out of the vehicle.

Her faith in him was heartening.

What followed was an intense five hours. Callum saw the gamut of small-town life all in one afternoon as St Felicity ministered to her flock. It wasn't the most efficient system he'd ever seen. Too much chatter and drinking of tea and eating of cake or whatever piece of home-made cooking was presented to them for his liking, but it appeared to be the ritual and with Felicity's advice ringing in his ears there was no way he was declining. He'd never eaten so well in his life.

He was going to have to do some serious working out when he got back to Sydney.

He followed Felicity's lead after earning her glare when he'd declined something at their second stop. It just wasn't done, apparently. And she was right, the patients were leery of him to start with so if eating food that was offered at all their dozen stops helped with the warming-up process then when in Rome...

That all changed when they got to their last call—Meryl's house. She didn't appear to have a last name or require any kind of formal address as Felicity's other patients had.

Just Meryl, apparently.

Her house was a small cottage with a deep bull-nosed veranda. Dreamcatchers and wind chimes of all types and sizes hung from the guttering. The pungent spice of incense prickled Callum's nose and a small shrine with a Buddha and a variety of candles and flowers was set up in one corner of the living room.

Meryl took to him right away. She was sitting in a big stuffed recliner and was possibly the most wrinkled person Callum had ever met. But there was a strength and agility to her movements that made him think she was probably younger than she appeared.

He stuck out his hand when Felicity introduced them. Her hand was soft but her grip was firm as she pulled him nearer, forcing him to lean in closer.

'Cal,' she murmured, immediately shortening his name in a husky voice that sounded like the product of a pack-a-day habit. She looked straight into his eyes, taking her time to study him. 'You have an unhappy aura,' she finally declared, releasing his hand.

Callum glanced at Felicity for an interpretation in case there was one other than the obvious—Meryl was a little nutty. She shot him the most faux innocent eyebrow-lift he'd ever seen in his life. He should have known that someone who lived in a house guarded by dream catchers was going to be a little…alternative.

'Meryl reads auras,' she said, a small smile playing on her lips.

That little knowing smile drew attention to her mouth and it was just about the sexiest damn thing he'd ever seen. All week he'd been trying not to think about that mouth and where she'd put it on his body. Her attitude towards him had helped. But now she was finally pulling the stick out of her butt it was impossible not to go there again.

Impossible not to want to familiarise himself with it again and kiss the smile right off that sexy mouth.

'Hmm, it's looking a little happier now,' Meryl mused.

Callum blinked at the running commentary on the state of his aura, pulling his gaze from Felicity's. He gave himself a mental shake. The last thing he wanted Meryl proclaiming was his aura's massive erection.

'Sit down here, Cal,' Meryl said, patting an old vinyl chair beside her.

Callum would rather sit outside in the car but there was

no way he could get out of this without looking rude. The normal rules of doctoring just didn't apply in the community, certainly not in a house that could have belonged in Oz.

He glanced at Felicity, who was obviously finding the situation highly amusing.

'What colour's Felicity's aura?' he asked, turning to give all his attention to Meryl. Thankfully, Felicity was on his right so he could see her smile slowly deflating.

Although he was sure she had no cause to worry. The saintly Felicity's aura was no doubt rainbowesque and probably smelled like strawberries and candy canes.

'It'll be the same as usual,' Meryl said, flicking her gaze to Felicity. Callum was inordinately pleased when the older woman raised an eyebrow. 'Or maybe not… It's *usually* so balanced but it does look a little…ruffled today.'

Callum smiled as the tables were turned and Felicity frowned and put a hand to her belly. Meryl's gaze cut back to him and he pressed his lips together so she couldn't see him gloating, although there was something all-seeing about Meryl that couldn't be easily dismissed.

Her eyes narrowed speculatively. 'You're staying at Luci's place, right?'

Callum nodded, feeling on solid ground with standard questioning. 'Yes. And she's staying at my place in Sydney.'

'And how long are you staying in Vickers Hill?'

'I'm here for eight weeks.'

'No.' Meryl shook her head slowly as her gaze darted all around his head before she peered into his eyes. It was more thorough than any of the dozens of specialists with their fancy high-powered microscopes had ever managed.

Frankly, it put an itch up his spine.

'You'll be here for much longer than that.'

Callum broke the eye contact with difficulty. No. *He was going back to Sydney*. To his harbourside apartment and his job that started in the New year. Vickers Hill was just a pit stop. A place for some clear air.

He glanced at Felicity, who wasn't looking so sure of herself now either. She appeared ready to deny it if he didn't.

'I can assure you,' Callum said, dredging up his most positive smile for Meryl. It wasn't one he'd used a lot these last two years and it didn't feel right on his face. 'I'm only here short term.'

Meryl just smiled and patted his hand. 'You'll see. It's okay,' she assured him. 'It'll work out. You were meant to come here. It's your destiny. It's in your aura.'

Callum didn't know what to say to that. Clearly Meryl wasn't about to change her mind and what did it matter what some crazy old lady on an incense high who read auras said?

He was in charge of his destiny.

'Right, well.' Felicity clapped her hands together. 'Let's get your blood pressure checked, Meryl.'

Callum vacated the seat, grateful to her for rescuing him from any more talk of auras and destinies and staying in Vickers Hill.

He could have kissed her.

He *really* could have kissed her.

Callum was looking out the passenger window of Felicity's car when she rolled to a stop in front of Luci's house. He still wasn't used to living in a place that was so country kitsch. It was a turn-of-the-century stone cottage with a chimney and a wraparound porch along which grew a thick bushy passionfruit vine laden with fruit. The entire garden was beautifully manicured and a riot of colour that reflected the froufrou decor of the interior.

Lots of lace at the dinky little windows and white shabby chic furniture complemented the exposed oak ceiling beams and the oak kitchen tops. It was a far cry from his sleek, minimalist apartment dominated by huge unadorned windows from which to admire the stunning water view.

Callum glanced at Felicity, who was staring straight ahead at some point on the road. They hadn't talked at all from Meryl's to here. He figured they were both lost for words. 'So… Meryl…she's a little…colourful?'

Her head snapped around to glare at him. 'And what's wrong with that?' she demanded. 'We can't all be hip, cool Sydneysiders.'

Callum blinked at her unexpected vehemence, holding up his hands to indicate his surrender. Her chest rose and fell markedly. 'Hey,' he murmured. 'It wasn't a criticism.'

She glared at him for a beat or two before returning her attention to the road and huffing out, 'Sorry.'

Callum sighed. Okay. *Enough.* Enough of this. Something was obviously bothering her and he couldn't ignore it any longer, hoping she'd snap out of it. He was going to have to mention the elephant in the room.

Or the car, as it turned out.

'You don't have to worry about me saying anything to anyone about what happened between us.'

That earned him another short, sharp, slightly askance glance. 'I didn't for a minute think I had to.'

Callum raised both his eyebrows. Okay…so what was this all about? It couldn't be his work. He'd been his usual competent, efficient self. He may not be fully resigned to his new career but he knew he did good work. The same way he always knew he did good surgery.

He was a Hollingsworth—they always excelled at what they did.

'Okay. Well…sorry. It's just…you've been angry at me all week and I thought… I just needed to reassure you, that's all. If that's what you're worried about.' He thought maybe, deep down, she was, she just didn't want to acknowledge it so it was worth saying again. 'I don't kiss and tell and what happened that night is between us only.'

'Good.' She glanced away, fixing her gaze on the steering wheel. 'Thank you.'

It wasn't exactly the immediate easing of tensions that he'd hoped it would be. Hell, if she was strung any tighter she'd explode. 'Only we haven't really talked about how we're going to handle it. You know, now that we're working so closely together, and maybe we should because I feel like we've got off on the wrong foot.'

Considering they hadn't put a foot wrong when they'd just been two strangers on a train, their missteps since had been ridiculous.

'I was planning on ignoring it.'

Callum surprised himself with a laugh at her candour. He didn't think she'd meant it to be funny—more like a morose statement of fact—but it was. 'Yeah. So was I.' But neither of them were doing a very good job. 'And then…'

He stopped himself before the words he'd been about to say slipped out of his mouth. They clearly hadn't been through his rigorous filter. It must be the after-effects of the incense. Or maybe the very present effects of her perfume. It was the one she'd been wearing *that* night. He hadn't really noticed it at the time but right now it was achingly familiar, taking him right back.

She turned her head and their eyes met. 'And then, what?'

His gaze dropped to her mouth. He should leave it alone.

Tell her it didn't matter. Walk it back. But the air in the car grew heavier as the space between them seemed to shrink and the urge to pull her ponytail loose slithered thick and dangerous through a head teeming with very bad ideas.

'And then you said Meryl reads auras and had this little half-smile on your mouth like you just knew it was going to throw me, and it was so damn sexy all I could think about was kissing you.'

'Oh. Right,' she muttered, her gaze falling to *his* mouth now. 'That doesn't really help.'

Callum shook his head and somehow, when he stopped, it had inched closer to hers. 'Not even a bit?' Her perfume filled his head and he could see the movement of her throat as she swallowed.

'I think what happened on the train should stay on the train,' she said, her voice husky.

'I agree.' And he did. Or he had, anyway.

'I mean it was…lovely but—'

'Lovely?' His gaze locked with hers as he quirked an eyebrow at the insipid description. 'Why don't you go all the way and tell me it was *nice*?'

She shrugged. 'It was that too.'

But that smile was there on her mouth again and heat flared in his belly. He gave a playful groan. 'You make it sound like we held hands and sang "Kumbayah" all night.'

She laughed, that great big sound she'd used so frequently when they'd been on the train but he hadn't heard since. 'How would you describe it?'

It was a leading question and they were playing with fire. He wondered if she understood how slim the thread was to which he was clinging. But she was looking at his mouth once more and he was pretty sure she'd angled her head closer because he hadn't moved a muscle this time.

In fact, he was barely even breathing.

'Hot,' he muttered, his voice thick in his throat, his gaze dropping to her mouth. 'Sexy. Mind-blowing.'

'Erotic,' she whispered, her pupils dilated.

Callum nodded as he lifted his hand and pushed back an escaped honey-blonde tendril. His fingers whispered across her cheek and jaw as they withdrew. '*So* erotic.'

'Oh, God,' she moaned, her voice low and needy like it'd been when he'd first slipped inside her. Her hands went to the lapels of his jacket and tugged.

Callum didn't need any more encouragement, his mouth meeting hers like they'd never been apart. Like they'd picked up where they'd left off at hot, sexy and mind-blowing, heading straight for erotic.

She smelled good and tasted better and he slid his palms onto her face, holding her steady so he could kiss her harder, deeper, wetter. He ran his tongue over her bottom lip and when she moaned and moved closer still, he thrust it fully into her mouth, his erection surging as her tongue stroked against his.

His heart pounded in his chest, his pulse whooshed like Niagara Falls through his ears and his breathing went from husky to laboured as his whole world narrowed down to just her. Her mouth. Her kisses. Her moans and sighs. The desperate grip of her hands on his lapels.

Just Felicity. In his arms. Again.

And God alone knew where it would have ended up had there not been a firm rap on Felicity's window that scared the life out of him and her also, if the way she grabbed at her chest as they broke apart was any indication.

He was expecting to see half the town with pitchforks out to save St Felicity from his clutches but it was just Mrs Smith from across the road, who'd introduced herself the day he'd moved in and had given him a friendly wave every day since.

She didn't look so friendly now.

'My God,' Felicity muttered under her breath. 'I think I just had a heart attack.'

Callum knew how she felt. What the hell was he doing? He was too old to be necking in cars, for crying out loud. They both were.

Certainly too damn old to be sprung doing it.

'Mrs Smith,' Felicity said, as she wound her window down.

Callum admired the note of cheerful innocence in her voice like nothing was going on here. Like maybe his neighbour hadn't noticed she'd had her tongue down his throat. But the delicious vibrato in her voice betrayed how very much *had* been going on.

'Flick Mitchell,' Mrs Smith said, a scandalised note raising her voice to a higher register. 'Dr Hollingsworth.' Her tone for him was rather more accusatory. 'This is hardly appropriate behaviour in broad daylight. I don't need to tell you that Vickers Hill prides itself on public decorum. Just because your parents don't live here any more doesn't mean you should let your behavioural standards slide. It's important to always act like a lady, Flick. I know your mother taught you that.'

It was on the tip of Callum's tongue to tell the old biddy he was more interested in Felicity being a *woman* than a lady but Felicity was nodding her head and saying, 'You're right, Mrs Smith, I'm terribly sorry. You have my assurance it won't happen again.'

Mrs Smith peered down her nose at him. 'And what about your assurances, young man?'

It had been a long time since anyone had called Callum *young man*. He was just getting used to Bill calling him *son*.

Anyone would think they'd been accosted by an angry

father with a shotgun instead of a little old lady from across the street, and a dozen different responses flipped through his head. They all died on his lips as Felicity turned pleading eyes on him.

Hell. He was a sucker for that look. Who was he kidding? He was a sucker for any way her face looked. He gritted his teeth and put his hand on his heart. 'I promise there will be no more public displays of affection between Felicity and myself, Mrs Smith.'

Because next time he'd make damn sure he dragged her inside first. Away from prying eyes.

She nodded, satisfied, but wasn't finished with them yet. 'I guess you'll be going home now,' she said pointedly.

'Yes.' Felicity nodded. 'Callum was just leaving.'

Callum didn't want to leave. He very much wanted to finish off the kiss that had been so rudely interrupted. But it was obvious the mood was in tatters and Mrs Smith wasn't going anywhere until *he* did. He glanced at Felicity, who lifted one shoulder in a slight *it's-not-worth-the-aggro* shrug.

'Right,' he said, reaching for the handle. 'I'll…see you tomorrow.'

She nodded but refused to meet his eyes. The last thing he saw as she drove away, apart from Mrs Smith's evil eye, was Felicity's stony profile.

They were back to square one. Worse than square one. If the kiss had been one step forward, this was definitely two steps back.

'Oh, God,' Felicity groaned into her mobile phone a few hours later. 'This is *so* bad. I'm never going to live this down. Why did it have to be Mrs Smith? Now the whole town's going to know. They'll have us married off by the end of next week.'

Luci's laughter floated down the line to her. She'd rung half an hour ago ostensibly to check on the house but also to grill Felicity over a little rumour she'd heard, courtesy of her mother. Poor Luci hadn't been able to get a word in edgewise over Felicity's self-flagellation.

'I say screw the town and just go for it.'

Felicity blinked. 'Well, look at you. Only a short time in the big city and you're completely corrupted. Mrs Smith would be horrified.'

Another laugh. 'Hey, haven't you been telling me to go for it? To move, to have an adventure, to get out of my rut? The same can be said for you, missy. It's been four years since Ned. You deserve a rampant public display of affection and you're twenty-eight years old, for God's sake. Unless…he is a good kisser, right?'

Good? The man was *sublime*. He must have been standing at the top of the queue when they'd been handing out the kissing gene. Ned had been a great kisser too so her bar was set very high. 'Ooh, yeah.'

'Oh, *really*? That good, huh?'

'Well…a girl doesn't like to kiss and tell.'

Which was a good reminder that Callum had said the same thing and there wasn't a lot she could tell Luci without telling her everything and she wasn't ready to do that yet. She didn't want to make it a thing.

The man was here for eight weeks—not someone to blow her precious reputation on. Plus his bedside manner kinda sucked and she was confused as to why something that should have been a major turn-off didn't seem to matter where her body was concerned.

'Anyway, I've been gabbing on and on about me and I haven't even asked you what's going on with you. How's Sydney? Tell me about Seb.'

'Oh, I hardly ever see him,' Luci dismissed airily.

Felicity had known her friend long enough to hear the tell-tale waver in her voice, indicating she wasn't being entirely honest, but Luci ploughed on, talking about her course and Sydney and the weather and her work, and Felicity let her go on while her mind churned through bigger issues.

Like why the hell she'd let Callum kiss her in broad daylight. The fact that she'd actually initiated it by pulling on his lapels was something she chose not to focus on.

She'd been cranky that he'd invaded her space today. After three frustrating clinics on the run, every second of which she'd wanted to shake him for his efficiency over humanity approach, she'd needed some time out.

And then he'd made that comment about Meryl. Although, to be fair, Meryl had been called much worse things than colourful and Felicity's irritation had, in truth, been more about her blemished aura and Meryl's predictions.

Most of the town thought Meryl was certifiable but she'd been right too many times for Felicity to discount.

So why, if she'd been so damn cranky at him, had she kissed him? In broad daylight? Blemishing much more than her aura?

And how was Vickers Hill going to react?

CHAPTER EIGHT

By THE TIME Monday rocked around again Felicity was on her last nerve. Between the speculation that was running rife in Vickers Hill—phone calls from her mother, whispers at the supermarket, unsolicited advice from just about everybody—and enduring another afternoon clinic with Callum's same robotic approach, she was just about done cutting him slack.

If they hadn't kissed on Thursday and tripped the Vickers Hill grapevine into overdrive, she may well have bitten her tongue for longer—it wasn't her place to comment on how he did his job. But they had and Felicity was just about out of her be-nice-to-the-locum store.

It was ironic that everyone thought they were having wild monkey sex when all she wanted to do was strangle him with his stethoscope.

Yeah, the man could kiss. But he *sucked* at connecting with his patients.

It was the last straw when Callum asked her to 'Send in the bunions when you're ready' as she was opening the office door to show a patient out. Felicity's vision went a hot, hazy red as her brain exploded and practically leaked out her ears. She slapped the door shut with the palm of her hand and turned on a dime to glare at him.

'Mr Dunnich,' she said, shoving her hand on her hip.

He glanced up at her from his screen and she hated the way her heart did a funny little leap as he peered at her through those sexy, rimless frames.

'He's the bunions?'

'No,' she said, her voice register sitting squarely in the frosty zone. 'He's *Mr Dunnich*. That's his name. Or Alf if you're ever invited to be that familiar.' Felicity doubted he would be. 'He's the one whose wife insisted he bring you roses last week, remember?'

'Oh. Yes…'

He was eyeing her warily now. It was obvious he knew he'd done something wrong but equally obvious that he was clueless as to what.

'She had a stroke two years ago and now he's her full-time carer,' Felicity continued, her voice low from the rough edge of emotion that had welled out of nowhere in her chest. 'The roses give her so much pleasure and he knows it.' Her voice cracked and she didn't care how insane she sounded.

Mr Dunnich wasn't just bunions to her.

Callum stood, his forehead crinkling. 'Is there something wrong, Felicity?'

'The person who was just in here with the *hamstring* is called *Malcolm*. The person before that with the *carpal tunnel* is *Stefanie*.'

Pressure built in Felicity's chest as her desperation for him to understand mixed with the emotions she always felt when she was talking about her patients. She sucked in a breath and blew it noisily out of her mouth before she totally broke down and her message was lost amidst incoherent accusations and ugly snot crying.

'They all have names. We don't refer to our patients as their body parts around here. They're *people*, not medical conditions.'

'God…sorry.' He grimaced, pulling his glasses off and throwing them on the table. 'I'm still adjusting to a new mindset. It's a bad habit.'

'Well, break it,' she snapped. Felicity understood that a lot of surgeons had that mindset. But a lot didn't so it was a choice. A bad one.

His jaw clenched. If Felicity hadn't gone to the dark side she'd have recognised it as a sign to back off. But this had been brewing for a week and she was all-in now.

'Have there been complaints?' he demanded, hands on hips.

'No. Country people don't complain, Callum. They endure. But these are *my* people. They're going to be here long after you swan off back to Sydney and I'm not going to sit around and watch you treat them so impersonally because you're too…'

A thousand adjectives came to mind, pumping through her head as quickly as her blood pumped through her chest. Some glimmer of propriety did prevail, however. 'Too… *cavalier* to take a personal interest in them.'

His green eyes turned to flinty chips of jade. 'I would defy *anybody* to say I haven't given them the very best treatment. I've been thorough and efficient and effective and I *really* don't like your tone.'

'What? Your city surgical nurses don't call you out on your behaviour?' she demanded, keeping her voice low, aware there was a waiting room full of people outside and very thin walls.

'I think they have a little more respect for their colleagues.'

'Oh, really? Well, guess what? You have to earn respect out here. It's not just given to you like some damn golden halo from on high. It takes more than a pair of scrubs and

I *will* advocate for my patients whether you like it or not. I've been biting my tongue for a week now but no more.'

'This?' he said, shaking his head in obvious disbelief. '*This* is why you've been angry at me for a week?'

'What? A little too trivial for you?'

He shook his head at her, his mouth a flat line. 'Oh, well, please,' he said, his tone bitingly sarcastic, 'by all means do let me have it all. I'd hate you to pop a lung keeping it all in.'

Felicity wasn't sure about popping a lung but she sure as hell felt like she was about to blow a vessel in her brain as her blood pressure hit stroke levels. She stalked over to his desk and stabbed her finger at the woodgrain surface.

'It's not about efficiency. There's more to being a good family practice doctor than thoroughness. A GP role is about *connection* and forming long-term *relationships*. It's about *community* and earning trust so that people can and *will* tell you stuff that they'd never tell anyone else because you're their doctor and they're scared out of their brains about something. For Pete's sake.' She shook her head. 'Don't they teach you any of this in GP school? Or does the big hot-shot city surgeon not need to listen?'

'Of course,' he snapped. 'I'm just not…the touchy-feely type.'

'You don't *have* to be. But you can't be robotic about it either. You're just going through the motions at the moment, Callum. Ticking the boxes. Frankly, your bedside manner sucks.'

'Oh, no.' He shook his head vehemently. 'It damn well does not. My bedside manner is great. *All* my patients love me.'

'Well, I'm sure they do when you're talking to them post-op when they're high on drugs and whatever surgical miracle you've performed for them.'

'Oh, yeah?' he snorted. 'This from St Felicity.'

Felicity had no clue what he meant but she wasn't about to get distracted from her point.

'Seriously. Just think about it for a moment. How much *actual* time would you spend with each patient, not counting the hours you're cutting them open? An hour? Two? In general practice, if you stick around a place long enough you're going to see that person multiple times over many years for a variety of different things. You're going to be there with them through good and bad, thick and thin. You're going to tell them they're pregnant or miscarrying, or have cancer or are in remission. You're the person they're going to trust with their lives. The one they're going to break down in front of and who they're going to look at with eyes that are desperate for answers and cures you just don't have.'

Felicity's breath caught as her throat thickened. Damn it. She was getting emotional again. But this stuff meant something.

'They *have* to be more than the sum of their parts to you, Callum. *That's* what being a good GP is about. Forget what they taught you in surgical school. None of it is relevant here.'

Even as she said the words she realised that was the crux of the problem for him. This career move had been forced on him by his eye injury and clearly his heart wasn't in it. It was a fall-back position for him, not a calling. Not like it was for Bill and Angela and Meera.

All the rage and anger that had buoyed her to say what she'd been itching to say flowed out of her, leaving her curiously deflated. 'Why are you even here, Callum? Is it really what you want? You don't seem to be very invested in the job and you're a long way from home so I'm wondering if maybe you're just running away?'

'No.' He shook his head. 'I'm not running away. I just needed a…circuit-breaker. A fresh start. Some clear air for a while. But I am going back. I *will* go back.'

Felicity studied his face. It was so grim and determined it spoke volumes. 'To prove yourself?'

He didn't admit it but she could tell by the tightening of his face that she'd hit close to the bone. 'You have a problem with that?' he asked, his tone defensive.

'No.' And she didn't. But it was fair warning. The man was good-looking. A great kisser. And knew how to melt her into a puddle in bed. It would be easy to get swept away by that and forget he didn't want this job or small-town life.

'But why become a GP? You could have retrained in another surgical speciality. Something that doesn't require a lot of precision. Orthopaedics. All hammer and chisels and power tools. Lot of grunt. Very manly.'

He laughed and it helped to ease the tension. Felicity was relieved. She'd been pretty harsh on him.

'Even that involves a degree of microsurgery and I just can't trust myself.'

'So become a physician. Plenty of specialties to sink your teeth into.'

He shook his head again. His frame was erect, his head was held high, but there was defeat in his gaze. 'I can't work in a hospital. There's that smell, you know?' He looked at her earnestly and Felicity nodded. She knew that smell. Like it had been scrubbed with disinfectant only seconds before you walked into it.

'I love that smell. It's been running through my veins since I was a kid. It's addictive. And it's associated with surgery to me. Having to set foot in a hospital every day for work and not go to the operating theatres would be torture. A constant reminder of everything I've lost. That

I'm living out the consolation prize instead of the dream. I can't do it.'

Part of Felicity wanted to tell him to harden up. That life wasn't fair. That it threw you curveballs. But she figured he'd learned that lesson plenty over the last couple of years.

'So you chose general practice.'

'Yes.'

And here they were.

'So *choose* it,' she said.

'Okay, fine,' he huffed, sitting in his chair, rubbing a hand over his eyes. 'What do you suggest to improve my skills? Teach me.'

She narrowed her eyes at him. 'Seriously? It's not rocket science.'

'Seriously. I mean it.' He nodded. 'Give me some pointers and I'll employ them for the remaining patients today. You can critique me at the end. Give me a score out of ten.'

Felicity suppressed an eye-roll. Just like a man to make it competitive. But she had to give him chops for taking what she'd said on board. Especially given its level of frankness. She'd known some surgeons in Adelaide who would have had apoplexy if she'd spoken to them the way she'd spoken to Callum.

The fact he seemed keen to improve was also encouraging.

'Fine.' A stray piece of her fringe fell over her right eye and she absently blew it away as she pulled up a chair. 'How about you start by calling them by their names? And *thinking* about them that way too. As *people* first. And instead of focusing on their problem and trying to solve it as soon as possible, then calling out "Next", like you've set a mental timer, maybe you could try a little conversation. Talk to *them* when they're here, *not* your computer screen, and about something other than whatever it is they're coming in for. The weather. The weekend markets. Their kids. Their grandkids. Their mothers-in-law. Harvest season. Mulberry pies. Anything.'

'Conversation, huh?'

Felicity heard the amusement in his voice and couldn't stop the smile that curved her mouth. She had first-hand experience of how good he was at conversation. 'Yeah. It's okay, we have time. Pretend you're on a train.'

He smiled too and she breathed in sharply as his whole damn face came alive. For a moment they just sat there smiling at each other, Felicity's hopes and *heart* floating foolishly outside her body somewhere. 'Who knows, you might even discover you *like* being a GP.'

His smile faded a little, a good reminder that Callum was only temporary and not to get carried away. Not to let herself become some kind of consolation prize—his words.

'How about we start with Mr Dunnich?' she said, forcing her legs to stand and dropping her gaze to her trousers, where she brushed at invisible creases.

'The bunions?'

Her head snapped up to find him grinning big and wide. The kind of grin that made Felicity wish she was still seated.

'And the roses,' he added quickly. 'And the wife with a stroke who he cares for. And adores.'

Felicity refused to laugh but she had to fight the urge as she nodded in acknowledgement. 'Correct.'

Callum felt suitably chastised as he waited for Felicity to get Mr Dunnich. If he'd known this was what had been bugging her all week he'd have had it out with her sooner. On Friday and again today he'd figured it was the kiss.

It was almost a relief it had been about this.

The fact the entire town thought he'd besmirched St

Flick was way beyond his scope of practise but the way he interacted with patients he could fix. The practical experience he'd had during his training had been very different from Vickers Hill. Most of his practical had been at the busy north shore practice he was heading to in the New Year. Scheduling was always tight and that's how he'd learned.

Get them in, get them out. *Next.*

He'd even been applauded for it.

The fact that it wasn't the way they did things here hadn't even occurred to him and he was grateful to Felicity for finally mentioning it.

Or perhaps cracking up about it was a better descriptor.

She'd asked him if a city nurse had ever called him on his behaviour and the truth was a nurse probably wouldn't have dared talk to him like that in one of his theatres. He'd been the surgeon and he'd ruled the kingdom. Not only that, he came from a long line of surgeons. The Hollingsworth name was well known in Sydney. And he'd been the heir apparent for a long time.

God. He sounded like an arrogant douche.

The door opened, pulling Callum out of his reverie. 'Ah, Mr Dunnich.' Callum half rose. 'Come and sit down.'

Mr Dunnich approached more tentatively than he had last time and Callum cringed internally. He'd been too busy at the computer to acknowledge Mr Dunnich last time until he had sat down and it was clear the man was wary of him.

Callum smiled and indicated a chair for his patient. 'How are you?' he asked as the old man sat.

Mr Dunnich shot a glance at Felicity, as if he was waiting for an interpretation. 'Fine, thank you, Doctor.'

Callum grimaced at how formal Mr Dunnich was this time. No *Doc* today. The fact that he was responsible for it didn't sit well at all. He obviously had some ground to make up and he was determined to do just that.

'How are the toes going?'

Mr Dunnich bent to take off his shoes. 'Much better,' he said. 'Those pills worked a treat.'

Callum performed the same examination on the toes as he'd done last week but this time, aware of Felicity's scrutiny, he commented on his patient's neatly pressed trousers. 'That's a perfect crease you've got going on there.'

'Oh…yes.'

'Do you get them dry-cleaned or iron them yourself?'

'Do it myself,' he said, pride strengthening his voice. 'Twenty years in the army when I was a lad. Some things you never forget.'

'Really? I might have to drop mine around too.'

Mr Dunnich glanced at him awkwardly and Callum grinned and winked. He was relieved when the old man and then Felicity laughed. 'Me too,' she added.

'Not on your life.' Mr Dunnich chortled.

'Please thank your wife for the roses last week. I took them home and they were perfect in Luci's house.'

'Oh, yes,' Mr Dunnich agreed cheekily. 'Luci's house was made for roses.'

'Does your wife have a favourite?' Callum enquired as he indicated Mr Dunnich should put his shoes back on.

'No. No one in particular but she does love the climbing roses best. Every morning without fail we have a cuppa out on the front porch so she can look out over the arbour where they all climb. Gets some Vitamin D too before the day becomes too hot. Except the last few days. Lizzy hasn't really wanted to.'

Callum frowned. 'Is she sick?'

'No, I don't think so,' he said, straightening now his shoes were back on. 'Communication has been hard since the stroke but I've got pretty good at understanding her. She says not. I think she's just kinda down, you know? I'm a little bit worried about her, to be honest. She's never been that kind of person.'

'That's no good.' Callum's medical antennae pinged. It had been such a long time since they'd done that. It was nice to have them back.

He flicked a glance at Felicity. Her brows were drawn together in a concerned V. Maybe Mrs Dunnich needed to be checked on. 'How about we add Lizzy to Felicity's home visit list on Thursday? Just to give her a once-over, put your mind at ease?'

Mr Dunnich brightened. 'Yeah?'

'Absolutely, Mr Dunnich,' Felicity confirmed. 'We're here to support you and Lizzy.'

'Okay, then, thank you. I'd really appreciate it. I'll make you some of Lizzy's rhubarb tartlets. I've got rhubarb coming out of my ears.'

'That sounds fabulous,' she agreed, and Callum wondered where the hell she put all that food if every Thursday was the same as the last one. Her figure was about as perfect as it got without a single sign of twelve different carbohydrate-laden snacks.

'Right, then, it's settled,' Callum said. 'Now, I think I'll write you up for a month's worth of the medication for your bunions and let's assess again after that. Sooner, of course, if the pain worsens. Does that sound like a plan?'

'Sure does, Doc.'

Callum couldn't deny how satisfying that *Doc* was as he turned to the computer and ordered the medication, the script printing out quickly. He pulled it out of the printer and handed it to Mr Dunnich, standing at the same time.

'See you next month, Mr Dunnich,' Callum said. 'And Felicity will see you on Thursday.'

'Call me Alf,' he said, also rising and holding out his hand, which Callum took. 'I'll make sure to have some extra tartlets for Flick to give to you.'

Callum smiled. The people of Vickers Hill obviously prided themselves on the gourmet reputation of the town, nestled as it was in the middle of wine country. They also seemed intent on making him fat.

'Or she might just keep them for herself,' Felicity said. Mr Dunnich laughed as amusement lit Felicity's eyes and they dared him to surrender to his fate.

'Rhubarb tartlets are my favourite. I would love that.'

Callum let out a breath as he sat at his desk after Alf left with Felicity. If the shine in her eyes was anything to go by, he'd nailed it. There had certainly been no tight-lipped, jaw-clenched, silent disapproval.

The door opened and he braced himself for his next patient—a torn ACL. *Oops*. No. *Jane Richie* was his next patient. But he needn't have worried, it was just Felicity.

'Now,' she said as she walked towards him with an I-told-you-so swagger. 'That wasn't so hard, was it?'

He rolled his eyes. 'You're a gloater, aren't you?'

'I have no idea what you mean,' she said, batting her eyelashes at him in an exaggerated manner with a big grin that transformed her entire face, and in that moment he saw the same thing that everyone else around here did— Flick, who was all things to all people. Who was popular with everybody and loved by all.

Who belonged to them.

It was a sobering thought. She'd been the girl on the train to him since the beginning but seeing her here in her natural habitat it was clear that train girl had been the aberration.

Still, he wasn't ready to let that version of her go either. There were obviously two sides to Felicity and he was privileged to have seen the side that obviously no one here had. 'Let me make it up to you for being so obtuse and… What was it you called me? Cavalier? Come to my place for dinner tonight. I'm a pretty mean cook.'

The remnants of her smile slid from her mouth as she sat on the chair Mr Dunnich had just vacated. 'No.'

'*Just* dinner.'

'No.'

'Are you worried about Mrs Smith?'

'No. I'm worried about us. Together. Alone. Somewhere near a bed.'

A thick slug of desire hit Callum low in the belly. He'd been thinking about them alone *on* a bed an inordinate amount of time ever since the kiss in the car. 'You think I can't control myself?'

'I think you know as well as I do that *neither* of us will be able to control ourselves.'

Callum liked it that she wasn't playing coy or trying to pretend there wasn't a thing simmering between them. She may have been trying to ignore it for a week but she wasn't in denial.

'And we're not going there.'

He frowned, getting his thoughts back on track. 'We're not?' It was the right thing to do given they had to work together and he was here for only a short period of time but…

'No. I'm going to be your friend.'

Callum didn't have many female friends. The ones he did have he didn't want to sleep with.

The same couldn't be said for Felicity.

'You are?'

'Yes. I'll take you touring on the weekends. We'll visit some art galleries and antique shops. There's some great lookouts and a heritage trail. We'll drink wine and eat gourmet food at a bunch of different wineries. It'll be fun.'

Not as much fun as drinking wine and eating gourmet food off her body. 'Okay…'

'Are you free on Saturday?'

'Yes.'

'Good. I'll pick you up at eleven.'

CHAPTER NINE

FELICITY WASN'T NERVOUS when she picked Callum up on Saturday. She was confident they could be friends, despite the very definite tug of her libido and crazy speculation from the entire town.

Her libido didn't rule her actions and the town could talk all they wanted. Felicity knew from old they would anyway. As long as she and Callum knew where they stood, the town could go on building castles in the air.

Of course, the second she saw him walking down Luci's flower-lined pathway her confidence nosedived. She didn't know if it was the riot of colour and prettiness all around him making him seem so damn male or the way he filled out his snug blue jeans, but her belly looped the loop.

Friends. She could do this. *They* could do it.

They had to. Vickers Hill was not the place to be reckless. To be the girl from the train. She would be here long after he'd left and she didn't want to be walking around with everyone talking about her behind her back. She didn't want to be an object of gossip or, worse, pity.

Besides, sex was easy. A friendship could be more enduring and, she suspected, less pain in the long run. Above all else, she sensed that Callum needed a friend more than anything now. He'd been through a lot and was still working things out. She had no doubt he could find lovers. But he was in Vickers Hill for a reason—for clear air.

Sex would just fog it all up.

Felicity braced herself as he opened the car door and climbed in beside her. She smiled and said, 'Hi,' trying not to notice the way his T-shirt fell against his stomach. It was difficult when she knew exactly what was beneath.

'Hey,' he said. She couldn't really see his eyes behind the dark sunglasses but she could feel them all over her. 'You look great.'

Felicity blushed, reminding her of how he'd made her blush on the train. She was wearing a dress she'd bought at Bondi with Luci. It was strappy and light in an Aztec pattern, baring her shoulders and arms. The skirt was loose and flowing, the hem fluttering around her knees.

'Thanks,' she murmured, returning her attention to the road as she engaged the clutch. She wasn't going to tell him he looked great too. She hadn't bought him here to flirt with him and if she said, 'You don't look so bad either', that's what she'd be doing.

She didn't want the time he had left here to be one long slow tease between the two of them until one, or both, of them cracked. She was genuine about forming a friendship with him. Absolutely certain that it was their destiny.

Or, if nothing else, sensible.

'Where are we off to?'

'Pretty Maids All In A Row cellar door,' Felicity said, pleased to be slipping into tour-guide mode. It was a role she often played for visitors. She loved Vickers Hill and the entire Clare Valley. It may be smaller and further away than the renowned wine-growing region of the Barossa but it was known for its foodie culture and many high-end restaurants.

'That sounds like a mouthful.'

'It is a little.' She laughed. 'But they have a Riesling to die for and my favourite menu of all the local wineries. They do this rabbit dish that will make you weep. But first I'm going to take you on a bit of a scenic drive around.'

'Sounds good to me.' He nodded. 'Lead on.'

By the time Felicity pulled into the winery car park an hour later she didn't think she'd laughed so much in her life. Callum had been an entertaining companion—very *Cal*like—as she'd driven him all around the valley to give him a good overview of the district that surrounded Vickers Hill.

During lunch—rabbit and a very fine Riesling—they talked a lot of shop. Callum was keen to know all the ins and outs of the practice and the different relationships and Felicity was happy to impart all she knew.

It was only when they were relaxing over dessert and she was feeling the buzz from her second glass of wine that things turned personal.

'So how come,' he asked, supporting his chin in his palm as he leaned his elbow on the thick slab of timber that made up the table, 'somebody hasn't snapped you up by now, St Felicity.'

Felicity laughed. 'St Felicity?'

'Yes. *Saint*.' He grinned. 'Vickers Hill's very own. You're the woman who can do no wrong, don't you know? I have a feeling that the town will apply to have you canonised any day now.'

If he only knew how very unsaintly her thoughts had been today he'd be shocked. 'I think I have to be dead for that to happen.'

'A trifling detail,' he dismissed with a flick of his hand. 'Seriously, though, were you born in Vickers Hill? Because your people do love you.'

'Born, bred and schooled. Stayed here until I left to go to uni in Adelaide to study nursing.'

'And you came straight back and have dedicated every waking moment of your life to the good people of the Hill?'

Felicity laughed. 'No. I've only been back for four years. I worked in Adelaide for just over seven years.'

'Whereabouts?'

'At the general hospital, in their emergency department.'

'And you came home because you were…' He raised both eyebrows. 'Over it?' She shook her head. 'Burned out?' She shook it again. 'I know,' he said, smiling, drawing attention to his lips, 'St Felicity was sacked.'

'No.' She laughed.

'It was drugs, wasn't it? It's okay, you can tell. You're secret is safe with me.'

'No,' she said, laughing harder. 'Try again.'

'Hmm.' He narrowed his eyes, his gaze roaming all over her face for long moments. 'I know,' he announced. 'It was because of a man, wasn't it? He broke your heart.'

Felicity's breath hitched at his startling accuracy. She hoped her face didn't betray how badly her heart had been broken as she forced joviality into her voice. 'Bingo.'

Callum's face morphed from teasing to serious in one second flat. 'Oh, God, sorry. I didn't mean… I shouldn't have been kidding around. That was…dumb.'

'It's fine. It was four years ago. I'm over it.'

It was a startling revelation to realise she *was* over it. The hurt had lingered for such a long time. But she could put her hand on her heart right here, right now and honestly say that all the feelings she'd had for Ned were no more.

She'd always *love* him in that nostalgic we-were-good-together-and-you-used-to-mean-the-world-to-me way. They'd had a lot of great times. There'd been a lot of love. But she was over the heart*ache*.

She was healed. And not crazy glued back together but actually fully knitted.

'How long were you together?'

'Four years. He—Ned—was a nurse. We went through uni together and we both worked in A and E. We were friends first and it kind of developed slowly from there. Crept up on us, I guess.'

'So how did it all go wrong? What happened?'

To this day, Felicity still didn't fully understand it. It had been so sudden. 'One day he just said he'd met somebody else. Just…' Felicity splayed her hands '…like that. We were a few weeks off taking a holiday to New Zealand. I thought he was going to propose.' She gave a half-laugh and shook her head, thinking about how damn clueless she'd been. 'On the day he dumped me I was asking him if his passport had arrived yet and he just blurted it out. "I've met somebody else and I want to be with her."'

His hand slid across the table and covered hers. 'I'm so sorry. That must have been devastating. What a total creep.'

His quick insult surprised a laugh out of Felicity. 'He said he hadn't meant it to happen, he hadn't been looking for it. For what it's worth, I believed him. He was never the kind of guy who was always looking over my shoulder, you know?'

He winced. 'We're all creeps, aren't we?' He withdrew his hand and placed both of them over his heart. 'I sincerely apologise on behalf of the entire male sex in that case.'

She laughed again. 'It's okay. I survived.'

'You did,' he murmured, his gaze locking on hers as he dropped his hands to the table. 'Kudos to you.'

'Oh, I licked my wounds for a long time, don't you worry about that. It was pretty messy for a while.'

'Did you never suspect?'

'Never.' Felicity had been completely blindsided by Ned's admission. 'Apparently he'd known her for a month.'

He blinked. 'Wow. That's a *big* call.'

'Yeah. But they got married a month later and have two kids so they must be doing something right.'

'And you came home?'

Felicity nodded. 'I did. Home to my old bedroom and my father's country music playing on the radio and my mother's home cooking.'

'Just what the doctor ordered,' he teased.

'Yes.' She'd put on six kilos in that first month. It had taken her another year to get them off. 'Then Dr Dawson gave me a job, even though I had no practice nurse qualifications. Sure, I'm Luci's friend so he knew me well and probably couldn't say no to me when I burst into tears in front of him one day, but I will be forever in his debt for that. He was a saviour. *Work* was a saviour.'

Work had got her through days when all she'd wanted to do was curl up in a ball. It had saved her from ringing Ned a hundred times a day, screaming and/or crying at him until she was hoarse.

'You were lucky, then.'

His voice was even but there was a gravity to his words and all the teasing light had dimmed from his eyes. Of course. Callum had never had that when his life had gone pear-shaped. She'd relied on work to get her through her grief but he hadn't been *able* to work. The mere fact he *couldn't* had been at the very crux of his grief.

'Yeah, I was,' she agreed.

'Well,' he said, tossing his head as if he was trying to shake off the black cloud that had descended around them, 'for what it's worth, I'm glad you weren't with that lying, cheating scumbag the day you stepped on the train.'

Felicity laughed. 'So am I.' The heaviness of the conversation suddenly lightened as good memories crowded out the bad. Sitting opposite him now, it felt like they were back in the dining carriage.

'What about you?' she asked. 'A woman ever broken your heart? No.' She shook her head. 'Let me guess. You do all the breaking, I bet.'

'I'll have you know a girl called Susie Watts smashed my heart to smithereens when I was nine years old.' He put a hand on his chest. 'She dumped me for Jimmy Jones because he had a bigger bicycle than I did.'

Felicity sucked in some air through her hollowed cheeks in an appropriately sympathetic noise. 'Ouch.' But the urge to laugh was overwhelming. 'I'm sorry. That's awful.'

He narrowed his eyes. 'You don't look very sorry.'

Laughter bubbled in her chest. 'No, I was just thinking…'

'Thinking what?'

'A guy called Jimmy Jones? He sounds like one of those bad boys some girls are fatally attracted to. Maybe it wasn't just his bicycle that was bigger.'

'Oh, no,' Callum groaned good-naturedly, shutting his eyes before opening them again. 'Kick a guy when he's down.'

She did laugh this time. 'Sorry,' she said, trying to make herself stop.

He drank his coffee and watched her patiently—intently— a smile turning the fullness of his lips into two plush crescents. God, he was *sexy*. The way he smiled was sexy. The way his hair brushed his ears was sexy. The way he tilted his head was sexy.

The way he looked at *her* was sexy.

'So, you didn't answer my question,' Felicity said when she'd pulled herself under control. 'Ever had your heart broken? In an *adult* relationship?'

He placed his coffee cup back on its saucer. 'Not really.'

'You more a play-the-field kind of guy?' Everything about him oozed masculine confidence. She could see him at some hip Sydney bar mobbed by women.

'There's been a couple of longer-term relationships but they were never love matches and when you're working long hours and studying all the other hours left in the day they tend to take a back seat until they fizzle out. They were light and fun and mutually enjoyable while they lasted. And then…'

Felicity waited for him to continue after his abrupt cessation. When he didn't she cocked an eyebrow and prompted him. 'And then?'

He shifted in his seat, sitting more upright, pulling his arm back and propping his bent elbow on the curved back of the chair. 'After the accident…people didn't really know what to say and frankly I was pretty awful to be around sometimes. Most people in my social circle were in medicine and a lot of them dropped out of the circle—I guess because I was the elephant in the room. I was their *what if.* A rather sad reminder of how you could be riding on top one second then on your butt the next.'

'Did they think it was contagious?' she asked drily.

He smiled. 'I think maybe they thought of me more like a bad omen. Surgeons are all about the successes. We don't like to talk about failures. We certainly don't like to be confronted by them.'

'And it was the same with women?'

'No. Ironically, my sex life had never been better.' He fiddled with his coffee cup for a moment. 'And I'm not very proud to say I kind of drowned myself in that for quite a while.' He shrugged. 'I was throwing myself a huge pity party and it wasn't like there was much else to do. Until I realised that about ninety percent of the action I was getting amounted to *pity* sex.'

'Oh.' Felicity wanted to reach out and touch him like he'd touched her, but he seemed so far away now. 'What about the other ten percent?'

'Some kind of sick sexual healing for the blind man thing.'

Felicity grimaced. 'Oh, dear.'

'Yes.' He frowned into his coffee. 'After that I kind of just stopped. It was a real downer for my libido.'

Felicity knew she shouldn't get into a conversation about his libido in case it veered into flirting territory but she was a sucker for a wounded guy and the nurse inside her urged her to try and turn that frown upside down. Soothe it right off his face.

'Your sex drive seemed in perfect working order to me,' she murmured, hoping her voice sounded light and teasing rather than coy and flirty.

'Ah, well,' he said, lifting his gaze squarely to her lips, sucking away all the oxygen between them, 'that's because you woke it up.'

Her mouth tingled under his intense scrutiny and she could barely breathe. She probably shouldn't feel so damn turned on, especially as he didn't look entirely happy about his newly roused libido.

But she did. 'I'm…sorry?'

He shook his head, his eyes lifting higher and locking with hers. 'I'm not.'

The words both pleased and petrified Felicity. Was it just a statement of fact or a subtle reminder of the thing they were trying to ignore? Luckily for her, a waiter chose that moment to clear their table, breaking their eye contact and the accompanying tension.

For now.

* * *

Felicity pulled her car up outside Luci's house at around four. She waved at Mrs Smith, who was in her front garden, watering her plants. The old biddy didn't even pretend to be minding her own business.

'Uh-oh,' Callum said. 'Bouncer at six o'clock.'

Felicity laughed at the idea of Mrs Smith in a black T-shirt with Security stamped across the front in big white letters. Not that she needed it—she'd taught at the primary school for almost thirty years. Nobody in Vickers Hill messed with her.

'Thank you for today,' Callum said as he undid his seat belt. 'I had a really great time.'

'So did I.'

And she had. They'd had their moments when teasing and banter had definitely branched into flirting but they'd pulled back and just enjoyed each other's company.

As much as two people who were trying to deny their sexual attraction could.

'We should do it again,' he said.

Felicity nodded. 'Oh, we will. By the time you get out of here I promise you'll have seen every inch worth seeing.'

She realised the potential double entendre about the same time as Callum, his eyebrows rising as he tried to suppress a grin. 'None of those inches include me.'

He laughed. 'Just checking.'

She rolled her eyes at him. 'Seriously? Mrs Smith is over there, probably trying to read our lips, so show a little decorum, please.'

'Of course.' He nodded and moulded his face into solemn lines but there was mischief in his eyes. 'So…my turn for the chauffeuring next time but I can't do next weekend because I'm on call.'

'That's okay. I'm actually going to an art exhibition on

Thursday night at Drayton's Crossing. We drove through there on our way to lunch? It's a friend of mine but if you want to come along it should be fun. You can drive if you want.'

'Ah…okay.'

Felicity gave a half-laugh. 'Your enthusiasm is overwhelming. It won't be MOMA but she's really good, I promise. She has sell-out showings in Adelaide but this is a fundraiser for the local fire service and she's a Clare Valley girl.'

'No, it's not that.' He smoothed his palms up and down his jeans, which was distracting as hell. 'I can't…drive at night on my conditional licence. My visual acuity and depth of field in my left eye deteriorates badly in the dark.'

'Oh, okay, sure.' She shrugged. 'So I'll drive. I don't mind.'

But she could tell that *he* minded. *A lot.*

'It's not okay,' he growled, shoving a hand through his hair. 'I feel like a damn teenager on a curfew.'

His frustration was almost palpable. He'd obviously lost a degree of independence as well as his career and Felicity wanted nothing more than to soothe him, but it was probably the last thing *he* wanted from her. A guy like Callum who had turned his back on a steady supply of pity sex probably just needed a bit of understanding.

Being able to jump in a car and drive whenever she wanted was something she always took for granted. Any restriction on that would be a constant irritant for her too.

'I can imagine that's a real pain in the butt.'

'Yeah,' he huffed, looking out his window for long moments. 'I've got used to taking a taxi everywhere in Sydney.' He glanced at her. 'I don't suppose they have any Ubers in Vickers Hill?'

'Ah, no.' Felicity smiled. 'But we do have an old-fashioned

taxi service and I'm perfectly fine to drive us to Drayton's on Thursday, I promise. Hell, this car's been there so many times it could do it without any assistance from me.'

'Fine. But I drive on our next daytime outing.'

Felicity nodded. 'It's a date.' *Damn it.* She cringed at her flippant choice of words, her cheeks heating. Way to make it awkward, Flick. 'Well, you know, *figuratively*, of course.'

He laughed. 'Of course.'

Between that gaffe and Mrs Smith starting to pace up and down her footpath Felicity just wanted today to be over. She'd had a great time but clearly it was only going to be downhill from here.

'Well… I'm pretty sure Mrs Smith is about to turn her hose on us so I think it's time I left.'

'Sure.' He reached for the doorhandle. 'Thanks again.'

He was out of the car before she remembered she hadn't given him the gift from Mr Dunnich. 'Wait,' she called out quickly before he shut the door.

He ducked his head back in the car. 'What? Mrs Smith is giving me the evil eye.'

Felicity smiled. Mrs Smith hadn't lost that schoolteacher glare—the one that could see straight through a kid and know exactly what they were guilty of. She reached over to the back seat and grabbed the plastic container with five of the most perfectly formed rhubarb tartlets she'd ever seen.

'This is from Alf. He made me promise I'd give them to you. Not keep them for myself.' She thrust the box of temptation into his hands. 'You have no idea how hard that was.'

'I appreciate your restraint,' he murmured as he took the container, looking at her with eyes that left her in no doubt he appreciated much, much more.

Unexpected heat arced between them like a solar flare.

'Don't,' she said, trying to mentally pull herself back from this different sort of temptation. 'There were six. I ate one.'

He chuckled and it oozed into the car all around her. 'I appreciate your lack of restraint too.'

Felicity's breath caught in her throat as his gaze turned copulatory. Was he thinking about her lack of restraint in bed that night? Because she sure as hell was. She swore she could almost feel the rock of the train around them again.

Then he was straightening, the car *actually* rocking slightly as the door shut. He waved at Mrs Smith, earning himself a scowl, before he swaggered down Luci's path like he was striding along a hospital corridor instead of a path lined with lavender and sweet peas.

Two weeks down. Six more to go.

CHAPTER TEN

THE DAYS FORMED a steady rhythm, which Callum was starting to appreciate. He'd thought he'd needed the pace and the unpredictability of the north shore practice to keep his mind off things. He'd thought if he slowed down, if he had too much time to be idle, he'd have too much time to dwell on the state of his life.

And probably in the city that would have been true.

But there was something surprisingly satisfying about the slower tempo in the country. It took his mind off himself more effectively than keeping a frantic pace ever had because it freed up his mind from multiple foci—a jam-packed appointment book or surgical list to get through each day—and allowed him the space to think more holistically. He wasn't skimming the surface. He had time to sink down deeper into the layers.

He realised now that he hadn't needed to keep physically busy—he'd just needed to be mentally challenged. That was what he'd always loved about surgery—the mental challenge of the detail involved—and now he was finding a similar appreciation in the way general practice involved the minutiae of people's lives. That they were, as Felicity had said, the sum of *all* their parts, not just the product of one.

Even in the mornings, when he wasn't at work, he didn't feel the constant churn of loss and regret that continually threatened to swamp him back home in those rare quiet moments. Life in Sydney and the constant mix of pity and expectation from people for him to *bounce back*, to be the guy he'd been before the accident, seemed a million miles away.

Everything back home had reminded him of what he couldn't have. Everything in Vickers Hill showed him what he *could*.

He'd come here hoping to break the cycle of mental self-flagellation, hoping to shrug off the old skin and grow a new one. A better one. A *thicker* one.

Deep down he hadn't thought that possible.

But as Thursday rocked around and he was lazily appreciating Luci's garden as he sipped his coffee, he was beginning to think it was very much possible. He was even beginning to think it was possible that he and Felicity could be friends.

At work it seemed possible anyway. They were getting on well and it was easy to keep her straight in his head in a place where she was so clearly 'the nurse'. From what she wore to how people treated her to what they called her, everything existed to create that mental barrier.

Everyone called her Flick and every day she was dressed in the same navy pants and polo shirt as the other staff, her hair pulled into the same low ponytail. People spoke to her with both respect and affection. At work she *was* Flick and through tacit agreement they didn't talk about the train or that weird moment in the car on Saturday. They kept things professional, and it worked.

Even the art show tonight was kept in perspective when both Bill and Julia as well as Angela and about a dozen of his patients were also attending. Yes, *she'd* invited him and he was going *with* her but it was merely an act of kindness extended to the newbie in town.

It was the embodiment of country hospitality. An invitation that could have been issued by any one of the practice employees. But it had been issued by her. By *Flick*. And he was looking forward to it immensely.

Unfortunately it wasn't *Flick* who picked him up. It was most definitely *Felicity*. In that little black dress from the train. Or maybe it wasn't the exact one. But it was similar. Figure-hugging, a great glimpse of cleavage, a very distracting bow on the side that looked like it might be the way in—and *out*.

Okay. Not the one from the train—he'd have remembered that bow.

Did she know how tempting that damn bow was? Had she done it on purpose? He supposed there weren't a lot of places or events in Vickers Hill that required dressing up so why wouldn't she when she had the chance? It was obvious from the train that she was as partial to getting all girly as the next woman.

He just wished she'd chosen the light and summery look from the weekend when she'd taken him to lunch at the winery. The whole girl-next-door thing suited her.

There was nothing girl-next-door about this dress.

Not the figure-hugging, not the cleavage, not the sexy high heels. Not that damn bow or the sway of her hips or the swing of her long, loose hair. This was a Pavlov's dog dress.

And he was salivating like crazy.

It certainly drove out the mushrooming frustration he'd felt as he'd waited to be picked up like some teenager who'd had his keys taken off him by his parents. The black cloud that had been building all afternoon had blown right away as he'd opened the door, and by the time he'd slid into the car seat beside her, it was long gone.

Music, low and sweet, flared to life on the radio as she started the engine. Her bangles jingled. Her perfume enveloped him, filling his head with her scent and a string of bad ideas.

'You look…lovely,' he said as she smiled at him.

'Thanks.'

She reached for her seat belt but not before he saw a tiny slip in that smile, a slight dimming of the sparkle in her eyes as she buckled up.

Had she been hoping for more?

Unfortunately, lovely was about as polite as he could get right now. The next level up was *sexy*. The one after that was not for polite company.

He was okay with being friends. He understood the reasons for it and thought it was doable. But he wasn't stupid enough to deny there was the possibility of a very different relationship if they chose to go down that path.

Which they hadn't.

'I'm worried about Lizzy Dunnich,' she said, as she drove off.

Callum dragged his mind out of his—and her—pants. It was hard to concentrate on shop talk when she looked like the woman from the train, but at least it would help him to keep the division between the two very different women straight in his head.

'Is she unwell?' Felicity had obviously decided to keep her on her home-visit schedule after she'd seen her last week.

'No. Nothing specific I can pinpoint. Just a feeling. Like Alf says, she's just really withdrawn. But Bailey— that's their Labrador—has taken to not leaving her side. I'm worried he knows something we don't.'

Callum hadn't owned a dog, growing up, and they'd never come into his realm of practice when he'd been putting on a pair of scrubs every morning, but he'd read enough anecdotal evidence about the canine-human connection to understand why Felicity was worried.

'You think she might be…'

'Yeah.'

The white of her knuckles around the steering wheel drew his attention. *My* people, she'd called them that day she'd finally exploded at him for his poor connection with the patients.

And Mrs Dunnich was one of them.

'She's eighty-six,' he said gently, staring at her profile. 'And she's already had one stroke.'

'Yeah,' she said again, her eyes glued to the road.

He wasn't telling her anything she didn't already know. Lizzy Dunnich didn't have a whole lot of ticks in her column.

But this one felt close to him too.

As a surgeon he'd had patients die. The last one, not long before his accident, had been a fifty-eight-year-old woman who'd presented with a dissecting abdominal aortic aneurysm. They'd rushed her to Theatre but he hadn't been able to stem the haemorrhage.

Her death had been a professional loss—not a personal one. He hadn't known the woman. He hadn't eaten home-made rhubarb tartlets from her family recipe. He hadn't met her husband. Telling him had been as awful as it always was, but his scheduled theatre list had been severely disrupted because of the emergency and he'd still had three more patients to deal with so the death had been quickly filed under 'Impossible save', as triple As too often were.

'Why don't I drop by on Saturday and see them? I'm on call so—'

'Oh, would you?' she interrupted, her voice charged with hope.

'Of course.'

Her exhalation was noisy in the confines of the car. 'Thank you,' she said, glancing at him quickly before returning her attention to the road.

Callum's night vision might be rubbish but he could still see the shine of unshed tears in her eyes. He'd never met a woman who wore her emotions so openly. Once upon a time that would have made him want to run as far away as possible.

Tonight it made him want to pull her closer.

Felicity was still stewing over the word *lovely* when they arrived at the art show. She shouldn't be. Callum's offer to see Mrs Dunnich should be dominating her thoughts and she should still be grateful for that but somehow his *lovely* resonated the most.

Now she understood his dismay that day when she'd described their time on the train as lovely. It was such an…insipid word.

It shouldn't bother her. They were *friends* and attracting Callum wasn't her aim.

Absolutely not.

She'd worn the dress for *herself*. Because she didn't get the opportunity to dress up very often and everyone else would be making the effort. Because she was single and one day she hoped not to be—Mr Right *could* be in Drayton's Crossing. Because rocking a little black dress was a marvellous thing and putting one on one of life's great joys. Like sexy lingerie and expensive chocolate.

She'd worn the dress for herself, damn it.

But then Callum had said 'lovely' and she'd realised she

might have possibly, somewhere deep in her subconscious, worn it for him…

'There's Bill and Angela,' Callum said, his hand at her elbow.

Felicity looked around the transformed space. It had Veronica's artistic signature all over. Gone was the quaint hundred-year-old farmers' hall and in its place was a high-class bordello. Hundreds of metres of rich burgundy velvet were draped artfully overhead and lined the walls to form a dramatic backdrop to the paintings. There was a heavy reliance on gold brocade, plush velvet chaises and art deco standing lamps covered with red chiffon shawls to create a seductive pink glow.

Curvy women dressed in corsets and fishnet circulated with trays of champagne and canapés amongst the crowd milling around the paintings.

It was hard to believe this was little old Drayton's Crossing. It could be in any posh city gallery anywhere in the world, and while she knew about three-quarters of the people in the room, there were certainly some she didn't recognise. Probably from Adelaide. Veronica's art was highly sought after and her exhibitions, regardless of location, were always well attended.

'You want champagne?'

The fine hairs on Felicity's nape prickled as Callum's voice, low and close to her ear to be heard over the noise, did funny things to her equilibrium. She was conscious of his presence behind her. His bulk, his heat, the waft of his citrusy aftershave. The warmth of his breath on her temple.

Her eyelids fluttered closed, she swayed a little as she fought the urge to lean back. Let herself drape against him.

And wouldn't *that* just give everybody something more to gossip about?

They weren't in a city gallery somewhere. They were in *Drayton's Crossing*, for Pete's sake.

Felicity locked her quads and cleared her throat. 'Yes, please.' Anything to remove the temptation of him from her orbit long enough to get back some control.

'Be right back,' he murmured. 'Don't go away.'

Not much chance of that with legs as useless as two wet noodles.

She watched him go. Somehow he seemed more hip, cool, stylish and sexy than any other guy in the room— even the arty types who clearly weren't from these parts. He was wearing a suit the colour of roasted Arabica beans that he'd teamed with a purple shirt, left open at the neck. No tie.

He looked the ultimate in casual, urban chic. And the way those trousers pulled across his butt as he walked away should be utterly illegal.

There was nothing *lovely* about it.

By the time he came back, Felicity was talking to an old friend from Vickers Hill and she was on much more steady ground. In fact, for the rest of the night, as they went from painting to painting, there was always someone she knew, someone to introduce Callum to and mingle with to prevent them from being alone.

Because they needed to avoid that at all costs. She wasn't stupid, she could tell people were openly curious, watching them and their every move. It was why she tried extra hard to project a friendly, collegial discourse between them.

She was careful about her stance and other nonverbal cues, she kept the conversation about the paintings and suppressed the urge to touch him, which was surprisingly difficult. She'd never realised how tactile she was in conversation until she had to physically stop herself a dozen times from touching Callum's arm.

She seriously deserved an award for her portrayal of *just-friends-nothing-to-see-here-move-along-please*.

Finally, she got to introduce him to Veronica. Felicity had been trying to get to her all night but her friend had been swamped with both buyers and well-wishers.

'V.,' Felicity said with a smile as her friend enveloped her in an enthusiastic, champagne-slopping hug. 'This is fabulous. You must be so pleased.'

'Absolutely thrilled, darl.' Big hoop earrings matched wild brown curls and the whole kaftan-alternative vibe Veronica had going on. Not for the first time, Felicity wished she oozed the same brash sexiness that was like a second skin for Veronica.

'I've sold just about every painting. Reckon the Clare Valley fire service will get about fifty k out of their cut by the end of the night.'

'That's amazing. They'll be giving you the keys to the valley next time you're home,' Felicity teased.

One of the things she most loved about Veronica was that she hadn't lost her connection with her roots. Her artwork may be hung in galleries around the world but at heart she was a small-town girl.

'As long as they're able to open every cellar door in the district then I'm fine with that.' Veronica laughed in her disarmingly self-deprecating way before turning her attention to Callum. 'Well, hello, there,' she said, as Felicity took a nervous sip of her remaining champers. 'So *you're* the guy she's doing.'

Felicity almost inhaled her drink at the outrageous statement. 'V.,' Felicity warned, coughing and spluttering on the bubbles that had almost gone down the wrong way as Callum threw back his head and laughed, seemingly unconcerned.

'What?' Veronica asked with a faux aura of innocence. 'All I was going to say is I approve, darling.' She eyed Callum up and down. 'If you've got to be in trouble with the town, might as well make it worth your while.' She held her hand out to Callum. 'Hi, I'm V.'

'Callum.'

'Callum, huh?' Veronica shook her head. 'You look like a Cal to me.'

Callum grinned and Felicity wanted to stomp on his foot. 'I get that as well.'

'I *bet* you do, darl.' Veronica laughed, tapping his shoulder lightly. She switched her attention to Felicity. 'He's good in bed, right? I can just tell.'

Felicity glanced around, hoping nobody was eavesdropping. She'd forgotten how outrageous Veronica could be. She had no filter and lived to scandalise.

'I am not doing him.' Felicity hissed, while Callum—*Cal*—chuckled some more. Which *was* true. *Currently*, she wasn't. 'The gossips have got it wrong as usual.'

'Well, you should make it right,' Veronica murmured, her gaze eating Callum up again. 'If you can't beat them, darling, you might as well join them.'

Felicity was beginning to regret introducing them. Veronica's attention was a little too lascivious for her liking as a spike of something that felt very much like jealousy prodded Felicity in the chest.

Thankfully she noticed a couple heading their way with an artistic fever in their eyes, clearly intent on monopolising the *artiste* for as long as Veronica was willing to put up with them. 'Oh, look,' Felicity said, tipping her chin at the approaching zealots, 'Buyers incoming. Don't let us keep you.'

She shot her insanely vibrant and attractive friend a sweet smile as she seized Callum's arm and pulled him away. Veronica laughed, clearly neither fooled nor insulted, blowing a couple of quick air kisses before turning her attention on her fans.

They ended up in a corner, near a standing lamp emanating a very distracting pink glow. The crowd had thinned slightly, which enabled them to have a little more privacy.

Not that that had been the objective.

She had no idea what to say to Callum after Veronica's directness. At least everyone else had been discreet about their curiosity. She slugged back the dregs of her champers and immediately wished she could swig another. But as she was driving she grabbed a soda water off a passing tray instead. Callum snagged a beer.

Felicity sipped and wondered whether she should mention Veronica at all—apologise for her maybe. Explain she lived to scandalise. But frankly she was still too embarrassed to head down that track.

'V. seems like a hoot.'

Well. That was settled, then. Looked like they were going to talk about her whether she wanted to or not. 'She is. Sorry about that. She loves to shock people.'

He shook his head, tracking Veronica's movements. 'I think she's fabulous.'

Felicity nodded. Yes. He would. Veronica was probably much more his type than she was. She could imagine him back before his injury with someone delightfully brash and flirty like Veronica. Someone who was socially outgoing, confident in herself and her sexuality.

'She's gorgeous, isn't she? So out there and…' Felicity cleared her throat of the sudden husky stricture threatening to close it right off '…sexy.'

His head swivelled in Felicity's direction, one eyebrow cocked. 'Sexy, huh?'

Heat suffused her face as he studied her like he was seeing her through new eyes, his gaze drawing her in as if they were the only two people in the room. 'A woman can appreciate sexiness in another woman,' she said, a defensive streak in her voice a mile wide.

He held up his hands in mock surrender. 'I totally agree. It's a kinda sexy thing to admit, actually.'

So she was sexy now instead of lovely?

Heat flared between them. She suddenly wished they *were* the only two people in the room. The thought was nine parts thrilling, one part panic inducing. She couldn't afford to lose her head in front of all these people and lose all the 'just mates' groundwork she'd laid over the last hour or so.

'Who, me?' she murmured, keeping her voice low and silky. 'Impossible. I'm *lovely*, remember?'

'Ah.' He chuckled, his lips twitching on the rim of his glass before he took a mouthful of beer. 'Sorry about that. It was a bad word choice.'

'Oh, I don't know,' she said, the irritation from earlier returning with a vengeance as she mimicked what he'd said that day they'd visited Meryl. 'You could have said *nice*.'

He glanced around before his gaze drifted to her mouth. 'Trust me, it was cleaner than what I was really thinking.'

The low admission rumbled from his lips and stroked her in all the good places. She should just leave that alone. But some devil inside her wanted to know what he thought of her black dress.

'Oh?' She hoped the vibrato in her voice didn't betray how very badly she *needed* to know.

'It's not really for…' he looked around again before returning his gaze to hers, lowering his head and leaning in slightly as his voice went down a register '…polite company.'

Felicity was beyond caring about polite as his warm breath stirred the wisps of hair at her temple. A wave of goose-bumps swept down the side of her face and fanned out across her neck. She swayed closer, as if he was pulling her with an invisible thread, locking them in a private little bubble amidst all the colour and movement around them.

'Maybe you should whisper it?' she suggested, turning her lips towards his ear, her voice almost as low and rough as his. She was thankful for her heels bringing their heights closer.

She swore she could *feel* his smile as he leaned in to do just that, his lips brushing her hair.

Felicity's breath hitched and something deep and low clenched down hard as he whispered a very dirty word. It wasn't Shakespeare. It was bald and base and primal.

Such a freaking turn-on.

'And for what it's worth,' he muttered, pulling back so he could stare into her eyes, '*you* are the sexiest woman in the room tonight.'

Felicity swallowed as her legs threatened to melt to jelly again and land her on her butt.

'*Ah*. Here you are!' Angela said, sliding an arm around Felicity's waist, seemingly oblivious to the mood. 'Cal, I need to borrow Flick for a moment. Someone has to come with me while I pay for my painting and stop me from buying another one. She's disciplined like that.'

Felicity didn't get a chance to refuse as Angela dragged her away, but she did glance over her shoulder to find

Callum had her firmly in his sights, carnal intent blazing from his eyes.

How they were going to get home without pulling over and jumping each other's bones she had no idea.

CHAPTER ELEVEN

THEY LEFT AN hour later. An hour during which Felicity spent as much time *away* from Callum as possible, mingling with other people as she fought to get her body back under control. Because, while it was clear now that their sexual attraction was never going to allow them to be the friends she'd hoped they could be, it didn't mean succumbing to their attraction was the right thing either.

There was no point getting close to him when it would be *her* heart bruised in the end. Sure, she could have a fling with him but the truth was she'd never been good at casual sex.

Feelings always came in to it for her. Not necessarily love but a very definite connection. That's just the way she was.

It was like a reverse superpower. Her kryptonite. It made her weak.

Before Ned she'd had three serious relationships. Two had lasted six months. One had lasted nine. She was an emotional person—she liked to be invested and committed to the men she dated.

She liked being attached to another person.

But Callum was a different prospect. He'd already admitted to not forming attachments. To having a string of affairs with women during his darkest hours. And he was still coming to terms with a lot of baggage.

It didn't take a brain surgeon to figure out she'd be the more invested of the two of them if she let this thing become more than what had happened on the train. And in her car. And here tonight. She already liked him way more than was wise, especially now he'd proved to be a halfway decent doctor as well.

And then where would she be? Vickers Hill had always felt safe to her. It was her home, the place she'd run to after Ned. The place where she'd come into her own and found her feet. She didn't want to have to run from it as well because it was too painful to stay.

So she wasn't going to go there. But…she was Callum's lift home so she had to find some way to reboot the direction of the night. Maybe her overwhelming desire to have sex with him *was* going to get in the way of a friendship but that didn't mean she couldn't be friendly.

And for that she had to steer the conversation. Because she had no doubt if she steered it the wrong way, Callum would merrily follow.

'Tell me about your brother,' she blurted out as she pulled out of the car park, hyper-aware of the intimacy created by the glow of the dashboard lights and the slow ballad playing on the radio. 'Sebastian, right?'

Callum frowned, obviously not expecting that after the tension that had been building between them. 'Seb,' he corrected. '*That's* what you want to talk about?'

Felicity did not take her eyes off the road. 'That's what I want to talk about.'

He didn't answer for long moments and Felicity held her breath. Was he going to call her on it? Was he going to slip his hand on her leg and turn her into putty?

Everything seemed to hang in the balance as the seconds stretched. Then he sighed and said, 'What do you want to know?'

She shrugged, gripping the steering wheel hard as relief coursed through her system. 'Everything, I guess. He is living with our Luci after all. I'm pretty sure she hasn't told her parents yet so I feel like someone should at least know something about him.'

'In case he's a serial killer?'

Felicity ignored the derision. 'Exactly.'

'Anything specifically? "Everything" is kind of broad.'

'Is he older or younger than you?'

'Three years younger.'

'And he lives with you?'

'No. He doesn't live anywhere in particular, he just crashes at my place when he's in Sydney.'

Felicity frowned at the section of road lit up by her headlights, conscious of dry bushland flying by in her peripheral vision. Seb Hollingsworth—who was living with Luci—was some kind of…drifter?

'So he's…homeless?'

Callum's low chuckle enveloped her, wrapping her up, reminding her how alone they were. Not that being surrounded by people had seemed to matter back at the art show either.

'No. He has a boat that he's doing up with plans to live on it, eventually.'

'Does he have a job to support that plan?' A thirty-one-year-old guy with no fixed abode wasn't exactly inspiring confidence.

'Yes.' Callum chuckled again. 'He's a community health physician, employed by the government. He travels around a lot, mainly in rural areas.'

'Which is why he doesn't have his own place?'

'Yes. That and the fact he's allergic to putting down

roots ever since his pregnant girlfriend was killed in a hit-and-run accident a few years back.'

Felicity blanched at the casual imparting of such a tragic tale, flicking a quick glance at him before returning it to the road. The awful news socked her right in the centre of her chest and tears pricked her eyes. 'Oh, God.' She absently patted her chest. 'How *awful* for him.'

'Yes. It was a terrible time. He kind of changed after that. Moved in a completely different direction. Sold their house, bought a motorbike and a run-down boat and started working away a lot.'

Felicity had no doubt something like that could irrevocably change a person. It seemed like both the Hollingsworth men were good at running away. 'Sounds like he's a bit of a wherever-I-lay-my-hat kinda guy.'

'Yeah,' he agreed. 'I think that sums him up perfectly.'

'Are you close?'

Right from the beginning, Callum had come across as utterly self-contained. It was hard to reconcile him having a sibling. If she'd been forced to guess she would have said he was an only child.

He shrugged. 'We're not bosom buddies. But we have a solid relationship built on mutual respect for us both needing our own space.'

Well…that was suitably vague… And sad. It seemed to her that the Hollingsworth brothers could have been a great support to each other during their respective tragedies if they'd come together instead of running away.

But, then, what did she know about sibling relationships? She *was* an only child.

'So,' he said, interrupting her thoughts, 'does Seb pass muster now he has a tragic backstory?'

He was teasing but Felicity didn't see the funny side. 'I don't think it's something you should be making light of,' she chided, aware that she probably sounded like some puritan but unable to easily shake off the lingering sadness of Seb's tragedy.

'Its fine.' He laughed. 'Every year for Christmas Seb sends me a brochure from the guide dogs society. We're blokes, we talk smack and joke about our problems, that's how we bond.'

Felicity rolled her eyes. *Men.* She'd always wanted a brother. Now she wasn't so sure. She wondered what Luci, fellow single child, nurse and sucker for a wounded man, was making of Seb.

'Well, does he or doesn't he?' Callum prompted.

Knowing more about Seb was comforting. She just hoped Luci's vagueness when she talked about him wasn't because she was falling for him. Luci was getting over a painful divorce and Seb Hollingsworth didn't sound like he was ready for a relationship.

Kind of like his brother.

'I'm not about to ring Luci and tell her to get out of the house.'

'Good.' He nodded. 'From what I can gather, she's fine with him being there anyway. And if she wasn't he'd have probably just crashed in the boat. Or, if he'd been absolutely desperate, at my parents' place.'

So Callum had parents in Sydney. 'They don't get on?'

He shrugged. 'Their relationship is a little…fraught.'

'They don't approve of his lifestyle?'

'They don't approve of his *career* choice. They're surgeons. In fact, *all* the Hollingsworths are surgeons,' he said, a core of something that sounded like bitterness infecting his voice. 'Seb chose something outside the field so he's always been a disappointment to them.'

Felicity couldn't begin to imagine her parents being disappointed in *anything* she'd chosen, let alone medicine.

The son of a train driver and the daughter of a dairy farmer had only ever wanted happiness for their child. They'd retired to the coast now but were thrilled that Felicity had found her niche in life.

'They must be very proud of you, carrying on the family tradition?' she observed.

'They *were*.'

'Were?' She sneaked a peek at his face, his profile contorting into a grimace, before she looked back at the road.

Surely they'd supported him during and after his injury?

'They think I've given up a little too easily.'

Felicity touched his arm without thinking, just as she would have done to anyone to express her empathy. 'I'm sorry.' No wonder Callum and Seb ran away from their stuff when there was no one for them to run *to*.

'It's fine,' he dismissed, with a shrug, dislodging her hand. 'I'm used to their indifference. We both are. They're just not cut out to be parents. Some people aren't.'

'But still…' She couldn't wrap her head around it.

'It's fine,' he repeated. 'Don't feel sorry for me. Seb and I grew up with a lot of privilege that many of the kids around us didn't. We didn't want for anything.'

Materialistically, maybe not, but Felicity didn't have to be a psychologist to know what kids needed most were engaged, interested, supportive parents.

'And I think we turned out kinda okay despite them. Well…' he shot her a lopsided grin '…*I* did at least. The jury's still out on Seb.'

Her mouth twitched. Callum Hollingsworth in full charm mode was a force to be reckoned with and she didn't have it in her after such serious subject matter to deny him a little lightness. 'Yeah,' she murmured, sneaking him another look. 'You're kinda okay.'

He grinned at her for a beat or two. Felicity's pulse

fluttered and her breath hitched as the moment stretched. She broke it by looking back at the road and the far reach of the headlights illuminating the ghostly white trunks of gum trees.

He didn't say anything for a while and the music filled the space between them. 'About before...' he said eventually.

'No.' Felicity shook her head. 'Let's not do this. Let's mark it up to champagne and vanity and never talk about it again. Okay?'

She held her breath, waiting for his agreement. What she'd do if he didn't, she had no idea. If he looked at her and said *Screw that*, what *would* she do? Probably pull the car over and do him on the side of the road.

'We seem to do that a lot,' he said after a silence that was loud enough to obliterate the music. 'Avoid talking about this thing between us. I'm not sure it's very healthy.'

'No.' Felicity shook her head again vigorously. 'Unhealthy would be flat-out denial. I'm not denying it. I'm ignoring it.'

'And by *it* you mean our red-hot sexual attraction?'

Felicity's fingers tightened around the wheel at Callum's unnecessary summation. 'Yes,' she muttered.

As if she needed any reminding.

'That. But you and I are *not* going there. So there's no point talking about what happened before because nothing happened.'

The fact he'd turned her on in a crowded room with just one, dirty, whispered word didn't count.

He gave a short, sharp laugh. 'Now, *that's* denial.'

Yeah. He had her there. But she only had two options and pulling the car over and having him prove that word to her wasn't a viable one. So she had to forge ahead.

With conversation.

Or turn the music up really loud and not talk at all.

She chose the latter.

Callum was still thinking about that trip home on Thursday night and their awkward goodbye when he dialled Felicity's number on Saturday morning from the Dunnich garden. It was a walk in the park compared to what he was about to tell her. He'd put up with a dozen awkward goodbyes in exchange for this one sad hello.

'Hey,' she said, her voice perky.

She'd used that tone of voice with him all day yesterday. *Perky.* So damn cheerful. It had been amusing then but it grated this morning.

He'd never met a woman so determined to keep him at arm's length.

'What's up?'

For a moment he didn't want to tell her. He just wanted to soak up the November sun beating down on his neck and get lost in the heady aroma of roses and the lazy drone of bees, knowing she was in his ear, breathing and perky.

'Callum?' she prompted, some of the perkiness dissolving.

His heart punched the centre of his chest with slow, precise jabs as he took a steadying breath. 'I'm at Alf's.'

There was a pause on the end of the line, a pause that was so damn loud he could practically hear every thought careening through her head. 'What's happened?'

Her voice was low, serious, resigned. All the perkiness was gone. It was matter-of-fact now. Professional. But he could also hear the slight huskiness. Could picture her big grey eyes growing bright.

'It's Lizzy.' Callum looked over his shoulder to the open back door. He could see Alf's silhouette as he talked on the phone in the central hallway. 'She's had a massive stroke.'

No pause this time, no grilling him for the details. Just, 'I'll be right there', and the phone going dead.

Callum put his phone in his back pocket and went inside, the cool and relative darkness a stark contrast to the bright morning outside. He pushed his sunnies on top of his head and headed for Alf, who hung up the landline as he neared.

'That was our daughter in Adelaide,' he said, his usually strong, slow drawl weak and tremulous as he stared at the device. 'She's going to let everyone know and then head up to us.' He glanced at Callum. 'Do you think she'll h…?' His voice wobbled and cracked. 'Hold on till then, Doc?'

Callum was surprised Lizzy had even lasted this long. Her breathing was affected by the stroke. It had improved since he'd placed some nasal prongs on and run in a trickle of oxygen but Callum didn't think she'd see out too many more hours.

He slid his hand on Alf's shoulder and gave a squeeze. 'I reckon she will, Alf.' Because he needed hope now more than anything.

He nodded, his lips trembling, suddenly looking every one of his eighty-plus years. 'Did you get hold of Flick?' he asked gruffly.

'Yes. She should be here shortly.'

'Rightio,' Alf said, staring at the door to his bedroom and straightening his shoulders as if he was going into battle. How did a husband say goodbye to a wife he'd been with for almost seventy years? 'I'm going back in.'

Callum nodded and wished he didn't feel so out of his depth. He hadn't done this in a long time—stood by and done nothing while a patient slowly slipped away.

He was used to action. To *saving* people.

But Alf had been adamant after Callum had diagnosed the stroke that Lizzy not go to hospital and produced an advance care directive that stated Lizzy didn't want any extraordinary measures taken to save or prolong her life in the event of another major stroke.

'She wants to be here with her family and Bailey by her side,' he'd said.

And Callum understood that, he just didn't know what Alf needed of him right now. It felt wrong to be witnessing something so intimate when he barely knew them. It felt like an intrusion. But he knew he couldn't leave Alf either.

It was why he'd suggested Felicity come and sit with Alf until his family arrived and the old man had jumped at the idea.

'Can I bring you in a cup of tea or something?'

'No, thanks, Doc,' Alf said, and quietly slipped into the room.

A well of uselessness swamped him, familiar and over-whelming. He'd felt like this after the accident when the extent of his injury had sunk in. He'd hated it then and he hated it now.

He had to be able to do something, surely?

He wandered aimlessly to the open front door, pulling his sunglasses down as the brightness jabbed into his per-manently dilated left pupil like a knife. He looked up and down the street, willing Felicity's car to arrive, for her to walk through the front gate.

She'd know what to do.

A mix of floral aromas tickled his senses as he waited and his gaze was drawn to the beauty of Alf's garden. It drifted to the arbour that arched over the gate and was cov-ered in climbing roses, and he wondered if these were the ones that Lizzy liked so much. They were pretty, a cham-pagne colour and smaller than the ones growing on indi-vidual bushes. Dainty and feminine. Very much like her.

An idea hit him then and he smiled as he strode back

into the house and searched the kitchen for a pair of scissors. Maybe filling her room with the aroma of her beloved roses could be his contribution?

Who knew what she could still hear, see and smell?

Locating some scissors in a drawer, he headed back out, stopping at the first bush near the front porch and snipping one of the blooms. The front path was lined with bushes and as he had no real idea what he was doing, apart from avoiding the thorns, he figured he might as well snip one from each. Clearly arranging flowers wasn't his forte but they didn't need to be pretty—they just needed to provide some joy and, hopefully, some peace.

For Alf as well as Lizzy.

He was halfway through when Felicity pulled up. The surge of relief that flooded his chest flowed cool and electric through his veins.

'Hi,' she said as she pushed open the gate and walked under the arbour.

'Hi.' She was in strappy sandals, denim shorts that came to just above her knee and a tank top. She was Flick and she was exactly who he needed. 'I'm sorry for calling you for this—'

She shook her head, interrupting his apology, her loose ponytail brushing back and forth between her shoulder blades. 'You did the right thing. Is she…?'

'No,' he assured her quickly, and her shoulders visibly relaxed. 'She's unconscious but hanging on. Alf's family are driving up from Adelaide. I thought he needed a familiar face to wait with him until they got here.'

'Of course.' She gave him a sad smile, her expression full of empathy. 'What happened?'

'We were all chatting out in the back garden. Alf and I left Lizzy and Bailey there, watching a couple of the magpies they feed frolicking in the sprinkler, so he could take me in and show me some of his wines. We'd been gone a couple of minutes when Bailey started to bark.' Callum wiped the sweat off his brow with the back of his hand. 'Alf knew straight away. When we got to her she was slumped in the wheelchair, unconscious.'

'Oh, no,' she murmured. 'Poor Mr Dunnich.'

'He's been really good. Stoic, you know?' Callum had no idea how long it would last.

'Yes, he's country down to his bootstraps. And what about you?' she asked, peering at him hard as if she was trying to see behind his dark shades. 'Are *you* okay?'

The question surprised him. No colleague had ever asked him if he was okay over a work situation. Sometimes things went wrong and you just got on with it.

But, as he'd learned over the last three weeks, that wasn't the way they did things in Vickers Hill.

'Yes. Thanks.' It felt surprisingly good to have been asked. He may not have known the Dunniches for long but he'd been incredibly moved by Alf's gentleness as he'd laid Lizzy on the bed and stroked her hair. 'Better now you're here.'

Maybe that was one of the things he wasn't allowed to say but it was true. And not in a *hey, baby* way. In a *human* way. She knew Alf and Lizzy and she knew him.

They were all connected.

She glanced at the scissors in his hands and the stems he'd already picked. 'I didn't know what else to do,' he said. 'All I really know about her is how much she loves roses so I figured…'

Overly bright eyes smiled at him. 'I think that's a really beautiful thing to do. Lizzy would love that.'

Callum's chest swelled. He'd felt like a clumsy fool with his black thumb cutting pretty roses in someone else's garden—completely conspicuous. But Felicity's compliment validated his instincts.

'You can leave them in the kitchen if you want. I'll find a vase for them in a bit.'

'I can do it,' Callum dismissed.

A tiny frown caused a little V between her brows. 'Oh… okay, sure. Thanks.'

It was Callum's turn to frown. She didn't sound so sure and he certainly didn't know the etiquette here. 'Is it? Okay?'

'Of course. I just…didn't think you'd want to stick around. You don't have to, you know. I've got this.'

She was letting him off the hook. Three weeks ago Callum would have taken that offer and run with it. Left the nurse to deal with relatives and the patient comfort stuff.

But he wasn't that person any more. *Thanks to her.*

'I'd like to stay…if you don't think it's intruding.'

'That would be great,' she said, her smile gentle, her hand sliding onto his arm and giving it a pat.

Callum glanced at it, surprised at how comforting it was. 'Is she in the bedroom?' He nodded and she edged around him, her hand dropping away. 'I'll see you in there,' she murmured.

He watched her disappear inside the house, the imprint of her hand still marking his skin. Kind of like the way she'd marked his life. In just a few short weeks the girl from the train had taught him more about himself than he'd learned in thirty-plus years. More about being a doctor. More about the things that actually mattered.

Whatever did or didn't happen between them he knew one thing for sure—he was *never* going to forget Felicity Mitchell.

Callum stepped into the room fifteen minutes later. He'd found a vase under the sink and arranged the blooms. It was never going to win a floral arrangement competition but it wasn't bad for his first time.

He placed them on an old-fashioned dressing table.

'Thanks, Doc,' Alf said. He was sitting on a chair beside the bed, holding his wife's hand. Felicity was sitting next to Alf, holding his hand. 'Lizzy loves her roses, don't you, darlin'?' he asked, patting her hand a couple of times.

'Do you remember that time Bailey dug up those new bushes she'd planted when he was a puppy?' Felicity asked. 'And how hard Bailey worked to get back into her good graces.'

Alf chuckled. Bailey, who was lying on the bed with Lizzy, whined and thumped his tail at the mention of his name but he didn't move his head from Lizzy's thigh.

Callum listened for the next couple of hours as Alf regaled them with stories about Lizzy and their life together. There was so much humour and love in every one but Alf's voice often cracked and Callum could only guess how hard it was for him to watch his beloved wife slipping away.

Her respirations changed as they chatted in the bedroom and by the time the first family members arrived Lizzy's breathing had slowed right down. There were more due to arrive over the course of the afternoon and Alf was praying that everyone could get here before the end, but deep down Callum didn't hold out much hope.

Callum and Felicity moved out to the kitchen to give the family time together. They didn't really talk much, just kept busy, making cups of tea and coffee and refilling them as often as required. At lunchtime Callum went out and bought some loaves of bread and sandwich fillers, which they turned into a couple of crammed platters, and later, for afternoon tea, they were able to rustle up enough home cooking to satisfy everyone.

By the time Lizzy took her last breath at four o'clock,

all the family that could be there were by her side. Callum marvelled at her staying power. He had clearly underestimated Alf's wife. It was as if she'd been hanging on for all her family before passing away.

They were washing up when Bailey howled. All the hairs on Callum's nape stood on end. Felicity's hands in the hot, sudsy water stilled. He waited for her to say something but she didn't, she just stood in silence for long moments. He wasn't sure what he should do but he wanted to do *something*. To give her some comfort. He knew how close she was to Alf and Lizzy but she'd held herself together today. He'd seen how hard it had been, seen her rapid blinking on more than one occasion as she'd comforted an upset Alf.

Tentatively, he slid an arm around her shoulders. She was stiff, like she might shatter into a thousand pieces, and for a moment he thought she was going to stay like that until he murmured, 'I'm sorry.' Then her shoulders suddenly slumped and her body leaned against his, her head resting on his biceps.

He dropped a kiss on her honey-blonde hair and they stayed there for a long time as he gently rubbed his hand up and down her arm.

A part of him wished he could do more but this, doing nothing, was somehow so much more intimate.

It felt right.

CHAPTER TWELVE

FELICITY STARED OUT of the window of Callum's car as he pulled up in front of her place and cut the engine. She'd offered to leave her car at Alf's so the large extended family had an extra car to get around in the next few days, which had left Callum to drive her home.

It was seven in the evening and the shadows of the gum trees in her front yard were just starting to lengthen. She and Callum had stuck around and notified all the right people and made the arrangements for Lizzy to be taken away. She'd wanted to free Alf and his family from the burden of it all so they could just grieve and hold each other.

Alf's 'I don't know what I'm going to do without her, Flick' ran on a continuous loop through her head. His devastation had reached inside her and squeezed her gut and still weighed heavily against her chest.

'We need to keep an eye on Alf the next little while,' she said. Felicity hadn't even registered the silence in the car until she broke it.

'You don't think he'd try to…'

Felicity shook her head, her gaze fixed on the shadows outside the car. 'No. But they've been together a lot of years. It wouldn't be the first time a spouse had died close on the heels of a long-term partner.'

'Good point.'

'I'll organise some community health services,' she said, her brain flipping through the options. 'And I'll mobilise the Country Women's Association.'

Felicity knew the CWA would rally around Alf. Lizzy had been the local president for about twenty years—Alf would never have to cook again.

'His daughter said quite a few of them were sticking around until after the funeral and she was going to stay on until Christmas. Apparently they're all going to spend it here with Alf.'

Christmas. It was hard to believe it was only five weeks away. 'That's good.'

They lapsed into silence again. Felicity looked at her house. It seemed so quiet and empty after the fullness of Alf's house today. She had never minded the quietness. It had been one of the joys of moving back to Vickers Hill after living in an apartment on a busy main road in Adelaide. But she didn't want to face the quietness now. She didn't want to be alone.

She turned her head to look at him. 'You want to come in for a drink?'

To say he looked taken aback by the offer was an understatement. 'There…seem to be a lot of reasons why I shouldn't.'

Felicity nodded. There were. But.

'I need a drink. A big one. And I don't want to be alone right now.'

His eyes searched hers for a beat or two. She wasn't sure what she was looking for but he must have been satisfied because he reached for the release button on his seat belt. 'I could definitely go a drink.'

Felicity was thankful as she unlocked her front door and Callum followed her into the house that she had no Mrs Smiths to worry about. Sure, people gossiped in her street too—where didn't they?—but her neighbours were mostly families, young mums too busy just getting through the day to worry about what Felicity was doing in the privacy of her own home.

'You were so good with Alf's family today,' he said from behind her as he followed her into her formal lounge room.

'Well, I've had plenty of practice,' she said as she poured them both a slug of her favourite whisky.

'Sure. I just figured you'd be…'

Felicity smiled to herself as she screwed the lid back on the bottle then turned, handing him his whisky. 'An emotional wreck? A blubbering mess?'

'I was thinking more along the lines of not quite so contained.'

She smiled again. Callum was treading carefully. 'Lizzy's death isn't about me and my feelings. It's about them. Her family. Me bursting into tears because *I'm* sad doesn't prioritise their grief and also puts the onus on them to comfort *me* during a time when they should only be thinking of themselves. It's selfish. Not helpful.'

'So you just…don't?'

'That's right.' She nodded. 'You just suck it up. Come home, have a drink and a long cry in the shower.'

Felicity looked into the depths of the amber fluid. The tears that had been threatening since she'd got the phone call this morning pushed closer to the surface. She blinked hard, swirled the whisky around the glass a few times before raising it towards him.

'To Lizzy.'

He tapped his glass against hers. 'To Lizzy.'

Felicity slugged back half of hers, sucking in a breath as the whisky burned all the way down. '*You* were pretty great too today,' she mused as she watched him over the rim of her glass.

He smiled. 'I had a good teacher.'

Felicity laughed. A short, sharp sound that was more wounded than joyous. It hurt. Deep inside her chest where it had been hurting all day.

He frowned and took a step towards her. 'Are you okay?'

'Nope.' Her voice wobbled, her smile wobbled. Everything wobbled inside as the soft concern in his voice undid her. 'But I will be tomorrow.'

A tear escaped. And then another.

'Felicity,' he whispered, placing his drink down on a nearby table and taking the step that separated them, his hands on her hips. 'Don't cry.'

She didn't want to, not in front of him, but crying came as naturally to Felicity as laughing. She'd thought the tears would hold off until she was alone. She was wrong.

'Sorry,' she said, embarrassed, dashing them away with her hands.

'Don't,' he said. 'Don't ever apologise for being who you are.'

It didn't help. The tears came faster.

'Hey,' he murmured, taking her glass and discarding it too before sliding his hands up her back, urging her against him.

Felicity went, shutting her eyes and bunching her fingers in his T-shirt, letting the tears fall. It was beyond her power to stop them.

'I'm sorry,' she repeated, the even thud of his heart comforting beneath her ear.

'Shh,' he said, his chin resting on top of her head. 'It's okay.'

It certainly felt okay, standing in the circle of his arms,

weeping quietly. Losing Lizzy had taken a little chink out of her soul, as had every patient she'd ever lost. It was inevitable for someone like her whose emotions were barely skin deep, but having Callum here with her helped.

She glanced up at him. She was close enough to his neck to see every individual whisker, to press her nose to his throat and inhale the citrus essence of him. Fill herself up with that instead of the echoes of Alf finally breaking down and whispering, 'My darling, my darling, my darling', like his heart was shattering.

She angled her head back until she was looking into his eyes, eyes that told their own story of loss right there for the whole world to see.

'Thank you,' she said, rising up on tiptoe and kissing him.

For being here. For being *there*. For being better. For being what she needed exactly when she needed it.

Like right now.

He eyed her warily as he pulled back, his hands moving to her hips and pushing her away gently. But Felicity held firm. The night stretched ahead of her and she didn't want to be alone for any of it.

'Felicity?' His hands branded her hips as his confused eyes searched hers. Was he trying to find some kind of meaning as to why she'd kissed him? 'I'm not sure we should be doing this.'

Felicity was very sure they *shouldn't* be but she wanted it anyway. And the accelerated thud of his heart beneath her palm told her maybe he did too.

'I didn't mean this to be—' He stopped abruptly, obviously finding the right words difficult. 'I was just...trying to comfort you.'

'I know.' She did. And she appreciated it.

But...

She raised her hand, tracing her fingers along his jaw and up the side of his face. 'I just need a different kind of comfort tonight.'

He stared at her for long moments before covering her hand with his and bringing it to his mouth, dropping a kiss on her palm. It was such a gentle gesture Felicity's eyes welled with tears again.

His mouth lowered and he kissed her, soft and slow, like their very first kiss on the train before it had turned hot and heavy. The tears spilled over, trekking south, his thumbs wiping them away as he cupped her cheeks either side of her jaw, his gentleness so sweet she sighed his name against his mouth.

He eased away slightly. 'Take me to the nearest bed.'

The low, gravelly request slid right between her legs and, without a word, Felicity took him by the hand and led him to her bedroom.

She turned as they crossed the threshold, seeing her bed in its usual unmade disarray. 'It's a little messy, I'm afraid I don't see the point in making my bed when—'

His mouth cut her off as his hands slid to her waist, bringing their bodies flush against each other. 'I don't care about mess,' he muttered, coming up for air, feathering kisses along her jaw to her ear. 'I just want to be inside you.'

Felicity's eyes fluttered closed. 'Oh, God,' she breathed, her hands on his shoulders. 'I want you inside me too.'

And then he was kissing her mouth again as he pulled at her tank top, peeling it off, and she was rucking up his T-shirt and hauling it over his head then reaching for the snaps on his shorts as he reached for hers, pushing them down his legs, kicking out of her own, their kissing stop-start as they shimmied out of their clothes.

Then they were naked and breathless and falling on

the bed together in a tangle of limbs and impatience, and
he was rolling her on her back, kissing down her neck to
her breasts, sucking each nipple in turn, making her cry
out and arch her back and forget everything about the day
except this moment.

Nothing mattered right now but how they could make
each other's bodies sing. Nothing mattered but him.

Her fingers tangled hard in his hair, holding him at her
breasts, begging him for more. And he gave her more.
More and more, his tongue taunting her until she saw
stars. Until she was so damn wet and tingly and restless
she was begging him to stop, begging him to finish it, to
thrust himself inside her and take them both where they
wanted to go.

Her nails dug into his back and she dragged his mouth
off her nipple. 'I want you inside me.'

He kissed her hard before mumbling, 'Condom,' then
heading back to torture her nipples some more.

Condom. *Right.* Bedside drawer.

Desperately she reached for it, crying out and arching
her back when he resumed what he'd been doing, only the
other side this time, his hard tongue circling and circling
and circling until her eyes were rolling back in her head
and her nipple was slippery and elongated, then sucking
it deep into his mouth, his teeth scraping against the tip.

Her hand found a loose foil packet and she snatched it
up, tearing it open as she pushed on his shoulder. 'Condom,' she panted.

He lifted his head and Felicity almost whimpered at
the relief, the cool air stiffening her wet nipples into tight,
hard cones. He grabbed the condom from her and shifted
slightly to his side, sheathing himself in one deft move.
Then she was reaching for him, grasping his shoulders,
pulling him over her, spreading her legs wide so he could

settle deep, reaching for his erection, exulting in his guttural groan as she squeezed all his glorious length, guiding him to where she was slick and needy.

'There,' she gasped as he nudged, thick and hard against
her, tormenting her with the promise of his girth. 'Right
there.'

'Oh, yeah,' he murmured, his voice a low growl. 'Right
there.'

And then he was sliding home and she was calling out
his name, wrapping her legs around his waist, asking him
for more, feeling every hot, hard glide, shivering and shaking with each thrust, tilting her pelvis to meet each one,
digging her fingers into his buttocks, revelling in the tremble through his thighs and biceps and the harsh suck of
his breath as the friction built and the tension mounted,
his arms hard bands of muscle bracketing her shoulders.

It wasn't long before the whole world started to unravel.
A tiny ripple that started deep and low became two, then
three. Then became stronger.

A contraction. Two. Three.

Then a shudder undulating along her pelvic floor.

Felicity gasped as the shudders escalated, increasing
in intensity until she could barely stand it, her eyes flying
open to find him watching her, their gazes locking in an
intensely intimate moment.

The moment of mutual release.

'Yes,' he muttered, his brow crinkled in concentration,
his biceps like granite in her peripheral vision, as his hips
pumped faster and harder. 'I can feel you. I can feel you.'

Felicity cried out, fighting the urge to shut her eyes as
she came, showing him all that she was as she flew apart.
He joined her in the maelstrom moments later, his eyes
wide open too, gifting her every second of his orgasm as it
slammed through his body, the wonder and intensity of it

reflected in his gaze until they were churned out the other end, sweaty, spent and utterly exhausted.

It was dark in her room but the red luminous figures on Felicity's bedside clock told her it was ten past one. She should be tired from the emotion of the day and the expended energy of the night. But she wasn't.

Callum was in her bed and while that was something she was going to have to deal with—*tomorrow*—she was going to enjoy it for the night. Like she had on the train.

She was tracing patterns on his chest as he stroked lazy fingers up and down her back. 'What do you see when you look at me?'

'Fishing for compliments?' Even rumbling through his chest wall straight into her ear, his voice didn't lose any of its amusement.

She smiled, her finger circling one flat, brown nipple. 'No. I'm being serious.'

His hand paused for a moment, missing a beat or two before continuing its steady pace. 'Okay. I see an incredible woman, a great lover and amazing nurse. I see—'

'No.' Felicity pushed off his chest, propping her head on her hand as she looked down at him, stroking a finger along his chin, under his bottom lip. 'I mean, what do you physically see? With your eye the way it is.'

He went very still. 'Oh. Right.'

Her finger paused on his chin. *Damn.* Way to kill the mood, Flick. 'I'm sorry. It's okay. I shouldn't have asked.'

Except lying here with him she'd realised she didn't know anything about the nitty-gritty of his eyesight. Mostly because he'd seemed so closed off about it but it seemed uncaring not to enquire.

Sure, it was easy to forget when looking at him that he had any kind of sight deficit. His misshapen, slightly dilated pupil and the fact he couldn't drive at night were the only indications. But it was hardly something *he* could forget. It wasn't like it was out of sight.

It *was* his sight.

'No. It's fine,' he assured her. 'You just took me by surprise, that's all. Nobody other than my specialists and the medical board have ever really asked.'

Felicity stroked her finger along his bottom lip. It was full and tempting. 'Didn't any of those women you shamelessly slept with after the accident ever ask?'

He smiled and she traced the curve of his mouth all the way to the corner and back again. 'They seemed more interested in bagging the blind surgeon than the details of my injury,' he said, his voice heavy with derision.

'Well, I'm interested,' she said, tapping his chin lightly.

'In the details or…' his hand slid onto her hip and lightly stroked '…bagging the blind dude?'

Felicity laughed, his tone light and more self-deprecating now. 'Huh. Been there, done that. Three times already tonight.'

His hand swept to her butt, scattering goose-bumps down the backs of her thighs and arrowing heat right between her legs. 'Fourth time's a charm.'

'Patience,' she teased, dropping a quick kiss on his mouth. 'Now, tell me how you see me.'

He sighed dramatically but kept up the drugging sweep of his hand from hip to buttocks and back again. 'At the moment, in the dark, not much with the left eye, you're kind of a dim blur.'

He was becoming a bit of a blur too as heat streaked to her pelvis. 'What about during the day? In normal light?'

'If I cover up my good eye, you'd be pretty blurred. The acuity in my left eye is shocking but my right eye compensates and if I'm wearing my glasses then the blurriness improves even further. But if you're standing on my left I probably wouldn't see you at all because my peripheral vision in that eye is pretty much nonexistent.'

The bitterness that had tinged his voice when he'd first told her about it was missing now. She wasn't sure if that was significant or just the result of three really good orgasms.

God knew, if she was any mellower at the moment from those orgasms and the very distracting stroke of his hand, she'd be floating away like a dandelion puff.

'They can't operate to help in any way?'

'They did what they could in the beginning. I've had quite a few surgical interventions, including laser work on my retina, but…frankly I don't think any of the specialists thought I'd have any kind of worthwhile vision so they're seeing it as a win.'

'And they think it's as good as it'll get?'

'It may improve marginally, in time but it's taken over two years to get where it is and most of that progress was made in the first year.'

'Are you still friends with the guy who bowled the ball?'

'Sure.' He shrugged. 'It's not his fault. It was a freak accident and I should have been wearing a helmet. I had one in my car but…'

Yeah. But…

Felicity was sure he'd done the should-haves and if-onlys over and over. It had been an expensive error in judgement and her heart went out to him. There was just something about this man that made her want to make it all better for him.

Enough bringing them down.

They had tonight and she was up for a little sexual healing.

'So, to recap,' she said, sliding her leg over and rolling

up to straddle him, settling her slick heat over his semi-hardness, 'what you're saying is you see things right in front of you reasonably well in reasonable light, especially if you have glasses on.'

He chuckled, his hands moving to her hips. 'Yes.'

'So...' she arched her back, lifting the hair off her nape and piling it high on her head, two-handed '...it's not so good at the moment.'

'I can see enough,' he murmured, the heat from his gaze like an infra-red beam fanning over her breasts, prickling her nipples to tight, hard buds. 'And I have a pretty good imagination.'

'Would this help?' she asked, letting her hair go, leaning forward at the hips, reaching for the switch that was looped through the wrought-iron lattice of her bedhead.

She flicked it on and sat back to admire the effect of a dozen tiny fairy lights, embedded in plastic hearts woven through the metal, glowing soft and pink.

It was kind of how she felt now. Her heart on a string, all happy and glowy inside her.

'Oh, yes,' he muttered, his gaze zeroing in with laser-like intensity, his hands sliding up her sides.

His singular focus was an instant turn-on. 'Light not too harsh?' she teased.

He shook his head as his fingers stroked the undersides of her breasts. 'It's perfect.' He cupped them fully. 'You're perfect.' He brushed his thumbs across her aching nipples. 'So beautiful.'

Felicity moaned as his rapidly swelling erection pushed hard against the knot of tingling nerves between her legs and she rubbed herself against him for maximum effect.

'God,' he groaned, vaulting upright, curling an arm around her waist and hauling her close. Felicity arched her back, offering her nipple to his questing mouth. She buried her hand in his hair, her eyes fluttering closed as his hot, wet mouth closed around her and she let herself get lost in the pleasure.

CHAPTER THIRTEEN

FELICITY WAS SITTING at the central island bench in her kitchen the next morning, reading the Sunday paper she had delivered to her door. A steaming-hot cup of coffee sat at her elbow as she tried to concentrate on some political scandal instead of the speech she had to give.

She'd heard the shower being turned on about fifteen minutes ago so it wouldn't be long now.

She'd been awake for a couple of hours, just watching him sleep, admiring the play of early morning shadows across his face and body. He looked so damn sexy in her bed.

When he was asleep. When he was awake. When he was thrusting into her, silhouetted by a fuzzy pink glow.

They would be memories she would treasure for ever.

But it couldn't be any more than another one-night stand. It would be too easy to spend the next five weeks in his arms and too hard to say goodbye. He wasn't ready. There were issues he still had to work out. And she didn't want to invest in someone who'd probably break her heart. It had taken her a long time to feel whole after Ned and she'd learned to be more guarded since then.

She just couldn't be the girl from the train here in Vickers Hill. She wasn't that reckless. Not in real life. Not with her reputation and not with her emotions.

'Good morning.'

The gravelly male voice coming from behind her ruffled all the tiny hairs on Felicity's nape. But there was wariness in his tone too. Was he feeling unsure after waking to an empty bed?

'Morning,' she said, not bothering to turn and acknowledge him, just slipping off her stool and heading for the percolator. 'Want a coffee?'

'Sure.' His tone was all wariness now.

She picked up a mug and poured him one, steeling herself to face him.

'Here you go,' she said, turning, mug in hand and a smile on her face. He was standing near the bench in his clothes from yesterday, except for his bare feet.

His hair was damp and he smelled like her shampoo.

Coconut had never smelled so damn good.

She slid his coffee across the bench, keen to keep something solid between them. 'Sit,' she said, leaning across to shift the newspaper out of the way.

Felicity didn't wait to see if he followed her command. She turned back to the percolator and poured herself another coffee. Her third for the morning. When she was done she made a beeline for the stool that was on her side of the bench and sat down, taking a sip of her drink.

He took one too and said, 'I feel like I'm about to get a "Dear John" speech.'

She shot him a nervous smile. 'Am I that obvious?'

He placed his mug on the countertop. 'Just say what you have to say, Felicity.'

She nodded. The direct approach was good. Rip that sticking plaster off and get on with it. 'Last night was...'

God, where did she even start with last night? The train had been good but last night had been better. It'd been emotional, not just sexual. A deeper connection born not just from what they'd shared yesterday but from three weeks of spending practically every day together.

And that scared the hell out of her.

'It's okay,' he said, his lips curling in a derisive smile. 'I think we can skip the compliments.'

'Okay.' She placed her mug down on the granite bench-top too. 'Last night was inevitable. It's been building for the last few weeks and after the train…well, I think we both know the train was never going to be enough when we've had to work together so closely.'

'*I* think if the next words that come out of your mouth are that you regret it or that *I* should regret it or that it was wrong or dumb or any other ridiculous statement then you should stop right there.'

Felicity gave a half-smile at his pre-emptive statement. His mouth was set in a hard line, his green eyes steely. He was even sexy when he was cranky. 'Nope.' She shook her head. 'No regrets.'

Never.

His mouth relaxed and his shoulders lost some of their tension. *Sexy, sexy, sexy.*

'But this can't become a regular thing,' she continued. 'I can't keep having sex with you and fooling myself that it's just some crazy interlude. Some mutual fun while you're here…that it'll all be okay. I'm just not built that way. I'm not the girl from the train. I was never really her. I'm just Flick from Vickers Hill.'

He didn't say anything for long moments, just stared at her as if he was trying to figure her out. 'Are you telling me…' he placed his bent elbow on the bench and supported his chin in his palm '…you don't even want to be friends?'

If only. Friends would make everything so much easier but that line was somewhere behind her now. 'I think I'm probably always going to want more than that from you.'

'Like…friends with benefits?'

She shook her head sadly. 'Like friends with *emotions*.'

Her admission sat him back, his arm dropping to the countertop. 'I see.'

She wondered if he did. Really did. 'You know what I thought last night when I turned those lights on? That that was me. That was my heart. Glowing all pink and beautiful inside my chest.'

He swallowed then, a light dawning in his eyes as the information slowly settled in. 'Are you trying to tell me that you're…?'

'No. I'm not,' she assured him. Quickly. Definitively. *She couldn't be.* It had taken her almost a year to realise she'd loved Ned. It would be preposterous to be in love with Callum after a few weeks. 'But… I *am* that kind of girl. Absence *doesn't* make my heart grow fonder. *Presence* makes it grow fonder and we can't keep doing this…' she waved her finger back and forth between them '…without…consequences. I *like* you, Callum.'

He was scheduled to leave on Christmas Eve and she was already sad about that day five weeks from now.

'I like you too.'

Felicity suppressed a snort. She didn't need to hear some quick-fire, city-slicker patronising response. He knew *exactly* what she meant. She folded her arms. 'A little *too* much.'

He dropped his gaze to his coffee as her point hit home and he fiddled with the handle. 'So we just…what?' he asked, glancing at her. 'See each other at work and that's it?'

'Yep.' Felicity nodded. 'Just colleagues…just two professionals. That's all.'

His gaze searched hers for what felt like an age, as if he was trying to assess just how serious she was. She didn't blink. Not once. Even though her hands were shaking around her mug and her pulse whooshed like a raging river through her ears.

'Okay. Sure. If that's what you want.'

Felicity nodded, amazed at her outer calm. 'It is.' Even though what she really wanted was for him to say, 'To hell with that,' pick her up and throw her down on her bed. The temptation to spend every night like last night almost overwhelmed her now she'd done herself out of the chance.

But he was going back to Sydney. He *had* to go back to Sydney. He had to work out what he wanted.

And living in a state of denial was preferable to living in a state of hope.

Two weeks later, in early December, Callum strode into the Parson's Nose—one of the many excellent gourmet pubs in town—searching the crowded room for his brother. If he'd been surprised to get a phone call from Seb—they had more of a texting relationship these days—he'd been utterly gobsmacked when Seb announced he was in Vickers Hill.

Today was Thursday, which was normally his day off, but Bill's brother had died a few days ago and the funeral was this morning so Callum had been covering for the old man. He hadn't minded and there had been the added bonus of seeing Felicity. But Bill had insisted he'd return for the afternoon appointments despite Callum encouraging him to take the whole day off.

Callum kept hearing from Julia about Bill retiring and all her grand plans for them but, as far as Callum could see, Bill wasn't ready to go yet. He certainly didn't seem to be in any hurry about finding a replacement.

'Cal!' Callum's head swivelled towards the voice and

he squinted, trying to locate Seb. Finally he clocked his brother, waving and grinning, near the bar.

Callum made his way through several groups of people as Seb slid off his stool. When he finally reached the bar he pulled his brother in for a bear hug as they slapped each other on the back. The circumstances of their lives the last few years had meant a lot of separation but it was always good to see him again.

'Missing me, dude?' Callum said as they pulled apart.

'Always.' Seb laughed.

They settled on their bar stools and Seb waved the bartender over, ordering Callum a local beer. They watched as he poured then they clinked their glasses together and toasted brotherly love.

'What on earth brings you to sleepy little Vickers Hill?' Callum asked, swiping froth from his top lip.

'Well, it's not the surf.' Seb grinned.

Callum laughed. 'No. Definitely not.' He sighed. 'I *do* miss the surf.'

'Maybe I should be asking what on earth brings *you* to Vickers Hill?'

His brother may be younger but, being the black sheep of the family, he was never one for taking things at face value and always the one to ask probing questions. Even as a kid he'd wanted to know the whys, whats and wherefores of everything.

'I needed some…clear air.'

Seb regarded him over the rim of his beer glass for a beat or two. 'Have you found it?'

That was a much harder question to answer. Trust Seb to be the one asking it.

'Yes. And no.'

Seb lifted an eyebrow. 'Now, that requires further explanation so spill it, big brother.'

Callum didn't even know where to begin. In five weeks he *had* managed to find clear air regarding his career. He'd arrived here conflicted, hoping like crazy that a change in pace and scenery would enthuse him for his new path.

And it had.

He'd seen a different side to what had felt like the yoke of general practice and he'd been a better doctor out here then he'd been the last two years in any of his placements.

Thanks to Felicity.

Felicity...

Yeah. The air there was *far* from clear. Pretty damn murky, actually. She'd been strict about their interactions and things between the two of them had been exactly as she'd wanted. They saw each other at work from one p.m. four days a week and rarely outside any more, apart from bumping into her at the shops or petrol station.

But that hadn't stopped the trip in his pulse whenever he heard her laughter or checking her out *every single time* she walked into the room. She'd been stringing tinsel up around the office all this week and she'd started wearing very distracting Christmas T-shirts and a red Santa hat with a cute white pom-pom on the end.

She seemed pretty damn cheerful, her easiness with him so effortless considering he had to check himself constantly. The urge to flirt, to slip into banter, to yank on that distracting white pom-pom was harder to suppress than he'd thought.

He had to keep reminding himself of what she'd said and who she was. She was a sensitive, empathic woman who'd taken him on to advocate for her patients and wasn't ashamed of how close her emotions bubbled to the surface. She'd got teary talking about her grandfather the first day he'd met her. Not to mention her reaction over Seb's fiancé and, of course, her tears for Lizzy Dunnich.

I'm that kind of girl.

That's what she'd said. And he was aware of it every day, watching her with the people she worked with and her patients. The way she cooed over the babies and clucked over the oldies, cheered over the wins and bossed the non-compliant with such a loving hand.

She *wasn't* like other women he'd met. She wasn't the kind he could play with and leave. Just walk away from and know she'd be okay. She'd told him she liked him. A woman had never told him she liked him. They'd confessed their love, their desire, their admiration. Their wildest sexual fantasies. But, looking back, he wasn't sure any of them had *liked* him.

And he'd never really told a woman he liked her either. In fact, he'd taken himself by complete surprise when he'd said it back. But it had felt right and he found himself not wanting to screw it up. To leave with her still liking him, even if it meant having to ignore his libido.

Because he *was* going back to Sydney.

He had to go back. He had a lot to prove.

'Uh-oh,' Seb said, waiting with a cocked eyebrow, clearly amused at Callum's prolonged contemplation. 'That bad?'

He glanced at his brother. 'There's this woman…'

'It's always a woman.' Seb chuckled.

Callum shook his head. 'Felicity isn't just any woman.'

'Felicity?' Seb frowned. 'Do you mean Flick? Luci's friend?'

'Yep.' And he told his brother everything.

'Well?' Callum asked after he'd run out of steam and his beer glass was empty.

'Well, what?'

'What do you think? Am I crazy?'

'Hell, Cal,' Seb groaned. 'Don't ask me. Luci has me so tied up in knots I don't know what to do any more either.'

'Luci?' It was Callum's turn to frown. '*My* Luci?'

'*Your* Luci?'

'I mean the one in my apartment?'

'Yes. She's the reason I'm here today. Her uncle died—'

'I know,' Callum interrupted. 'I've been covering the morning appointments for her father.'

With Felicity.

'Right. Well, she came back for the funeral and I know coming back and facing the town again was hard so... I thought I'd be here for her.'

'You *know*?'

Seb shrugged and, if Callum wasn't very much mistaken that was a smile breaking across his brother's face. 'We...talk. We've got close.'

Callum blinked. Could Seb actually be taking an interest in another woman after all this time? He hoped so. His brother had been to hell and back. 'Good for you. You've been through a lot, man. You deserve to be happy.'

Seb looked him straight in the eye. 'So do you, Cal. So do you.'

Callum appreciated the sentiment but his loss had been nothing compared to Seb's. 'Well,' he said, changing the subject, 'I'm sure Luci is very pleased to have you here.'

'Oh, she doesn't know yet. I only made up my mind this morning and jumped an early flight.' Seb checked his watch and quickly downed the dregs of his beer. 'So I'd better get going. The funeral should be over by now.'

He stood and Callum followed suit. They shook hands and shared another bear hug. Seb mumbled something about spending Christmas together and then he was striding out of the pub, his 'So do you, Cal,' lingering in his wake.

* * *

Felicity pulled up outside Luci's the day before Christmas Eve, a bunch of nerves knotting so tight in her stomach she feared it was going to burst open under the tension. Or she was going to throw up.

One or the other.

Callum was leaving tomorrow. In the morning. He'd be back in Sydney by lunchtime.

Out of sight, out of mind, right?

Fourteen hundred kilometres out of sight. Although she doubted even the North Pole would be far enough to keep him out of mind...

She glanced at the lavender growing along Luci's front path. She didn't know why she was here.

No. That was a lie. She knew.

The little farewell party they'd thrown Callum at lunch today just hadn't cut it. Giving him a polite hug good-bye in front of all their colleagues had seemed too impersonal considering what had transpired between them. She wanted to say things to him—personal things. Things she couldn't say in front of everyone at work. But still needed to be said.

Private things.

That she wished him well, that he was going to be all right. And a brilliant GP. That she was pleased their paths had crossed and there were no hard feelings.

That she'd *never ever* forget their night on the train.

After weeks of keeping every thought and feeling strictly under wraps, she couldn't let him leave without telling him that. She had to *know* he knew.

The last few weeks had been an exercise in self-control and, somehow, she'd managed. *Just.* But with him leaving tomorrow she couldn't deny the strong pull to *see* him one last time.

To just…*look* at him.

So she'd jumped in her car and driven straight here. Hell, she hadn't even bothered getting out of her uniform.

This last time felt ridiculously momentous and Felicity took a deep breath. It caught in the thickening of her throat as her trembling fingers reached for the doorhandle. She fumbled it then stumbled out as if it was her first ever step.

She was hyper-aware of everything around her as her pulse throbbed through her temples. The sun warm on her shoulders, even at almost seven in the evening after a record run of high temperatures and concerns about bush fires. The trill of insects. The laughter of kids somewhere up the street.

The smell of lavender and meat roasting from one of the nearby houses.

'Good evening, Flick.'

Felicity startled at the imperious greeting from behind her, her heart pounding in her chest at being sprung again by Mrs Smith.

Did the woman have some kind of sixth sense? She was only coming to talk, for crying out loud.

'Evening, Mrs Smith,' she said, plastering on a smile as she turned to face the woman who she was quickly coming to think of as her nemesis. Even standing on her footpath in a baggy house dress and hair rollers she somehow still managed to look like the stern teacher who had taught Felicity in grade four.

'You here to see Dr Hollingsworth?'

'Er…' Felicity tried to figure out a response that would cause the least amount of ire from Vickers Hill's self-appointed defender of virtue.

But Mrs Smith didn't wait for any further elaboration. 'He's leaving in the morning.'

'Yes.'

'Back to Sydney.'

'Yes.'

She made a tutting sound. 'You left your run too late, my girl.'

Felicity blinked. 'My…run?'

'He's been here for two months. And you're not getting any younger.'

What the ever-loving hell…? Had Mrs Smith just implied she'd been left on the shelf at the grand age of twenty-eight?

'I'd been married for almost ten years and had three little kiddies by your age. You should be settling down with a nice local boy. What about Ed Dempsey? He's had his eye on you for a while.'

Ed Dempsey? He had his eye on every woman with a pulse. Plus she'd never quite forgiven him for putting a green frog down the back of her shirt when she'd been four.

'There's nothing between Dr Hollingsworth and I.'

'So why are you here on his doorstep at the last minute?' A sudden light dawned over her wrinkly face and Felicity felt nine years old again under her eagle-eyed gaze. 'Ah, I see,' she sniffed. 'You know…' she glanced around her as she made her way towards Felicity '…you can't expect him to buy the cow if he's getting the milk for free.'

Felicity gaped at her old primary school teacher as she contemplated hacking off her ears to unhear what had just been said. *'Mrs Smith.'*

'Oh, you don't think I know what you young people get up to these days?' She stepped off the footpath and Felicity resigned herself to a lecture about the perils of premarital sex from her ex-teacher. 'Why, I…'

She didn't get to finish her sentence and for a brief moment, as Mrs Smith stumbled, relief flowed like coolant through Felicity's system. Unfortunately, she didn't regain her footing and despite Felicity lurching for her as Mrs Smith looked around wild-eyed, desperately trying to grab hold of something, she fell hard on the road on her left side.

She cried out in pain. 'Mrs Smith!' Felicity threw herself down beside her, her annoyance forgotten. 'Are you okay?'

'No,' she managed through clenched teeth, rolling onto her back, groaning in pain as she grabbed her hip. 'I'm not.'

Out of habit, Felicity placed her fingers on the pulse at Mrs Smith's wrist. 'Where are you hurt?'

'It's my damn hip,' she snapped, raising her head as if she'd be able to see a bone sticking out or something before giving up and dropping her head back onto the road on an annoyed hiss.

Felicity was relieved to feel a strong, regular pulse, and slid her hand into Mrs Smith's to give it a squeeze, whether the older woman wanted the comfort or not. She glanced down to find Mrs Smith's left leg was markedly shorter than the right and badly externally rotated. *Damn.* Felicity would bet her life the older woman had sustained a fractured neck of femur.

'Anywhere else?'

'Isn't that enough?' Mrs Smith grouched.

Felicity pressed her lips together to stop herself smiling. 'Okay, hang on a sec.' She pulled her phone out of her back pocket and dialled Callum.

'Felicity?'

She ignored the husky query in his voice. And the tug down deep and low inside her. 'I'm outside. Opposite. At Mrs Smith's. She's had a fall on the road and I'm pretty sure she's fractured her left NOF. Can you give some help, please?'

She could have handled it herself if she'd had to but it made sense to have as much medical support as possible.

'On my way.'

The call was hung up in her ear and she quickly dialled the ambulance station, which, thanks to her home visit schedule, was on speed dial in her contacts. She was ending the call as Callum crossed the road. He was wearing shorts that came to his knees and an ab-hugging T-shirt and was carrying a couple of pillows.

Her heart missed a beat or two.

'You've called an ambulance?' he asked as he knelt on the road, his knees pressing into the bitumen. He didn't look at Felicity as he smiled at the older woman, who was noisily sucking air in and out of her lungs.

'They're ten minutes away.'

He nodded. 'How are you going, Mrs Smith?'

'I've been better,' she said, although the cantankerous edge had obviously been weakened from the pain. 'Think I might have broken my hip.'

'I think you're right,' he murmured, slipping a pillow under her head.

'What's your pain level if one is the mildest and ten is the worst pain you've ever felt?' Felicity asked.

'A hundred,' Mrs Smith panted.

Felicity believed her. Her brow was deeply furrowed and there was a ring of white around her tight mouth. Mrs Smith might be a bit of an old busybody but they bred them tough out here and she was one of the toughest characters in Vickers Hill.

'The ambulance will be here soon,' Callum soothed. 'We'll get you some pain relief and have you on the way to hospital in a jiffy. You think you can hold on for a bit longer?'

'I'll be fine,' she dismissed, her voice gruff, but she squeezed Felicity's hand harder.

Finally he looked at Felicity, their gazes meshing, a question in his eyes she was too afraid to answer.

'We'll support her pelvis in a sling when they get here,' he said, breaking their eye contact. 'I brought out a sheet to fashion one but we'd better wait for the magic green whistle to arrive before we attempt anything.'

'Agreed.' Pain relief was their priority before they attempted any kind of handling. She just wished she could have a magic green whistle for their situation. One that took them back to that night on the train and turned them into two normal people with no baggage and open hearts.

'Did you hit your head, Mrs Smith?' he asked, and Felicity was grateful that Callum's medical training had taken over. Grateful for any distraction from the question she'd seen in his eyes and from the answer she could no longer deny.

Why are you here?

Because I love you.

CHAPTER FOURTEEN

BY THE TIME the ambulance had departed it was well and truly dark. Then it was just the two of them standing in the middle of the road bathed in the silent strobing of red and blue lights as they faded down the street. The neighbours who had milled around had since melted away to their homes.

'You want a drink?'

Felicity shook her head. She needed to go now that she knew the answer to the question. She certainly didn't need to drink alcohol around him, lose her inhibitions and blurt it out.

She loved him.

It was insane and the timing sucked. It was too soon and he was leaving—he *had* to leave—but it was there nonetheless. Like a light blinking inside her, sure and steady. She was in deep.

Too deep. Too soon.

And losing him was going to hurt about a thousand times more than losing Ned ever had. No amount of crazy glue was going to put her heart back together after this.

Damn.

'Okay. But I'm assuming there's a reason you came over?'

She nodded. Not that it mattered now. 'No… I just wanted to…say goodbye.'

He shoved his hands on his hips. 'You said goodbye at the party.'

'I know. But...'

'But what?'

Yeah, Flick. But what?

Stupid tears pricked the backs of her eyes and Felicity was grateful for the night. 'I don't know...it felt too public.'

'So come inside.'

She shook her head, standing her ground. 'Here's fine.'

He looked around him pointedly. 'This isn't public? We're in the middle of the street. And...' he smiled suddenly and Felicity's breath hitched '...I'm reasonably certain Mrs Smith has the entire neighbourhood bugged.'

Felicity gave a weak half-smile despite the raging torment kicking up a storm in her gut.

A smile had never hurt so damn much.

She glanced at her car. It was three paces away but her legs were shaking so much it may as well have been on the moon. There just didn't seem to be enough oxygen between them. 'Mrs Smith ruined the mood.'

'She has a habit of doing that.' He regarded her for long moments before holding out his hand. 'Give me your phone.'

She frowned. 'What?'

'You look kind of undecided so let's ask Mike.' He waggled his fingers at her. 'Modern-day coin toss, remember?'

Felicity knew she should just walk away. But he was so damn sexy, smiling down her like that in the dark, being all flirty and charming and reminding her of that night on the train.

Playing dirty, no matter how obvious. And she was weak. No. More than that. Where he was concerned she was *feeble*.

She reached into her back pocket, tapped in her code and handed it over, her fingers trembling almost as much as her legs. He took it, navigating quickly to where he needed to be.

The light from the screen bathed his face in a sexy glow, highlighting his mouth, the dark outline of his whiskers and casting shadows under his chiselled cheekbones.

His gaze met hers as he brought the phone up to his mouth. 'Mike, should Felicity go to Callum's house for a drink?'

'Are his intentions honourable?'

The stylised British accent seemed loud in the hush that had fallen over the neighbourhood. Felicity's lungs burned as she held her breath and he held her gaze.

'They are, Mike.'

'One drink should be okay.'

He grinned at the quick-fire response as he passed the phone back, his face fading into the night again. 'Mike has spoken.'

Felicity let her breath out in a slow, husky exhalation. 'I think it's time I stopped letting Mike make these kinds of decisions.'

'Oh, I don't know. I think he's been on the money so far.'

Felicity sighed. 'Callum—'

'Oh, come on. Besides, I have a gift for you that I was going to drop off in your mailbox in the morning and now I can give it to you personally.' He put his hand over his heart and added, 'Please...' for good measure.

And not just any old *please*. There was a vibrato to it that floated gossamer fingers around her good sense, wrapping it up in an iron web.

'Okay. Fine. But I'm *not* having a drink. You give me the gift then I'm going.'

He smiled and nodded, clearly pleased with himself. 'Absolutely.'

He led the way up the path lit by subtle solar lamps, the

scent of lavender infusing Felicity's senses. It was hard to believe that Luci would be back tomorrow.

God, she had so much to tell her!

Felicity's nerves tangled into a knot as the door clicked shut behind her. 'Come in. Take a seat on the couch. I'll be right back.'

Oh, no. No way was she going to sit on Luci's cosy couch in her homey living room. She needed to be where she could make a quick escape.

She needed to be *vertical*.

'I'll wait here,' she said, grinding the soles of her sensible work shoes into the parquet floor of the entranceway.

He shrugged. 'Suit yourself.'

Thankfully he was back quickly, placing a package no bigger and sightly bulkier than a business card in the palm of her hand. It was wrapped in pretty flowery tissue paper. 'I couldn't resist it when I saw it in town the other day.' He grinned.

His smile would have been infectious had Felicity not been hyper-aware of the confines of the small alcove in which they stood and the fact the only light in the house was coming from behind them somewhere, which only seemed to enhance his nearness, his broadness, his sexy citrus essence.

She made a concerted effort to concentrate on the wrapping as her fingers fumbled it uselessly. When finally she conquered it she pulled it back to reveal a cheap-looking plastic badge boasting the word *Saint* in tacky diamantés.

'Now it's official,' he teased.

Felicity surprised herself by laughing. She'd been hoping it wasn't something sentimental lest she cry. She needn't have worried. The badge struck just the right note. Light and funny but still sweet and thoughtful.

'You think I should wear it to work?'

'Sure. Here.' He grabbed it from her. 'Let's see if it goes with the uniform.'

'Everything goes with diamantés,' she protested as his plan became clear, but it was too late, he'd stepped right in, opening the back clasp of the badge and fingering the open collar of her polo shirt.

It brought him a hell of a lot closer and she realised she was being hemmed in. The solid door behind her, his solid chest in front of her. Her pulse skipped madly. Goosebumps swept up and down her neck where his fingers accidentally brushed, rippling out in a hot wave to her breasts, beading her nipples into tight, hard peaks.

'There.' He stepped back but not all the way. He was still closer than he had been.

Closer than was good for her sanity.

'I think it looks perfect.'

Felicity breathed in deep, her oxygen depleted again. 'I doubt Bill would agree.'

'I think Bill would think it was amusing. Angela would think it's hysterical.'

'Yeah.' Knowing both of them, Felicity had to concede the point. 'I guess they would.'

They lapsed into silence, the lightness that had swirled around them moments ago quickly dissipating as awareness of the low light and their closeness set in again.

'So,' he prompted after long moments, 'you came to say goodbye? Before Mrs Smith so inconveniently broke her NOF?'

Felicity fixed her gaze on his shoulder. 'Yes.'

He nodded slowly. 'It's hard to believe it's been two months. It went quickly.'

'Yes.' It had and it hadn't. These last ten minutes, with her chest bursting and her heart breaking and him within touching distance, had felt like an age.

'I guess Meryl was wrong,' he murmured, shoving his hands in his pockets. The action pulled his T-shirt flat against his belly.

Felicity shrugged. Their visit with Meryl seemed a million years ago right now. 'First time for everything.'

More silence. 'I've never really said thank you,' he said, after the silence had stretched about as far as it could without snapping in two. 'The way you took me to task that day. You made me a better doctor.'

Felicity glanced at him, surprised by the statement. But the huskiness in his voice and the earnestness reflected in his gaze showed his sincerity. 'Its fine,' she dismissed. 'You'd been through a lot and you were grieving for your lost career. You'd have figured it out, I'm sure.'

He shook his head. 'No. I don't know that I would have.' He shuffled a little closer, his gaze dropping to her mouth. 'Thank you, Felicity.'

Oh, God. He was going to kiss her. Look away. *Look away.*

He was *thankful* and *grateful*. While she was *in love*. It was all so screwed up.

Look away.

But she couldn't drag her eyes off him. Thankfully, though, she still had some use of her legs and she took a step back. Or tried at least. Her shoulder blades met the door with practically no distance put between them at all.

'I'm going to miss you,' he said, his hand reaching for her, pushing back a chunk of hair that had come loose from her ponytail as they'd treated Mrs Smith, his palm lingering to cup her face. Her eyes fluttered closed. 'Are you going to miss me?'

She was going to miss him with a hunger that would gnaw away at her insides. She just knew it. Breaking up with Ned had been hard—she'd lost a friend as well as a lover. But Callum was an entirely different beast. There'd been no slow build-up to their relationship. No dawning realisation. It had been a headlong rush and she'd fallen hard and fast. And that was going to smash through her life like a wrecking ball.

'Yes.'

She didn't trust herself to elaborate as her eyes opened. And then she couldn't, even if she wanted to, because his head was lowering. Slowly. Inexorably.

God...why did she want his lips on hers so *freaking bad*?

'You said your intentions were honourable.'

It was supposed to sound strong, assertive, but came out all weak and breathy. More a plea than a last-ditch attempt to derail the inevitable.

'They were,' he muttered, his lips almost brushing hers. 'I swear they were.'

And then they were on her and opening over hers, hot and hard and sure, his ragged breath loud in her ears as he demanded entrance to her mouth, his tongue sweeping inside, stroking along hers as his hands went to her waist and his body aligned with hers—hot and hard and sure.

Her pulse hammered and her breath tangled with his as she tried frantically to drag in air. His thigh slid between her legs, pressing in hard, and she moaned as heat flooded her pelvis.

'God...you taste so good,' he murmured against her mouth, and his voice was so deep and dark and needy it filled her head with heat and need and sex. She knew if they didn't stop right now they'd be on the floor in seconds and it wouldn't be sex this time, it would be making *love*, and she couldn't bear for that to be one-sided.

Rallying reserves she hadn't known she had, she tore

her mouth from his. 'Callum,' she panted, pushing on his chest, desperate for some distance. 'Stop. Please, stop.'

His mouth was wet and his eyes were a little glazed as he backed up and she breathed more easily. 'Why?' he asked, his hands slipping off her waist, one shoving through his hair.

Because I love you, you idiot. 'Because I can't think, I can't be…rational when you do that. And you're leaving in the morning.'

He gazed at her for long beats before scrubbing a hand over his face. 'Maybe I could stay? I know Meera's back from maternity leave in the New Year but maybe she'd like some more time to be with her baby?'

Felicity blinked. *'What?'* Blind hope surged in her heart even as her head rejected it.

Maybe I could stay?

No. He needed to go. And it was just plain cruel to taunt her with empty possibilities.

He shrugged. 'I like it here. I like working here. I like that *you're* here.'

'No.' She shook her head, hardening her heart, refusing to let herself be carried away by his lust-induced sentiment. 'You can't hide here, Callum. It's bad enough you ran away here.'

He took a step back, clearly surprised by her frankness, although surely he was used to her speaking her mind by now? He shoved a hand on a hip. 'I was after clear air.'

She shrugged. 'You say potato…'

'You ran away too, Felicity, when you came here after Ned.'

'I wasn't running *away*. I was running *to* something.' She shook her head. 'Look…you had this brilliant life and career and you knew what you wanted, then it got blown all to hell. I knew what I wanted too and it also got blown all to hell, but I'm out the other side of it now. You're still in the middle. You said when you first came here that you had something to prove. So go home and prove it,' she said, goading him.

Goading him to leave her.

It hurt, damn it. So *freaking* much.

'Prove that being a GP is what you want.'

'It is what I want,' he snapped.

He turned away from her then, striding into the kitchen behind, placing his fists on the edge of the bench as he reached it. Felicity followed him at a slower pace. His shoulders were hunched, his head hung low between them.

'It's what you want *here*, while you're hiding away in Vickers Hill,' she said, gentler this time, speaking to his back. 'Wanting it *here* is easy. But you have to face the real world, Callum. The people that matter. The only way you're going to know if it's what you *really* want is by going back home. To your *surgeon* parents and your *surgeon* friends and their dinner parties full of shop talk about their latest surgical feats. Because it's only by going back to your old life that you'll know for sure.'

He didn't say anything for a long time. Finally he raised his head and slowly turned to face her. He leaned his butt against the bench and crossed his ankles in a casually deceptive pose but every inch of him was tense. 'Come with me.'

Felicity blinked, her heart beating hard in her chest, as hard as it was bleeding. A part of her wanted to snatch his offer up, throw caution to the wind, just as she'd urged Luci to do.

But this was *love*. And hers was too big to risk on a man still sorting his life out.

She wanted to be with him but she needed to know she

wasn't another consolation prize. The consolation woman that came part and parcel with the consolation job.

'No.'

'I like you. I think there's something between us. I think it could be more.'

Felicity sucked in a breath as his rumbled admissions played havoc with her sensibilities. The man obviously knew how to push all her damn buttons. She wondered if he had any idea how much his vague, noncommittal words hurt.

She swallowed. 'No.'

God, how could such a little word be so hard to say?

He cocked an eyebrow. 'You don't want to live in Sydney? I have an apartment on the harbour. And if you're worried about a job—don't be. With your qualifications and experience you could walk into about a dozen jobs straight away.'

'No.' She said it more firmly this time as he didn't seem to be getting the message.

'*Why?*' he demanded.

'Because you have a lot of things to confront and you don't need me hanging around muddying the waters. You need clear air back in Sydney too. I'm not going to be your distraction. A way for you to avoid facing up to the issues.'

'So you don't think there could be more between us?'

Felicity had told herself she wasn't going to cry when she came here tonight but she was just about at the end of her emotional tether. She wanted nothing more than to take up his offer. If only he knew how much it was killing her to keep denying him.

She cleared her throat of the sudden thickening. 'Of course I do.'

'So come with me,' he repeated. 'Or are you too married to this place to contemplate leaving?'

'No. I don't have a problem with leaving Vickers Hill. I'm just not doing it for someone who's in the middle of figuring out his life.'

'Well, I'm *really* sorry I'm not together enough for you,' he said, sarcasm dripping from every word.

'I don't expect you to be, Callum. I understand you've been through a lot. I'm just saying I'm not getting involved while you're in the middle of it all.'

Felicity rubbed her hands up and down her arms. How could she feel cold when it was still so damn hot?

'There's enough pressure on relationships these days as it is,' she continued, 'and we're not going to survive if somewhere down the track, when you come out the other end of this, you decide that I'm not what you want. That I was just a symptom of your deep unhappiness at the time. One that you're stuck with. I don't want to become collateral damage or be your consolation prize, like becoming a GP was.'

'You would never be that,' he denied quickly, taking a step towards her. *'Never.'*

Felicity took a step back, hardening her heart to the flicker of hurt she saw scurrying across his face. She didn't doubt his sincerity but he still needed time and space, whether he knew it or not.

'Please, just come to Sydney and let's see how things go?'

His words were a cruel blow. *See how things go?* She was in love with him and he wanted to test the waters.

'No.'

'*Damn it*, Felicity. You want to. I can *see* it in your eyes. Why are you being so stubborn?'

Felicity didn't have the emotional energy to go round and round the houses with him. She needed to end it— sever it. Here and now. And she knew just how to do it.

'Because I'm in love with you.' The words came out on a rush of pent-up emotions and clanged into a heap between them. It felt good to get it out even if Callum was staring at her like she'd lost her mind. 'And I want more than "Let's see how things go". You can't give that to me and I'm not settling for less. I'm sure as hell not moving halfway across the country for it.'

He took a step back, looking more and more horrified as his butt met the bench again. 'But…it's only been two months. That's…*crazy*.'

Felicity nodded. 'I know. Trust me, *I know*. But it's there anyway. You want to know something crazier? I think I fell in love with you on the train.'

He took a deep breath and let it escape as he shoved a hand through his hair. 'I…don't know what to say. I really like you, Felicity, I—'

'It's fine,' she interrupted, shaking her head. His horror would be comical if it wasn't currently tearing her heart into tiny little pieces.

She didn't need him trying to stumble through a quantification of how much he *liked* her.

'I know. I understand. Really, I do. But that's why I can't do this. Why I can't move to Sydney with you. And why I'm leaving now.'

He didn't say anything. Just stood there, his face a mix of confusion, shock and disbelief, and all the broken pieces of her heart splintered.

She blinked hard as her emotions threatened to take over. She needed to get through this without breaking down. 'Thank you for everything,' she said. 'I will *always* remember and cherish our night on the train. And I *will* miss you.' She stopped, cleared the quaver in her voice. 'Have a good life, Callum. Be happy. You deserve it.'

And then, because she really was about to lose it, she turned on her heel and slipped out of the house.

He didn't try and stop her.

CHAPTER FIFTEEN

Two months later...

CALLUM STOOD ON a balcony overlooking Sydney Harbour.
Not his. A friend's. Taking a breather from another excru-
ciating dinner party. A murmur of conversation, an occasional laugh and bluesy notes from a top-of-the-range
system oozed out into the night air. A light breeze ruffled
his hair as the lights on the harbour blurred on the surface
of the water courtesy of his compromised night vision.

'Cal?' He turned to find Erica—or maybe it was Angelica?—standing in the doorway, smiling at him. 'Entrées are
being served.'

He nodded. 'Okay, thanks. I'll be right in,' he assured,
then turned back to the view. He could sense her lingering in the doorway but refused to be hurried. It was rude
but he wasn't good company tonight.

He'd told Kim, a thirty-three-year-old mother of four,
she had breast cancer today. She'd sat deathly still in the
chair as if he'd gutted her while Josh, her husband, had
yelled at him then openly wept.

Try as he may, he couldn't get it out of his head. And
being here wasn't helping.

Go to dinner parties, Felicity had said. Except tonight
he just wanted to be with her. Not at this banal event where

everyone was trying to out-surgeon each other. Where they always tried to out-surgeon each other.

It had been hard to start with—reconnecting with the old crowd. And their stories had stirred the old fires, but not like before. He'd spent two years during his GP training burning with envy and resentment that he wasn't in the *club* any more.

And then he'd gone to Vickers Hill…

Why did they keep inviting him back? *Because you keep saying yes, doofus.*

Maybe he needed to say no every now and then. Maybe he needed to start socialising with other GPs. Except not those at his current practice because that wasn't really working out. His billable hours had halved and he'd already had a couple of 'friendly chats' with the head of the practice about picking up the pace.

But how could he have only spent five minutes with Kim and Josh today? Felicity would never have forgiven him.

He'd never have forgiven himself.

God, he missed her. Dreamed about her. Woke up at night aching for her. Had almost called her a dozen times. Had wanted to call her today. To tell her about Kim. To share his utter helplessness and hear the soft note of empathy in her voice.

To hear her say he could do this.

A ferry horn wafted towards him from somewhere on the water and he shook himself out of his funk, throwing back the rest of his whisky and making his way inside.

He took the indicated seat next to another woman whose name he didn't remember. A sumptuous feast was served courtesy of some up-and-coming catering firm in high demand amongst the urban professional set. Absently he wondered what Kim and Josh were eating tonight.

Was it possible to stomach anything after such news?

The talk turned to shop, as it inevitably did, and Callum let it whirl around him. It took a strong stomach to dine with a bunch of surgeons as the nitty-gritty of all kinds of blood, guts and gore was openly discussed.

'What about you, Cal?'

Callum glanced in the direction of the query. It was from Allan, one of the guys he'd gone to med school with. Allan was a transplant surgeon.

'You save any lives today in the eczema, allergies and asthma trenches?'

There was general laughter. Allan's attitude was typical and one that had dogged and bugged him during his training, but it flowed off him now.

'No. I told a woman she had an aggressive form of breast cancer.'

As a party killer it worked a treat. Callum could almost hear the loud scratching of a needle across a vinyl record as everyone fell silent.

It was bliss for about two point five seconds before Roger, a facio-maxillary surgeon, said, 'You should refer her to Charlie Maddison. He's an excellent breast surgeon.'

'Or Abigail,' Allan added, which garnered a lot of murmured support.

The conversation moved on to breast surgery. No one asked her name, her age or her prognosis. Whether she was married or had kids. Not even the name of the oncologist he'd rung and personally spoken to, arranging for Kim and Josh to go straight there and see her immediately. Nope. They'd moved on to the biggest tumours they'd ever removed.

His phone vibrated in his pocket and he pulled it out, grateful for the interruption, concealing it under the table a little as he glanced at it. He smiled when he saw it was a text from Felicity.

They had been texting back and forth a few times a week for a while now, after some initial radio silence. But with Luci and Seb all loved up and talking wedding bells they'd been included in group texts and it had gone from there.

It wasn't the kind of communication he craved but she seemed to want to keep it light and he was happy for any kind of contact. She usually sent him a picture with Meryl or Alf or any of his other regulars and he'd taken to sending her pictures of the beach and the view from his balcony because a crazy part of him hoped it might just convince her to rock up one day.

Not even her unexpected *I love you* doused that particular fantasy. Not when he missed her so damn much. Okay, it had shocked him at the time but she *had* prewarned him she was that kind of girl.

Callum smiled as he read the text—Mrs Smith says hi—and tapped on the attachment. The image opened up to reveal a selfie of Felicity and Mrs Smith, their faces smooshed together. Felicity was cross-eyed and making a fishy mouth with her lips—so very *Flick*—while the older woman glared suspiciously at the camera.

A niggle took up residence in his chest as he devoured every detail. Felicity had her saint badge on her collar and Mrs Smith was sporting one on her collar too. Her diamantés spelled out *Security*.

He laughed out loud. He couldn't help himself. It was the first time since talking to Kim and Josh he'd been taken out of himself and his lungs suddenly felt too big for his chest.

'You okay, man?' Allan asked.

Callum looked up to find everyone at the table staring at him as if he'd lost his mind.

Maybe he had.

Was he okay? *Hell, no.* If he wasn't very much mistaken, he was heads over heels in love with a chick who'd just sent him a fishy-lipped selfie. The realisation hit him like a tonne of bricks as he glanced at the woman beside him. She was gorgeous and a renal surgeon to boot. But he couldn't imagine her crossing her eyes and scrunching up her face while posing with a cantankerous old woman.

Wow. He was in love with Felicity. He'd been fooling himself that his feelings had been milder, that he'd merely been *missing* her, ignoring the emptiness inside, going through the motions because he'd been determined to prove that he could come back from his injury as if nothing had ever happened.

But it hadn't worked. Because his entire focus was screwed up. Literally and figuratively. He'd been blind to what was important.

Felicity.

The niggle grew to the size of a fist, pushing on his sternum. Who knew love could feel this *bad*? Like a freaking heart attack!

He stood up, pushing his chair back abruptly. What was he doing *here* when she was *there*? Why had he ever left?

Because she'd made him. She'd sent him away. To sort his life out. To work out what he truly wanted.

If you love something, set it free.

Well…mission accomplished. And he didn't want to feel this empty ever again. Felicity filled him up and he didn't want to spend a second longer away from her than he had to.

'Cal? Are you okay?' Allan repeated, his forehead creased.

Callum dumped his napkin on the table. 'I am now, Allan. I'm sorry but I've got to go.'

'Hey, where's the fire?' Erica—Angelica?—joked.

'In Vickers Hill.' He grinned.

Everyone looked a little mystified as he walked away but Callum didn't give a damn as he strode out of the apartment. For the first time in two months—hell, in almost three years—everything felt right.

Felicity had set him free. Because she loved him. Now it was time to go back. Because *he* loved *her*.

It was almost seven when Callum finally caught up with Felicity the next evening. He'd been travelling all day but he felt completely energised. He'd gone straight to her house in his hire car, the speech he'd been rehearsing all day bursting on his tongue, only to be told by a neighbour she was at Luci's, watering the garden.

Callum knew from Seb that Felicity was taking care of Luci's garden while they waited for a buyer in a market that wasn't exactly thriving. Undeterred by the setback, he'd driven straight to Luci's and pulled up outside her house ten minutes later.

He experienced a strange sense of déjà vu as he cut the engine. The street was quiet and the cottage looked as pretty as a picture, the waning sun glowing a lovely honey hue on the brickwork. He half expected Mrs Smith to tap on his window, narrow her eyes at him and call him 'young man.'

He spied Felicity watering the lavender further up the path, her back to him, buds from her phone firmly plugged into her ears. He climbed out of the car and headed towards her, content to stand on the footpath near the front gate and just watch her. Her ponytail swung as she moved her head to whatever beat was being piped into her ears.

A stream of dying sunlight caught the hose spray at the

right angle, causing rainbows to dance in the fine mist. She'd told him once that her heart was a pink light glowing inside her and now he knew how she felt as rainbows filled up his chest.

It was a fanciful notion. Utter romantic nonsense. But he didn't care.

She turned then and his breath hitched as she spied him and went very still. 'Callum?'

It wasn't quite the rapturous welcome he'd been dreaming about but it was *Felicity* and he was here with her and that's all that mattered right now. 'Hi.'

She didn't do or say anything for long moments, just stared at him. 'What are you…doing here?'

'I rang Bill last night.'

She eyed him warily as she twisted the nozzle to cut off the spray. 'Why?'

'I asked him for a job.'

'You…did?'

Callum nodded, pleased to hear the first sign of a squeak in her voice. A good sign, he hoped. 'He offered me his. I'm taking over his share of the practice. He's finally retiring.'

She walked towards him, frowning and nonplussed. 'But…he didn't say anything today.'

'I asked him not to.'

An even bigger frown. 'Why?'

'Because I wanted it to be a surprise.'

She'd reached the gate but kept firmly on her side. 'You did?'

He smiled as her frown lines smoothed out and her tone lightened.

'Yes. I wanted to tell you myself.'

'You did?'

He laughed then. The entire time they'd been acquainted he'd never known her to be monosyllabic. Quite the contrary.

'Yes. Because I love you.' The words came much easier than he'd thought they would. He'd thought saying it for the first time would be terrifying but it was easy.

Things always were when they were right.

'You set me free and you were right to do so. I needed that. I needed to go home to know what I wanted. To be sure. But now I know and I'm back. Because I'm yours. If—' his heart thundered in his chest, suddenly unsure of himself '—you'll have me.'

She stared at him, reaching for the gate and wrapping her fingers around the curved metal. She looked lost for words but the glassiness of her eyes said more than words ever could.

'Felicity?'

'Is it what you want?' she asked, fierce suddenly. *'Really?'*

He nodded. 'It is.' He slid his hand over the top of hers. 'You and me. Here. In Vickers Hill.'

She glanced at their joined hands before returning her gaze to his face. 'What about your job? Your apartment?'

'I resigned today. It wasn't working out there anyway since a bossy nurse taught me patients needed more than five minutes with their doctor. I have to go back for a month and work out my notice but then I'm moving here. And we'll keep my apartment as a holiday home. We can rent it out or leave it empty. I'm sure Seb and Luci wouldn't say no to bunking there while they figure out where they want to be. I know Luci's not keen to have the baby on the boat.'

She smiled then. It was only small but it was progress. 'Seems like you have it all worked out.'

He shook his head. 'No. I don't. Not really. None of it means anything without you and I'm completely terrified now you haven't thrown yourself at me that you've found a six-foot-nine, rugby-playing boyfriend, so can you please just put me out of my misery already?'

Their gazes locked and in that moment he could see love shining in her eyes. Love for him. *Only him.* He hadn't seen anything more beautiful in his life.

She pushed gently on the gate. He stepped back as she stepped through and joined him on the footpath, their bodies almost touching.

'You're the only one for me,' she murmured.

Relief flooded Callum's system. It coursed fast and cool through his chest and flowed hot to his groin. He smiled, slid a hand on her waist, drew her closer, their bodies aligning in perfect synchronicity.

His gaze dropped to her mouth as anticipation tightened his belly.

'Good evening, Dr Hollingsworth,' a familiar authoritative voice said from across the road. 'Flick didn't tell me you were back in town.'

He groaned under his breath and Felicity laughed as he plastered a smile on his face. 'Mrs Smith,' he said. 'I see you've recovered fully.'

'I see you're not back in town for more than five seconds and you're already taking liberties.'

Her disapproving gaze fell to where his body was pressed against Felicity's. *Too damn bad.* There was no way he was stepping away like some guilty schoolboy. Not now he had Felicity exactly where he wanted her.

'Indeed,' he agreed cheerfully. 'And I intend taking liberties as long as Felicity will let me, Mrs Smith, because I love her and she loves me. Consider yourself warned.'

He dipped her then, ignoring both Felicity's surprised squeak and Mrs Smith's scandalised gasp.

'Callum,' Felicity whispered, clutching at his arm while trying not to laugh. 'You're going to give her a heart attack.'

'Lucky for her we know how to do CPR.' He grinned.

Then he kissed her—long and dirty—claiming her mouth with deliberate indecency, giving Mrs Smith something really juicy to gossip about.

Because he didn't care who said what—this was right. This was for ever.

EPILOGUE

One year later...

THEY HELD THE WEDDING in Luci's back garden. Although it wasn't Luci's any more—Callum had bought it the day after he'd dipped Felicity in the street and kissed her, and they'd been happily living in sin together ever since.

Much to Mrs Smith's chagrin.

Seb and Luci and little Eve travelled to Vickers Hill for the wedding. As did Felicity's parents and Bill and Julia, who interrupted their RV trip around Australia.

Felicity wore a pink dress and, thanks to Alf Dunnich, a garland of glorious pink rosebuds in her hair. And, in a few days, they'd be heading to Sydney for two blissful sun-drenched weeks at Callum's apartment where, with any luck, they'd make a honeymoon baby.

The first of many.

Felicity couldn't have been happier as she said, 'I do', and she kissed her new husband in front of all their family and friends.

And somewhere from on high Meryl, who had passed away while Callum had been working out his notice in Sydney, was nodding her head and saying, *I told you so...*

* * * * *

If you missed the first story in
THE CHRISTMAS SWAP *duet*
look out for

WAKING UP TO DR GORGEOUS
by Emily Forbes

And if you enjoyed this story, check out these
other great reads from Amy Andrews:

IT HAPPENED ONE NIGHT SHIFT
200 HARLEY STREET: THE TORTURED HERO
GOLD COAST ANGELS: HOW TO RESIST TEMPTATION
ONE NIGHT SHE WOULD NEVER FORGET

All available now!

MILLS & BOON®

MEDICAL ROMANCE™

THE ULTIMATE IN ROMANTIC MEDICAL DRAMA

1016/03

MILLS & BOON®

EXCLUSIVE EXCERPT

Could a miracle in maternity reunite paediatrician
Max Ainsley with his estranged wife, Annabelle
Brookes, in time for Christmas?

Read on for a sneak preview of
THE NURSE'S CHRISTMAS GIFT
*the first book in the heart-warming
festive Medical quartet*
CHRISTMAS MIRACLES IN MATERNITY

"It's still there, isn't it, despite everything?"

Annabelle frowned, moving under one of the street
lamps along the edge of a park. "What is?"

"That old spark."

She'd felt that spark the second she'd laid eyes on
Max all those years ago. But he wasn't talking about
way back then. He was talking about right now.

"Yes," she whispered.

She wished to hell it weren't. But she wasn't going
to pay truth back with a lie.

"Anna..." He took her hand and eased them off the
path and into the dark shadows of a nearby bench.

She sat down, before she fell down. His voice...
She would recognise that tone anywhere. He sat beside
her, still holding her hand.

"You've changed," he said.

"So have you. You seem..." She shook her head,

unable to put words to her earlier thoughts. Or maybe it was that she wasn't sure she should.

"That bad, huh?"

"No. Not at all."

He grinned, the flash of his teeth sending a shiver over her. "That good, then, huh?"

Annabelle laughed and nudged him with her shoulder. "You wish."

"I actually do."

When his fingers shifted from her hand to just beneath her chin, the shiver turned to a whoosh as all the breath left her body, her nerve endings suddenly attuned to Max's every move. And when his head came down, all she felt was anticipation.

THE NURSE'S CHRISTMAS GIFT by Tina Becket

Available November 2016

www.millsandboon.co.uk

MILLS & BOON®

Why shop at millsandboon.co.uk?

Each year, thousands of romance readers find their perfect read at millsandboon.co.uk. That's because we're passionate about bringing you the very best romantic fiction. Here are some of the advantages of shopping at www.millsandboon.co.uk:

* **Get new books first**—you'll be able to buy your favourite books one month before they hit the shops

* **Get exclusive discounts**—you'll also be able to buy our specially created monthly collections, with up to 50% off the RRP

* **Find your favourite authors**—latest news, interviews and new releases for all your favourite authors and series on our website, plus ideas for what to try next

* **Join in**—once you've bought your favourite books, don't forget to register with us to rate, review and join in the discussions

Visit **www.millsandboon.co.uk**
for all this and more today!